Fidarsi é bene; non fidarsi é meglio . . .
'To trust is good; not to trust is better . . .'

OLD ITALIAN PROVERB

PROLOGUE

Wannsee, near Berlin, February 1945

THE FILM'S quality was poor, even allowing for the makeshift projector and battered portable screen. The 'set' was badly lit, the focus variable, the print grainy. The only part no one could argue with was the action. That was all too obviously, hideously real.

Seven months earlier, in July 1944, a group of highly placed plotters had tried to kill Adolf Hitler and take over the reins of government. They had failed and had paid with their lives. This film of their mediaeval torture and abject deaths had been released for limited circulation to key servants of the Nazi régime, to teach them what awaited those who betrayed the Führer's trust, and somehow the crudity of the production helped to underline the insanity of it all. To think that Hitler had personally overseen the filming and editing. A madman's home-made film for showing to captive audiences in still, cold offices such as this.

Scene. A half-starved man in prison clothes is hoisted high by muscular executioners. His eyes to camera are lost, hollow, wide, and his long legs flap clumsily – he cannot help himself – like those of some rangy marshland bird in take-off.

Scene. The man is now dangling from a meat hook set into the whitewashed brick wall. Jerking and writhing. His face, which the camera moves in on hungrily, is no longer blank but contorted; the eyes now bulge like independent, bloated creatures, competing with the tongue in contest in horrors of the flesh.

Jumping jellyfish. Standartenführer Heinz Ludwig Keppler fought to keep his eyes on the screen and could not get that

1

strange phrase out of his mind. He had come across it from
watching American movies, both in Germany and during his
frequent visits to the U.S.A. before the war. It was a piece of
slang, so far as he recalled, expressing surprise or disbelief.
Yes, but here also eyes like slippery, repellent, translucent
jellyfish in their extremity, trying to leap clear of the agony,
the humiliation, the enforced rush towards extinction. The
camera backed away, probed around, carefully showing all the
minutiae of what slow strangulation does to a human being,
lingering on the deepening bite of piano wire as it tightened
around the man's neck, gloating over the urine stain spreading
on the crotch of his striped prison trousers. It just went on
and on. In its way, the camera loved the event.

Keppler closed his eyes momentarily, feigning tiredness in
case anyone noticed. Of course, he knew that even at the end
of a long working day he could not do so for more than a few
seconds without being accused of squeamishness and lack of
political zeal. A servant of the State who could not bear to
watch traitors die might be assumed to share their weaknesses
deep in his heart. So went the Nazi régime's logic. The Standartenführer knew the other men in the room, and suspected
that at least one was watching the audience rather than the
screen, noting every gesture and nuance.

When Keppler opened his eyes once more, a new face was
on the screen. This time it belonged to a well-known and
respected general, a man of sixty with many victories to his
credit, who just a few months before had been praised in all
the newspapers and propaganda newsreels for his heroism and
his 'fanatical' loyalty to the Führer and Fatherland. Of course,
the General's Nazi fervour had actually been a front, a cover
for his involvement in plans to kill the very man he swore love
for. The general had been a military gigolo, a deceiver for the
noblest of reasons.

The general's was still recognisable as a good and brave
face, despite the emaciation and the gauntness born of terror;
in its way his face represented all that was best and most
virtuous in the German military tradition. Then suddenly it
too was hauled aloft, the wire looped around the hook in the
wall so that the general's final, awful dance of death could
begin. Keppler felt like crying out in protest and despair. What
he actually did was to purse his lips in righteous approval of

this shining example of 'patriotic justice'. Then he lit a cigarette with a very slightly shaking hand.

Ten minutes later, that part of the ordeal was over. The
main lights were switched on by a smartly turned-out young
SS orderly and the nine men in the viewing room sat blinking
in the brightness. They were all hard men, the cream of the
Criminal Police, but none of them could hide the fact that
they were disturbed and repelled. Even Gruppenführer Müller
– the man they called 'Gestapo' Müller, who had organised
the showing and was to deliver the speech to follow – seemed
a little green around the gills. Whether because of his own
shock or, more probably, in a calculated move to add to the
effect of his words. Müller waited for something like fifteen
seconds before he clasped together his spade-like peasant's
hands and started to speak.

'What you have just seen is both a warning and an assurance,' he began. 'A warning, of course, of what happens to
those who betray the nation's and the Führer's trust. And how
is it also an assurance?' Müller permitted himself the thinnest,
chilliest of smiles. 'Well, gentlemen, let us say that it illustrates
the fact that we Germans have gone too far to turn back. We
can never rejoin the community of so-called civilised – read,
decadent – nations. Just as we have shown no mercy to those
who resisted or betrayed our national-socialist state, so the
Allies also will be merciless with us if we allow them to defeat
us and take us prisoner. Gentlemen: *They know what we have
done. Honourable surrender and survival are not possible. We
are irrevocably committed to resistance, to saving the
Reich . . .*'

The Gestapo chief, the man who had held Germany and
Europe and half of Russia in his iron torturer's grip and even
in Hitler's shrinking empire could still have tens of thousands
killed whenever he chose to pick up the telephone, paused
once more with heavy meaning. He wore spectacles, his eyes
glinted myopically, but there was nothing of the student or
the intellectual in him. His face was much more like the slaugh-
terman's, witness to the price a man paid for working days
and nights in the darkness among the tormented and the
broken, the dying and the dead.

'They know', Müller repeated. 'Versions of this film are in
circulation. The Allies are bound to find examples. Just as

they will find evidence of what has happened in the ghettos, the prisons, the concentrations, in fields and forests and ravines where – I will not be mealy-mouthed, gentlemen – where we have killed for Germany. The Allies may forgive our German women, our children, our peasants and factory workers, even the troops of our regular Wehrmacht, but they will never forgive those who have worn the black uniform of the SS and hunted the enemies of the Führer, as we have, driven traitors to deservedly miserable deaths.'

A department head from Criminal Records (Inland) just behind Keppler cleared his throat and shifted uncomfortably in his seat. Although they had been incorporated into the SS-dominated apparatus of terror long ago, not all the senior officers in the criminal police were Nazis. Few were exactly liberal, but many were just conscientious civil servants, bemused by what had happened since 1933, trying to do their essential jobs as best they could and, yes, sticking their heads in the sand if that was what it took to keep their peace of mind, at times even their sanity, intact. Keppler liked to tell himself that was what he had done these past twelve years. His self did not always believe him.

Keppler stayed solid as a rock, still and calm. He could not afford to be any other way. It was a talent of his since child-hood, the result of growing up in a crowded cold-water flat with seven other children and parents who beat a noisy child. In the Keppler household, Heinz made himself *ganz klein und hässlich*, small and ugly as the old German saying went, and even though he was no longer small and certainly not ugly, he felt like becoming like that now, so inconspicuous that he could sneak away and no one would notice. Müller was Keppler's father to the life, bull neck and bloodshot eyes, surveying the few creatures on earth over whom he had absolute power, wondering which victim he would choose to wield the strap on tonight. The difference was that Müller was rarely drunk, which Keppler's father had been most of the time, and the Gestapo boss's whims led not to impulsive clips round the ear or an impromptu beltings, but to the system-atised, premeditated infliction of agony, death, enforced silence. Müller was stone-cold sober. Stone cold.

'Thank you, gentlemen,' Müller concluded his address. 'There will be a meeting in the morning to discuss the transfer of key domestic and international records, including the Interpol files under Keppler's care, to places of safety in South Germany.' He looked at Keppler. 'Standartenführer, I should like to talk with you immediately after this meeting to consider certain special logistical problems involved in the move.'

Keppler nodded mechanically. Müller made comments to a couple of other officers, then rose and strode out of the room, flanked by his assistants. The crew borrowed from the propaganda ministry started to tidy away the projector and the screen. No one could bring himself to speak. Men dispersed quietly to their offices, to their departments. Most would be off home immediately, but Keppler guessed that more of them than usual would risk being caught by the British bombers while sinking a few glasses of schnapps in some bar on the way. Anything to wipe away the impression of those faces, those bodies, those eyes . . .

Forty minutes later, Standartenführer Keppler, fat briefcase in his gloved hand, walked down the driveway and turned into the leafy suburban street. He left behind him the villa at number 16 am Kleinen which housed the archive over which he reigned, supreme except for Müller and, above him, the stratospheric heights of Kaltenbrunner, head of all security organs in the Reich, the most powerful policeman in Hitler's Germany. Müller was enough to worry about for now. In contrast to Kaltenbrunner, who spent an increasing amount of time on 'urgent business' in the 'Alpine Fortress' in South Germany – holed up in a comfortably-converted hunting lodge with his Hungarian mistress, word had it – Müller was close, ever-present, always watching.

Resplendent in his black uniform and greatcoat, still looking for all the world like the confident, promotion-hungry, Nazified technocrat he had once been, Keppler strode away through the softly falling snow, boots crunching on the thin patina that was already settling on the pavement like silver leaf. He was very good at keeping up appearances; he had done that especially well during his private meeting with Müller just now. In fact, it was his main hope of survival.

Five minutes' walk would bring him to the Wannsee station. Twenty minutes more, barring an early air raid and chaos on the transit system, until he arrived at the apartment. She would be waiting for him there, they had agreed. She still needed him, despite everything. She still seemed to care. Maybe she even still loved him. In the old, carefree days of arrogance and ambition, he had never thought about that. Times changed, and patriotism became a disguise, ambition gave way to terror of failure, strength deteriorated into many subtle kinds of weakness. Parts of a man died.

Keppler's flat was on the third floor of an old, greystone block in the Kantstrasse, where once there had been a thriving, colourful community of writers, artists, and fashionable people-about-town, including Party officials with a taste for bohemian pleasures. Now much of the street had been demolished by the bombing; only a few shops stayed open, and a basement dive called the *Groschenkeller* which looked as if it would keep on serving its beer and cheap cognac until the end of the world came. Which might not be too far off. Keppler had lived here for eight years, and he liked it. It would be hard to leave.

His key turned in the lock with a nice, solid click. Strange how safe 'home' felt, even when you knew about the bombs, the 3 a.m. raids by the Gestapo; knew that home was no guarantee of any kind of security any more.

Keppler walked straight in to the spacious living room, noted that one small lamp had been left on by the sofa near the window. There was gentle music playing from the radio, a slow, slightly jazzy number that he didn't recognise. It sounded American. God forbid that she should have tuned in to AFN or Luxembourg; that was an offence punishable by death. He put down his briefcase, called out softly, 'Helen?'

When there was no answer, he sighed and walked through to the bedroom. Sure enough, there she was, asleep on top of the bed in her day clothes.

'*Mein Schatz*,' he said. 'Treasure.' And he leaned over, touched her on the forehead and ran one finger very gently over the skin. Her eyes opened.

'Heinz. I was tired. I'm okay. What's the time . . . ?'

'Eight. I had to stay late.' Should he tell her about the film? Not unless he had to. Just Müller's lecture and the all-important meeting afterwards. 'Müller lectured us about how we were all marked men, the Allies will have our hides,' he told her. 'We have no choice, as the élite of the State, but to

6

buckle down and save the Reich at all costs, abandoning all thought of self-preservation.'

She smiled sleepily. 'You have heard that one before.'

'But this time the madmen mean it.' He would have to tell her, to show why he was taking such an extreme course of action. 'I won't go into details,' he continued, 'but I'll tell you that they showed us an unspeakable film of what they did to the July 20th traitors. The slightest deviation, the tiniest suspicion . . . it could happen to any of us.' Keppler was surprised at the way he had to catch his breath, at the dry fear in his voice. 'Helen, we have to get out. To stay is more dangerous than to go.'

She looked at him with curiosity. There wasn't much other expression in her eyes; perhaps a dash of pity. How Keppler hated that. In the old days she had been in awe of him, she had wanted him. And, God, how he had wanted her and taken her. It seemed so long ago . . .

'How?' she said simply. 'How can we both leave? That's always been the problem.'

Keppler took a deep breath. There was a pain in his chest but he knew it was fear, not physical disease. 'Müller asked to see me privately after the lecture', he said. 'Important news. He is making me responsible for sifting and destroying certain extremely sensitive and secret Interpol records. Those to be destroyed include files that are dangerous for us, and also for certain very important people in Britain and America.' He paused for a moment, aware that he was talking too quickly, almost gabbling. 'It is a marvellous opportunity, darling. I plan to select some of the most sensational documents, dealing with a quite explosive matter, and sell them in exchange for our freedom and our future, Helen. Certain interested parties, especially in Britain, will do anything to gain possession of the files I'm talking about. Including presenting us with a one-way ticket out of the Third Reich! First you . . . you will go westward and be my intermediary, because you can travel freely. Müller would never allow me to do that. I know too much.'

She was alert now. Her body was still relaxed, her movements lazy, like a cat's, but she was totally concentrated.

'It won't be easy. Who shall I approach initially?'

'No problem. I have the names of people in authority who

will receive you. And then, once the groundwork has been done, there is someone in particular, a man named Sutton I used to meet at Interpol conferences before the war. British. I shall insist that they use him to get us out of this hell-hole.'

'I'm glad you have made your decision at last,' Helen said. She touched his thigh, stroked it gently, smiled up at him.

Keppler closed his eyes in mingled pleasure and shame, hunched over like a penitent boy. 'I know it will feel better when I feel in control of things again. The important thing is to act. Soon we shall be together, really together.'

She said nothing for a long moment. Then she smiled lazily. 'I think we both need a drink,' she murmured. 'And then you can tell me everything. Slowly and systematically. If I am to take these risks, I have to know.'

'I'm sure that when we are in London, I'll be myself again,' Keppler said. 'It's this feeling of helplessness . . . we'll want each other.'

She took her hand away from his thigh. 'You're depressed. I know that can lead to temporary disturbances. We all know that. Don't worry, Heinz.'

'But I do worry,' said Standartenführer Heinz Keppler.

She smiled at him. Here he was, about to abandon his country, send a shockwave through at least two other nations, and his main concern was his precious virility.

'You'll get your . . . manly power . . . back', she said. 'There'll be a place in the sun. Now,' she added, sliding off the bed, her manner becoming brisker, 'do you think this Sutton person is trustworthy?'

Keppler took her arm to lead her into the living-room. The commentary from the radio, he noticed with relief, was Hungarian, German-controlled Radio Budapest.

'Trustworthy?' He puffed out a little laugh. 'He's the most fearsomely honest policeman I ever met. And he's very clever too. A rare combination in a big-city cop.'

'Sounds interesting,' she said. 'When did you last see him?'

Keppler shrugged. 'Maybe six years ago, maybe a bit more.'

'People change. You've changed.'

'Not the Suttons of this world. Not the terriers, the dogs who never let go.' Keppler paused uneasily, as if a thought had just occurred to him. 'You do want to go West with me, Helen? You're willing to take the risk?'

'Yes, Heinz. God knows I've taken plenty already. Rest assured.'

If only he knew, Helen von Ackersberg found herself thinking, *if only he knew how many risks and with whom. If only he knew that this was just another twist, another stage in the process. The beginning of betrayal for him, for her a mere permutation. But maybe this one would see her home and free. Out of here. Provided for.*

CHAPTER ONE

'WHY DID YOU KILL those men?' George Sutton demanded. 'Why did you turn your deck-guns on the lifeboats of the *Doria*? Were you following orders from your superiors, or are you just a cruel, murdering bastard?'

The tall, even-featured Englishman spoke in German with a kind of a metallic weariness, almost as if he was bored. Except that his pale blue eyes stayed alert and fixed on his victim's like a raptor's on its prey.

The German P.O.W. sitting opposite him was a former U-boat commander, a few years Sutton's junior, sharp-featured and pointy-eared, almost elflike in appearance. It seemed ridiculous that anyone should be accusing him of anything more heinous than organising a dance at the fairy ring.

'Sergeant,' he drawled, emphasising Sutton's humble rank in a crude attempt at one-upmanship, 'according to the Geneva Convention I don't have to discuss these details with you or anyone else. I repeat for the hundredth time that I'm prepared to tell you only my name and rank. So far as the rest goes, I must remind you – since astonishingly you remain ignorant of this basic fact – that like every officer of every nation I was and remain bound to obey the orders of my commander.'

'Aha. Grand Admiral Doenitz was your commander. So you're admitting the order to fire on the lifeboats came from him?'

Sutton rested his chin in his hands and waited. He didn't seriously expect his man here to answer that question, but it was good to let him stew a little more, shiver in silence. The walls of the prefabricated army hut where Sutton was conducting the interrogation didn't offer much protection against the damp, insidious cold that was the curse of the

10

Scottish coast even in early March. Besides, the chairs in the room had been placed cunningly so that Sutton got most of the heat from the small War Office issue stove, the German as little as possible. It was all part of the battle to break down his resistance.

Sutton counted mentally to fifty, then sighed.

'*Herr Kapitänleutnant*,' he continued heavily, returning his victim's sarcasm, 'you may be right about the technicalities of the Geneva Convention – as you probably know, I'm a policeman by training, not a lawyer – but I do know very well that machine-gunning innocent people who have abandoned ship comes under the category of a war crime and is punishable by death.' A grim smile. 'The order for you to be hanged would not be signed by Grand Admiral Doenitz, unlike the orders of the day in the German Navy, but you would be every bit as dead once that trap-door opened underneath you, believe me.'

'The winners of wars have the habit of making their own laws,' the German said. He tried to flash Sutton a devil-may-care grin, but the way his hands clasped each other until the knuckles drained white betrayed his growing tension.

'Oh, don't give me that shit', Sutton murmured, again without any particular passion, as if the man had just made a bad joke. He paused, jotted a few more notes on his pad. He knew very well that the German across the bare table from him was gradually losing his nerve. Having expected to sit out the remainder of the war peacefully in a P.O.W. camp, the man now found himself having to answer for an action under-taken almost three years previously, when he had turned his guns on the survivors from a Canadian freighter torpedoed just off Newfoundland. The Kapitänleutnant couldn't know that the British had already decided against hanging him. In fact, Sutton's job was to gather evidence for the post-war crimes trial of the German naval commander, Doenitz, but to have let his victim into that particular secret would have spoiled the game completely.

'Listen,' he said after a while, 'we've got all the eye-witnesses we need to convict you. If you co-operate, though – give us a few harmless insights into your command structure, who was responsible for what orders – I'll do my best to get

11

them to go easy on you. Tell me the truth, do you really want to swing for Doenitz?'

Sutton kept chipping away at the man's resistance in his accurate, methodical German. His grammar was a touch too perfect, his command of slang not quite a native speaker's, because originally he had learned the language at night school in the East End of London, and he had never had the leisure to spend more than a few weeks at a time in the country itself. Nevertheless, his accent was remarkably authentic. Sutton's facility in foreign languages, despite his never having got beyond an elementary school education, had puzzled many colleagues and irritated some. It particularly vexed the ones who had been to public schools and to Oxford and Sandhurst. For them, working-class boys like George Sutton could never be seen as intelligent, only possessed of a low cunning. The in-born, instinctive feel for alien thought-patterns and speech-rhythms that enabled Sutton to master German was often dismissed as a parrot-like mimicry, something that indicated a lack of character, even an unpatriotic nature.

Sutton repeated: 'I asked you, do you want to swing for Doenitz?'

'*Schweinerei* . . .' the German protested.

'Rubbish! I'll tell you, the biggest *Schwein* is the Grand Admiral himself. He's only too happy for poor arseholes like you to carry the can for his orders.' Sutton leaned forward and his manner took on a kind of rough, barrack-room frankness. 'Doenitz is not going to be the big boss for much longer, you know. The war's almost over. A few weeks, my friend, and he'll be just as deep in the mire as you, facing questions in some little room somewhere – no more fancy uniforms and limousines and yes-men to pass his orders on to the scum who do the actual killing and dying. Soon Doenitz will be down to a pullover, regulation trousers and dirty underwear. Going to save your neck then, is he? Or are *you* saving *his*?'

That last sally had hit home, Sutton could tell. The German was still refusing to talk, but his face had paled even more, and his attempt at a superior smile was getting less convincing by the minute. He's a tough enough bastard, thought Sutton with a certain professional respect, and he's probably still Nazi to the core, but he's only human, and he's beginning to wonder if he really wants to die for Grand Admiral Karl. I'll get him yet, he told himself.

'I demand to be returned to my quarters,' the German said at last. It was a brave, if rather pathetic, attempt at a fight back.

'All in good time, eh? The night is young,' said Sutton with a grin. Then his eyes fixed as if by chance on the packet of Gold Flake cigarettes that lay on the table beside his notepad. The German had been casting intense, longing looks at them for the past hour. The time had come to switch completely to the soft approach. 'Let's have a smoke, relax a bit, shall we?' he suggested.

Despite himself, the German's answering look was grateful, hungrily appreciative. He even crept his chair forward a little so that it was closer to the stove, and Sutton didn't order him back as he would have done five minutes previously.

Sutton was sliding two cigarettes from the packet when there was a knock at the door. He cursed quietly, paused, then put them back.

'What is it?' he barked.

A plump, bespectacled face appeared around the door.

'Sorry to disturb you, George. Urgent message from the C.O. You're to drop whatever you're doing and report to him on the double.'

Sutton was tempted to give him an earful, and had the interloper been anybody but Eric Daniels, he might have indulged himself. But Daniels, with his middle-aged school-boy's face, was a decent bloke. So instead he grunted, uncoiled his lean form from his chair, went over to the door. He spoke to Daniels in broad Cockney to make it harder for the prisoner to follow the conversation.

'Did he tell you what it was about?' he demanded. 'Me and old matey here were getting on famously until you stuck your bleeding great schnozzle in. Christ, it's gone seven at night. Are you telling me the major's still on the job and stone-cold sober?'

Daniels grinned slyly. 'I can't guarantee the last, but he's certainly in his office, and it looks to me as if someone, some-where, has put a rocket up his backside.'

Sutton nodded, glanced at the nicotine-starved German,

who looked ready to climb up the wall, then shrugged his shoulders.

'All right,' he said grudgingly, 'I'll be over in a jiffy. Just let me wrap things up with Attila the bloody Hun here.'

'I have the feeling the major may be telling you something that's to your advantage, George.'

'That'll be the day.'

Daniels chuckled and said he would be in the mess later if Sutton wanted to drop by. When he had gone, Sutton spent a few moments wondering whether he felt like being nice or nasty to the U-boat commander. It was a close decision, but for tactical reasons he decided to be nice. He tossed the long-withheld cigarette across the table, watched with satisfaction the German's vain attempt to keep some dignity as he scrabbled for it.

'There you go, Kapitänleutnant, *sir*. Have a cough for Doenitz. Maybe we'll have a bit more to talk about next time. I have to be off now – something more important to do than helping you save your own skin – but don't forget that I could turn out to be the best friend you've got. I may even be the only one, in fact. *Auf Wiedersehen*.'

He called in the guard from the ante-room and told him to escort the prisoner back to his quarters. Then he threw his greatcoat over his shoulders, began to run through the driving rain to the camp administration block a couple of hundred yards distant. He was more intrigued and excited by the C.O.'s summons than he would ever let Eric Daniels know, but he was also way past letting himself hope that it might mean a ticket out of this dump, something worthwhile for an old man in his forties to do at last. Sutton squelched into the outer office, conscious of the fact that he must look like a drowned rat, not caring very much if he did. Despite the place's vomit-green walls and spartan, bureaucratic ugliness, it was an oasis of sophistication and comfort compared with the rest of the camp. It had an open fire in a grate in one corner, decent arm chairs, and the small telephone switchboard gave a luxurious sense of connection to the outside world.

Clerk-corporal MacIntyre was on duty tonight. The tiny, wiry prince of the orderly room looked up from his copy of the *Scottish Daily Express*, granted Sutton the usual hostile sneer. MacIntyre believed that all the camp's interrogators, most of whom had been recruited from schools and colleges, were effete intellectuals, and if there was one thing he couldn't stand, it was effete intellectuals. The fact that Sutton had been a policeman in civilian life made no difference; after eggheads, MacIntyre, who was proud of being bred in the lawless slums of Glasgow, hated coppers the most.

'He's nae pleased to be kept waitin' this time o' night, the major,' said MacIntyre, jabbing a bony finger at the door of the C.O.'s office. 'The major's nae pleased at all, I'll tell ye for nuthin'.'

Sutton ignored the warnings of impending doom, which were part of the corporal's little routine. 'I'll just go straight in and see what he wants then,' he said.

'He's nae pleased.'

The knock was followed by a long silence, then a bellowed instruction to enter. Sutton opened the door, stepped forward and saluted the officer, who was hastily sitting back down at his desk and wiping his moustache.

'Sir,' he rasped. 'You asked to see me.'

Major Skeffington looked at him strangely for a moment, as if puzzled as to why Sutton was here at all. He was in his late fifties, a regular soldier brought out of retirement to run this P.O.W. camp. His job meant that he acted as a sort of combined turnkey and entertainments officer to a bunch of Nazis – and interrogators for that matter – who were far younger and more intelligent than he was. The challenge alternately terrified and bored him. Even from where he was standing, just inside the doorway, Sutton could smell whisky on the major's breath and guessed that Skeffington had just ditched the bottle in the office filing-cabinet. Totally pointless, since everyone in the camp knew about the major's weakness for spirits. If he had felt any affection for Skeffington, Sutton might have pitied him. Since he didn't – the man was incompetent and lazy, a bigot and a bully – he could only trace a sense of faint disgust.

'Ah, Sutton,' the major mumbled. 'Yes, yes, I did. You took your time getting here.'

'I was in the middle of an important interrogation, sir,' Sutton answered crisply. 'I had to wind it up and then ensure that the prisoner was safely returned to his hut. You will be aware of the procedures, sir.'

'Of course I know the bloody procedures, sergeant. Don't be insolent.' Skeffington's tongue tripped over the last word. He wasn't too far gone yet. Only slurring one word in ten.

'Sorry, sir.'

Sutton waited for Skeffington to get on with his explanation for the interview, but none was forthcoming. The major had a double chin, red veins in his nose and cheeks, and a gap between his front teeth that you could poke a stick through. His eyes were at the same time doleful and poisonous, like those of a snake with a perpetual thirst. At the moment he was staring at his desk-top.

'Well, I suppose you're wondering what all this is about, then,' he said eventually, toying with a badly chewed pencil and still resolutely refusing to look Sutton in the eye.

'Well, yes. Of course, sir. As you know, I have expressed my desire to be transferred to a more active kind of service – '

'Tell me, have you been happy here, sergeant?' Skeffington cut in, ignoring Sutton's answer and darting him a look of furtive hostility.

'Happy, sir?' Sutton asked incredulously. 'I'm afraid I don't follow.'

'Come on, man. You're well over forty and you've seen a bit of the world. You know what I mean. Some people like it here, some don't. What about you?'

'Well, sir . . . then the answer is no. I haven't been very happy. I have tried to do my job as efficiently as possible, though.'

Skeffington's gaze dropped back down to the table and became sadder than ever. 'I'm sorry,' he said thickly. 'Very sorry. Sorry you're not the type who fits easily into a team.'

Sutton decided that the major was hoping for some kind of absolution, an assurance that the sergeant's unhappiness had everything to do with Sutton's own psychological peculiarities and nothing to do with Skeffington's methods of leadership. He clammed up tight, said nothing. It just wasn't worth asking for trouble when salvation might be at hand.

'Be that as it may,' the major said after a long, pained silence, 'I mean, happy or otherwise, I daresay you'll be relieved to know that you are being transferred as a matter of some urgency. To London. A man from Scotland Yard, of all bloody places, rang me half an hour or so ago and demanded

that I despatch you down there forthwith or suffer the consequences. Rude bugger, he was.'

Sutton could have leapt for joy. He had guessed that he
might be transferred to some other branch of the corps,
perhaps one involved in more active service, despite his age.
Never, even in his wildest daydreams, had he thought he
would be summoned back to the Yard. What the hell was
going on?

'May I . . . er . . . ask the name of the officer who made
the request, sir?' he said, trying to sound calm and indifferent.

'It wasn't a request, it was a bloody order. Authorised at
the very highest level, he said.' Skeffington glared hard at
Sutton, then looked down at his memo pad for support. 'This
chap was called Rudwick. Sir James Rudwick. Mean anything
to you?'

'Yes indeed, sir. He used to be my immediate superior when
I was an officer in the Metropolitan Police.'

'Well, it looks like you're in for a jolly reunion then, doesn't
it?'

Sutton doubted it, given the manner of his parting from
Rudwick and the man's personality, but he was hardly going
to bare his soul to Skeffington.

'I expect it will be interesting, sir. Did he – er –
discuss . . . ?' Sutton probed.

'No, he certainly didn't. Blighter wouldn't give me any idea
what it was about. Just said he'd cleared it with the War Office,
paperwork to follow, and you're to report to him at Scotland
Yard within forty-eight hours. I've already told MacIntyre to
organise you a booking and a travel warrant for the first down
train from Inverness tomorrow. All right? They said your
services would be required for an indefinite period of time.'

Skeffington was getting close to the end of his tether. His
puffy eyes kept flitting towards the filing cabinet and its secret.

'Very well, sir,' said Sutton. 'Will that be all, then?'

Skeffington nodded absently. 'Good luck to you, I suppose,
Sutton,' he said. It was an odd way of wishing a man well.
The major did not rise or offer his hand. 'We'll see you when
we see you, if at all. Think of us up here among the hailstones
and the heather, while you launch yourself into the fleshpots
of London, eh?'

'Yes, sir.'

Sutton left the room. MacIntyre's eager little eyes swivelled towards him enquiringly.

'As you bloody well know already, I'm off down to London,' Sutton said. 'To see an old friend.'

'Aye, well. I suppose if ye've got a friend, ye'd best keep the bugger sweet. They don't come along every minute for miserable bastards like you.'

Sutton came close to smiling, but didn't want to give the man the pleasure. 'What happened to your loved ones, Mac? All wiped out in a bicycle accident, were they?'

When Sutton arrived in the sergeants' mess, Daniels was seated at a table, nursing his usual pint of warm, watery beer. Sutton, as was his habit, grabbed a jug of tea and joined him.

'I assumed you'd be sending Attila back to his dungeon and signing off for the night.' Daniels said. 'You know I thirst for intelligent conversation, and you're the next best thing.'

'Cheers. You never discard a joke just because you've used it before, do you, Eric? I can see you were brought up right.'

He downed some tea. Daniels chuckled, then looked at him shrewdly. 'Well, George, What did the major want?'

'Mainly, I think the major wanted a drink.'

'Quite. But what did he want from you?'

'Oh,' Sutton said casually. 'I've got orders to go down to the Smoke. I'm to report to the Yard.'

'Good grief. That's extraordinary news, isn't it?' said Daniels, moved and, he was ashamed to say, surprised at what Sutton had told him.

Daniels knew, like most of the camp, that until eighteen months or so ago, Sutton had been a high-flying senior officer at Metropolitan Police headquarters with work that included government committees, foreign trips and Lord knows what else. The trouble had started when Sutton's wife had been killed in the Blitz – there was more to it than just that, the gossips said – and he had hit the bottle in a big way. Some colleagues in the force had tried to protect him, including his boss, Sir James Rudwick, but in the end he had been forced to resign. Down the slippery slope to sergeant-interrogator at this camp on the Moray Firth, with a sergeant's pay and terminal boredom. Sutton had now got the booze and the grief under control, but it had cost him dear. Sutton made his particular sour kind of jokes, smiled his wry smile, but Daniels

18

reckoned he could count on the fingers of one the number of times he had seen his friend manage a real, honest-to-God belly-laugh.

'Come on then, George. What's the S.P.? You know I can keep a secret.'

'I don't know myself,' Sutton said. 'All I know is, I have to leave first thing tomorrow morning.'

'Back to the old Alma Mater.'

'Something like that. After six months of pushing for transfer to active service, perhaps they decided the Met counted as a theatre of war.' Sutton saw Daniels eyeing him suspiciously, and lifted his hands in protest to say, 'I really and truly don't know any more than I've just told you. They wouldn't tell the major anything over the phone. I don't blame them, either.'

'Well, George, it could be a whole new career.'

'Who knows?' Sutton said with a shrug. Both he and Daniels knew that his careful indifference hid unexpressed hope, even longing. Not that Daniels envied Sutton anything from a career point of view. He was a complete and unashamed civilian who couldn't wait to get back to his cosy little niche teaching languages in a grammar school near Manchester. 'They might even make me twelfth man on the cricket team at the Yard. Or maybe it's the second eleven for poor old George . . .'

'I don't know, George, you're younger than most of the Middlesex side, even when the younger boys come back from the war.'

Their arguments about cricket were a form of therapy. A brief debate on the merits or otherwise of Middlesex's projected post-war side – especially Simms, Edrich and Compton – followed. Daniels followed no particular county team. He just liked to talk.

'Oh well,' said Sutton at last. 'You're not going to have time to think about such sublime matters from tomorrow. You're going to have to take over our friend the Kapitänleutnant with the big brown eyes.'

Daniels groaned. 'The bastard who machine-gunned those merchant seamen when they took to the lifeboats? Christ, there's a nasty piece of work if you like.'

'He's what the system made him. Hitler Youth from the age of thirteen, weekly lectures on the duty of Germans to do everything the Führer tells them – and their right to do anything they bloody well please to so-called sub-humans or enemies of the *Volk*. What do you expect, Eric?' Sutton sipped some tea. 'But he's scared for his hide. He may even be developing the semblance of a conscience. The main thing is, you need to get all the evidence you can about where his orders came from – when, how they were enforced. We want a picture of the entire chain of command, right down to the exact names and dates, even if it's just guidelines on how often to empty the bilges. The legal branch is screaming for evidence against Doenitz. They want him to stand trial alongside the rest of the top Nazis.'

'I'll do my best. Trust me to get stuck with him. He's more your cup of poison.'

'Just keep worrying away at him. I'll write up my report tonight, which should help you a bit. Unofficially, and strictly between you and me, I'll tell you I was intending to spread a rumour around that he was starting to sing. His Nazi friends in the camp don't like collaborators, especially the real super-Nazi fellows, and if they believe he's telling us classified information, they'll probably rough him up a bit. That could force him to run to us, if it gets bad enough. Anyway, the important thing is to divide the bastards amongst themselves, pit them against each other. You manage to get your villains falling out amongst themselves, you've won half the battle. Old C.I.D. wisdom.

'Ah, George. Once a copper, always a copper.'

Sutton sipped his tea with every appearance of calm. There wasn't a single night when he didn't come in here and want some of that beer, or a tumbler of whisky. No one who hadn't been through the long, lurid nightmare of alcoholism could ever know what it was like to desire something so much, or what it cost to deny that desire.

'So they say,' he murmured. 'So they say.'

CHAPTER TWO

THE SO-CALLED Inverness-to-London 'express' was crammed full of men in uniform of every possible nationality, most of them young, most of them in high spirits, all of them sick of war and of being cogs in the huge machine that had almost – but not quite – beaten Germany and Japan to their knees. None of them showed much interest in a forty-two-year-old sergeant of the Intelligence Corps who didn't laugh, rarely spoke and certainly wasn't inclined to join in sing-songs.

Sutton sat quietly in his seat by the window, spacing out his cigarettes at one per hour, watching the countryside slowly turn from bare moorland to rolling hills as they travelled southwards from the Highlands to the border. Around Edinburgh all was mutable shades of sepia and grey-black in the late afternoon light. There was plenty of time to see everything. Before the war, speed records had been achieved on the old LMS line from London to Scotland; these days, with the railways overstretched and short of staff and rolling stock, the once-proud trains moved painfully slowly, and timetables were correctly dismissed by the general public as bad works of fiction. Between the Scottish capital and Berwick-on-Tweed the train's pace wound down to barely above a brisk walk. Night had long since fallen when they stopped at the pretty little town right on the border between England and Scotland.

The woman who got on at Berwick wrenched Sutton out of his trance-like state. She was in her late twenties, dark and slim as far as could be told, because she wore a bulky woollen coat. The thing that really attracted Sutton's notice was her eyes, which instead of being hazel or brown, to go with her complexion, were a piercing shade of blue and disturbingly alive. She explored the carriage once, catching his eye as she passed his compartment, then a few minutes later re-appeared and slid open the door.

'Mind if I squeeze in? I know it's pretty bad in here, but everywhere else is even worse,' she said in a pleasant but firm voice. The accent was London suburban.

'You can sit on me knee if you like, darling,' said the sailor next to Sutton. He was big, with a face like a pink pudding, hardly out of his teens and cocky as only the young, strong and stupid can be.

'Don't you listen to him,' his mate told her with a scoff. 'He's just an old letch. You'll be safer in my lap.'

The woman was faced with eight hawklike pairs of male eyes, all glued to her, probably mentally stripping her where she stood, but she handled herself very well. Without another word, she hauled her suitcase over to the window.

'It's all right,' she said briskly, refusing to be provoked. 'I'll sit on my suitcase, thanks.'

Sutton got to his feet. 'You can sit here if you like,' he said. 'You look as if you could do with getting your head down for a bit.'

The pudding-faced sailor chortled lasciviously.

She looked at him, then at Sutton, frowned. A second later she had made her decision and said simply, 'That's very kind of you, sergeant. Thanks very much.'

'Hey, why don't you come and get your head down here, love,' said the sailor, pointing at his groin. His mate spluttered with laughter and began to make gestures mimicking masturbation.

Sutton turned, looked down at him as if the boy was two years old and had just done something in his trousers.

'Are you going to behave, sonny?' he asked softly. 'The lady bought her ticket, she's entitled to travel in peace and quiet.'

'Who are you talking to, grandpa?' the sailor snarled, bridling but not getting to his feet.

'You. Who else?'

'There's fifty blokes from my ship on this train, mate. You take me on, you take on all of us. We just come off a convoy from Russia, and . . .'

'I'm not taking you on – unless you insist. I'm just reminding you of your manners. Do you get my meaning?'

Sutton's eyes locked with the young sailor's, like animals meeting in a forest clearing, sizing each other up. The first, crucial instant of contact told Sutton that the boy didn't have what London villains called the 'bottle' to face up to him alone. With his mates might be different, but they weren't here at the moment. It was all bravado. God knows, Sutton had worked for long enough with real hard cases to know when there was genuine violence in a man's eyes, the kind who doesn't care how much damage he inflicts or receives, just so long as the volcano inside is allowed to erupt. Under the circumstances, why let it go any further? He decided to ease the boy off the hook, give him an opportunity to back down.

'Listen,' said Sutton, making an effort to be paternal without being condescending. 'You're going on leave, you're excited. All right. But let's all have some consideration for each other, shall we?'

The sailor reddened, eyed his mate out of the corner of his eye, obviously checking on the chances of getting help from that direction. The other boy didn't react.

'Just having a laugh,' he said defiantly. 'What's wrong with that? You never had a laugh with a tart?'

'You're calling the lady a tart?'

'You know what I mean.'

'Of course I do. Apologise to the lady. Say, I'm sorry I was rude to you and I didn't mean to call you a tart.' Sutton could feel so much pent-up anger coming out of him. He was almost frightened of himself, watching himself but somehow unable to intervene and calm down.

'A tart's – '

'Just do it. Apologise.'

Sutton's hand had gone out to touch the boy's shoulder, forcing him gently but inexorably down in his seat. His face was impassive, but inside a voice was saying, why are you doing this? Why bother? – She doesn't care? What are *you* getting out of this?

The boy decided to admit defeat, but he practically choked on the words when he said, 'I . . . apologise, don't I?'

'Say the words I told you to say.'

Eventually the boy spat them out one by one.

'Good lad,' Sutton said, and moved aside to let the woman

take his seat. Seemingly unaffected by the incident, she stepped past him side-on. Something about her careful avoidance of physical contact was, Sutton realised, far more erotic than a normal touch or a nudge.

'Excuse, son,' she said coolly, taking her seat beside the sailor. She crossed her legs with a rustle of stocking, smiled. The sailor blushed, bit his lip in embarrassment and suppressed fury, looked away.

Sutton lifted her case up onto the luggage rack. She thanked him, and busied herself pushing her soft shoulder-bag into the corner of the seat to provide a makeshift headrest. It was as if the sailor did not exist for her now.

'All right?' asked Sutton.

'Thanks. Very good.'

Sutton settled down on the floor, using his kitbag as a pillow and stretching his body out between the others' feet. He fancied he could feel the sailor boy's boot twitching, itching to crash down on his neck or his chest, but perhaps he was imagining things. He couldn't help admiring the woman's legs. He wondered if he should say anything more, but within moments, unexpectedly, Sutton was fast asleep.

A jolt shook Sutton into wakefulness out of a dreamless sleep. He had read somewhere, maybe in one of his wife's magazines, that you always had dreams; it was just that you often didn't remember them. If he didn't, it was fine by him. His eyes adjusted to the darkness in the compartment, and there was the woman staring down at him, puffing on a cigarette. She looked serious and self-contained, just as she had when he had first seen her. She seemed friendly enough, as far as he could see.

'The station sign says we're in Newcastle-under-Lyme,' she said. 'Where's that when it's at home?'

'Somewhere in the Midlands,' he answered vaguely.

' "Somewhere in the Midlands, our gallant boys are stopped in a railway siding. Who knows when they'll finally reach their destination . . . ?" ' she intoned in a passable imitation of a Pathé News announcer. 'Anyway, you should be able to do better than that. You're in the Intelligence Corps.'

'You know your unit identification badges.'

'Come on, any girl worth her salt got to know all the regimental badges as soon as war was declared.' Her look was cynically amused. 'That way she knew who was in the glamour outfits, who wasn't.'

'Important, eh?'

'Women are romantic about these things, always have been. And because they're romantic they're quite prepared to be bloody cruel.'

Sutton let that one pass. 'Don't you travel this way very often, then? I can tell you're a Londoner.'

She smiled. 'One up for the Intelligence Corps,' she said sardonically. 'I'd never been north of Watford before the beginning of this month.'

'And what's your verdict on the wild and woolly north?'

'I daresay it's all right in summer, but there's not an awful lot to do at nights, I can tell you. I've just spent a couple of weeks looking after my sister's family while she had her appendix done. She went and married a farmer from the border country, poor thing. Sheep, sheep and more sheep.'

'You should try the Highlands of Scotland if you're fond of sheep.'

She didn't answer. Instead she went back to looking out of the window, frowning as if she had already revealed too much of herself too quickly. She crushed her cigarette out in the ash-tray and ran one hand through her hair before turning back to face Sutton.

'I suppose I'd better show some manners,' she said. 'My name is Rose Wesolowski and I'm pleased to meet you.'

'Polish?'

'He was.'

Sutton didn't feel like exploring the past tense straight away. 'George Sutton,' he introduced himself. 'And by the way, does the Intelligence Corps count as a glamour unit?'

'Could be worse. Better than the Pay Corps or the Engineers. Just.'

'And what about Mr Wesolowski?' Sutton probed gently.

'I thought so at the time,' she said with a wistful look in her disturbing eyes. 'How much more glamorous can you get than the cavalry? Like all the rest of them, he escaped from Poland in the nick of time, et cetera et cetera. Adam looked like Charles Boyer, kissed your hand all the time, and the fact that he didn't speak more than half a dozen words of English made him all the more attractive and mysterious.' She laughed, but with a bitter edge to it. 'It was only when he learned to speak English a bit better that I realised his main interests and topics of conversation were himself and glorious Poland. In that order. Our little boy came third, and God knows about me.'

Sutton tensed. 'You have a kid?'

'He's three and a half. And if you're still wondering my husband was killed "somewhere in Italy", which I've since been told was Monte Cassino. Thinking, as ever, of himself and Poland, he tried to storm an enemy machine-gun post single-handed. He got lots of them, but unfortunately they got all of him. The government-in-exile gave him a very nice medal, or rather they sent it to me through the post with their sincere condolences. I get a little widow's pension.'

Sutton got to his feet, wincing slightly from the pain in his back and neck. He did a few shoulder exercises to loosen up the muscles, then lit a cigarette. The engine ahead was hissing gently. A few hardy souls were stretching their legs on the freezing platform. The young sailor was sound asleep, his head resting on his mate's shoulder. He looked very young, even innocent in his way; despite the slack-jawed stupidity of that face, Sutton felt a stab of regret for having humiliated him, then chided himself. What's the matter? Getting sentimental in your old age, George?

'You married?' she asked.

'My wife was killed in the Blitz.'

'I'm sorry. Kids?'

'No, no kids.'

'Not much to look forward to on this leave, then,' she said matter-of-factly.

'I suppose not. But this is official business, anyway.'

'Oh, got to see a man about a dog, hush-hush and all that?'

'That kind of thing,' Sutton agreed, and laughed at the dead-pan absurdity of her delivery. He liked her sense of humour and her toughness.

As if to show her other side, she suddenly said, 'I didn't intend to play down your loss. Your wife's death, I mean. I suppose that because of Adam I think I'm entitled to be a bit callous.'

'I understand,' Sutton said. And he did. He really did. In many ways it was like looking in the mirror, talking to this

26

woman, except that somehow she had kept more of a vital spark of life going than he had. She didn't let too many people see it, he suspected, but it was there if you looked.

He found out that she lived in a 'sort of all right' little flat in Mornington Crescent with her son, that she had been a nurse but now she worked for the Ministry of Food as a filing clerk. Her boss was a darling and had fiddled her two weeks' compassionate leave so that she could look after her sister's family during their crisis. As for her own child, he was staying with mother in Ruislip. He spent a lot of time there.

'I'm surprised you stayed close to the centre of London. Especially with the flying bombs this past year,' Sutton said.

'It took me twenty-three years to get out of Ruislip in the first place,' she told him firmly. 'It'll take a bloody sight more than a few doodlebugs and a shortage of babysitters to send me back there. Yes, I know it's not the kind of thing nice young widows are supposed to say to strangers on trains, but then I gave up trying to be nice years ago.'

'When you left Ruislip?'

'Oh no, well before that. You see, I realised that for people in Ruislip and Hounslow and all those places, being "nice" hides all sorts of nasty secret things.'

'I won't ask for details.'

'You don't have to. You *know*,' she said. 'That's the reason I decided to talk to you. Not because of the trouble with that boy there in his sailor suit, by the way – I could have sorted him out on my own, thanks very much.'

At last she smiled. It spread slowly and took its good time to enter her disconcerting blue eyes, but when it reached them they sparkled like aquamarine, deep and dangerous as well as inviting.

Some time after midnight when the train pulled into King's Cross, Sutton and Rose Wesolowski walked through the ticket barrier together and then stood awkwardly on the busy, crowded concourse. Fellow-arrivals streamed past them, while waiting passengers, mostly servicemen, stood smoking and drinking tea, or crammed onto the rows of bench seats under the station clock.

She looked around. 'There are the sailors from the boy's ship,' she said. 'They're terribly drunk, I think.'

27

Twenty yards from them were a bunch of young men in the uniforms of naval ratings, gathered like noisy schoolchildren on an excursion, except that there was no teacher in sight to supervise them. They were handing round cigarettes, boxing with each other, talking far too loudly. He couldn't see the boy he had faced down as they came south of Berwick, but he suspected he must be in there somewhere. Were they staring at him, nudging each other, or what?

'Well, it's been a pleasure,' he told Rose. 'It helped to pass the time.'

'Yes. I really get bored too. On trains.'

She was waiting, so he said it: 'How are you actually going to get home?'

'On my own two feet, of course. I've been finding my own way around through the blackout for five years now. My husband was hardly around at all for the last two. Where are you off to?'

'Paddington. There's a lodging-house there I usually stay in when I'm in London. I rang up and reserved a room. They know me and they don't mind if I turn up in the middle of the night.'

She nodded, and for the first time she seemed shy.

'I could walk you back,' he said then. 'You said you lived in Mornington Crescent? It's not far, and I'll be able to get a bus on to my digs. Or an underground from Great Portland Street if the trains are still running.'

There was a moment's hesitation. 'All right,' she said. 'If it's not too much trouble. I know I said I'm used to it, but to tell the truth I've never liked the dark much, and then there's the suitcase . . .'

'Come on.'

'You're sure it's not too much trouble?'

'Don't be so *nice*, all right?'

Sutton examined her face carefully, trying to fathom what was really going on behind the awkward politeness, but actually it was harder to divine her true feelings than it had been when they had first met on the train. Hell, let her get back to her flat and her child and her job and whatever was left for her of Adam Wesolowski, war hero. And let George Sutton see her to her door, then make his way to Paddington to that spartan but clean room in the lodging-house. There he could keep himself to himself and think whatever he needed to think about Jeannie.

He picked up her suitcase and his own kitbag, and they set off up the wide expanse of the Euston Road. They walked slowly, turning north half a mile along at Warren Street underground station. There were some suspicious-looking characters around – the usual late-night drunks, plus some tarts and their pimps, but no sign of the gang of sailor-boys. Rose talked quite a lot, constantly assuring Sutton that she was more than capable of looking after herself. She travelled where she liked, she said; she ate and drank wherever took her fancy. She had worked as a nurse, after all, and got used to seeing men when they were sick, naked, helpless and altogether ridiculous. If they gave you any trouble, there was a *look* you could give men that saw them off.

They arrived at Mornington Crescent and were walking around the curved terrace towards her flat. She stopped at a wrought-iron gate set in a wall, behind which some steps led down into the basement.

They stood silently for a moment. Then Sutton said, 'I'd better go or I'll miss the last train.'

'Why don't you just miss it? I made trouble for you. The least I can do is give you a bed for the night.'

'Listen – '

'It's up to you, George. You're a widower, I'm a widow. We're not doing anybody any harm. No one has to do anything they don't want to.'

'I'm not an easy man, you know.'

'I'll risk it', she said, and pushed the gate open.

Sutton followed her down the dark, steep steps, waited while she fumbled with her keys and finally let them into the flat.

Inside the door was a narrow, bare hallway. The first room on the left was a tiny bedroom containing a child's bed, some Beatrix Potter pictures fixed to the wall, a basket filled with well-used toys.

'That's Jimmy's room. I'm lucky to have the space; the bloke from the housing office must have liked the look of me, because he could have moved me to a smaller place when Adam was killed, but he didn't. At least I get a bit of peace once the boy's in bed.' She moved towards the living room.

'Put the case in my bedroom, will you? It's the next one along. I'll go through and put the fire on and see what there is in the cupboard. Should be a drop of something.'

She laughed as she walked ahead of him into the living-room. As she went through the door, she put on the light, took off her coat and tossed it carelessly onto a sofa.

Sutton obediently dumped the case in her bedroom. It was unfussy, almost spartan, except for the little touches like an embroidered bedspread and an antique brass lamp. The lamp was there because she liked it, and no other reason. Sutton sniffed the air. The whole flat was damp and musty after two weeks without being aired or attended to.

'Come on through!' he heard her call out. 'Or are you spellbound by the beauty of your surroundings?'

When Sutton walked into the living-room, he saw how much of Rose Wesolowski he had missed during their hours on the train. She had spent the whole journey wrapped up in a thick, shapeless utility overcoat. Now, looking at her standing at the far end of the room with her hands on her hips, in a chic woollen sweater and tight skirt, he realised that he had somehow picked up a stunning woman. And he hadn't even been trying!

'Seen a ghost?'

'No. An apparition, but very much alive.'

She giggled, indicated some bottles on the table. 'There's whisky, but only the American kind, Jack Daniels. Or there's a tiny bit of gin. Or Algerian red wine.'

'I'd prefer a cup of tea.'

'Aha.'

'I don't drink. Not any more.'

'Well, I do. But I'll put the kettle on for you.'

She went out into the kitchen, lit the gas ring and put a big enamel kettle on to boil. When she came back into the living-room, she poured herself two fingers of Jack Daniels and raised her glass in a toast.

'Since this is courtesy of the PX, let's say, long live our glorious Allies,' she said, and took a grateful sip. She must have noticed the longing in Sutton's eyes, because her tone suddenly changed, became softer. 'Serious trouble with the demon drink?'

Booze doesn't agree with me. In fact, at one stage we

disagreed so violently that it damned-near killed me. As it was, I had to give up my job in C.I.D.'

'Was that painful?'

'I was a good copper. I liked the work. And it had been eighteen years of my life, give or take a month or two.'

'Oh, most policemen have got a problem dealing with ordinary life in my experience – little details like their families, their women.' she said.

For a moment Sutton felt insulted, then he realised that she was telling the truth. She wasn't even looking at him but just staring into her glass of whisky, as if she had stated a simple fact, a way of the world.

'You've been involved with coppers, have you?'

'Oh, I've met all sorts. I've got no problems with them, so don't worry. Unless you've by any chance got a problem with women, George . . . ?'

'Not the sort of problem that would bother you.' Sutton shot back sharply before he had time to think.

She winced. 'I suppose I asked for that. But I do fancy you. Just for tonight.'

Sutton felt a mixture of anger, lust and pity. He couldn't help but reach out, take her arm, pull her towards him.

'You, Mrs Wesolowski, are about as romantic as a declaration of war,' he said. 'And I bet you drive a lot of men mad.'

He kissed her gently on the lips, smelled the whisky on her breath. She stroked his back, then pulled away, but only so that she could lead the way through to the bedroom.

'It's bloody cold in here,' she said briskly. 'We'd better get our comforts worked out before we start anything, hadn't we?'

The first thing she did was to light the gas fire in the wall near the bed. Then she took her shoes off kicked them into the corner. Finally, as smoothly and easily as if she were reaching for a coat from the cupboard, she slid her hands inside Sutton's army greatcoat, pulled him towards her with a sudden, fierce need. He felt her pelvis thrusting against his groin, her lips searching for his and finding them.

'Come alive for tonight, Sergeant George Whoever,' she murmured huskily. 'After tonight you can do what you damned well like.'

Soon adept fingers were snaking inside his battledress trousers, probing his hardness. Rose Wesolowski was not slow.

She quickly twisted out of her knickers, and Sutton eased her skirt up until it was way up around her waist and warm flesh met flesh, tip of cock homing into her luxuriously dark, damp mound, guided by her gentle but insistent hand. He was already easing himself inside her when they tumbled onto the bed together in a kind of controlled dive, her legs wrapped around him. She moaned with pleasure and the beginnings of the most intense stages of arousal as his cock pushed in deep, rested and then began the rhythmic motions of pleasure.

He liked Rose and desired her, but he knew that this was as far as it would go. A brief encounter, a celebration of his release from Scotland. He would probably never see her again. At that moment, though, this realisation didn't make him want her any the less. To him if felt like the first small episode in a new life, mysterious and good. He was having his first woman since his wife's death. He was reporting back to Scotland Yard, the prodigal son returning from exile. After the long, lean stint on the Moray Firth, Sutton's cup seemed to run over. And in Rose Wesolowski's neat little kitchen, the kettle she had put on to make his nice, sober cup of tea boiled completely dry.

CHAPTER THREE

SUTTON had got used to waking early; without the disturb-
ance of alcohol, his body returned to the animal rest and
activity patterns of childhood. What he wasn't used to – not
any more – was waking up and finding a woman in bed by his
side.

He was still wearing his watch. Tut-tut, he thought.
Gentlemen didn't wear watches in bed, just as they were
supposed to rest on their elbows when they mounted a lady
for pleasure. Thank God he wasn't a gentleman. It was just
gone seven and he had slept only three hours thanks to Rose
Wesolowski. He smiled, lay looking at the smooth, pale back
with its almost masculine, broad shoulders. She had turned
away from him in sleep, and her bare right arm was draped
over the far edge of the bed. The gold-plated bracelet on her
wrist glistened faintly in the very first grey light of day.

Sutton swung himself out of bed slowly and carefully, so as
not to disturb her, padded to the small bathroom that lay just
off the kitchen. Rose had left the gas fire on – strictly against
the fuel-saving regulations – but it was still bloody cold in
there, and the linoleum was as chilly to the feet and as treacherous as a frozen pond. After emptying his bladder, Sutton
turned on the light over the sink, looked at himself in the
mirror, and was shocked by what he saw. He remembered
how before they had gone to bed Rose had said, *come alive*,
with an urgency that he hadn't understood. But now, perhaps,
he did.

The actual flesh was not so bad. The army haircut was pretty
drastic, but Sutton still had a good head of fair hair. As for
the lines on his face, at his age they were considered to be
evidence of character. There really wasn't much to complain

about in the features as a whole, which included a good strong mouth and nose, and not even a hint of a double chin. Okay for forty-three next birthday. Jeannie had thought he was handsome, and there had never been any shortage of girls who shared that opinion, before or after he got married. So what was wrong? Why did he feel so uneasy when he looked at himself?

After a short while it came to him. Normally when he faced a mirror – say, when he went to shave in the morning – he was prepared for what he saw, or bleary from sleep, or used a tiny travelling mirror that showed only his chin or his upper lip. This was the first time in a long while that he had caught his entire reflection in a mirror when he was wide awake and, maybe because of the night he had spent with this woman, defenceless in a strange kind of way.

'Jesus,' Sutton muttered to himself, and he blinked. 'Where've you been?'

It was the eyes, he thought. They were dead. He honestly wondered why Rose had brought him back here to her bed. Maybe she had felt responsible for him after the trouble in the train. Maybe dead eyes were the fashion this year. Or maybe she just liked going to bed with strange men.

Sutton saw the safety-razor a moment later, when he looked down at the sink. It was stainless steel, the kind you couldn't get over here. Sure enough, the words 'MADE IN USA' were stamped on the handle. He opened up the little cupboard, confirmed that there was a packet of spare blades in there, plus a shaving brush and some men's cologne whose label told him it had been manufactured somewhere in Maryland.

No wonder Rose Wesolowski had plenty of Jack Daniels in the house, and no wonder she had been very clear that Sutton would be staying just the one night.

'We're all entitled to a fling from time to time, you know,' Rose said from the doorway. 'Particularly when we've just got engaged.'

Sutton turned and saw her standing there. She had thrown a dressing-gown over her shoulders. It must have kept out some of the cold, but it didn't conceal her full, large-nippled breasts or the tempting curve of her belly.

'I've never been called a fling before,' Sutton said, and closed the cupboard door. 'It's quite flattering. I just hope

34

your G.I.'s not in the habit of dropping by for a spot of breakfast, because I don't think he'd be too pleased to find me here.'

'He doesn't know I'm back yet. He won't find out until I choose to tell him.'

'And when will that be?'

'Oh, I don't know.' She smiled at him mockingly. 'Don't flatter yourself you're the reason I'm not telling him yet. As it happens, I'd like a couple of days on my own, just with Jimmy, before I see him.'

'You like things your way, don't you?' Sutton said.

'I suppose I do. Don't you?'

Sutton laughed. 'And what does your G.I. think about that?'

'Oh, he's a nice, gentle man. He's got perfect manners, he works very hard, and he's in line to take over his dad's grocery business in California when he gets out of the army. There'll be a house and land, a car, a great future for Jimmy – and it's all a long way from Ruislip.'

'That again. Is it all you care about?'

' "Judge not, that ye be not judged," Sergeant George,' she said with a laugh. 'Were your intentions entirely honourable when you walked through that front door?'

'No, they weren't. I admit it,' he said.

'Of course they weren't. Now, my G.I. doesn't get exclusive rights to my charms until he signs that piece of paper and starts giving me cheques to cover the housekeeping. If you've got the time, we can do again what we did a couple of times last night. I'm not a good little American housewife yet.'

Sutton grinned. 'Well, I'm not in London until I choose to let them know, either. That's the beauty of the war. Everything's always going wrong, so there's always plenty of excuses.'

'Who needs excuses?' she said.

The fortress-like Gothic building on the Victorian Embankment had once seemed as familiar and welcoming to Sutton as the house he was born in, but today, as he approached Scotland Yard along the wide street by the river, he could feel its brooding, implacable quality. In its power and severity it was like a monastery or the headquarters of a militant religious order which never forgave those who transgressed.

Sutton had felt defiant, even cocksure, when he finally left Rose Wesolowski's flat earlier that morning. Now, passing through the lobby doors and finding himself inundated with the sights and sounds and sensations that had been such an important part of his life for so many years, he felt his confidence ebb and a knot of fear and loss begin to harden in his stomach.

Ever since he had entered Peel House for his ten-week induction course back in '26, just after the General Strike, the raw boy from the East End had stood in awe of the Yard, had longed to be a part of the legend known the world over. Scotland Yard had been the headquarters of the London Metropolitan Police since 1890, a famous landmark in the city, but also far more. It stood for power and glory, law and order, efficiency and integrity, and also moderation and sobriety – all the Victorian virtues.

George Sutton had wanted the power and the glory, and he had got it, by hard work and clever playing of the promotion game. He had never stopped to ask the price. The road through 'E' Division at Bow Street, weary hours on the beat and in boring courtrooms, to C.I.D., then to the Yard at last and the rank of Detective Chief Inspector and aide to the Commissioner, had been a long and testing one. He had worked all hours, studied and read and watched and listened, learned how to fight with words rather than fists, to protect himself from the infighting and jealousies that got more savage and dangerous the closer he came to the top. He had become a senior man, the rising star they called 'the boy wonder'. His persistence in language classes had led to his selection for international work, bringing travel to Interpol conferences as a junior member of the British delegation, and once the war came he found himself sitting on little-known but surprisingly influential committees co-ordinating the work of his own C.I.D., the Special Branch, and the counter-espionage people at Leconfield House, headquarters of M.I.5.

So there he was, Jack the Lad from Stepney, bright and hardworking with an unaccountable flair for languages. There had even been talk of teaming him up with the quiet, deceptively jovial Chief Inspector Smith, an ex-Yard man now with the security service, whose prowess at arresting spies over a period of six or seven years had given him the nickname

'Spycatcher'. Bound for glory, was George Sutton, as many of his colleagues had enviously noticed.

Then, one afternoon in the autumn of '43, Sir James Rudwick, once Sutton's mentor and protector, had bowed to pressure from other senior officers and formally requested his resignation. For two years now Sutton had believed that he would never set foot in Scotland Yard again.

Sutton was deep in thought as he stepped out onto the landing along the corridor from the commissioner's offices. Then, with a shock, he realised someone was calling his name. He rounded on his heel, swinging his kitbag almost like a weapon, looked to his right. Just a few yards away stood Jim Garfield, a man he had known quite well during his years here. With Garfield was a younger man, broad-shouldered and square-jowelled, wearing an unusually well-cut suit and a look of permanent disdain. Both men carried thick bundles of files under their arms and looked as if they spent a lot of time in corridors close to the offices of the great and powerful.

Garfield advanced on Sutton, looking a little sheepish but apparently glad to see him. To be fair, he was not one of those who had lobbied for Sutton's resignation when there had been the trouble about his drinking.

'Lord, Lord, George, my old mate . . . How's things?' Garfield said.

'Hello, Jim. Sir James wanted to see me when I was next in London, so here I am,' Sutton shrugged. He liked Garfield well enough, but he knew the man gossiped in the Red Lion after work. Every drinking man in at the Yard would know before the pub shut tonight that George Sutton, former boy wonder and now disgraced, was back in town.

'Oh, that's typical of Sir James,' Garfield said. 'Decent stick, doesn't forget people in a hurry. Look, I'm sorry I didn't see you before you left. It all happened so bloody quickly, didn't it?'

'Yes. Still, the army hasn't been so bad,' Sutton lied. 'Except they don't play cricket up in the wilds of Scotland. Oh, and the sheep start looking rather attractive after a while.'

'Ha! Very good, George. You always were one for the dry humour, as I remember.' As if to avoid any more of Sutton's dry humour, he turned and indicated his companion, who was staring coolly at Sutton as if he were trespassing in an exclusive private club. 'George,' Garfield said awkwardly, 'meet Henry Bardwell. Henry's on the Security Liaison Committee with me. He – '

'I think that's enough, don't you, Jim?' Bardwell cut in smoothly. He had an educated accent and looked, when you took the time to study him, as if the only question he'd ask if you wanted to buy his mother would be, cash or cheque? 'You know what they say about careless talk,' he added pompously.

Garfield chortled, winked at Sutton. 'Come on. Old George here was a founder member of the same committee. Not much he doesn't know about our dark secrets.'

Bardwell nodded and smiled a tight smile, but said nothing. He was obviously just waiting it out until this unexpected interruption came to an end. Sutton knew the type well.

'Ah well, got to dash,' said Garfield uncomfortably. 'Conference. You know how it is once you get to so-called senior rank.'

'Had a promotion since we last met?'

'Made Super last August.'

'Congratulations.'

'Tell you what, pop round the Red Lion if you're free later.'

Sutton felt a huge weariness. People like this knew about him and alcohol, and they just kept pressing. He didn't feel like explaining about booze yet again. In any case, he wasn't sure which was more irksome: Jim Garfield's patronising bonhomie or that shark Bardwell's cold-eyed stare. Bardwell was Special Branch, even junior M.I.5, from 'F' section, internal subversion. Anyway, he was certainly minor public school, probably ex-colonial police, the kind who always looked right down their noses at the likes of Sutton.

'I'll see how I'm fixed,' Sutton said. 'Give the boys my regards anyway.'

'Sutton . . .' Bardwell said suddenly, just as they were about to part. 'I think I've heard of you, now I come to think about it. I must say I'm surprised to see you here.'

'There you go,' Sutton answered sweetly. 'No accounting for the strange whims of our masters along the corridor, eh?'

Bardwell nodded unsmilingly, turned away.

'Well, George. Must dash,' said Garfield.

'Of course. My best to Lilly.'

'Oh yes. She'll be glad to know you're all right.'

'Goodbye, Jim.'

''Bye, George. Don't do anything I wouldn't do.'

That's a bit limiting, thought Sutton as Garfield and the
other man set off up the other corridor on their way to their
self-important world of meetings and conferences and memos
and telephone calls. Apart from the odd few beers in the pub,
Jim had always lived the blameless life of an early Christian
saint, pure in thought and deed. There were times when Sutton
had envied him his little semi-detached house in Dulwich, his
bull-nosed Morris in the garage, his wife and . . .

Better not take that one too far, Sutton thought. Dangerous
territory, even after Rose Wesolowski.

When Sutton was ushered into Sir James Rudwick's office, the
Assistant Commissioner (Security) was standing facing away
from the door, gazing out of the window over the embankment
with his hands clasped behind his broad back. It was, Sutton
knew, his normal stance when receiving insolent underlings or
difficult equals.

Sutton cleared his throat, said in a firm voice, 'Good
morning, Sir James.'

Rudwick waited for a moment more, turned at a leisurely
pace, registered the expression of amusement on Sutton's face
but did not react.

'George,' he said with a faint smile, rocking on his heels
and keeping his distance for the moment. 'Good to see you
again. How are you?'

No handshake, no embrace of the prodigal son. It was as if
Sutton still came to this office several times a week and his
presence was in no way remarkable.

'Not bad, sir. A bit tired.'

'I'm not surprised. It's the very devil travelling by train these
days.'

As if you'd know, Sutton thought, with your official car and
chauffeur.

They were both tall men, Sutton six-foot two, Rudwick
perhaps an inch shorter. There any similarity ended. While
Sutton was fair-haired, even-featured and, despite his forty-
two years, still almost as lean and trim as the amateur cricketer
he had been in his youth, Sir James was sixty and all trunk
and head, with walrus jowls and a barrel chest. The overall

impression was of a giant's torso welded onto a dwarf's limbs. he had a thick moustache, of the kind fashionable in Edwardian times, especially in India, where he had been first in the army and then in the police for many years. All in all, despite his physical oddity, Rudwick seemed typical of the solid, patriotic English officers who had conquered and now ruled the British Empire – a bit snobbish, perhaps a bit out of touch with modern life, but essentially decent and above all determined to do their duty whatever the circumstances. Sutton had always found him crusty but straightforward, and a lot more intelligent than his blimpish appearance led people to believe. He had come to like and respect him during his last years at the Yard.

Rudwick was wearing the dark brown tweed suit he always wore in the spring. He was comfortably predictable, like the clock in the drawing room or a belligerent but loyal family dog.

'Take a seat, George, old boy,' he said, easing himself down behind his big mahogany desk. Sutton sat down in the chair facing him across the desk-top. 'We'll look after you. We've fixed you up with a very comfortable furnished room in Holland Park, all expenses paid, three meals a day, and so on. You can get some rest – ' he sifted among the papers on the surface in front of him, frowning, then found what he was looking for – 'after we've had our chat.'

'I have a place in Paddington I use, sir.'

'We'd like you to be in one of our own places, if you don't mind. It makes things so much easier from the point of view of the paperwork,' Rudwick said without taking his attention from his papers.

'I see, sir.'

Rudwick looked up then, gave him a wintry smile, sat back in his chair and formed his fingers into a steeple.

'I don't think you do quite see, actually, George,' he said. 'Of course, I couldn't say anything on the phone to that dreadful major in Scotland, but I can tell you here and now that you have become a very valuable commodity all of a sudden. You are to be looked after, wrapped in tissue paper, cosseted.'

Sutton didn't ask the question Rudwick was so blatantly

cueing him for. He fished a packet of cigarettes out of his pocket. 'Mind if I smoke, sir?'

'If you must.' Rudwick looked distinctly offended. 'Look, old boy, I know you like playing games, but there's such a thing as normal curiosity. Don't you want to know why George Sutton is suddenly so welcome in these parts once again? Good God, man, if I were you I'd be breaking down the door to find out what's going on.'

'Well, I'd like to know, yes. But I'm sure it's a story you'd like to tell in your own particular way, sir. I'm a very patient man, as you know.'

Rudwick shook his head in a gesture of affectionate despair.

'Your two winters in Siberia obviously haven't softened you, George.'

'Did you expect them to, sir?'

Rudwick looked away and glanced at the framed sepia photograph of his wife and two sons that he kept on his desk. It had been taken in India just after the First World War and showed them sitting in wicker chairs on a lawn while a servant brought them afternoon tea. Everyone was staring at the camera like actors composing themselves for a flashbulb to pop. The servant alone seemed totally oblivious and natural, as unconcerned and neutral as the table, the teapot or the grass. Sir James always referred to that photograph in sticky moments, as a Catholic plays with his rosary or a Buddhist repeats his mantra.

'I suppose you have every right to be a little spiky, George,' he said after a while. 'That whole business of your leaving wasn't easy on any of us. You were one of my best officers, perhaps the very best, but can't we let it be water under the bridge?'

It was true that Rudwick had thrown Sutton to the wolves only because the pressure to fire him had been too great. Throughout Sutton's career there had been the superior Bardwells, who thought of him as jumped-up cockney, and the Jim Garfields, who for all their decency didn't understand the edge of defiance that stopped him from being a faithful pipe-and-slippers breadwinner who came home every night to his dinner and after ten years of marriage called his wife 'mother'. When Sutton had overstepped the mark neither group had had much compassion for the boy wonder.

41

'Perhaps we can. Anyway, to what do I owe this . . . trip back upstream?'

'Not bad, George. Not bad.' Rudwick grimaced at the bitter little joke. 'Now, I want to discuss an Interpol matter – or at least, Interpol is our starting point. First of all, I want to ask you whether you recall a German police officer named Keppler – Heinz Keppler.'

Sutton thought for a moment, then nodded. 'I remember him, yes. He came to London for the '37 Interpol Conference. After that, I met him at Interpol H.Q. in Vienna after the Nazis took control of Austria and got their hands on the Interpol apparatus there. The last time I saw him was in Berlin, spring of '39, just before I was transferred to Security.'

'Fine. What do you know about him, eh?'

'Not too much,' Sutton said. 'He was a records man, as I recall. Bit of a man for the high life. I think I took him on a night out up West the first time we met. Spoke good English, with an American accent. Must have been there. A little above average height, good build, brown hair. Duelling scar on his right cheek. Wore glasses and didn't like having to. His weakness was vanity.'

'Spoken like a veteran of a hundred identity parades. Did you and he become . . . er . . . friendly?'

Sutton looked at him in surprise. 'Not especially. We had a few drinks together – in Berlin he bought the booze and the dinner on his department's budget, they were so keen to court us. Apart from the standard Nazi spiel, he spent a lot of time trying to convince me that he was just a simple, honest copper like you and me, not one of your thugs. He got pretty insistent about it after his eighth glass of *schnapps*.'

'Were you convinced by him?'

'You must be joking. He might have got a bit maudlin when he'd had a few, but he was one of Heydrich's shining stars all right. Like the rest of them, everything he said or did gave the impression that the sun shone out of the Führer's bum. Mind you, I say he gave the *impression* . . .'

'Quite. So he was just another face at the conference, a chap you had a drink with, might chat with about professional matters in common, consult if you had a problem he could help you with, that sort of thing. No different to your French

42

or Dutch or Swedish counterpart. There was nothing you could call a special relationship between you and Keppler?'

'No. I spoke his language, of course. But there were others I spent more time with and certainly others I was more fond of. Where is all this leading sir?'

'It's leading, George, to the fact that whatever impression he made on you, you certainly made quite a lasting impression on Herr Keppler, who is now, by the way, a Colonel in the SS and controls the Interpol records. In fact, he has contacted us from inside Berlin and has made very specific and special reference to George Sutton. What do you think of that?'

'He must be round the twist, sir.'

'That had occurred to me as one explanation,' Sir James said drily. 'Except for this . . .'

Rudwick took a key from his pocket, unlocked one of the drawers in his desk, reached in and took out a buff-coloured file. From the file he removed a printed magazine-style publication and handed it to Sutton.

The magazine was professionally printed and very slickly designed. It dated from the autumn of 1944 and the interesting thing about it was the title: *Internationale Kriminalpolizei*, International Criminal Police. It described itself as the German language edition of the 'sole official publication of the International Criminal Police Commission – better known to the world at large as Interpol'.

'Just in case, like most people, you thought Interpol faded away when the war broke out,' Rudwick explained. 'In fact, the Germans have kept the whole thing going strong, even managed to keep police forces from neutral and occupied countries affiliated. The Germans have always insisted that they are just "looking after" the files and the organisation until peace comes. Of course, almost no one is convinced that that is their actual intention. You were transferred from Interpol liaison duties just before the war, weren't you, George?'

'That's right. May '39. It's all in my record.'

'Just confirming it,' said Rudwick. 'Then you know that the Nazis finally took the organisation over lock, stock and barrel in '38 when they invaded Austria and occupied the organisation's offices in Vienna.'

'Yes, sir. That's the year I visited Vienna and saw Keppler

the second time. He was one of the many Nazis who were suddenly swarming all over the shop, telling everybody what to do and generally behaving like cocks of the walk.'

'Which they were, George. S.S. General Daluege had actually been elected President of Interpol the previous year. But once the Germans were physically established in Vienna as occupiers, the real head of Interpol – the man who controlled the files that had been so painstakingly built up over fifteen years – was Daluege's ultimate boss: Reinhard Heydrich himself, head of the Nazi secret police.'

'I would have thought that it was obvious at the time what was happening. I've always wondered why the democratic governments didn't object, or even demand that the headquarters and the archives be transferred elsewhere. Say, to a neutral country.'

'You forget, George, that these things take time, and that they need something close to unanimity to be enforceable. Interpol was more like a professional private club than a truly international organisation. The head of the Vienna Police Department simply invited other police chiefs and national forces to join. Nothing to do with governments. In fact, we liked to think the system was better that way, less "political". We couldn't predict that a bunch of bad hats like Heydrich and his cronies would move in and take advantage.'

'Not being able to predict the way dictators behave seems to have been a speciality for our political leaders at that time, if I may say so, sir.'

'What are you getting at, George?' Rudwick asked irritably.

'I'm thinking of Mr Chamberlain and the Munich Treaty. "Peace in our time" and all that. He and the rest of them believed that Hitler would play fair with us if only we played fair with him.'

'I see you're an expert on international politics – with the help of seven years' hindsight, of course,' Rudwick said tartly.

Sutton smiled. 'After my visit to Vienna that summer, I did make much the same point in my official report. It seemed to me to be as plain as the nose on your face. I grew up in Stepney. If you always insist on playing fair in the streets around where I spent my childhood, you'll soon find yourself in very serious trouble.'

Rudwick sighed and continued.

'The forces involved had always accepted that whoever was in charge of the Austrian police automatically took over the presidency of the organisation. After all, the Austrians provided a building, clerical and administrative staff, and more than their fair share of the running expenses. When the Germans annexed Austria, the head of the German police was appointed police chief in Vienna and that was that. Unfortunately, Heydrich turned out to be a Nazi of the very worst sort. His ambitions went far beyond anything we could imagine, George. It was Heydrich's clear intention to create a vast storehouse of information, culled from Interpol's files and using any new material that came his way through his control of the organisation. Information equals power for honest policemen pursuing criminal investigations – hence our enthusiastic support for Interpol up to that time. However, information is also the lifeblood of the secret policeman, the spy – and the blackmailer. All very low forms of life.'

'So what have the Nazis been up to these past six years?' Sutton asked.

'In December 1941, just after we went to war with Japan, the Interpol offices and archives were transferred to a suburban villa in Berlin. Immediately next door happen to be the administrative offices of some key Gestapo departments. A nice coincidence, eh?'

'Coincidence be damned.'

'Precisely. With the Nazis occupying most of Europe and planning to divide the world up between themselves and Japan, Heydrich and his S.S. henchmen were preparing the way for the creation of a huge apparatus of repression, using the Interpol organisation and the files as a key component.'

Sutton nodded. 'So the cosy club where honest coppers from different countries could exchange information and pictures of their kids, help each other catch villains, once a year swap stories over a few beers at the congress, becomes a pillar of Nazism, a way of controlling the lives of millions of ordinary people.'

'That was undoubtedly Heydrich's long-term goal: to have a file on every wretched citizen of the Nazis empire.'

'And after he was assassinated?'

'Then Kaltenbrunner, his successor, eventually became President of Interpol. Vice-President and Director of the organisation's International Bureau was S.S. General Arthur Nebe, head of the RKPA – the Reich Office of Criminal Police. And on the next level beneath him was our old friend Heinz Keppler.' Rudwick drummed his fingers on the desk. 'Well, there you have the situation as regards Interpol.'

There was a pause. Sutton lit another cigarette. 'This is all very interesting,' he said, 'but I'm sure you're not giving me this lecture just to increase my knowledge of the subject – especially as it's obviously no bloody use to me in the position I hold at the moment. Sir, I'd now appreciate it very much if you would tell me what you want from me?'

'In a moment, George. I have something else for you first,' Rudwick said crisply. From the original folder he produced a sheaf of typewritten documents that had been stapled together in the top left-hand corner in perfect civil service style. He passed it over to Sutton.

The sheets were, on closer examination, photographic copies, stamped on one margin 'IKPK', the initials of Interpol in German, and on the right with the smaller hand-stamp of an eagle and swastika plus the imprint 'Abt. III(X)'.

'I know about Section III – that's the criminal administration department. But what's this "X" business?'

'Used to be under Nebe's personal supervision. It's now run by Keppler to all intents and purposes, or so he says. It's where all the so-called "sensitive" Interpol files are kept.'

'What happened to Nebe, by the way?'

'We're not sure,' Rudwick admitted. 'We think he was involved in the plot against Hitler's life in July 1944. He could be dead, he could be in prison.'

'So Keppler is following in Nebe's footsteps in more ways than one. Well, well,' said Sutton thoughtfully.

He read through the documents. The first was a report of a raid on an apartment in Brussels in October 1941 by Belgian Sûreté officials backed up by a couple of Germans who were described as 'observers' from Gestapo headquarters in Berlin. There followed an autopsy report on one Albert Lapentière, described as thirty-eight years old, a Belgian citizen, an 'itinerant criminal' usually resident at the address that had been raided. Lapentière had been absent from his home when the police raided it, but he was found two days later in a cheap hotel room near the city's Midi station, poisoned, probable suicide but foul play not completely ruled out. A brief résumé of the criminal's life was attached, which revealed that he had been marginally involved in extreme right-wing politics as well as operating as a con-man and occasional thief in Belgium, the South of France, and – here Sutton's interest was sparked – London.

'Got around, didn't he?' he said to Rudwick.

Sir James just nodded gravely and told Sutton to finish reading.

A blurred photograph showed a plump-faced man with neat hair and the alert, serious expression of an ambitious young businessman or an up-and-coming politician. According to the document Lapentière had made a handsome living and enjoyed the acquaintance and confidence of 'powerful friends who cannot be named'. This phrase was asterisked and a hand-written note explained: 'See details of documents found in subject's apartment. These are *very strictly secret* and can be perused only on personal application to R.H.'

That was all. Sutton looked up. 'R.H. is Heydrich?'

'Right, George.'

'So where did this come from?'

'From friend Keppler, of course. George he's been in touch with us in the past week or so, through a neutral intermediary.'

'Anyone I know?'

'Not . . . yet, George.' Rudwick began to toy with a sphinx paperweight by his blotting pad. 'In fact, these are not the only papers we have received, but they're all I can show you. The documents in general are actually rather important and embarrassing from . . . a political and historical point of view. Our people want them, and Keppler has them.'

'I'm beginning to catch your drift. Well, Keppler has obviously changed his mind about Hitler. Or has the prospect of defeat changed his mind for him?'

'Does it matter, George? The important thing is that he has some material that is of vital importance to this country's security, and he's named his price for allowing us to have it.'

'Which is?'

'A one-way ticket out of Berlin before the Russians get there, and our assurance of his safety and future comfort.'

'Jesus Christ. Those mysterious papers found in the

Belgian's flat must have been strong stuff. What were they, sir?'

'I can't tell you, George.'

'Ah. I see.'

There was a taut silence.

'Well, what *can* you tell me?' Sutton asked softly. 'Or did you get me here just to reminisce a bit about Keppler, authenticate an Interpol document, hear what Keppler's doing these days and then pick up my hat and coat and clear off back up to Moray Firth again?' Sutton lit his third cigarette of the interview, ignoring the slight pain in his chest as his lungs protested.

'George, this is an extremely delicate matter,' Rudwick said. 'We have to tread very carefully. If I had invited you down here merely to pick your brains, because it was necessary for the task in hand, then I should have done so without the slightest compunction, no matter how much you might complain or bluster. However, that is not the case. You are very much needed and will, I hope and trust, be very much involved. As I said when we first began this conversation, you are a very valuable man.'

'All right. I'm listening.' Sutton drew the smoke down into his lungs, stared hard at Rudwick, trying to read his face but seeing only a mixture of exasperation and cool command, very much what could be expected from a senior officer with all the advantages of class and rank facing down a disgraced subordinate.

'You see, Keppler was very, very impressed with you when he met you years ago at the Interpol meetings. George, he wants to get out of Berlin and he wants you to go in there and escort him to safety. In fact, I may as well tell you now, he insists you're the only man who'll do. You're the only man he'll trust to get him back to us and not try anything on with him.

The room suddenly went very quiet, as pregnantly still as the eye of a storm.

'Sir,' said Sutton eventually, 'that's ridiculous, I'm just a copper. A flatfoot. Mr Plod.'

'That's not my opinion, or that of your present outfit. Don't think the powers-that-be haven't been keeping an eye on you these past couple of years,' Rudwick told him with a smile.

'You've been wasted in the P.O.W. camps, and now's your chance to show them why. These are the people who consigned you to the scrap heap, and you can prove them wrong! George, I believe firmly that you have the skills and the courage required. You know Germany. You speak the language. All you need is a little extra training and some pukka papers.'

'You're serious aren't you?'

'Never more so in my entire life. Why else go to all this trouble with you? We want what Keppler has, and we'll save his skin too if that's part of the bargain. He insists that you're the only man he'll deal with and time's running short. The only answer is for you to go into Germany and bring him out.'

Sutton shook his head but said nothing. Rudwick continued, unfazed.

'You're a good choice, George. You're bright and resourceful, and you've got guts.' Rudwick got his feet, began to walk over to the window. Sutton stayed where he was. 'I've always regretted having to let you go. It was one of the most painful decisions I have had to make. At the time I had no choice, the way you were hitting the bottle, but that need not be the end of it.'

'I don't understand.'

Rudwick turned back and faced him. 'I have made representations to the authorities and they have agreed to make an offer to you, one which I wholeheartedly welcome, George, they have agreed that if you go on the mission to Berlin, on your return you will be reinstated in the police force without a stain on your record, same rank and full pension rights, just as if you had never been away. Should you choose to take early retirement, you will receive a generous cash gratuity, tax-free. But more than that, I know that you are a patriotic Englishman to your fingertips, and I give you my word that this material, and Heinz Keppler, are considered of the utmost importance to the security of this country. I *give you my word*, George.'

Sutton stared up at the ceiling, trying to think rationally, imagining what the future would be like if he refused this offer. Back to the Moray Firth for another miserable few months, and then demob and then what? A clerical job somewhere, alone in a furnished room, waiting for a Rose Wesolowski to come into his life every now and again and give him the illusion that it was worth living. After about half a minute he looked down and met Rudwick's enquiring gaze. The Assistant Commissioner's eyes were alert, as unblinking and calculating as a cat's.

Sutton crushed his butt out in the ashtray. 'So how the hell do I get into Berlin?'

When Sutton had left his office, Rudwick sat quietly for a full minute. Then he shook himself, as if casting out an unclean thought. He got to his feet, strolled over to the cabinet in the corner and poured himself a large brandy from the decanter. It was not yet quite noon, but extraordinary situations call for extraordinary measures. In this case, he thought, a double.

Glass in hand, he walked over to the telephone on his desk, picked it up and asked the switchboard operator to connect him with a Whitehall number.

'Rudwick here,' he said when he got through. 'You'll be pleased to know that our man has agreed. Yes, of course this line is secure, don't be such a scare-monger, Ronald. Tell Simon, will you?'

Rudwick listened carefully, shook his head.

'No, I don't think he'll change his mind. He's not the type. However, I do think if we could arrange a little meeting to impress him with the importance . . . yes, while the P.M.'s away in Paris would be perfect. It took a long time to convince him, I had to show him the material about the Belgian to add authenticity. I know it's a risk . . . well, perhaps you're right and it doesn't matter what he knows . . . You know that's up to Simon. I don't want to know about it. Goodbye, Ronald.'

When Rudwick replaced the receiver, there were deep lines of concern and distress etched in his heavy face. Big Ben began to strike twelve in the distance. It was a bright, cold day, the kind of a day that could be classified either late winter or early spring. He picked up his brandy and walked across to the window overlooking the embankment, and stood there for some time, staring down at the figures in the street below.

The men and women scurrying past Scotland Yard seemed, unless Rudwick was mistaken, to have slightly more of a lightness in their step these days. Why not? Victory was within the British people's grasp at last after five and a half long, weary years of struggle. Peace would arrive along with the spring flowers. It was so hard now to remember the dark days of 1940 and 1941 when many of these same people had given up all hope of beating Hitler, and some important Englishmen had cast around for ways of saving something from the disastrous defeat that had then seemed inevitable.

Yes, some had faltered when Britain had stood alone against the apparently overwhelming might of Hitler's armies. But on the surface, at least, the nation had remained united and defiant. Gazing down on the ordinary men and women in the London street now, Rudwick knew once more with sudden force how vital it was that they continue to believe in the myth of a united wartime Britain. If for any reason the general public came to suspect what had really been plotted – and almost made real – more than four years previously by some of the most powerful and respected men in England, there would be cries of outrage and treason. Lives and reputations would lie in tatters. There might even be treason trials. It mustn't be allowed to happen.

Rudwick crossed back to the cabinet and refilled his glass, looked at the photograph of his wife, the two sons who were serving in the army now. He thought of the honourable peaceful retirement he and Lady Rudwick could look forward to, with visits from their children and grandchildren, a garden full of roses. Perhaps he would write a book of memoirs about his life in the Indian and British police forces. He had earned his ease, surely? Did he deserve to lose everything he had earned in a long life of service to his country, all because of one foolish mistake?

Rudwick thought of Sutton and took a long sip of brandy. You're a good man, George, he said to himself, but this is a matter of survival. I'm sorry, bloody sorry, because I've always liked you, but this bullet has your name on it, George.

CHAPTER FOUR

GEORGE SUTTON left his kitbag at the digs in Holland Park, took an underground train to Tottenham Court Road and there changed to the Northern Line that took him directly to Finchley. When the train emerged from the tunnel after Highgate, two stops before his destination, he was surprised to see that the sun had broken through the leaden afternoon sky. It shone on the prosperous modern suburbs of North London now, while he waited his chance to cross the Barnet Bypass. He watched, his face a hard mask of exhaustion, as a convoy of American army trucks travelled past him at speed. When they had gone, he made his way to the far side of the road and walked along the grass verge to the cemetery gates.

Inside the neat, municipally tended suburb of the dead, Sutton paused and smoked yet another cigarette. It was almost a year since his last visit to Jeannie.

A young woman with a boy of three or four passed him. The child looked at Sutton, saw his uniform, crooked his tiny fingers into the shape of an imaginary gun and fired pretend bullets straight at Sutton's stomach. His mother pulled him away and offered him a little smile of embarrassment before hurrying on. She was pretty, with dark hair tucked under a headscarf, big brown eyes, nice legs.

Sutton threw away his cigarette butt and walked slowly along the well-kept path that ran between the graves. Some were quite fresh, he realised, and a glance at some headstones told him that many of the dead were pitifully young. The V-1s and V-2s had sown a fresh crop of death in the final stages of the war, even more indiscriminate and terrifying than the havoc wreaked by the Luftwaffe's manned bombers. He had been told of a block of flats not far from Highgate station that had been demolished by a German flying bomb one peaceful afternoon the previous autumn. Jeannie's grave, he realised with a shock, was probably no longer considered new.

Just on the left now. Sutton turned automatically off the main path, continued for another few yards. Then he stood still, took off his cap, silently said: 'Hello, love.' His lips were moving, and he knew it, but he didn't give a damn if someone saw and thought he was out of his mind.

The plain granite headstone gave away no more than the bare facts. It read simply:

To the memory of
JEAN HARRIET SUTTON
beloved wife of George
Departed this world May 19th 1943
Aged 35 years
Sadly Missed

As always, Sutton read it through several times, searching for extra meaning and finding none.

'Well, I went to bed with a woman last night, Jeannie,' he said. 'The first one since you died. I liked her, she was almost as barmy as me, which sort of made it all right. We've both lost our other halves. Anyway, it was a comfort for both of us.'

He stood without saying anything for a few seconds, watching his breath curl in the chilly air, rubbing his hands, then continued.

'That's not all, Jeannie. I'm going to Berlin. I'm going to save a Nazi and some bits of paper. Sir James Rudwick, no less, got me away from Siberia specially. Safety of the Realm involved. I couldn't turn him down, could I? What else would I be doing with my life anyway?'

After that, there wasn't much more to be said. He had kept up to date, that was the main thing. If she'd still been alive, maybe by this stage Jeannie wouldn't have cared a damn what he did. Nevertheless, he needed to tell her all this.

Despite the thin sun overhead, the air was cold and the wind cutting. His tiredness made him feel extra vulnerable in the cold. It was a good afternoon to wrap up warm and take a brisk walk, perhaps, but no kind of a day for standing around communing with the dead.

'When – I suppose I should really say if – I get back from Berlin, I'll come and see you again,' Sutton said. 'I'm still trying to forgive both of us, love.'

The stupid thing was, she probably wouldn't even have left him when it really came down to it. But Jeannie had always dearly loved a cuddle and a good time, and there hadn't been a lot of either for her at that time.

Sutton walked quickly as far as the cemetery gates, then stopped and caught his breath once he was out on the road again and free of the dead. On his way back to the underground station he realised he had said nothing to Jeannie about Rudwick's offer to give him his old job back. Maybe because it was that job that had killed their marriage – and her. A wave of sadness and remorse overcame him at the memory of Jeannie as she had looked standing on the doorstep of their rented house about a mile from here, just before he had left for work. With another hour to go until she had to set out for the school where she taught domestic science, she had been furtive and nervous. He had been in a hurry, irritable, knowing something was wrong but unwilling to spend the time on it when there was so much else to do. As he had been about to dash out of the door she had taken his arm, tossed her dark hair, looked him straight in the eye.

'George, why don't you take a couple of days off? I've got half-term coming up. We could go away, spend some time together. Just you and me.'

He knew now that she had still loved him enough to try to get back what they had once had, but at the time he had already been fixed on his very important task for that day, an inspection trip to Guildford. He would probably be staying the night there. So he had said, 'Sometime soon, eh? We'll talk about it,' and given her a peck on the cheek, and not even looked back on his rush down the street. He had even felt relieved at not having to worry about her for a while, not being forced to face her accusing looks, her complaints about how little time they spent together. He had felt a kind of guilty freedom.

Eighteen hours later they had woken him up to tell him Jeannie was dead. A stray bomb had fallen on the bedroom where she was sleeping. It wasn't until later that he found out that the bedroom wasn't in his house but at the house of a man she worked with. She had been in bed with him.

Well, technically he was a free man, Sutton thought bitterly. He could jump off London Bridge and there would be no comebacks. He could throw himself in front of a bus in the full knowledge that there was no one else he need worry about or feel responsible for. He could work twenty-four hours a day if he wanted to. He could take a trip to Berlin.

CHAPTER FIVE

CLYDE TOLSON's puffily handsome features were composed in an attitude of masculine calm as he waited in the Director's antiseptically clean outer office. The white handkerchief in the breast pocket of his dark suit was crisp and newly laundered, the creases in his trousers immaculate as ever, a supreme example of attention to the FBI's rigid dress code. At the moment he was staring intently at the white plaster death-mask of John Dillinger that had sat here at FBI Headquarters in Washington DC for more than ten years in a big glass case. Right next to it were displayed the notorious outlaw's silver-rimmed spectacles which still bore the scar of an FBI agent's bullet, his straw hat and his corona cigar, the last still wrapped in cellophane as it had been when retrieved from the pocket of the corpse. Tolson liked to review that grim, tiny museum from time to time if he was kept waiting out here. It reminded him of the old gang-busting days, when John Edgar and he and the rest of the boys had known exactly who the enemy was, and how to fight him. These days, since the Bureau had gotten involved with spies and politics, well, he was not so sure how he felt any more. But for John Edgar, he might have been tempted to go back to the General Services Administration. There was a price to being helper and friend to the greatest living American and Tolson was prepared to pay it.

Tolson rose automatically as the door to Hoover's office opened. Usually, as Associate Director and closest friend of the Director, Tolson could walk in with just a knock, but when Hoover had summoned him this time, he had specifically asked him to wait. Everything about this two-thirty appointment had been portentous. Tolson was curious, puzzled, and more than a little anxious. The afternoon already reeked of conspiracy, of shadows and the rancid underside of human life.

He had expected to see Hoover himself, but instead he was forced to greet W. H. Drane Lester, one of the other Assistant Directors who was not well known for his closeness to Hoover. Suddenly Tolson was afflicted by a surge of jealous indignation that he had been excluded from John Edgar's room by Lester, of all people. What could Hoover possibly have had to discuss with Lester that Tolson was not permitted to witness? Lester was a nobody, had never even been to dinner with the Director, let alone accompanied him on vacation, as Tolson had been doing for years. Nevertheless, he favoured Lester with a dignified smile, extended a hand in greeting.

'Tolson.'

'Lester.'

They shook. Already Tolson could see John Edgar hovering by his huge, polished, empty desk. With a final nod to Lester, he moved past him and into the room, closing the door behind him.

'Gee, Clyde,' was the first thing Hoover said, jerking a thumb at the five-feet long sailfish he kept stuffed and mounted on the wall by his desk. 'You know, we've been working too hard. How long is it since we got down to Florida and battled it out with one of those babies?' He shook his head. 'All work and no play. It's been a long war.'

'It sure has,' Tolson agreed, joining him by the desk and standing easy. 'Maybe this summer. We still have the Japs to beat.'

The flurry of disquiet that Lester's presence had aroused was over now. Tolson was his usual unruffled self, perhaps the only FBI employee who ever felt completely at ease in the boss's presence. With other underlings Hoover played power games, but not with Tolson, his oldest and most loyal servant, his eyes and his ears, his friend. With Tolson he could dare to be himself.

The Director's famous bulldog features creased in a grim smile at Tolson's remark about the Pacific War. At fifty, the lips that had once looked oddly sensual had taken on the look of caricature, as if they were rubber, detachable. They no longer fitted the ageing face that surrounded them. Hoover was beginning to look froglike. Not that he had ever been handsome – that had never been his appeal, and neither would he have wanted it to be. But now, slowly, he was becoming positively ugly, and perhaps somewhere that hurt him, made him feel uneasy.

'And after the Japs, the Communists, Clyde,' he rasped. 'The enemies of America never sleep.'

The gleaming expanses of Hoover's glass-topped desk were furnished with only three items: a photograph of Hoover's dog, an old-fashioned stand-up telephone, and a framed copy of Kipling's poem, 'If'. The Director glared at each in turn, as if wondering which particular prop he needed this afternoon, selected the phone, picked it up.

'Bring the machine I ordered through, will you?' Replacing the handset, he perched on the corner of the desk and returned his attention to Tolson.

'Clyde,' he said earnestly, 'I need your opinion on some important political questions.' He cleared his throat. 'First, I want you to tell me how you would envisage the postwar role of the former Ambassador to England, Mr Joseph Patrick Kennedy.'

'You mean with regard to the Bureau's operations?'

'No. We have certain uses for each other, the Bureau and Kennedy, and that will undoubtedly continue to be the case. But I mean in general, so far as his career is concerned.'

Tolson smiled his boyish, open smile. 'Well, that's pretty easy. I guess he'll get back to making money. What else has Joe Kennedy's life ever been about? He must be one of the richest men in the country, and he just keeps on making it.'

'Sure he does. But why, Clyde? For what?'

'Why? Oh, he's ambitious, likes power and success. Also, we know he likes what guys like him think of as a good time, especially when it comes to enjoyment of the, ah, female sex.'

Hoover smiled coldly. 'For more than twenty years Kennedy's been able to purchase all the female flesh he wants. He doesn't need yet more money for that.'

'Okay,' Tolson said amiably. His chief's sarcasm just bounced off him. He knew his place, and he liked it. Let Hoover be the genius who made the great leaps of deduction. Tolson was happy to be his sounding-board. 'Okay,' he went on, 'I know Kennedy has political ambitions. Hell, he's done us a few favours for which he'll expect recompense. Especially, he's built a few useful bridges for us with the kikes in the movie business out on the coast. He seems to get along with those types okay.'

Hoover's barking laugh cut into his speculations, reduced him to silence.

'Are you kidding? He hates Jews!' Hoover spat out. 'Oh, he can do business with them. He needs them, so he pretends they're fine fellows – at least to their faces. But deep down, Clyde, I can tell you he loathes the kikes because they killed Jesus. That's what the priests told him when he was a kid. Joe Kennedy may have two hundred million dollars in stocks and bonds and real estate, he may have been to Harvard, and he may have the ear of the President, but deep down he's just a barkeep's boy from East Boston with money in the bank, a Mick made good. You want to know what that means? You want to know what's really important to him?' This time Hoover didn't even go through the motions of waiting for Tolson's answer. 'The future, Clyde. For his family, and especially his sons.'

Hoover slid off the desk, began to pace around the room. His excitement was sudden, raw electricity, comparable to ungovernable lust. Tolson could trace it in his intense eyes, in the colour that came suddenly to his cheeks, in his hands, which seemed to grasp at each other while he was in motion, as if they had lives of their own. Tolson watched him, waited for him to get to the real point of the meeting.

'He's like a tribal chief, Clyde,' Hoover said. 'An Irish chieftain. Sure, Joe knows he's far too crude, too tainted by his past, to make a career for himself in Congress. But he can make sure his boys get there – and beyond.'

The FBI Director's eyes narrowed, the hands tensed. Then they relaxed and his eyes widened into a kind of wonderment that was almost childlike.

'Joe Kennedy's reason for adding incessantly to his wealth is very simple,' he said. 'He intends to use that money to turn the Kennedy clan into the nation's most powerful family. To be specific, Kennedy aims to buy one of his boys the presidency of the United States.'

'That seems kind of a little crude, if I may say so,' Tolson answered cautiously.

Hoover chuckled. 'It is,' he said. 'Kennedy is a simple soul,

Clyde. He knows how power works. He knows what his money can buy, and he knows that all you have to do is to find out who pulls the levers of power and then either buy them, or frighten them into doing what you want. Plus, the raw material isn't bad. All his kids are pretty smart except the weak-minded one who's kept out of sight. They're pretty, and they can turn on the Irish charm when it suits them, just like their old man. Most important of all, they have a two hundred million dollar private political fund. Think about it. Why should he fail?'

'I knew he had plans for Joe Jr. But the kid's dead. He was posted missing on some mission for the Airforce last fall.'

'A small setback. The old man's got eight more where he came from, including another three boys. So Joe Jr gets himself killed in action. There's Jack next in line – he's got a dead war hero for a brother, plus he already made a good showing with that PT story in the Solomons.'

'It'll take time to groom him. He's maybe twenty-seven. Too young to run for the Senate.'

Hoover shook his head. 'I know for a fact that Joe intends to have Jack run for one of the Boston districts in the House elections next year. Sure, he had Joe Junior all set up – the kid was even on the state delegation to the Democratic convention in 1940 – cocky enough to refuse to support the straight FDR ticket, too. Anyway, the old man's transferred his hopes and the power of his open wallet to Jack, and he's in a hurry. There'll be a Kennedy sitting in Congress after the mid-term elections, come hell or high water. It'll just cost Joe a few hundred thousand more than he originally planned, that's all.'

For the first time Tolson looked really uneasy. 'Chief, are you saying you want to stop the Kennedys in their tracks?' he murmured. 'I would foresee a few problems with that.'

'Stop them?' Hoover stroked the glass surface of his desk, grinned at Tolson. 'Why no, Clyde, this is a free country, the greatest democracy the world has ever known.' He walked around to the other side of the desk, leaned on it, resting on his knuckles and peering intently at his Associate Director. 'For years now I have been keeping a detailed file on the Kennedys. It is now a foot and a half thick, plus there's other material. It makes fine reading, I can tell you, and it's one of my most important projects, Clyde. It will be our nest-egg in the future if that future belongs to the sons of Ambassador

Joe. All we need to do is to keep it up to date, so that if Jack or any other Kennedy makes it to the White House we can be certain – absolutely certain – that the interests of the nation and of the Bureau we are privileged to serve will be borne in mind at all times.'

Tolson nodded to show he understood. This was familiar territory. He and the Director had an agreement; Tolson was the keeper of the secrets, the one man permitted to know anywhere near the full extent of the dirt that Hoover kept on virtually every major figure in American public life. Tolson fixed things where necessary, if the Director didn't want to be personally involved. He knew that the information his chief controlled was the source of Hoover's, and therefore his, power and security of employment. Not even the most determined President would dare to offend the all-knowing J. Edgar Hoover, and who would dare to try to sack him when he could ruin them with a word, a leak to the press, a threat of disclosure or even prosecution? So Hoover wanted everything he could get on the Kennedys. Fine. Tolson would give the orders.

'It's a major priority, Clyde,' Hoover emphasised. 'Maybe the biggest priority, outside the area of actual Communist subversion, that I can think of at the moment.'

Tolson was still nodding when the door opened and one of the young agents from Hoover's personal staff walked in, carrying a large recording machine of the latest design.

'You took your time,' Hoover snapped.

'Sorry, sir. It had to be brought up from the basement,' the young agent said. 'Should I plug it in?'

Hoover nodded sullenly. They waited in silence while the machine was connected up, switched on. When it was all ready to function, the aide was dismissed with a wave. He moved softly out of the room, quiet as a young penitent.

Once the door was closed, Hoover advanced on the machine. 'Listen to this, Clyde,' he said eagerly, and switched it on.

After a few seconds there was a click, and the room filled with recorded laughter. The sound quality was not of the best, but you could tell the laugh belonged to a young man who was a little drunk. Then came the sound of ice clinking in a glass, or a tumbler being placed down suddenly and hard on a solid surface. The laugh became an animal grunt. A woman's voice, with an attractive foreign lilt, maybe Scandinavian, squealed 'Jack! Wait . . . I am not ready, you naughty . . . ah . . . please . . . aah . . .'

They listened in silence. Tolson began to blush, slightly at first and then developing into a pink fulness, like a fresh suntan. He was a shy man when it came to sexual matters, and he had never gotten used to the idea of this kind of eavesdropping. Here he was, privy to two people in a hotel room making love with a wild abandon that he had never imagined even in his dreams. For his part, Hoover was pacing the room, his hands clenched tight behind his back as if to prevent them from wandering, his jaw set in a lock of puritanical distaste. On the recording, whatever was happening certainly had nothing at all to do with puritanism. The woman was letting out little pants and moans of delight, in between giving the man explicit instructions about how to move, where to put his hand, his mouth, his . . . his grunts were getting louder. The sounds of bedsprings under strain were accelerating as the man moved towards his climax. It was then that Hoover stepped forward and snapped off the machine.

In the quiet that followed, Tolson proceeded to clear his throat with great thoroughness.

'May I assume that was . . . Jack Kennedy, chief?' he said at last.

'It was indeed. John Fitzgerald Kennedy, who his father believes is fit to be a future President of the United States. His tryst with that . . . lady' – Hoover couldn't keep the loathing out of his voice – '. . . was recorded in 1942. Her name was Inga Arvard. She was under suspicion of being an enemy agent.'

'Yes, I recall that case. I thought we decided to confine ourselves to more . . . routine surveillance measures.'

There was something close to mischief – or was it triumph? – in Hoover's hooded eyes.

'Officially that was the case, Clyde. Nevertheless, I'll tell you now that I personally used that pretext to authorise the wiring of the hotel room where Kennedy was meeting Arvard. I knew she wasn't really working for the Nazis, but the official suspicion meant that I could legitimately gather important evidence of the younger Kennedy boy's amatory exploits. I have kept this as my personal concern, Clyde, until now.' He clapped Tolson on the shoulder in a gesture of man-to-man frankness. 'But this is moving up to become a top priority, and now I'm choosing to involve you. Because I need to work hand in hand with the only man I can trust.'

Tolson was moved. He signified his sense of honour by pursing his lips, nodding. Then his look became a little doubtful.

'With all due respect, sir,' he said, 'this kind of behaviour is not – unfortunately – uncommon in our public life. I mean, senators, congressmen, members of the Supreme Court and the cabinet, even FDR himself . . .'

'I know. Evidence of philandering is nothing so special. It's not absolutely decisive. You and I know there are very few men in public life, outside this building at least, who actually practise and actively uphold the values they claim to treasure. The President, cripple or not,' Hoover added with a touch of brutality, 'is no angel in that department. But there are worse things.'

Hoover reached into his drawer and pulled out a piece of paper, handed it to Tolson.

Pasted to the sheet was a yellowed clipping from a newspaper. It had been neatly labelled, 'EXTRACT FROM "THE WEEK", LONDON, 13th SEPTEMBER 1939', and beside it was a note in the Director's own neat handwriting: 'TO CONFIDENTIAL KENNEDY FILE, PERSONAL ARCHIVE – J.E.H.'.

Urged on by Hoover, Tolson read the clipping:

There are those in high places in London who regard it as axiomatic that the war must not be conducted in such a way as to lead to a total breakdown of the German régime and the emergence of some kind of 'radical' government in Germany. These circles are certainly in direct touch with certain German military circles – and the intermediary is the American Embassy in London (after all, nobody can suspect Mr Kennedy of being unduly prejudiced against fascist régimes and it is through Mr Kennedy that the German government hopes to maintain 'contacts' . . .

He glanced up at Hoover, his square Mid-Western face furrowed with doubt.

'Chief,' Tolson said slowly, 'I remember this incident. This was written, what, ten days after Germany and England went to war. That paper was just a Commie scandal sheet run up by some Red. We checked all this stuff. We knew Kennedy wasn't so nuts about the British, especially being an Irish boyo from Boston, but that stuff was just too wild, too hard to prove or disprove. And . . . well, chief, it is not the job of the F.B.I. to make foreign policy, after all.'

'Very true, Clyde. I can always rely on your memory. But what if we were wrong to dismiss that story?' Hoover said. 'What if that scandal-sheet was telling the truth – in fact was actually understating Kennedy's involvement. What if his activities were really far more treacherous and damaging than anything even the most fever-brained Commie mud-slinger could imagine? How about that?'

'I don't exactly follow, chief.' Tolson's reply was guarded. When he started to have serious reservations about one of Hoover's schemes, he also started becoming more formal, putting that 'chief' between himself and his old friend.

'You don't have to follow, not all the way,' Hoover said. His eyes narrowed. His hands stabbed the air as he continued, 'But tell me, what wouldn't you do to get your hands on documents that showed beyond all doubt that Kennedy betrayed Britain in its hour of need – in fact, that he conspired against the British will to resist and against the person of the Premier, Winston Churchill? That he directly opposed the wishes and instructions of his own master, the President of the United States?' Hoover paused, breathing heavily. 'This is dynamite, history-making material, Clyde. For a number of people, but mainly for the Kennedy clan, it's political and personal poison. The world may forgive a dalliance with a good-time girl. It will not forgive a full-blooded affair with Hitler.'

'We're talking about while Kennedy was Ambassador to London, right?'

'Absolutely.'

'Lord . . . . Chief, you have these documents in your possession here in Washington?'

As if a spell had been broken, Hoover began to move around the room once more, driven by that restless, oddly sexual energy. He came to rest by the window that overlooked

Pennsylvania Avenue, stared out of it for a short while, then turned back to gaze intently at Tolson.

'If I did, would I be picking your brains?' he said quietly. 'No. This is a strategy meeting, Clyde. I need your support. No more questions. Just answers.'

The loyal Tolson gloomily accepted the implied rebuke. He believed implicitly that J. Edgar Hoover was the finest American alive, but he hated breaking the rules, and he suspected very strongly that what Hoover was working up to would involve doing just that. This was no harmless bull session. Tolson was going to be involved in this project whether he liked it or not.

'I see that, Chief,' he said. 'Okay,' he added, sealing his assent.

'Good. Let's drop the actual Kennedy business for now,' Hoover said briskly. 'And if you have any appointments planned for this afternoon, cancel them. We have a lot of other matters to discuss, and it's going to take time.'

While Tolson got on the internal phone to his own office, Hoover pressed a button on the wall and told the aide who appeared in response that they would like coffee and cookies on the table and that they weren't to be disturbed for the next two hours. F.B.I. agents were forbidden to eat or drink at their desks under pain of dismissal or transfer to a remote station, but Hoover allowed himself a few obvious privileges, and this was one of them. He rationalised it by saying that, since he had a separate coffee-table and chairs across the office from his desk, it was not unmannerly to partake of refreshments there when he was especially busy. For a while he stared out of the window again, admiring the early shows of snowdrops and daffodils across the Avenue. It promised to be a fine spring in Washington. He wondered what it would be like in weary, tormented Europe, crucible of horror and source of the power that he sought.

When Tolson was free, Hoover invited him to sit down in one of the easy chairs surrounding the coffee-table.

'Right now I need to discuss two further areas with you,' he said. 'First, the International Criminal Police Commission. I just spoke to Drane Lester because he was our delegate to the '37 Interpol conference, you may recall. I was asking him about Interpol and about the various officers from other

65

countries he met over in Europe.' Hoover leaned forward confidentially. 'I didn't tell him, but I'll tell you, what I really needed to know. I actually wanted to find out about two men, Clyde. One is a guy named Keppler, a German, and the other and Englishman called Sutton. Both men are police officers who were closely concerned with Interpol before the war.' He frowned. 'These are people I would have wanted to work with if we'd gotten as intimately involved with Interpol as I wanted us to, instead of leaving the field to those darned Nazis. But the fact is that we are now involved with these men anyway.'

'They're here? In the States?'

'No, no.' Hoover said, shaking his head, a patronising smile spreading over his face. 'That's precisely the point, Clyde. That's our problem. You will remember that our government in its wisdom has ruled that the F.B.I. may not operate outside the territory of the United States and its dependencies. Okay, South America's accepted, but that's the back yard. Which is why certain powerful politicians stomped on our plans to take a dominant role in Interpol. It would have given us too much power! If we had joined, the Bureau would have acquired a legitimate means of extending its counter-subversion activities beyond the borders of this country, and then those pussy-footing pinkos in the State Department would have had to mind their rears! We'd have been able to confront the enemies of America in their lairs, Clyde. That's why they stopped us. It was too much of a threat.'

Hoover's eyes flashed with electric indignation. Then he leaned over, poured coffee for himself and his Associate Director, added cream and sugar in the right amounts to each cup, like the parent who knows his family's tastes. He broke a cookie in half and popped a piece into his mouth.

'Oh, they say we'd be making U.S. foreign policy. Hogwash!' Hoover growled. 'Joe Kennedy can make his own foreign policy, as we now know. Morgenthau can make foreign policy. Bill Donovan and his rich kids at O.S.S. have joined the party too in the past couple of years. Hell, everyone else has the right to play games overseas. But not the F.B.I. Not the most effective, loyal, incorruptible body of American manhood God sent, with all our wealth of experience at fighting crime and foreign subversion, oh no!'

'It's a scandal, sir,' Tolson agreed lamely.

'A scandal? It's a *conspiracy*. Let me tell you, Clyde, that I have got wind that people from another department of the U.S. government may have a chance of access to the Kennedy material I mentioned. Have you any idea what they will do with it? They'll suppress it, maybe destroy it, to *protect* Kennedy and the Democratic Party! That's political chicanery, Clyde!'

'Which, ah, department, chief?'

'Never mind. But tell me, Clyde, when it's for the good of America, we are entitled to co-opt any individual, no matter how reprehensible his record and his habits. Isn't that right? Wouldn't that be justified for the greater good?'

The pleading quality in his boss's voice was childish, almost pitiable. Tolson felt his heart leap, for all his doubts. How could he ever refuse this man, who time after time had saved America from evil?

'Well, chief, if we're really sure it's necessary, I guess the common good takes precedence. We have, for instance, offered deals to certain gangsters when necessary to apprehend particular felons or breaking major crime rings.'

'Exactly.' Hoover sat nodding with satisfaction, his spleen well-vented for the moment.

'Yes, Clyde, that's the way it has to be. 'We're going to teach those smartasses in the State Department and O.S.S. a thing or two. We're going to find a way of bringing the full extent of our power to bear, and we're going to finish up in possession of information that will put the Kennedy clan at our mercy forever. They won't dare *break wind* without my say-so!'

'Okay, chief. Then what do you want me to do?' Tolson asked. He added quite huffily, 'Do you require information about the Kennedys, or Interpol, or what?'

'This is all connected, Clyde. Allow me to follow all the threads. I've been thinking very carefully,' Hoover assured him. 'I'll tell you exactly what your immediate job is. I want you to find out everything you can about the Navy's Intelligence operations around the New York waterfront, and especially the Navy's links with some well-known figures in organised crime.'

'Chief, we're moving very fast here. We're moving all over the place, and I'm not clear,' Tolson said. 'Can you tell me what this is *really* about or do I have to piece it together for myself?'

'Later, Clyde. Later you'll see. This is really very delicate. Trust me. Meanwhile,' Hoover added, his voice rising on a gust of infectious enthusiasm, 'meanwhile we're talking Mob, and we're talking someone right at the top.'

The Kennedys, the Nazis, the State Department and O.S.S., and now the Mob. Where was it going to end? Tolson thought nostalgically of the mementos of John Dillinger outside in the spotless anteroom. You had known where you were with Dillinger. Guy robbed a few banks, he crossed a state line in a stolen car, and there you were. A hunt, a hail of bullets, a terrific write-up in the press. Those were the days.

'Yes, Clyde,' Hoover exulted. 'Right at the very *very* top.'

CHAPTER SIX

'STRIKE ME if it isn't Mrs Sutton's little boy, George, the scourge of the criminal classes,' said the overweight man drinking at the bar of the Coach and Horses. He patted the empty barstool next to him. 'Park yourself here. What's your poison?'

Sutton made a deprecatory gesture, stayed standing. 'I want to have a word with you, Harry. In private.'

Harry Stone looked around in mock surprise. The Coach and Horses was one of the big pubs built in the 1920s. It was only six o'clock and the taproom, almost as large and every bit as cheerless and cold as an aircraft hangar, was empty except for an old couple hunched over their milk stouts. 'Ain't this private enough for you, mate?'

'No.'

''Streuth. Careless talk costs lives, eh?'

'You always did have a taste for melodrama, Harry. I just want us to wander next door to your scrapyard, shut ourselves in the office for a while and have a téte-à-téte. I'll buy you a drink afterwards. That's a promise.'

Stone shrugged, downed the rest of his whisky, called out to the barman to say he'd be back in a bit.

Twenty yards up the street from the pub, the two men arrived at a chain-link gate bearing a sign: 'H. STONE. GENERAL DEALER AND PURCHASING AGENT. CASH BUSINESS ONLY EXCEPT BY PRIOR ARRANGEMENT.' Stone, already slightly the worse for booze, fumbled for his keys, eventually managed to open the padlock that secured the gate. 'There she goes.' Sutton followed him between the piles of old motor-bikes, abandoned gas cookers, bedsteads and other junk that lined the path to

69

the tiny corrugated-iron shack that served as Stone's office. More fiddling with locks, and they went inside. There was a rickety kitchen chair behind the desk, in front of it a moth-eaten armchair with a brick replacing one of the casters. The most impressive part of the decor was a big, solid-looking, if somewhat battered steel safe in the corner. God knows what Stone kept in it, but it looked businesslike.

Stone indicated for Sutton to sit himself down there in 'the customer's seat, you know', and reached up into a first aid cabinet on the wall crudely marked with a red cross. From within it he produced a half-bottle of De Kuyper gin and a couple of chipped cups.

'Gin all right? I haven't managed to stock up on whisky this week,' Stone said.

Sutton shook his head. 'No thanks, Harry.'

'Tee-total at your age, George? Got religion or something, have we? Blimey, you and I have sunk a few together in the past.'

'I've given it up, Harry, all right?'

Something about Sutton's voice made Harry Stone nod thoughtfully. His incipient double chin wobbled as he unscrewed the top of the gin bottle and poured a generous measure into one of the cups. 'Suit yourself,' he said with an attempt at dignified tolerance.

Sutton hoped the alcohol had some antiseptic effect, because that cup looked as if it was a breeding-ground for every kind of germ known to man – and a few probably known only to Harry. He lit up a Gold Flake and was amused by Stone's relieved, thank-God-you've-still-got-vices look.

'How's tricks, Harry?' he said. 'Still the biggest fence east of Aldgate?'

Stone laughed, waved a hand to indicate the surroundings. 'Me, George? Can't you see all the signs of prosperity and respectability? I got meself a lovely little earner these days, all legit and above board.' To give him his due, he couldn't keep a straight face when Sutton grimaced in disbelief. 'Well, mostly. The bottom sort of fell out of the, er, second-hand goods market pretty early on in the war, but there's plenty of other ways to earn an honest quid, especially helping citizens to circumvent certain irksome rules and regulations when it comes to the purchase of essential items, if you get my meaning.'

'Black market, eh?'

'I'm a middle-man,' said Stone, looking hurt. 'A general agent.'

Sutton dropped the subject. He wasn't here to investigate the man's business or to persecute him, but to pick his brains. Stone was the fourth old criminal acquaintance he had called on this afternoon, and so far his quest had been fruitless. Failure made a man tired and irritable. Added to which, Sutton had got out of the habit of hoofing it around the streets of the East End. He was still in good shape for a man of his age – certainly compared with the likes of Harry Stone – but he wasn't a twenty-five-year-old copper any more, and almost two years of facing POWs across a desk had done nothing for his physical stamina.

Stone wore a smart navy double-breasted overcoat over a silver-grey check tweed suit, brown Oxfords, and an electric-blue tie with what looked like a masonic symbol on it. On closer inspection it turned out to be a large, interestingly-shaped gravy stain.

'You're dressing better these days, Harry. Your shoes almost match your suit,' said Sutton, changing the subject. Actually, when Sutton said 'better' he was drawing a fine distinction between dressing unspeakably, as Stone used to, and merely dressing badly, as he did now, but it did the trick. Harry beamed with pride.

The two men had been born a couple of hundred yards apart in Stepney. Stone was six months older. They had gone to the same schools, joined the same street gangs, kicked the same footballs around the alleys. Eventually one had joined the police, the other had gone to work in the underworld. It happened that way around here all the time, like a balancing law of nature. They had continued to meet from time to time. Sutton had been careful never to personally put Stone behind bars, and he had sometimes used him as an informer during his CID days. Sutton was fond of him. Harry had never been involved in any violence, he was good to his old mum and his widowed sister, and somehow he really didn't seem to know how to live any other kind of life but this.

'Ta, George. You're a gent.' Stone swallowed some gin. He

ran one plump hand through his thinning, mousey-coloured hair and pursed his lips. 'Listen, I heard about your missus, and I'm sorry, I really am. As for you getting slung off the Force, it was a bleedin' scandal if you ask me. And they say there's no honour among thieves, eh?' He could never resist a little quip, even when the subject was dead serious. It had cost Stone a few fat lips in his time, and he was lucky it hadn't cost him more. 'You're in the army now, I can see,' he added hastily. 'All right, is it?'

'Not so bad. I've been stationed in Scotland. That's why you haven't seen me around the manor.'

'Christ. What do they get up to up there on a Saturday night? Caber-tossing?' Harry genuinely had no notion of how life was outside London. He guessed it was like Regent's Park Zoo only a bit more untidy.

'If they still got the strength after they've finished chasing sheep.'

'Tell you what, I'm lucky I got certified unfit for active service. Cost me a bleedin' fortune, mind you, but it was worth it. Scotland? I ask you.'

Sutton glanced at his watch. He had told Rudwick he was going to pay his respects to Stepney, but he would be back at his digs by about seven. Time was pressing. 'Listen, Harry, I need some information,' he cut Stone short.

Stone nodded as if it was what he expected, but his eyes were suddenly wary. 'You're not on the strength at the Yard any more, George. What's the story? Not out to do some individual harm, are you, because you know I don't like that kind of thing.'

Sutton shook his head. 'Don't worry. No rough stuff. It's something I want to put my mind at rest about, that's all.'

'All right.'

'Oh, and I'm skint. I can't give you any money. Just a drink.'

''Streuth. I'm a bleeding charity now, am I?' Harry grumbled, but there was no real resentment in him.

'Up to you how you see it. I just don't happen to have any ready cash.'

'Well, I'll help you if I can because it's you, George, because we was kids together. Don't you go puttin' it about that Harry Stone gives free rides.'

'I won't. Now, I want to know if you remember a villain called Albert Lapentière, also known as Pierre Dubois and Jean-Luc Gössens. Belgian, sometimes pretended to be French if he thought it would open a few more doors. A con-man and occasional thief. He used to do London before the war as well as Brussels. Paris and the South of France. Thirtyish, respectable-looking, had a way of getting in with society circles.'

'Still around, is he?'

'Not at all.'

But Stone was thinking too hard to catch the inference. 'There *was* a bloke I used to see around,' he said. 'Flash Albert, they used to call him. He particularly went for Americans, turned on the old Frog charm. One of the things he did was, he had this con where he'd flog tickets for a sweepstake supposedly on behalf of anti-fascist refugees – there was other blokes involved in this, he weren't doing it on his own – and somehow the prizes would always end up going to people who were related to or in business with the organisers, know what I mean? Flash Albert had some very good connections. There was also cons to do with dummy companies belonging to exiled Spanish aristocrats, which would become amazing earners once the Reds lost the civil war, so Albert said. Them companies did a roaring trade towards the end of the Spanish war, of course, when it was odds-on Franco's mob were going to win and capitalism'd be back in business. People thought they were being clever, getting a bargain. The companies was worthless, of course, but they looked great on paper.'

'This sounds like my man. Did you ever handle anything he pinched?'

'George, that is not a kosher question.'

'This isn't official. It's personal, I promise.'

Stone nodded. 'All right. I know people had him fingered for a burglar, but he wasn't. He didn't actually do over the drums in question, did he? He used to let the villains who were planning the job in on all the security precautions, tell 'em where the stuff was, if the owners was away on the grouse moors or the South of France, that kind of thing. Through his connections. Got his percentage for that, see?' Stone flashed Sutton his artful dodger smile. 'And don't ask me how I know all this.'

73

'All right. He had access to some big houses, anyway. Any in particular you remember? This is important, Harry. Think carefully.'

'Kensington, Belgravia, you know. Being foreign he could pull the wool over their eyes. I heard his dad was a dustman back in Brussels, but how's your average English upper-class twit going to know the difference? Albert always had a good story, I'm told. Never went too far, never claimed to be aristocratic or anything like that, just a successful businessman who knew his way around, liked a good time and knew which knife to use for the fish course. If any of them toffs suspected he was a bit bent, they probably thought it was rawther interesting and fraightfully exciting.' Stone's upper-class drawl was excruciating, but Sutton got the point.

'You're sure you can't be more specific about the posh people he used to meet? Any politicians, for instance? And you said something about Americans.'

'Come on, I didn't know him that well. When I saw him around here he was usually drinking with Mosley's boys, fascists. Fact is, I sometimes thought to myself: Harry, I thought, this bloke's got a pronounced taste for statuesque young men in uniforms. He might well be a bit of a ginger, you know?'

Sutton nodded. A 'ginger beer' was Cockney rhyming slang for a queer, a homosexual. Anyway, queer or not, he had the right man. Surely Harry could be made to remember more. 'That's interesting,' he said. 'But I want to get back to his connections up West, the society people. Come on, Harry. Anything will do, even it seems as if it's not important.'

'Let's see . . . I'll tell you what, I heard he knew the Yank ambassador, wossisname, Joe Kennedy. Kennedy's daughter used to like going to parties where there was blokes like Albert, a bit shady. She loved a touch of low-life. He got invited to the embassy a few times, met the old man and they got on all right. He reckoned Joe was no more than a successful con-man himself. Old Flash Albert used to boast about all his hobnobbing when he come down here drinking, and you know how word gets around.' Stone frowned. Old Albert was a bit of a prick, if you really want to know. I wonder what become of him? Went back to Belgium, did he?'

'For a while. He's dead now.'

74

'Oh. Natural causes, or did someone decide they didn't like his face?'

'Does it matter, Harry?'

Stone shivered. 'I suppose not. It's getting a bit chilly in here, George, know what I mean?'

'Get back to the pub and have one on me,' Sutton said. 'I've got to go.' He put a ten-shilling note on the desk between them.

Stone shook his head. 'Keep the money. I'm not short of the readies at the moment, old son. I've had what they call a good war.' He winked. 'And you never know, there might come a day when I need you to do me a favour.'

'Leave it out, Harry. If you mean what I think you mean, forget it.'

Stone was grinning broadly, but there was something about the way he looked at Sutton that showed he wasn't just trying it on. 'Just my little joke, George. But seriously, I want you to know you can get in touch if you're ever in real schtuck,' he said. 'All the resources of my business empire are at your disposal.' He gestured meaningfully at the safe in the corner. 'What's mine is yours, and discretion guaranteed. Let's say it's for old times' sake, shall we, George?'

Sutton realised that Stone's eyes were moist with tears of nostalgia. He was, in his bent way, absolutely sincere. 'That's very kind of you, Harry. I'll remember what you said.'

'I mean, everything's changing so fast these days,' Stone went on, dabbing his eyes with a filthy handkerchief. 'After the war everything'll go to blazes, I know it. The old times when we was kids together, they wasn't so bad . . .'

Sutton got to his feet, looked down at Harry Stone, his fat face and his ridiculous tie and the empty cracked cup that had held his gin.

'How bad do you want them to be, Harry?' he said.

He had been moved by Stone's offer, and relieved that he had managed to make a few of his own connections about Rudwick's mysterious Belgian, because it put him just that vital bit ahead of his superior's game. Now that sense of satisfaction was suddenly lost: in its place he felt sadness and anger and regret.

'We went barefoot with the arses hanging out of our trousers,' Sutton growled. 'Our old men beat our mums black and blue every Friday night after they'd pissed away half their wages at the pub. Half our brothers and sisters died before they were old enough to go to school. Those times made a criminal out of you and a fool out of me. How bad's that, Harry?'

CHAPTER SEVEN

A PHONE CALL came to the comfortable house in Holland Park at eight-thirty that night. It was Rudwick.

"Evening, George. Feeling better? Good. I'll be coming to fetch you in half an hour. Comb your hair and shine your shoes because we have an appointment.'

The car was Rudwick's personal Daimler, driven by his chauffeur. Sir James was sitting in the back seat like a well-fed walrus, sleek and self-satisfied.

'You'll do,' he said, examining Sutton's turn-out. 'I suppose we can hardly expect you to look like a proper soldier, can we? After all, you're a policeman.'

'Was.'

'Come now, George. Still tetchy? You're going to get what you asked for. You should be glad. Unless, of course, you've got cold feet about the whole thing?'

Sutton shook his head, didn't ask where they were going. He settled back into the leather upholstery, stared out of the window. They had turned left into Kensington High Street and were heading for Knightsbridge, towards the West End or towards the government offices in SW1. There was something cussed in his nature that made him want to irritate Rudwick, refuse to be predictable and eager. Maybe it was childish, and then again maybe it had something to do with keeping some distance.

Nothing more was said until they were driving along the Mall.

'Not far now,' Rudwick murmured. He surveyed Sutton shrewdly through his narrow eyes. 'I thought we should go as close to the top as possible. I want you to know that this is a serious business, and I want you to hear it from the horse's mouth.'

'So where exactly are we going, sir?'

'Downing Street, George.'

'The Prime Minister?'

Rudwick chuckled indulgently. 'I'm afraid he's elsewhere at the moment, but a member of his staff will be there, along with any others necessary. We could have met at my office, but – '

'Dear old George wouldn't have been quite so impressed.'

'I suppose so, yes. What's wrong with making sure you know the importance of all this? Is that trying to impress you?'

'It certainly is. Keep it up and you might even get somewhere.'

'Tell me,' said Rudwick, carefully looking away from him. 'Do you still harbour resentment about what happened? The business after Mrs Sutton's death, the way you resigned from the Force?'

'I wouldn't be human if I didn't have feelings about it, Sir.'

'I want you to know I did my best, George, and I've never ceased defending you. But you went too far for a man in your position. You had some quick promotions, you were too ambitious, and you came from the wrong kind of background. You made enemies, George. You were too good.'

Sutton nodded wordlessly. Rudwick's voice was gentle, almost soothing, but it made no difference. Strange how as you grew older your view of the world changed so drastically. When he'd been a young constable straight out of training, if anyone had told him you could make enemies by being too *good* he would have laughed in his face. Now he knew it to be true – in fact one of the most important truths of life. But he also knew there were no excuses. Never mind the trauma of Jeannie's death. He knew the rules, and he knew they applied to himself as well. You lost control, you overstepped the mark, and you paid the price. Second chances were rare. He should make some kind of reply, he decided.

'I know all that. And I'm grateful, sir. It did matter that you defended me, despite the eventual outcome.'

'Well, those buggers who forced your resignation will be surprised at this turn of events. If they could see you now, George!'

Sutton smiled sourly. The Daimler turned the corner into Downing Street and drew up outside the front door of the Prime Minister's London residence. The policeman on permanent duty outside Number 10 recognised Rudwick and saluted, while the chauffeur opened the rear door for them. There were a few members of the public and a pair of frozen-looking journalist types in the dark street, and they made a feeble move towards the car. Within seconds, however, Rudwick and Sutton had been ushered inside by a bespectacled civil servant, who had appeared at the door as if by magic. It was all over very quickly, like a hanging or a bank robbery.

Like many visitors to 10 Downing Street, Sutton was immediately struck by how much room there was behind the narrow street frontage. Not that there was much time to inspect the warren of corridors; the same man who had opened the door for them was fussing about, almost pushing them up the stairs.

'His Lordship has a committee meeting in twenty minutes, Sir James,' he told Rudwick. 'I shall be interrupting rather rudely if you're not finished by then.'

At no time did the man acknowledge Sutton until he was about to knock on an upstairs door. Then he looked Sutton over with a kind of a surprised alarm, as if he was seeing him for the first time and deciding he didn't much like what he saw.

'Would you care to remove your coat . . . er . . .'

'Sutton. Sergeant Sutton, if you like.'

'I see. Well . . .'

'No thanks. It's still a bit chilly, even in here.'

The man coughed, straightened his tie, knocked.

'Enter!'

The voice from inside was almost Churchill's in its gravelly vibrancy, but not quite. Like an actor imitating him.

When they entered the small drawing-room there was a fire in the grate and armchairs arranged in a semi-circle. Two men were standing expectantly with sherry glasses in their hands.

'Ah,' said the one nearest them, the one with the deep, pseudo-Churchillian voice. 'Sir James, of course, and this must be Mr Sutton.'

He took a step towards Sutton, and a big hand was extended. It had greying hairs on the back and its grip was strong. The man's face was vaguely familiar to Sutton, perhaps from newsreels long ago, or from a magazine such as *Picture Post*. He was in his hearty mid-sixties, broad-shouldered and slim-hipped still, with thick eyebrows and pale blue eyes that could be described either as serene or as cold, depending on what you thought of their owner.

'This is Lord Frawley, George,' said Rudwick. 'And this . . .' another man was moving slowly forward at a shy shuffle '. . . is Simon Marjoribanks, a, ah, special adviser to the Home Office.'

Rudwick winked. He meant that Marjoribanks was something to do with M.I.5. It was a tired euphemism, and in the present company it was theatrical and a bit condescending and Sutton didn't like it at all. As for Frawley, yes, he remembered now. He'd been a plain MP before the war, one of the leading supporters of Chamberlain. Later Frawley had been kicked upstairs to the House of Lords, but he was obviously a clever politician who always found a way of sticking close to the centres of power, as his position here proved.

'Lord Frawley is a senior member of Mr Churchill's staff,' Rudwick explained, as if he understood the process of identification that was going on for Sutton. 'He may have dropped out of the newspaper headlines, but that doesn't mean he's not here at Downing Street a lot of the time. More than the Prime Minister, I've heard tell.'

Frawley laughed, but his pale eyes sparkled.

'I trust we can rely on Mr Sutton's discretion. You've already started gossiping, Sir James.'

Rudwick laughed too. Sutton had a not altogether pleasant feeling of intruding on a private club of men who knew each other and had taken a few hostages together. Marjoribanks, somewhere in his mid-fifties and the youngest of the three, also seemed the quietest. That didn't necessarily mean, as Sutton had learned in his dealings with Whitehall, that he wielded the least power or that he might not know a lot more than the other two put together. Rudwick and Frawley were very physical men in their different ways; Marjoribanks looked more like an academic, or even a scholarly monk, with his bald pate and nervous, unworldly smile. The shock came when he turned surprisingly intense eyes on Sutton and from between his thin lips whipped a voice like a steel hawser.

'Come on, Lord Frawley, don't beat about the bush. We want Mr Sutton to know that he had better be discreet. He signed the Official Secrets Act years ago, and he's bound by it like the rest of us until the day he dies,' Marjoribanks said. 'In my case, I'll say now that he'll get trouble from me, personally, if he doesn't keep this whole matter to himself. He seems to have decided that what we're asking him to fetch is worth risking his life for. That's his decision, freely arrived at. What else is there to say?' He took a sip of sherry, looked appraisingly at Sutton.

So the priest was a warrior-priest. Well, well. Sutton made a mental note not to cross this man. For all his ascetic looks, here was a man whose answers to life's problems were probably direct and, Sutton's instincts told him, if necessary violent.

'Indiscretion is not something I've ever been accused of, Mr Marjoribanks,' Sutton said. 'A few other things, but never telling tales out of school.'

Marjoribanks stared him out. 'Glad to hear it.'

'Drink?' said Frawley. 'I'm doing the honours. Best to keep it all between the four of us, I thought. No flunkeys or footmen to inhibit the conversation.'

'No thanks,' said Sutton in response to his enquiring gaze. Frawley, to his credit – or perhaps he had been expecting the refusal – simply nodded and passed on to Rudwick: 'The usual?'

The usual was a large whisky and soda. When Rudwick had his drink, at Frawley's suggestion they all took seats.

All three men's eyes were suddenly on Sutton, weighing him up.

'Well,' said Frawley, 'how do you feel about meeting Herr Heinz Keppler again?'

'It's not something I'd have gone out of my way to arrange, under other circumstances,' Sutton said carefully. 'In fact, I have to admit that I think Keppler's a waste of effort.'

Frawley smiled mechanically. 'I can see why you think that. You have strong anti-Nazi principles, do you, Mr Sutton? I don't think you are alone in this room in that. But it is sometimes both possible and necessary to keep those principles in one hand and at the same time very selectively – of course – use people whom we personally find distasteful. That is the situation regarding Herr Keppler. In other words, we are not interested in Keppler as a human being, only in what he *has*. Do you understand that?'

Before Sutton could say anything, Marjoribanks cut in with that unexpected, aggressive edge: 'Listen, Sutton, this man has information we can't afford to get out into the big, wide world. There's no shortage of nations and individuals who would use it to harm the interests of this country. I'd have thought that was enough. I can't seriously believe you'll let us and your country down.'

Marjoribanks set his glass down on a small, round Georgian table with a force that made it sway a little. He folded his arms.

'Sir James says you were probably his best officer, and you've got all the skills required. Quite honestly, I'd still send you even if circumstances were different. I don't have any people precisely cut out for this job.'

There was silence. Frawley said affably, 'Mr Marjoribanks is perhaps a little blunt at times. That comes from his craft, which is not one in which diplomacy plays a large part. What he's really saying is, he expects a man like you to put duty first. Now, I'm a politician. I know there has to be a deal, and the deal is that you get your country's thanks, and the reward of rehabilitation in the service you love. You risk a lot, but you stand to gain a great deal too.' He smiled encouragingly. 'Now. Any more questions? I shan't be able to spend much longer with you, I'm afraid.'

'Feel free, George,' muttered Rudwick to his left, and took a sip of whisky, scratched his nose.

'One small thing.' Sutton did not look at him, but the two other men opposite. 'And I'm aware that we have an agreement that's binding – on both sides. May I ask whether this business involves a third power, apart from Germany?'

Marjoribanks' eyes suddenly narrowed. He seemed about to speak, but Frawley intervened quickly: 'I can say that the information will be damaging not just to this country but to at least one major ally, yes,' he said.

'And is that ally aware of the existence of the material?'

A quick exchange of glances, an almost imperceptible shake of the head from Marjoribanks.

'No, not to our knowledge,' Frawley said. 'According to Keppler, we are the only government he has contacted. We don't believe it will be necessary to involve anyone else at this stage. Later, of course, when the material is safely in our hands and we have had the chance to evaluate it . . .' Frawley made an airy little wave with one hand which implied that perhaps they would share the information and perhaps they would not. His gesture summed up the whole attitude of self-assurance, an instinctively secretive and devious way of living that was completely alien to George Sutton, despite his police training and his thorough self-education. He would have to live with these people; but he could not, deep down, understand them.

'That's enough, I think,' Marjoribanks said. 'From now on it's got to be yea or nay. No more disclosure.'

Frawley and Rudwick both nodded. Sutton realised he had not got around to mentioning his conversation with Harry Stone, or the story about Kennedy. Nor did he feel inclined to do so now. Best for him to keep quiet, and keep ahead of them.

'Fair enough,' Sutton said. 'So it's just me.'

'And the intermediary, of course,' Rudwick put in. 'The same one who made the approach to us. This . . . person . . . can move freely between Germany and Switzerland and, well, now that the border between France and Switzerland is open, everyone's life is suddenly much easier.'

'There'll be help for you from our own man in Switzerland, Mr Sutton,' Frawley said. He looked at the clock on the mantelpiece. As if on cue, a knock came on the door and the owlish civil servant who had shown them in looked into the room.

'Committee time, Lord Frawley,' he said. 'They're champing at the bit.'

'Very well, Hoskins. I'll be along in a moment.'

Frawley got to his feet and offered Sutton his hand.

'Well, Mr Sutton, thank you for coming this evening,' Frawley said, keeping up the polite fiction that the encounter had been for his benefit rather than Sutton's. 'And good luck. It's good to know you're a man with a head on your shoulders, not just an automaton who goes in like a bull in a china shop. A privilege to meet you.'

There were handshakes all round as the meeting broke up, and within a few minutes Frawley was striding towards some committee room in intense conversation with the civil servant, as if Sutton had never existed. Marjoribanks excused himself quickly and without further comment.

'That was extremely interesting, George,' Rudwick said once they were back in the Daimler. 'I knew you wouldn't let me down. You can see the kind of level at which the decisions are being made. This is vital to the national interest, don't you see? Vital.'

To Sutton it sounded almost as if Rudwick were trying to persuade himself, but he let it pass.

'I remember Lord Frawley when he was an M.P.,' he said.

'As Ronald Frawley, he was a Member of Parliament, yes. He succeeded to his father's title and seat in the House of Lords three years ago. A very distinguished man and a great patriot, George.'

'I recall him as a very strong supporter of Mr Chamberlain, sir. He used to make speeches about how we needed to understand Germany's legitimate grievances, about how Herr Hitler was just trying to get his people a place in the sun. Seems strange to see him there at Downing Street under Mr Churchill. He was very anti-Churchill in the early days.'

'People change, George. What seemed reasonable a few years ago obviously doesn't make the same sense now. Many distinguished and patriotic men thought Hitler was sincere in those days. They believed that, since he was in charge in Germany and wasn't going to go away, he had to be accommodated somehow. It was all years ago, anyway.'

'As you say, sir.'

They drove on for some time without speaking. Then Rudwick said, 'I'm glad you've seen Mrs Sutton's grave and visited your old haunts. We start to make serious preparations now, George. Noses to the grindstone and no more gadding about London. We'll be keeping you rather under wraps from now on.' He let out a short laugh. 'Not so much the Nazis we're worried about – they're pretty much played out. But there's plenty among our so-called friends who'd give their eye teeth to have what Keppler's offering, and to have Keppler as well, for that matter. Fortunately, they're in the dark about all this, and we intend to keep it that way.'

The more Sutton thought about the meeting at Downing Street and its consequences, the more it seemed to him that he was being isolated, like a bacillus or a laboratory animal – both of which were, of course, carefully cultivated, and ultimately expendable.

'Things will really start to move quickly now, George,' said Rudwick. 'You've got people to see and things to do. We start first thing tomorrow after a hearty breakfast.'

'Like the condemned man.'

There was a brief, uncomfortable pause. Then Rudwick said, 'Or the honest craftsman, George. The honest labourer worthy of his hire.'

CHAPTER EIGHT

THE AUBURN-HAIRED WOMAN was in her mid-thirties and had the healthy colouring and sleek body that spoke of skiing every winter, swimming and tennis in the summer. There was also something about her that whispered quietly but insistently, money! As she walked along the Spitalgasse in the spring sunshine she wore a camel-hair coat of elegant cut with an Italian silk scarf at her throat, a sable fur hat, and a pair of patent-leather pumps. In almost any other European city at this time, Countess Helen von Ackersberg might have been the object of curiosity or envy or even hostility. But this was Berne, capital of neutral Switzerland. Elsewhere the world continued to suffer and starve and drown in its own blood, but here the good life went on with relatively few inconveniences.

As befitted her well-kept appearance, the countess seemed unhurried. She turned left at the old Käfigturm, once the city lock-up, and walked towards the river Aare. Just before the river she turned into a sidestreet off the main thoroughfare and began to windowshop at the expensive little jewellers and clothes stores. The sandstone buildings were honey-coloured in the sharp light. After a few minutes spent gazing in the window of a milliner's next to a café, she noticed the reflection of a man standing across the street. He was looking at his watch, as if waiting for a friend who was late. The countess recognised him but gave no sign. Casually she took a few steps to the door of the café and went in.

There were two other customers. One was an elderly Bernese with a small, ugly dog. The other was a young man sitting in the corner deep in his reading of the *Züricher Zeitung*. She approached his table.

86

'Joe!' she exclaimed, as if the encounter were a pleasant surprise.

He lowered his newspaper, smiled.

'Sit down, Helen,' he said quietly. 'We're okay. I've got two guys out there covering the place.'

'I saw one.'

Her voice was slightly husky, her English fluent with only a very small hint of Swiss-German sing-song. She had been born into a patrician family in Basel, according to the autobiography they had on file, but had lived for twelve years in America, spending four semesters at Vassar before returning to Europe and easing into what had seemed to be a very suitable marriage with the late Count von Ackersberg. The story of that marriage – like her relationship with Heinz Keppler – remained a mystery to Joe McCarr.

McCarr glanced in the direction of the waitress, saw that she was still in conversation with a young Swiss dandy at the counter.

'It's okay,' the countess said. 'You don't need to give her a hard time. I'll have some coffee when she's ready.'

McCarr nodded. He took a sip of his own coffee, made a face to indicate that it was cold.

'So how's it all going?' he asked.

'Good news, Joe. I spoke with my contact at the embassy. Sutton's coming. It's all fixed.'

McCarr flashed her a relieved smile. He was around thirty, with a square, open Irish-American face and the muscular body of the oarsmen he had been in his college days. He had ears that stuck out slightly, and a moustache; which gave him a more than passing resemblance to Clark Gable and had made him very popular with certain young women. But he wore his good looks without vanity. The amiable exterior concealed a serious nature and a controlled violence that made him a formidable intelligence operative.

'Terrific,' he said. 'When's he due in town?'

'A week or so. He's being briefed in London at the moment. Then me we meet, and so on and so forth.'

'And so forth is right.'

'Joe, you guys have got to move in fast.'

'We will.' The waitress finally appeared and McCarr ordered coffee in his excellent German. He might look like a pure-bred Mick, but his mother was from Hamburg. Maybe that was where the occasional edge of brooding introspection came from.

When the waitress had gone to fetch their order, McCarr jabbed a finger at his newspaper.

'The Russians are still poised just thirty or forty miles from Berlin,' he said. 'Who knows? The whole damned Reich could collapse like a house of cards any minute. What happens if we're too late? Has Keppler thought of that?'

She shrugged. 'He thinks of that all the time. But the word in Berlin is that Zhukhov's troops are still busy mopping up, securing their supply-lines. There's still a hell of a lot of Germans between the Oder and Berlin, and they'll fight like demons. They know what's happened to the people in the eastern provinces the Soviets have captured so far. Not nice. There's time, don't worry.'

'There'd better be. It's a pity he needs this Sutton so badly. That means we get to go at the Brits' pace, *and* persuade them to cut us in on the action.'

'Heinz believes in friendship. And he thinks of the British as gentlemen.'

'Where's he been the past few years, for God's sake?'

'On the other side,' she said. 'That's the whole point.'

'Sure. Ignorance is bliss. I guess that would have helped him keep his illusions,' McCarr agreed with a laugh.

There was a pause while the girl clattered the cups down before returning to her boyfriend. McCarr studied Helen von Ackersberg. She was smart, she was sexy, with that hair, those big green eyes and that alabaster skin. Not for the first time, he wondered what she was like in bed. And not for the first time, he thought of her giving that body to a Nazi, of all the things about her he didn't understand, and the speculation stayed theoretical. McCarr liked his women to be both pretty and pretty straightforward. Whatever else the countess might be, uncomplicated she was not.

'You happy?' he asked.

'Happy?'

'Is this whole thing all right with you? This is over and beyond the call of duty. It's a different ball-game. There's Sutton involved now, and me.'

She surveyed him coolly, took a sip of coffee. 'I brought

the message. I agreed. If it hadn't been all right with me, I wouldn't have acted as go-between. I'd have suddenly become seriously indisposed. You know that.'

'Just checking. The boss tells me to check, ask if the countess is happy.'

'Well, there's always reason to worry. I don't know Sutton, of course. He's just a cop. I hope he's not too much of a liability. He's planning to travel as a Swede, to cover up his less-than-perfect German. I guess that's okay. Probably best if you do too. Your German's too classical for a Swiss.'

'I spent six weeks in Nebraska once. I'll be just fine as a Swede.'

'Dear Lord, I hope so. Anyway, I've told you everything I know about Sutton, and it's not much. How about you?'

McCarr pursed his lips. 'We've done our own checking since you told us about him. Turns out there are a few problems, though not in the areas you mentioned.'

'Yes? What is it? One eye? One leg? Deaf and dumb?'

'Worse, in a way. Turns out Keppler's picked a drunk. A reformed one but a drunk all the same. Sutton was forced to resign from the British police a couple of years back. There was stuff to do with the death of his wife, I don't know the whole story. Of course, Keppler couldn't know that. He hadn't seen the guy for years. Anyway, he's been in disgrace, interrogating German POWs in some God-forsaken hole.'

'But is he any good?' She smiled. 'In action, I mean.'

'So long as he stays off the booze, I guess so. But with drunks that's always a big "if".'

'He doesn't sound too terrific. Strange. Heinz seemed to think he was the best cop he'd ever met. And coming from him, let me tell you, that is praise.'

'Maybe Keppler judged him well,' said McCarr with a sigh. 'No one's saying Sutton's got no brains. None of our sources think that.'

'And who exactly are your sources, Joe?'

McCarr paused, played with his cup. 'Oh, contacts in London. Plus the FBI. The boss contacted Hoover, got some background on both Sutton and Keppler, just to be sure. The Bureau was closely involved with Interpol, as you know, and Hoover had ambitions to challenge the Germans for control at one time. He has files on all the foreign officials.'

'Heinz loathes Hoover. That's one reason why he's insisting on dealing with Sutton and the British. He thinks Hoover's too devious, too ambitious.'

'He's entitled to his opinion,' McCarr said with a crooked grin. 'We only went to the Feds because we needed information. And Hoover's hands are tied. He can't operate on foreign soil. If he could, he would, but he can't. He'd love to get his hands on that material Keppler's got. It sounds like it could be political dynamite, and deep down J. Edgar is a political operator.'

'And your people?' the countess said quickly.

'We want joint control of whatever comes out of this. We want to make sure it's not abused. Any more questions?'

Her laugh was a little forced. 'I suppose not. I just wanted to have some reassurance. I wouldn't take this risk for J. Edgar Hoover. I wouldn't even take it for you, Joe.'

'How about for Keppler?'

'Next question, please,' she said. 'I seem to have got myself into a rather sordid scenario, don't I?'

'No, Helen,' said McCarr. 'Inside Germany right now, there are GIs dying because they chose the wrong moment to cross the road. That is sordid. This is complicated – and weird, I'll admit. But it's necessary. Someone's got to have that information. It's there. It won't go away. I want it to be us. And we're none of us innocents; we're all doing this of our own free will.'

'You're a rational man.'

'I believe there are good and bad governments, and my government is a good one.'

'Otherwise you wouldn't be here,' said the countess.

'Right. It's that simple.'

CHAPTER NINE

T HE BULLET-PROOF limousine's powerful engine purred through the peaceful countryside of upstate New York. There were snowdrops by the side of the road, but J. Edgar Hoover was oblivious of nature.

'Jim, we're due at one-fifteen in the warden's office,' he told the black chauffeur. 'One-fifteen. Not one-twenty. Not even one-sixteen. Got that?'

'We'll be all right, sir,' the driver said. James Crawford had been driving Hoover for many years, and he was almost never late. Nevertheless, Hoover always harassed him, and it was more than his job was worth to show resentment.

'We'd better.'

The FBI director's famous bulldog features relaxed slightly, but his thick fingers still drummed on the sill of the car's window. He turned to Tolson, who seemed to be dozing lightly in the other corner. It had been a long drive up from New York City after an intense couple of days' work there. Tolson was five years younger than his boss, but he didn't have Hoover's stamina.

'This is hard, Clyde. Hard. But there are jobs only we can take on. Others lack the will, or if they have the will, they lack the integrity to remain unsullied by contact with corruption.'

Tolson nodded. 'I understand how tough this must be for you, chief. I'm with you, you know that.'

'Thank you, Clyde. Your support is so important. Gee, to have a man I can trust completely the way I do you, that's a rare thing among men.' For a moment it seemed as if he was about to brush away a tear. Then his jaw hardened. 'Well, soon we'll take that vacation. We'll go to Miami, or maybe the Coast.'

Hoover's watch told him it was one-twelve when they stopped at the gates of Great Meadows State Prison. Built only thirty years previously in imposing classical style, it lay among parkland cradled by green hills. Among the criminal fraternity it was known as 'the country club' because it was relatively modern and comfortable, and because of its deceptive architectural grace. But it was still a high-security jail, housing some of the nation's toughest wrong-doers.

A minute to get inside the gate, another minute to walk to the warden's office, Hoover calculated.

'Very good, Jim,' he told the chauffeur. 'You're some boy when you get behind that wheel and no mistake.'

There were three black agents in the entire FBI: Hoover's driver, Hoover's receptionist/doorkeeper, and Hoover's personal messenger. The director had been brought up before the First War, when his native Washington was still very much a Southern city, and the rules and the prevailing attitudes were small-town Dixie. He'd got used to having Negro staff, and maintained the tradition in his professional life.

Security at Great Meadows was tight, and the preliminaries took a little longer than Hoover had expected. But Warden Morhous had got used to dealing with outside agencies since Lucky Luciano had been transferred here in '42. He knew it didn't pay to bend the rules. Vernon A. Morhous had been in the prison service for close on thirty years, and Hoover guessed correctly that he was a no-nonsense man who did things by the book. He decided to take things easy during the first part of the meeting, save his heavy artillery for later.

Morhous rose from his chair when Hoover and Tolson were shown into his simply-furnished office. They shook hands.

'I'm glad to meet you, Mr Hoover, Mr Tolson. Let me say I've always admired the work of the FBI under your energetic leadership,' he said with a Yankee gruffness that made it clear the compliment was no empty flattery. 'You've made a lot more work for me and my men, and that's just fine!'

Hoover took the only guest's seat while a warden was despatched to find one for Tolson.

'Well, Warden Morhous, I've heard plenty about you too,' he answered. 'And I wish we had more men like you in the service. Sticklers for the rules, goes without saying, but always willing to be flexible when circumstances demand it.'

The warden made no comment. His thin, pepper-and-salt moustache might have twitched a little in a suppressed smile. Conscientious he may have been, but he didn't lack a dry sense of humour.

A chair was brought in and Tolson seated.

'And how is the prisoner Luciano?' Hoover asked then.

Morhous shrugged. 'The prisoner Luciano is in good fettle,' he said. 'I have to admit that, compared with other hoodlum types I have encountered, he shows a degree of charm and intelligence, rare commodities in such circles. If I didn't know his record, it would be hard to conceive of him as one of the country's most dangerous and ruthless mobsters, but then I've been in this line of work long enough to know that appearances are almost always deceptive.'

'Sure, Luciano can charm the birds off the trees,' Hoover interrupted him. 'He's in jail, he knows any bad behaviour on his part will lose him any chance at all of parole. So he'll be as good as gold, the best little Sicilian altar-boy you ever did see.' Hoover licked his puffy lips. 'You cross Luciano, though, and you'll suddenly come to bad harm. Not from Charlie Lucky, goes without saying. From another source, no connection – not that you can prove, leastways.'

The warden looked uncomfortable. 'Mr Hoover,' he said with sudden primness, 'I have agreed that you may interview the prisoner on Federal business. However, I have my responsibilities and I insist that there should be a guard present.'

'Warden, one of my stipulations was very specifically that there would be complete privacy.'

'I know. But I've had time to consider. I have to account for your safety while you are in *my* prison, Mr Hoover. Whatever we say about the prisoner's character, you never know . . .'

There was something close to contempt in Hoover's snort of irritation. The mask was slipping.

'Luciano wouldn't dare touch me,' he snapped. 'Tom Dewey was the one who put him behind bars. If Dewey were to walk into his cell right now, maybe Luciano wouldn't be able to resist, maybe his hot Sicilian temper would make him violent. Not with me. I'm just a cop, even if I am the director of the FBI. He knows that and respects it.'

Morhous took a deep breath. 'I must insist.'

'I'm sorry, Warden,' said Hoover, his eyes narrowing to slits. 'I insist on complete privacy. Associate Director Tolson will be there with me, and he is armed. That is sufficient precaution. If I am not permitted privacy, I can assure you I won't rest – in Albany, or in Washington – until I gain access on my terms.' His teeth bared in an intimidating smile. 'Warden, I think you're at a stage in your career when you'll either rise to dizzy heights – or sink back into the depths whence you came. I'd like you to bear that in mind at this moment. I can assure you that eventually I will get to see Luciano alone. All I have to do is to pick up the phone.'

The warden looked down at his hands. 'I guess you know what you're doing, Mr Hoover,' he murmured.

'I most certainly do, Warden. Thank you for your cooperation. It will not go unremarked.' A rare smile creased Hoover's face, then disappeared as quickly as it had come.

Hoover and Tolson were shown into the small room between the Warden's office and the Steward's office that was routinely used for confidential interviews between law enforcement officers and prisoners who had decided to cooperate with the police in some way. It was bare, with just a table and two chairs on each side. Hoover chose the chairs facing the only window, gestured for Tolson to join him there, sat down and waited.

In this room, Hoover knew, over the past three years Luciano had met with his criminal associates – Meyer Lansky, Frank Costello, the waterfront boss 'Socks' Lanza and others – as part of a daring and highly irregular cooperation between the Mob and Navy Intelligence. First Luciano, issuing orders from his cell, had helped stop sabotage and strikes, and generally ensured that the docks ran smoothly for the war effort. Then he had arranged for his Mafia contacts in Sicily to aid American reconnaissance parties that were landed there. Finally, when Allied forces launched a full-scale invasion of Sicily in September '43, Luciano had used his influence and prestige to ensure that all possible aid was granted to the American army by Mafia groups in the 'old country'. Charlie Lucky had been the Mob's New York boss, but his influence ranged far beyond. That's why Hoover had come here today.

Five minutes passed while Hoover waited and considered

his situation, occasionally exchanging a tight smile and a word or two with Tolson. Then the door opened. A guard put his head in.

'Ready, sir?'

'Ready, son.'

The guard stepped aside and into the room walked the most powerful criminal in America, perhaps in the world, hands in his pockets and dressed in plain, light-blue prison garb.

Charles 'Lucky' Luciano – real name Salvatore Lucania – entered slowly, almost regally, looked at Hoover for a long time without speaking, then greeted him with a slight bow. It was play-acting, Hoover recognised. Charlie was going to make like the 'man of respect', the old-fashioned Sicilian cavalier. Okay. What did it matter?

'Take a seat, Luciano,' he said roughly. Neither he nor Tolson had risen to acknowledge the gangster.

Luciano pulled the chair away from the table and turned it slightly to one side. He gave a comfortable little wave of one well-manicured hand, a wry grin.

'Welcome to my humble residence, Mr Hoover,' he said simply, in a voice that had learned a strange kind of culture. The Lower East Side influence remained strong, but he had dignity. 'It's not much, but – ' Luciano shrugged.

Hoover glared at him stonily. 'It's better than the other place – in Dannemora.'

'True,' Luciano agreed readily. 'It was real cold there. And a long way for my family and friends to come to visit. This is really okay, considering.' A pause. The brown eyes became shrewd. 'So. To what do I owe this honour, Mr Hoover? The big G-man drops by to pass the time, eh? You come with the free pardon? You gonna admit your mistake? It wasn't a fair trial? Governor Dewey decided he's gonna make it up to me?'

There was bitterness now in the man's eyes, despite his easy smile. In 1936 Luciano had been given Thirty to Fifty on a flimsy vice charge. Thomas Dewey, then D.A. for Manhatten, had whipped up the press, public opinion, the jury, and got Lucky behind bars – not for his many real crimes but on a count on which the proud, curiously fastidious mobster was least guilty, as anyone who knew the underworld would agree. He had never cared for pimping, but unfortunately some of his underlings had. Dewey had managed to weave a web of

circumstantial evidence that connected Lucky with the running
of a chain of whorehouses, called 'compulsory prostitution'.
There'd been enough to convince the jury, and Dewey had
scored a victory that had helped to propel him to the
governor's mansion. Hoover knew all the details, but he didn't
care a fig how the conviction had been secured. So far as he
was concerned, Luciano richly deserved to be in jail, and he
would be the last man to claim that ends didn't justify means.
It was only that the ends had changed in this case. J. Edgar
Hoover wanted something from this man.

'Sorry, Luciano. Nothing like that. You're wrong about the
free pardon.'

'I kinda figured I might be,' Luciano said. His face with its
chipmunk cheeks, blue chin and wide mouth – imitated in so
many gangster movies – creased in grim hilarity.

'But,' Hoover continued slowly, 'I know you've been coop-
erating with the authorities. That's why I'm here. Because of
the waterfront. The help to our boys on Sicily.'

'Don't say you're going to give me a medal!'

A forced laugh. Hoover smiled. Tolson smiled. 'Come on,
Luciano.'

Lucky turned cool. 'Okay,' he said crisply, 'I do my best. I
been done an injustice, but I'm a good American, whatever
they say. Okay, some people don't like the way I make a
living, but I'm a hundred-and-fifty-percent behind the war
effort. And, you know, some of my best friends are Jews.'

Hoover knew that much too well. Meyer Lansky, the Mob's
accountant, for instance. One of the hallmarks of Luciano's
criminal career had been his ability to reach beyond the Sicilian
and Neapolitan communities in order to recruit allies and
associates. It was a factor that had made him a new, more
dangerous kind of threat to law and order.

'That's all true, Luciano,' Hoover soothed. 'And I know
that when you promise, you deliver. It's why I'm here.'

'Real nice of you to say that, Mr Hoover.'

Their eyes met. Two kings negotiating. One might be a
captive, the other the captor, but there was no denying that
even in this dismal room, facing almost an entire lifetime in
jail, Lucky Luciano knew himself to be any man's equal. He
was waiting, his head cocked a little to one side, looking calmly
at Hoover.

'I have a proposition,' said Hoover at last.

'Sure.'

Suddenly it was Hoover who felt unaccountably insecure, though he knew he had the power, the gift beyond price to bestow. He steeled himself and went on.

'I need something and someone, Luciano. I want some papers – and if possible the man who has charge of them.'

'You want him alive?' Luciano asked, as if he was establishing whether Hoover liked his hamburgers with or without onions.

'I don't want his corpse, let's put it that way. Mostly I want the papers.'

Luciano frowned. 'Sounds kinda routine. I don't ask why you can't arrange this job yourself.'

'The man and the documents are in Europe. Worse, they're in enemy-held territory. In Berlin.'

Luciano didn't bat an eyelid.

'I get the point. The arm of the FBI don't reach that far. But the arm of other government agencies, maybe. Don't we have an army, Mr Hoover, don't we have secret agents behind the enemy lines?'

'I want those papers and the man for myself, exclusively,' Hoover said with deliberation. 'I don't want any other government agencies involved. Security reasons.'

Luciano threw open his hands in mock-sympathy. 'It's a lousy world. Who can you trust, uh?'

'I want to know if you'll do what I ask,' Hoover said throatily, almost choking on his anger and humiliation. 'That's all, Luciano.'

'It's not easy, Mr Hoover. I have contacts in this kind of business – the recovery business, you know – in Europe.' Luciano sighed. 'But the price gets higher all the time, of course, and to operate inside Nazi-held territory, well, that's hard. You know I would do anything for my country, but under the circumstances I also feel entitled to ask what my country will do for me.'

'Parole,' Hoover growled. 'If you agree to help me, I'll personally ensure you're out of jail within a year, Luciano. If I don't intervene, you can guarantee you'll be in this dump till you're seventy.'

Luciano made no response to the clumsy threat.

'Say, six months from the time you get your man and his papers, I get parole,' he said with deceptive mildness. 'And no deportation. I love America, and I don't want to have to leave the United States just because of a little legal detail like citizenship.'

Hoover was beginning to sweat inside his winter-weight suit. He was not a man used to asking favours. He demanded; others followed. But he loved secrets, and the power they gave him.

'That's a tough demand,' he said a little lamely.

'You think your proposition is like a trip to the corner store? I'll have to call in a lot of favours with some very hungry people. And the man who might do this for me – I say might – is a very, very special person.'

'Okay,' Hoover said. He turned to Tolson, signalled for the Associate Director to hand him the briefcase he had been guarding since they entered the room. He unlocked it, took out some papers. 'The name of this man I want is Heinz Keppler. He's a cop, a Gestapo man, and he's in charge of some very valuable records. He's in Berlin. Can your guy handle that?'

'He can,' said Luciano with a proud smile that was almost fatherly.

Hoover looked at him hard. 'Are you serious? We're talking about just one man?'

'Right. A onc-man army, Mr Hoover. Don't worry about a thing, eh?'

'You have to realise Keppler won't be alone. I've got details of a group of people who . . .'

'Let us have those details. We have them, you don't need to worry. Take my word for it. You can trust me and my man both.'

'If it turns out I can't, it'll mean at least twenty more years in the Pen for you, Luciano. I can personally guarantee it.'

Luciano's eyes glinted momentarily, registering his distaste at Hoover's crudity. Where he came from, threats were an art form, courtly and indirect. What was this childish bluster from one of the most powerful men in the government?

'Mr Hoover,' he said, his voice still polite, 'this is a kind of a business deal, sure. It is also, for me, a matter of honour. You know that I am a man of influence, that I have a reputation to consider every bit as much as you do. Let's have some respect for each other, eh?'

Hoover stared at him coldly. 'I accept that this is a deal. That's all. Hard, cold convenience. What do you want, a kiss on the cheek?'

The insult was well-chosen, but the Mafia chief only smiled all the more affably. Any Sicilian knew that only a fool responded to an insult with anger or blows. The wise man appeared to accept it, and then waited his opportunity to avenge it.

'Up to you, Mr Hoover. Okay, I do your recovery job, you arrange parole. And no deportation.'

'That's the bargain, yes.'

'At least I know where I stand. I'm only sorry I can't offer you and Mr Tolson a drink to seal the bond, Mr Hoover. Maybe another time,' said Luciano.

Hoover got to his feet, looked at him with barely disguised loathing. 'Unless you do this job right,' he said, 'there isn't going to be another time.'

CHAPTER TEN

'VERY GOOD, Herr Salvesen. Welcome back to Switzerland.'

'*Dankeschön*. It's a great pleasure,' said George Sutton, trying out his Swedish-accented German.

He slipped the Swedish passport that identified him as Gustav Salvesen back into his coat pocket and proceeded to the exit door of the single-storey building. The dummy-run was over. Herr Salvesen had successfully completed a voyage by boat to Paris, then from Orly airfield to Zurich. And now there should be someone to pick him up and take him on to the next stage.

In the pale sunshine outside the terminal building there were several people waiting. The woman in her sixties with a poodle would have been nicely incongruous. A young couple, the young man with only one arm, showed no sign of recognition. Neither did a bald, middle-aged man who was smoking a pipe and reading a newspaper. Then, suddenly, he looked over the top of the paper, made to return to it, did a double take.

'My God. If it isn't Gustav Salvesen. I mean, am I right?' he said in stunningly bad German.

'Why, yes, for a moment I didn't recognise you,' Sutton said, making the agreed answer.

A brisk handshake. The man murmured: 'Hello. My name's Simpson. We'd better talk German until we're safely into the car. All right?'

'Fine.' Sutton agreed. Then he said at normal speaking volume, 'As it happens, I was about to hire a car to get to Berne. Are you still based there? If so, I would be grateful for a lift.'

'Of course. What a stroke of luck for you. As soon as the

100

chap I'm due to meet arrives, we'll be on our way. Get you to Berne in no time.'

A minute or so latter, a large man in a tweed coat appeared with his travelling-bag. He greeted Simpson respectfully, they all shook hands and the necessary introductions were made. Then they strolled out to the car, a porter following with Sutton's suitcase. The big man who had also got off the plane was an embassy chauffeur who had been flown to Paris and back just to give Simpson someone to 'meet' and give a lift to Berne – along with his 'old friend' Salvesen/Sutton.

Soon the three men were established in an Austin sedan with non-diplomatic numberplates, heading towards the Berne road. When they were well clear of the airport, Simpson stopped and told the chauffeur to take the wheel. He settled in the back with Sutton. It was a hundred miles or more to the Swiss capital, so they would have plenty of time for a briefing.

'We'll see you settled and fed at your hotel, and then tonight you'll be introduced to your travelling-companion.' Simpson leered as if it were expected of him. 'Extraordinary girl. Have you been given the low-down on the lady in question?'

Sutton shrugged, irritated by the man's schoolboy gaucheness:

'Helen Joanna von Ackersberg, born Zweig, Basel, Switzerland, 1910. Swiss citizen. Lived in America from the age of eight to the age of twenty. Married Count Erich von Ackersberg, landowner, born 1902, German citizen, in Berlin in 1933. Ackersberg is said to have been an opponent of Nazism, at least after a few years experience of the régime. Called up in 1939, rose to the rank of Oberleutnant before being killed on the Russian front just before Christmas '43. Countess von Ackersberg may already have been the mistress of Heinz Keppler by that time. Anyway, once she had been widowed Keppler fiddled her a nice vague job liaising between the International Red Cross here and its German branch, the DRK, which is itself controlled by an SS officer. More to the point, what this job – little more than a sinecure – enables her to do is to travel freely to Switzerland and thus act as Keppler's intermediary.'

'Very good. I hadn't intended to put you through your paces

so soon, but there you are. She's going to be a jolly useful companion, and she's a smasher too.'

'What I can't understand is how she comes to hop into bed with a Nazi,' said Sutton.

'Women, old boy. Who knows why they do these things? Look at Unity Mitford. Good family, lovely girls, all of them. Then Unity got a thing about the Führer and went completely cuckoo. At least the countess doesn't seem to be actually batty. Eccentric, I'll grant you, in her choice of paramours. Perhaps Keppler has good qualities to compensate.'

Sutton didn't recall any, but he decided not to dispute the point with the garrulous Simpson. He unbuttoned the jacket of his severely Swedish but very well-tailored dark suit, adjusted the gold-rimmed spectacles he had been forced to wear to make him, London had said, look more like a Red Cross dignitary. He had drawn the line at a monocle.

'You're clear about everything else, are you?' Simpson continued. 'With any luck, things should be absolutely straight-forward. Two Red Cross workers enter the Greater German Reich on an errand of mercy, pick up friend Keppler and his case filled with goodies, then exit smartly westwards.' Simpson wagged a finger at an imaginary naughty little boy. Since he wasn't actually looking at Sutton, it took a moment before it became obvious who he was referring to. 'But for Our Dear Lord's sake, don't get caught. The Swiss, the Swedes, and the Red Cross would all be furious. We'd deny all knowledge of you, naturally,' he added cheerfully.

Sutton asked where he would be staying. Simpson told him it would be a good-class hotel near the *Bundeshaus*, the Swiss parliament building.

'Blessed if I understand all this,' he said. 'I have to bung the chits back to your friend Rudwick directly for your expenses. Pretty irregular, but I suppose it has to do with the irregularity of the entire bloody business.' Simpson shook his head incredulously. 'The countess turned up, all she'd do was give us Lord Frawley's name and yours, refused to tell us anything. So I phoned up Frawley and from then on he organised everything, just told me to keep my mouth shut and give him and his people all the help they needed. Not a bloody thing in writing.' He snorted like a horse in a frosty dawn. 'Been operating on trust ever since the countess arrived on my doorstep. The thing is, my family has connections with Frawley. He's certainly been a tremendous help to me in my career, so hey ho, it seems a small favour to look after another protégé of his. To whit, you, Mr Sutton.'

'I suppose it does. They put me up in pretty basic digs in Holland Park. How come the sudden extravagance?'

'Oh, Gustav Salvesen's supposed to be independently wealthy, old chap. Got to keep up appearances, stay in character, or you might as well not bother. As for the hotel, it's perfect – popular with middle-ranking neutral diplomats, officials from the classier international charities, you know the sort of thing,' Simpson said airily. 'Might as well enjoy yourself a bit before you go into the lions' den. Not often HMG foots the bill for a fellow to live in this kind of style. I draw the line at champers, though. I *do* have to justify expenses, even if it's only to Rudwick.'

Sutton decided he didn't like Simpson much. Too much talk of connections, too much help from Lord Frawley in his career. Simpson was all upper-class heartiness, but Sutton had a feeling he was unreliable except to people who helped him in his career. It was unlikely that an ex-CID man, reformed drunk-turned-agent from the East End came into that category. 'I'll play it any way you want', he shrugged. 'Quite honestly I don't give a bugger.'

Ahead of them the road zig-zagged steeply down towards a small town nestled beneath the mountains on yet another turquoise Swiss lake.

'I say, Bignal, slow down a bit, will you?' Simpson told the driver testily.

The big man shrugged, then gently pressed the brake.

'They told me you were no picnic,' Simpson said to Sutton then. 'They didn't tell me you'd be quite as indigestible as all this.'

CHAPTER ELEVEN

SUTTON did not order champagne when he was left alone in his hotel room in Berne. Instead he admired the fresh daffodils and hyacinths in their vases in the salon of his modest suite, the fine covers on the bed in his bedroom, then undressed and drew the hottest, deepest bath he had had in six years of fuel-saving, water-hoarding wartime austerity. The wicked sense of freedom and self-indulgence was almost as relaxing as the soothing water. Then he stretched out luxuriously on the bed and fell asleep.

When he awoke it was dark, and someone was knocking on the door. It was Simpson and the chauffeur, who was beginning to look suspiciously like a bodyguard.

'I see you took your chance for some rest,' he said. 'Excellent. You have to build up your strength. What with the briefings and the . . . ah . . . Swedish lessons, you're going to be a very busy man between now and Easter.'

They waited in the salon while Sutton dressed in his sober suit and tie and put on his spectacles.

'Aha, Herr Salvesen!' said Simpson. 'Amazing what glasses can do for one's appearance. Now, I suggest that you and me and old Bignal here – ' he indicated the chauffeur ' – nip down to the bar and sink a snifter. The countess isn't due till seven-thirty, which gives us an hour to put our heads together. Sound all right?'

'A bit public, isn't it?'

'All under control. You can't live like a bloody hermit, you know. It'll all be very natural.'

Simpson disappeared into Sutton's bathroom to answer a call of nature, leaving him alone with Bignal, who relaxed visibly when his boss left the room.

'I think I know you,' he said suddenly in a rumbling South London voice. 'Didn't you used to be with CID at Lewisham nick before the war?'

'Yes. That's right. '31 to '33.'

Bignal nodded. 'Thought so. You put my brother away for armed robbery. Fifteen years hard he got,' he said matter-of-factly.

'I'd say I'm sorry, but I can't find it in me.'

'That's all right, squire. Me brother was a total bloody lunatic. A real tearaway. He should've joined the civil service like me. I've got a secure job. I travel around, see the world.'

That seemed to be the limit of Bignal's conversation. In the minute or so before Simpson's return, he said nothing. He stayed silent all the way down in the lift, and in the bar nursed a single lager while Simpson hit the whisky and Sutton drank good Swiss coffee. On reflection, Sutton decided that Bignal was probably one of the happiest, least resentful men he had ever met. Interesting. Even from the way he held his beer glass; it was also clear that he could kill anyone he was told to, with his big, bare hands.

Helen von Ackersberg was late. Simpson was on his third whisky when he got to his feet and called out, 'Countess!' She acknowledged him, and eyes swept to his right to take in Sutton, but their expression did not change.

Sutton got up from the table as she approached. Helen von Ackersberg was quite tall, about five foot eight, with auburn hair worn fashionably long. Her eyes were cool, though not hostile, her jaw firm. The only sign of vulnerability was in her lips, which were full and expressive. In her green calf-length dress and matching pillbox hat she looked sleek and expensive. He was still in a slight state of shock when she reached out her hand towards him.

'Ah, there you are, Herr Salvesen,' she said in English with a clipped American intonation. 'I see you have made the acquaintance of Mr Simpson. It's lucky there are very few Germans left in Berne these days. They would not approve of cosy chats with English diplomats.'

'As a neutral, I believe I can speak to whoever I wish,' said Sutton with a pompousness that he thought was nicely in character for Salvesen.

It was a very slow night in the hotel bar. Three stodgy-looking Swiss businessmen conducting a gloomy, monosyllabic financial conversation over beers with aquavit chasers. A man with a younger woman, probably an illicit girlfriend. All were some distance away and cocooned in their particular concerns.

'We just bumped into your colleague, Mr Salvesen. He was telling us about the refugee problem in Western Germany,' Simpson announced. 'This is something we shall have to deal with once the war is finally over.' He got to his feet. 'And now, I'm sure you have your Red Cross business to discuss.'

Then the pair of Englishmen marched out as if they had other, more important business. Sutton was due to rendezvous with them in his room afterwards.

'I'd better order you a drink,' said Sutton. He was irritated to find himself disturbed by the Countess's beauty, her real elegance. The encounter with the woman on the train had not been like this.

'That would be nice,' Helen von Ackersberg said simply. 'Relax. This is just a social event. We can make of it what we like.'

She smiled when she said it, but it was also a kind of reproach. This woman liked being on top, Sutton realised. Then he wondered about the need evident in that voluptuous mouth. Maybe she also longed not to be stronger than her men.

He ordered her a gin-and-tonic and another coffee for himself. Life without the usual crutch was pretty easy until a situation like this one. Even a small whisky would have relaxed him, he knew.

'So we're going to Berlin,' he said quietly, because he had to occupy himself somehow and get the thoughts of whisky out of his head. 'London outlined things for me. Simpson's filled in most of the rest. They make it sound like a picnic, but then they would, wouldn't they?' He paused. 'You're experienced. You know what things are like in Berlin. Anything you have to add?'

She caught his gaze and held it. 'The problem will not be getting in, but getting out. Even if the Gestapo gives us a thorough inspection on the way in, we should be all right. But on the way out, with Heinz and the documents . . .' She lit a cigarette, made a doubtful gesture.

106

'They'll be reluctant to tangle with a full SS colonel,' Sutton said. 'Keppler's fixed himself up with valid papers, hasn't he?'

'Yes. But nothing's certain these days. And it's not easy to just slip away without anyone noticing.'

'I suppose that's up to Keppler. Do you believe he can pull it off?'

'I think so. But, of course, for the people he works with, suspicion is a way of life.'

'Tell me more.'

'There's Kaltenbrunner, the man who took over from Heydrich, who's head of the SD, which includes the Gestapo. He's also technically head of Interpol. More important is Müller – he runs the Gestapo, they call him Gestapo-Müller. Heinz worked with him in the Munich police force. He says Müller is uncanny; he can read a man's soul.'

'I've served under a few blokes like that. Is Keppler under observation? If so, in a routine way, or more systematic?'

'He doesn't know. I mean, I think they're always spying on each other at Wannsee. But he's certain Müller's keeping an eye on him. We have to bear that in mind.'

'He's not just imagining things?'

'Heinz does not imagine things,' she said wryly.

'All right. I have met him, remember, Countess von Ackersberg.'

'Call me Helen, please.'

For the first time there was a hint of warmth. She obviously meant to put him at his ease, but instead Sutton realised that his left fist was clenched on the table, his knuckles white with tension.

'All right . . . Helen. I don't know if you're aware of the details, but I only met Keppler a total of three times before the war, always on official police business. It's not exactly a lifelong friendship.

'He respects you. He believes you have integrity and courage.'

Sutton nodded, unsure of what answer to make. He remembered Keppler's face, pink and fleshily handsome, with a ready smile but watchful eyes. The man had always stared at himself in windows, in mirrors in bars and washrooms, whenever he got the chance. At the time Sutton had been amused, seeing the German's vanity as a foreign foible, the same continental narcissism that made Frenchmen wear hairnets in bed and Italians wax their moustaches. Now he sensed in himself a kind of fierce anger born of envy for the man who had got a woman like Helen von Ackersberg to share his bed.

'Aren't you flattered?' she said suddenly.

Sutton frowned.

'Countess – Helen, it's hard to know what to say to that. Keppler, as far as I could tell, was pretty good at his job. I can't say I respected the police force he was part of. I'm here to do a job. What he thinks of me – or what I think of him – is relevant only in so far as it helps me to bring this project to a successful conclusion.'

It was almost impossible for him to keep the judgement out of his voice, even though Sutton chose his words carefully. God knows, he sounded pompous enough even to himself, but there was no point in pretending. He could see tension in her jaw, a holding-back, as if she were longing to say something in defence – whether of herself, or Keppler, or their relationship he could not tell – but instead she downed her drink like a man.

'I understand.' An arch smile. 'I'd like another gin-and-tonic, please.'

When a drink came, Sutton tried a conciliatory gesture.

'Look, let's make one thing clear. I don't like this job much, but I'm determined to carry it through. I don't want to let personal prejudices get in thc way.'

'In the way of what?'

'Of doing what we – and especially I – have to do. My government doesn't like your friend Keppler, but it needs him. I suppose I could say the same. I volunteered. I've got my reasons too.'

The countess smiled thinly. 'I suppose I'm not allowed to ask what they are.'

'Well, I could never resist a challenge. And, of course, I like to travel. Especially in Germany. I used to go on bicycle tours there when I was a young CID man, you know. So this whole thing's perfect, really.'

'I see,' said Helen, and made a sour face. She lifted her glass. 'I see you have the typical British sense of humour. Ah well, cheers! Here's to peace.'

Sutton took no more than a taste of his coffee. 'One thing

about you interests me especially,' he said then. 'Since it's my turn. There's something I'm curious about.'

She looked at him sharply. 'Well?'

'How did you come to work for the Red Cross, if you don't mind my asking?'

There was a hint of relief, and of the practised response when she said quickly: 'Oh, I've lived an extremely privileged life. First as a little rich girl in Switzerland and the States, her daddy's darling, and then as a landowner's wife over here. I get bored easily, I like adventure, and I happen to believe that because of the advantages God gave me, I ought to help, in however small a way, to limit the suffering that we humans have decided to inflict on ourselves in the twentieth century. Does that satisfy you?'

Sutton nodded. Not a word about the fact that she only started to work for the Red Cross after becoming Keppler's mistress. Perhaps it didn't matter. Perhaps it was natural for her to omit something that was a little embarrassing. He wished he understood that. He wished he understood the rich. Above all, he wished he understood women.

The countess looked at her watch.

'I must fly. A dinner engagement. Did Simpson tell you?'

'No.'

'Anyway, this was a pleasant way for us to make each other's acquaintance. Simpson will fix up some work meetings later in the week, so he tells me. He's got a little flat somewhere we can have secret assignations and pore over maps and so on. Now,' she added quietly, 'when we say goodbye, act like we've known each other for ages and find each other really quite boring. . . .'

They got to their feet. Sutton found her hand extended towards him, was about to shake it, then realised he was meant to kiss it. He reddened, bowed from the waist and pecked the ring finger in the best continental style he could muster.

'Very courtly. *Sie sind ein richtiger Kavalier, Herr Salvesen. Auf wiedersehen!*'

'*Auf wiedersehen, Gräfin von Ackersberg. Und hoffentlich recht bald.*'

'Your Swedish accent is better in German. Confusing, isn't it?' she murmured.

'But convenient.'

CHAPTER TWELVE

THE NEXT MORNING Sutton had breakfast in his hotel room – rich-roasted coffee, fresh *brötchen* with jam, and real scrambled eggs. After five years of rationing he savoured every mouthful. He was thinking about the Countess von Ackersberg, wondering what it would be like if she were there with him eating breakfast, preferably without her expensive clothes on, when the door opened and two strangers walked in on him without knocking.

Sutton rose, clutching his napkin. He wondered fleetingly if these could be German agents, but he felt no fear, more puzzlement. One of the men was bespectacled, scholarly-looking, forty-five to fifty; the other was younger, athletic type in a beefy kind of way. He had already guessed their actual nationality by the time the bespectacled man spoke. The voice was educated and precise and unmistakably American.

'Mr Salvesen?' the man enquired with an open but knowing smile.

Sutton stared at him, told himself they weren't brandishing guns. There was no violence in their manner, though there was aggression of a subtle kind. He nodded cautiously. 'Yes. Can I help you, gentlemen?'

Yanks. What was going on, for Christ's sake? Never mind. He had to play this game, whatever it was, very calmly, despite the fast beating of his heart, the flush he could feel in his face.

'Mind if we have a talk with you, Mr Salvesen?'

'Gentlemen,' Sutton began, 'I am unfamiliar – '

They had already sat down on the sofa opposite his breakfast table.

'Thanks. You've got nothing to be worried about,' said

110

spectacles. 'You know, I'd say Mr Salvesen speaks very good English, wouldn't you, Joe?' he remarked to his friend.

'Right. Perfect, even.'

There was an uncomfortable silence. Uncomfortable for Sutton, that is. The Americans seemed totally unperturbed.

'My name is Dulles. Allen Dulles,' the bespectacled man introduced himself. He indicated his companion. 'This is Joe McCarr.'

'Pleased to meet you,' said McCarr.

Sutton stayed where he was for the moment, looking hard at them but making no answer. 'You are American?' he said. 'If you have official matters to discuss, perhaps you would like to make an appointment.'

'Oh, we don't want to disturb you. Please get on with your breakfast,' said Dulles-spectacles. 'I know food in, er, Sweden has been a little monotonous these past few years. I'd hate to spoil your enjoyment.'

He smiled encouragingly.

'Please leave,' Sutton said.

'We really need to talk to you.'

'I am going to call the management,' Sutton said, and made for the phone. The man named McCarr rose to block his way. Dulles put a gentle restraining hand on his fellow-American's arm.

'We're expecting David Simpson at any moment,' he said. 'We wouldn't want a scene, and neither would he. Would he, Joe?'

'Absolutely not. He'll be here very soon. Maybe even now . . .'

There was a noise outside in the corridor. The door flew open, and Simpson strode into the room with Bignal at his heels. He was nevertheless panting audibly and his hair was slightly out of place.

'Why, *David* . . .' said Dulles with exaggerated politeness, rising to greet him. 'You got our call. How good of you to come so promptly.'

'Bastard,' Simpson hissed. 'Molesting people in hotels. You people just don't know how to behave. I'll have your guts for this, Allen. I swear it. This man is a friendly neutral – and if he's anybody's, he's mine!'

Dulles grinned. 'I'd say that if George Sutton's anyone, he's his own man. And we want to talk to him. And you.'

There was another pause. Both Simpson and Sutton were still on their feet. Sutton indicated that he was prepared to walk out, McCarr or no McCarr. The diplomat hesitated. He looked at Dulles.

'We can deal with it now or later, but we'll deal with it,' said the American. 'Why don't you sit down, both of you. Relax. This is just a friendly chat between Allies.'

Simpson's face was turning a shade of puce, but he had obviously decided to confront this problem now.

'Bastard,' he repeated, but he took a seat all the same.

'Look,' said Simpson, 'This is outrageous.'

Dulles raised an eyebrow. 'You think so? David, since when has it been okay for you guys to keep something of this importance from your honoured cousins? I've consulted you about everything I've been up to lately. We've cut you in on the lot. That's what we mean by inter-allied cooperation.'

'I don't know what you mean, Allen,' Simpson snapped. 'All I'm saying is, you can't go around barging in on, on – '

'David,' Dulles said, shaking his greying head, almost embarrassed at having to cause his friend to inflict such shameless lies on them all, and to no avail. 'We know everything. Sutton. Keppler. Helen von Ackersberg.'

'The countess is a respected Swiss citizen!'

'She's very much more complicated than that, David,' said Dulles quietly. 'And actually she's ours, has been for a long time. Please, let's stop beating around the bush. How do you think we got to know about friend 'Salvesen' here?'

'Ah.' Simpson nodded miserably. 'She's been working for you?'

'For two years now.'

If what Dulles said was true, and from the look on his face it seemed as if it was, then Simpson knew there was no way out. 'All right,' he said, 'if I can believe you on that score, what's this visit about?'

'Quite simple,' Dulles answered, relaxing back into the sofa. 'We want in, as they say. David, dear man, we want fifty percent of whatever Heinz Keppler is selling. And we want participation.'

Simpson watched him, his face a mask, made it clear he refused to comment yet.

'We propose the team that goes to Berlin consists of George Sutton, Helen von Ackersberg, – *and* Joe McCarr, Dulles explained, just in case Simpson had missed the point.

Sutton decided to make his move. It was obvious the plan had been blown wide open, and maybe he would have to accommodate himself to whatever situation arose. But for a moment he had to express something of his own will in this.

'This wasn't what I agreed too,' he growled. He looked at McCarr. 'I've got nothing against this man, but I don't know him. I was told I would be going in alone with the woman.'

Dulles nodded easily. McCarr did not even indicate that he had heard anything untoward.

'The way things are now, this has to be a joint effort,' Dulles explained patiently, as if to a troublesome child. 'We don't intend for you to shake us off. And I assure you that Mr McCarr here is a very handy man to have around.'

'Tell me more.'

'He's one of our most experienced covert operators, with several successful missions inside occupied Europe to his credit.' Dulles paused. 'Tell me, have you ever killed a man?' he asked with soft emphasis.

'No,' Sutton admitted. 'But I can look after myself.'

'Well, as it happens. Joe is a skilled operator, OSS trained. Any kind of real trouble, I'd trust him to get you out of it. And, if you're concerned, he speaks perfect German.'

The look of disgust had not left Simpson's face. Sutton said quietly:

'If I have the choice, then I don't want him.'

Simpson nodded. 'Allen, this is ridiculous. You know we share everything with you. This one's our territory, though. Keppler's our man. My colleague here's right,' he said, slapping Sutton on the shoulder in a saloon-bar fashion, as if they had known each other for years, 'We don't know Mr McCarr and it complicates things terribly.'

Dulles' manner changed suddenly. The urbanity disappeared; his face became hard as a street-fighter's.

'David,' he said with deliberation, 'you and I know some things don't get shared – and that this could be one of them. I'm telling you right now that even if I have to call Washington and get Bill Donovan in on this one – for that matter, if it takes action by the President – I aim to make sure Joe goes along to Berlin. I have some idea of what's involved, and I know it could be dynamite for America as well as Britain.'

'Of course, but – '

'I have to say two things, as politely as I can,' Dulles continued stubbornly, ignoring Simpson's protests. 'First, we can't afford to rely on anyone's good will, even a trusted ally's when vital American interests are involved. No gentlemen's agreements, not any more. If the situation is as we understand it to be, it could seriously jeopardise our international standing – and ruin a few reputations. Second, this mission *needs* a skilled man like Joe, an experienced agent who can handle crises and violent situations. We mean to ensure the files and this man are successfully brought to the West. Now, do you understand my reasoning and the grounds for my insisting on a joint venture?'

Simpson nodded slowly to signify that he did, but that he still didn't like the situation. 'All right.' He turned to Sutton. 'I think we should ask our American friends to leave now. I'll stay here. I don't want you talking to any more strange men.'

'I wasn't talking. Not until you turned up.'

Dulles and McCarr stood up.

'We'll be in touch later,' Simpson said curtly.

'Fine, David. I realise you've got to go through the channels. I'm not out to make things difficult for you.'

'Goodbye, Allen.'

Sutton said nothing by way of farewell.

'Goodbye, Mr Sutton,' said Dulles in an aggrieved voice. Was he genuinely hurt, or was it just a manoeuvre?

'Yes. Goodbye,' Sutton answered grudgingly.

Dulles had not finished. He moved to within Sutton's reach.

'Listen, please,' he said. 'I realise you probably think this is unforgivable. But I still want to mention that I've checked you out, talked to people from our FBI who met you on Interpol business, and found you're a much-respected man in your field. We'd really feel it a privilege to work with you.'

'Thanks for the compliment. I'd still prefer to work alone, Mr Dulles.'

'We all have to make compromises', Dulles said. The stubborn, hard look had returned to his face, like a shutter coming down.

Sutton kept his face expressionless, but he was aware that this man Dulles, whoever he was, had a power that went beyond mere force or even cleverness. He was one of the world's just men, damn him, and that made him very hard to resist.

Simpson left Sutton on his own in the room for a while, insisting that he lock the door. He had Bignal with him when he came back. He had recovered some of his composure, but there was still a hunted look about him.

'So, did you sort out our ally?' Sutton asked with acid directness.

Bignal was sent into the corridor to guard the door. Simpson sat down on the sofa, hunched like a schoolboy who has brought home a bad report and is wondering how to break the news to his doting parents.

'It all depends what you mean by "sort out",' he said. 'I've talked to one or two people here. The trouble is, I can't really discuss things with them in any kind of detail, because the business is so bloody hush-hush. But I've got a phone called booked to Frawley in London in half an hour.'

'What do you expect to come out of that?'

'I don't know yet.' Simpson hesitated. 'Look, the more I think this over, the more I realise the Americans have got us over a barrel.'

He slid into the clipped, mannered upper-class cockney imitation of pre-war 'fast' society when he was nervous. Sutton, who knew the real cockney only too well, would have been amused under different circumstances.

'I don't see that. Keppler will only deal with me. And if Helen von Ackersberg refuses to cooperate under the conditions we want, then there's no deal and so a good chance the files will fall into the wrong hands. That'll damage the Americans as much as us.'

Simpson nodded, lit a cigarette with a gold lighter.

'You see, it's more of a political problem now, George,' he murmured. 'Now they know and they *demand* to be involved, and Allen Dulles refuses to take no for an answer, it becomes big politics. Big, old boy. I mean, it was all right while they weren't supposed to know. We could have pleaded any old excuse – security risks, lack of time, whatever you like – but now it's in the open and we can't do that.' He smiled painfully. 'We've been caught with our trousers down. Bad enough when that happens with the enemy. When a friend catches you, it's totally disastrous.'

'I think you're saying we have to take that Yank with us.'

'George, I'm saying we could well be forced to,' Simpson said. 'They've got us by the privates, under the circumstances. This whole business works on the basis of favours, pros and cons. We have to be realistic.'

Sutton sighed, stared at his hands. He almost wished he was back in Scotland, having a cup of tea with Daniels and discussing the hypothetical first cricket season after the war.

'Pros and cons,' he repeated softly. 'And what if I say I won't work with the Americans?'

'George, you're beyond that, believe me.'

Sutton turned and looked at Simpson carefully. The man was smiling his genial country squire's smile, but the eyes were strangely hard and impersonal.

Then Simpson relaxed, or appeared to.

'We're all in this for keeps. National interest and all that. Can't always choose our bedfellows, you know.' He rose from the sofa and glanced at his watch. 'My phone call with London is due on the embassy's scrambler at ten. Got to go. Look . . . I hope you don't mind if I leave Bignal here to keep you company. He tells me you put his brother in chokey.'

'I did. He was pretty good about it.'

'Oh, Bignal's a sound chap.' Simpson laughed, clapped Sutton on the shoulder. 'Useful man to have on your side.'

Simpson went to the door and called Bignal into the room.

'Get Mr Sutton any papers, magazines, whatever else he wants,' he ordered. 'Have 'em sent up.' Simpson turned back to Sutton, smiled apologetically. 'If the Yanks are on to you, who else might be?' he explained, closing the door behind him.

Bignal lowered his bulk into an armchair. He seemed perfectly at ease.

'Do you mind if I ask you something, sir?' he said slowly after a while, with a shy grin.

'No. I don't mind. Within reason.'

116

Despite his physical menace, Sutton found Bignal comforting. He was from the streets Sutton knew intimately. Bignal's face, his mind, his voice, even his capacity for simple violence, were all familiar and understandable to him.

Bignal leaned forward, clasping his big hands together. There was something close to excitement in his bovine eyes.

'Y'see, Mister Sutton, I've always wanted to know whether it's true that when they knocked over Wolski's diamond warehouse in the Garden – you remember, it was in the old king's jubilee year – they had someone on the inside. I don't reckon they could've done it any other way, and I've always been dyin' to ask someone in the know. I can ask you, can't I? I mean, it's ten years ago, and I'm a civil servant now, aren't I?'

CHAPTER THIRTEEN

At Dulles' spacious apartment in the Herrengasse, the waiting was beginning to gnaw at them all. Dulles tapped his pipe out in the ash tray by his chair.

'They'll do it. They know I meant what I said,' he stated throatily.

Joe McCarr sat hunched forward on an antique chair, his chin resting on one bunched fist. 'I'm going. I know it,' he said. 'Sutton or no damned Sutton.'

'Oh, it'd better be Sutton,' the countess said. She sat down, smoothed her skirt over her elegant knees. 'We'd need time and plenty of it to persuade Heinz to change his mind. He's set on giving himself up to Honest George Sutton, and that's that.'

'You don't think he'd come with just you and me? Especially with the right kind of persuasion. I'm talking about you, Mata Hari.'

She shook her head. 'The only person who could twist Heinz around their little finger would be Gestapo-Müller – he could scare the pants off him – or maybe the General Manager of the Züricher Bank, who could offer him the security of Swiss francs in a numbered account. You overestimate my charm, I can tell you.'

Dulles cut in irritably on their nervous banter. 'Look, the British will go along with us. They don't have any other choice.'

'Oh, no?' said McCarr. 'If they can think of one, however unlikely, my guess is they'll go for it.'

'That's enough of that!' Dulles snapped. It wasn't like him. He threw up his hands in unspoken apology. 'Listen, they won't get Helen if they refuse us, and without her they don't get Keppler.'

'Maybe we don't either,' the countess said. 'Heinz doesn't know I'm working for you. He thinks he's dealing just with the British, and he's not going to like it if I turn up with Joe here and no Sutton. For some reason, he trusts the British. He's obsessed with them and their "fair play".'

'I guess that if we have to, we'll consider taking Keppler out of there against his will,' Dulles said.

'In a trunk or something?' she asked incredulously. 'Are you serious?'

'Do you have a better idea?' Dulles waited for an answer, but none came. 'Okay. Then the British will go along,' he said firmly. 'Even if I have to get FDR on the phone to Churchill. It's high time we started to be treated as equals. We've done our share in this war, in the Intelligence field as much as any other, and we're not going to have the British ignore and patronise us any more. This Keppler affair threatens our reputation every bit as seriously as theirs. Can you imagine what a fuss the British would have kicked up if someone had claimed to have that kind of dirt on one of their ambassadors?'

'I think all of us realise what's at stake. Changed your mind about that coffee?' the countess asked.

Dulles caught himself in mid-bitch, grinned. 'Why not, dammit, Helen. It's something to do . . .'

The phone rang ten minutes or so later. Dulles made a conscious effort to handle the call with calm and style, and mostly he succeeded.

'Yes. Okay, David. That's very, very good. I'm glad there are no hard feelings. Sutton will be all right? . . . Sure. I realise it will need some work. Helen and Joe are very sensitive to that.'

He put the phone down gently, turned to the others with a look that held infinitely more relief, and realistic resolve, than triumph. Dulles' ascetic face said all too clearly: sure, I'm delighted, but this is just the start.

'Four o'clock. They've fixed a safe house for the meeting, to show who's boss, but what do we care about that? Ladies and gentlemen, we're in!'

McCarr grinned. His muscular body had relaxed visibly.

'I always said I'd be a hero. I knew I'd be the first American into Berlin.'

'The first American *male*, you mean,' said Helen.

Dulles chuckled, looked at the clock on the mantelpiece.

'Well, it's ten after twelve. I guess we could decently grant ourselves one – and I mean one – Martini. A sober celebration to mark the end of the first act.'

CHAPTER FOURTEEN

Rome, Italy

'C'MON, BABY. Give it to me. I don't feel a thing. C'mon. Harder, harder . . .'

The young American soldier looked down at the girl's bobbing head. He grinned, titillated by the sight of his own cock sliding in and out of her busy mouth. She was doing everything she could: tongue stuff, little nibbles with her teeth on his shaft, all the tricks of the trade to get the job finished quickly and collect her occupation lira. But he was having a good time on his last night in Rome. He wasn't about to finish yet, for sure. He closed his eyes briefly as her ringed hand snaked under and caressed his balls.

'Hey . . . I like that . . .'

He stroked the top of her hair, then grabbed a handful of dark, greasy ringlets, pushed her in on him still further. The camp bed creaked. She let out a small squeak, wriggled, paused and uttered something throaty and muffled in Italian. It wasn't complimentary.

He laughed. 'You want money, kid, you work hard. Hard, *capite*?'

The room was about ten feet square and damp, with an oil lamp burning in the corner to show a bed, a table, a crucifix on the wall, a curtained closet in the corner that must contain a washbasin. It was in a tenement building in the Travastere district – immemorially Roman, poor and dirty and a long, long way from Minneapolis. The American was just a kid, arrogant in his ignorance and his hot, young stud's eagerness for sexual experience. To him the whore was like a bottle of beer from the PX, to be paid for, savoured and thrown away.

Most of the guys felt the same about the girls in Europe. Hell, you could get killed by the Nazis tomorrow. Meantime you had the right to grab yourself a real good time.

The girl had refused to undress, though she had coaxed him into nudity without trouble. In fact, there was something very appealing about being stark naked with this fully-clothed chick going down on you. Plus, in every other respect she was really hot, treating him with a nervous respect, as if he was someone special, a special client. She had wanted to know all about him before they fucked, where he was from, where he was being posted; she had been kind, told him she did it at a special price for Americans because they had liberated her country from the fascist Antichrist and all kinds of crazy stuff like that. He didn't understand a word, but he sure understood what she was doing to his meat, and he loved it.

'A–y–y–ah!'

The young American was starting to buck. He held tight to her hair and rode, eyes closed again, keening with pleasure. Soon, despite all the Chianti and the cheap brandy, he was going to make it, and whatever the bitch did he was going to shoot right into her pretty little mouth, because he wanted to do that once in his life. Now twenty-four, Second Lieutenant Eddie Avery had spent a frustrated adolescence in the back seat of his dad's '39 Buick with girls from nice suburbs who were pink and clean and never let you go farther than a hand on their tit. Once one had brought him to come in his pants, as a big favour and because she wanted to get engaged, but this was something else. This was another world.

'Aaaahhh!'

He did not hear the tiny rustle of the curtain in the corner behind him. In the gathering explosion of a climax that was moving right up through his legs, into his belly, of a spurting, jetting impulse in his groin, he did not even see the flash of the blade that moved across in front of his throat. He felt the hand over his mouth, but then there was only a terrible wrenching and hotness in his throat and he was drowning, drowning in a burning wetness that was not sperm from within his loins but blood pouring down his bare chest.

It was over in seconds. The girl recoiled, gagged, rolled back, pawing at her hair and her shoulders, which were

122

covered in blood. She did not scream or cry out, though her black eyes were wide with horror.

The corpse toppled, finally pushed aside by the man with the knife. He moved forward quickly to the girl as if to comfort her. He was looking at her with a kind of pity, that was certain. She stared up at him, still gagging as if she had something she would never be able to get out of her throat. Wordlessly, the man put his hand over her mouth. The blade sliced hard across her throat and he held her while she shuddered her way to eternity and went still.

The man relaxed, got to his feet. His white shirt and trousers were blood-spattered, but that did not concern him. He checked the American's uniform, neatly folded on the chair by the bed, and noted with relief that it was unmarked. He had done everything efficiently. He looked at the girl's body and swiftly crossed himself out of habit. Then he opened the curtain and began to undress. A thorough wash, and he could leave this place as a new man on the first leg of a long journey.

A few minutes later he emerged from the alcove in clean clothes that he had kept stored there. Working quickly but unhurriedly, he took the money, personal belongings and documents from the dead lieutenant's uniform, then packed them into a nondescript leather bag. The bloody clothes were left where they lay. He was almost ready.

Last of all, he cleaned his knife, as meticulously and unemotionally as a man who had just finished skinning a rabbit or slaughtering a lamb. It was a six-inch, slim blade, always honed to butchery-sharpness and with a stiletto point. It was an unusual blade, but the really curious thing about it was the handle, which was made of hard glass shaped in the form of a triangle. When it caught the light it was a reflecting prism. That was how he had got his name in the business.

Ask around, from Queen's to Catania, and only a select few would know his real name, Johnny Coletti. But mention 'Prism' and even law-abiding men would nod and avert their eyes, maybe say a silent prayer. Prism had killed so much, all kinds of people, and always he carried that same strange blade.

God protect us from Prism, men would mutter. When Prism has orders, when there is a contract and Prism is the executioner, there is nowhere to hide and death is assured. He is a chamaeleon, a man whose face changes like the colours of that evil glass in his knife. He never kills for pleasure or without necessity, but he is a perfect hunter and a perfect killer.

They said he was Luciano's man, that Charlie Lucky loved him like a son and saw him as his heir. But they also said, those who really knew, that even Charlie Lucky was just a little afraid of Prism.

On the way down the hallway towards the stairs, blade back in its sheath and bag in hand, Coletti knocked on a peeling door three times in a pre-arranged way. Waiting in that room were two poor, desperate men who would dispose of the corpses somewhere in the Alban Hills. They had been paid well by their standards, in black-market spam and cigarettes. They had never seen, nor would they see, Johnny Coletti, and knew nothing of the fact that this was a very special murder. Murder worthy of Prism himself.

Back in his elegant bachelor apartment in a mansion block near the central station, Coletti looked through the contents of Lieutenant Avery's wallet and pockets. Avery had been born on December 18th 1920 in Minneapolis, and was attached to field security. But the prize – the reason why this man had been singled out – was that he had documents transferring him to the German theatre. Thirty-one Americans had passed through the whore's room in the past four days; the lieutenant had been the winner in a fatal lottery. There was a nine-year gap in their ages, but to Coletti that wasn't a problem. For some time, he studied a photograph he had found in Avery's wallet. This was his family. Cheerful, corn-fed Americans, as the lieutenant himself had obviously been. Suckers, Coletti sneered. Civilians in every sense of the word, not people worthy of any respect. Even their sexual habits were everyday, he reflected, recalling Avery's performance with the whore. His finely sculpted nose wrinkled in distaste.

Come midnight he was almost ready. He had packed a bag with shaving-kit and civilian clothes. Hidden in its lining, for emergencies, was a Swiss passport identifying him as one Roberto Partolini, bank courier from Ancona. Those few items, along with Avery's papers, uniform and weapon, would be enough. They had to be. After all, he had the chain of contacts made available to him by Charlie Lucky.

124

The man who sat at his table, carefully collating all the documents and calculating his chances was of normal height by American standards, which made him tall for a Sicilian. He was quite stocky, but without an ounce of fat on his powerful body. Everything was solid muscle, and radiated power in even distribution, from his feet to the tips of his hands, from his taut, flat stomach to the eyes that were watchfully alive.

Yet under most circumstances there was nothing inhuman about Johnny Coletti. At home in New York, where he had lived from the age of seven to the age of twenty-five, at social gatherings in Sicily and Rome, he was known as a polite and charming man with a good sense of humour – though always with the utmost respect for others' age and position. Many mothers had tried to marry their daughters off to this amiable young Sicilian with his wit, his exquisite manners, and the glamour of America still surrounding him like an aura of well-being and hope. When none had succeeded, there had been rumours about his sexual tendencies. But the few men who knew him well were aware that he had normal, healthy appetites, and that he preferred to take his pleasures where he found them. A wife and children would only tie him down. The day would come when others did his killing for him, and maybe then he would marry a nice girl and do his duty as a family man. Perhaps after this big job for Charlie Lucky. Hey, he was getting soft, Coletti caught himself. Dangerous. Be careful. Those were not thoughts worthy of Prism.

By twelve-thirty, Coletti was ready to relax. He lit a cheroot, eased back in his chair and listened to the sounds of the street: music, laughter, snatches of conversation and song, political arguments, cars and trucks and animals, and somewhere a woman scolding her husband or lover for his uselessness in rich Roman dialect. He found the sounds comforting, familiar. There had been just such sounds in Little Italy, in Palermo. He was impassive, however, as he got to his feet and walked to the door of the room. He went out, locking carefully behind him, moved quietly along the hallway, gently jangling his keys, until he arrived at another apartment door. He entered without knocking.

The woman from Milan lay naked on the bed, resting on her stomach and reading a magazine. She glanced up and smiled. It did not seem to concern her that Coletti did not smile back for the moment. She knew he was tense. It was always like this before he went away on business. But she knew how to relax him.

'It's late,' she said in her husky, Lombard-accented voice. 'How do you know I'm not too tired for you?'

And then he did smile, boyishly but with an element of ungainsayable power.

'I've never known you to be too tired for me.'

'True. Never.'

The woman's name was Claudia. She was tall, blonde, pale, like so many northerners, with a perfect skin which fascinated men from the south. Her only blemish – if blemish it might be – was a neat little mole on her right thigh, an inch or so from the soft, golden bush of pubic hair. She rolled over on to her side, revealing herself, looking straight at him, aware of her magnetic animal beauty.

'We'll have some wine,' said Coletti. It was part of their game. 'Fetch some, Claudia. I'll watch you. You know I like that.'

And he sat down, loose and easy, on the sofa. He had time now. Plenty of time for this last pleasure. He was not like Eddie Avery, a slavering, eternal adolescent who engaged in crude couplings because his sensibilities went no further. Coletti savoured his women, treated them well, had always done so – even the cheap girls who had flocked to him when he had first become one of Charlie Lucky's boys, a young praetorian guardsman to a bootlegger who lived like a king.

Claudia giggled, slid provocatively from the bed and went to fetch wine. It would be a crisp Frascati of the best, aromatic quality, Coletti's favourite. Appreciatively he fed his eyes on her elegant haunches, her lithe, muscular back, admired the firmness of her breasts, which moved gently with the movements of the rest of her body. Finally, the long, fair hair that fascinated him. Sicilians might give children to dark, strong girls with child-bearing hips, but their lust, and his, was for the blonde and slender, the pale lover and not the dark mother. He had bought this woman for pleasure alone, not for breeding. She was his for as long as he kept the gifts and the money flowing. They enjoyed each other in bed and out, a civilised arrangement in barbarous and dangerous times.

She reached Coletti's seat, stood by him, then handed him the wine with a soft sigh.

He thanked her in his painstakingly correct Italian with its gentle American overlay.

She stood, her mound of venus very close his face, and waited while he tasted the wine.

'Very good,' he pronounced. 'I hope you like it too.'

'I love it.'

She laughed, slowly tilted her wine glass and poured its contents over her stomach so that a glistening river ran down the skin into her loins and among her pubic hair. She pressed her thighs together and made a small sound of delight.

'It tastes better in me than in you, I know. Just try . . .'

She guided his head towards her, still laughing.

Her scent was almost overwhelming in its musky warmth, her skin so soft. Coletti began just below her navel, enjoying the bouquet of wine and flesh. The extra bouquet. He moved down, taking his time, licking so very gently, with quiet murmurs of appreciation that she answered with tiny massagings of his head, until he reached her downy bush and began to probe with his tongue. The pressure of her fingers on his skull increased a little. She could not wait, could not resist guiding him to her bud, where the tongue really began to work and the wine really to taste.

This was Johnny Coletti at play, giving and receiving pleasure. There was a peculiar intensity to it, like the intensity of carnival, the ancient farewell to flesh before Lent. Soon Johnny Coletti would cast off thoughts of pleasure and give over his being to Prism. Prism had no time for amusements, no time for love; only for the job in hand, orders given by his *capo*. To change from Coletti into Prism was like moving from light into darkness, good into evil, life into death.

CHAPTER FIFTEEN

THE WOMAN was undoubtedly German, but her face was dark as a gipsy's, tanned by working in the sun and weather. Her stubby peasant's hands clutched a frying-pan as she stood in line, shivering beneath her ragged overcoat. The child on her hip was perhaps a year old. It did not cry. The scene might have been more human if it had. The woman shuffled forward, her eyes haunted and defeated but still searching the front of the queue for a sight of the thin goulash the relief workers were ladelling out to the other waiting refugees.

The open-air soup kitchen had been set up close to the edge of the Tiergarten park. Heinz Keppler had arranged the rendezvous here, not knowing that the area would be filled with these pathetic, homeless creatures. For some months now, German civilians from the eastern provinces had been flooding westwards, by train and on foot, with their bundles of possessions, pushed by the brutal Soviet advance into East Prussia, Silesia, Posen. They were mostly simple farm-labouring folk, often from the huge feudal estates of the Prussian aristocracy, and almost as primitive as the Slavs who were now driving them from their homes. Keppler examined the woman's face: the government might call her 'German', but there was inferior blood there, a trace of Polish or Wendish ancestry. So much for the 'master race' idea. These people were lost in Berlin, exiled from the plains and marshlands where they had laboured dully for their lords for hundreds of years. Keppler felt disgust and contempt mingled with routine pity.

The woman with the child was now staring at his smart greatcoat with its silver-lightning shoulder flashes, his polished boots and cap with the death's head badge, at his well-fed face. Somewhere far behind her dead eyes burned an atavistic violence nurtured by many centuries of oppression, veiled hatred against the aristocracy that had always disposed of the lives and lands of peasants such as these. The Führer had ensured now that they had been driven from their land altogether, and the SS was his most visible representative. Keppler would have bet that this woman – was she thirty, forty, fifty? – would gladly tear him limb from limb with her hard little clawlike hands. The advancing Russians were frightening enough for members of the Nazi élite like Keppler, but what would such dispossessed Germans do to them if they were given the chance? With a shiver that had little to do with the cold March wind, Keppler turned away and took a sudden interest in the anti-aircraft battery two hundred yards in the opposite direction.

Helen was late enough to stretch his already taut nerves even tighter. For several minutes before she actually arrived, Keppler was almost certain that she had been arrested on her arrival back in Berlin from Switzerland and was betraying everything she knew to Gestapo-Müller's interrogators. If she did not tell them immediately, there would come the cigarette burns, perhaps the electrodes on her nipples, or pack-rape in shifts to break her down. Keppler knew all the techniques. Perhaps the big men in trenchcoats and homburgs would soon be converging on him from different directions, cutting off his lines of escape. God knows, there was always the chance that one or other of them would be picked up. That was why, since deciding to defect to the British, he had made it a rule that he and Helen see each other as little as possible, and pretend that their affair was going off the boil. They met in the park, for drinks in cafés, behaving like lovers haggling over the final details of their separation. Keppler had put the word about in the department, had made up stories of new women in his life.

When Helen von Ackersberg reached him, he smiled wanly and gave her a peck on the cheek.

'Were you followed, darling?'

'I don't think so. You?'

'There may have been a tail. If there was, then I lost him

129

at the Zoo station. I made it look as if it was his fault he lost me, rather than deliberate on my part.'

'God, it will be good to get away from this madhouse, Heinz.'

She was talking about Gestapo-Müller's goons, but she was looking at the refugees. In her fur-trimmed coat and hat, expensive brogues and silk stockings, she felt every bit as conspicuous as Keppler. The looks she got from the line of refugees said, *SS officer's whore.*

'Let's move on,' the countess said.

They walked slowly eastwards, towards the Stadtmitte subway station. Even after Stalingrad there had still been lovers strolling hand in hand in this venerable park, and proud, elegant Prussian officers exercising their horses. The Count von Ackersberg had ridden here whenever he was in Berlin, and sometimes his wife had joined him. Now there was no time for love; and the officers had either been slaughtered in action, like Erich, or executed by the SS in the terrible blood-letting that had followed the plot against Hitler's life the previous July. Keppler knew that only too well, for he had helped process many of the charges against them. He had never told Helen the whole truth about that. It was just one of the countless shameful things he had done in order to survive.

'How does it feel to be in Berlin again? Do you wish you could stay in the West, in Switzerland or even France?' he said.

The countess forced a smile, touched his arm. 'Heinz, you know I'm determined to see this through.'

'You're wonderful,' Keppler said. 'I am a lucky man, and I don't deserve it.'

'Why not? Have you been such a terrible man that you should get caught here in this death-trap?'

A few dozen *Volkssturm* volunteers, home guardsmen drawn from among pubescent boys and rheumy old men, were comically drilling with wooden rifles under the orders of a massively fat Wehrmacht Feldwebel who sported an artificial leg. Hitler planned for them all to die – from pale, runny-nosed kids to avuncular pensioners. This was no more than training for mass-suicide.

'So, darling Helen. What news from the West? Is everything going smoothly?'

She nodded. 'Like a dream. Sutton has arrived. In ten days or so he'll be ready. Will you be all right until then?'

She said nothing about McCarr or the American involvement. There had been endless discussions about that; in the end it had been agreed that it would be best to present Keppler with a *fait accompli*. No surprises at this stage – only when he was so far in he couldn't pull out.

'I'll have to be.' Keppler paused uneasily. 'Once I know for certain when you're coming, I may go into hiding at the cottage. To forestall any moves on Müller's part. Days, hours, even minutes can make all the difference if he decides to move in.'

'Are the problems with Müller so serious?'

'Maybe. I can't tell for sure,' Keppler said with a frown. 'Sometimes I think that if he really suspected something, he wouldn't leave me – or either of us – at liberty. Then again, perhaps he is giving me enough rope . . . You must realise, Helen, that a lot of senior officers are preparing to bolt. No one's talking about it openly, of course – we're all supposed to be steeling ourselves to die heroically at our posts in the capital of the thousand-year Reich, blah-blah-blah – but in reality we all know exactly what's going to happen, which is that in three or four weeks' time it's going to be every man for himself. Those who can are hoarding foreign currency, getting themselves fitted out with exotic passports, preparing routes to South America and other safe places. It's only human nature.'

'I realise that. But why is Müller taking such an interest in you? If he had every officer under his command watched, he'd have no men left to operate his terror for him.'

Keppler grimaced. 'Charmingly put, my dear,' he said. 'Perhaps, rightly, he feels that my position in Interpol gives me international status that he has been denied, or perhaps he's plain jealous. As their empires shrink, men such as Müller are liable to get tetchy – and start clutching at straws. Believe me. I know the type well.'

'I remember the cottage at Nikolaussee,' the countess said suddenly. 'We spent some good times there.'

'There'll be other idyllic places, Helen. Perhaps we shall

131

go to the tropics. Africa. Asia. Australia. Where would you prefer?'

'I . . . I haven't thought about it, Heinz. I can only see as far as the end of every day.'

He squeezed her hand. 'Understandable. Just do your job and leave the planning to me. One day you'll be rich again, with a beautiful house and everything you want.'

She nodded wordlessly, then checked the time.

'Heinz, I must go back to the Health Ministry. I daren't be late. They report to the Gestapo on everyone like me in positions of special trust.'

'Very well. We'll meet again before you go back to Berne. And then – ' He clapped his hands together and tried to look as if he had not a care in the world. 'And then it will be non-stop to London.'

She tried to laugh too. They had passed the anti-aircraft battery and were walking through an avenue of luxuriantly budding linden trees. The last spring of the Third Reich promised to be a battle of flowers as well as soldiers.

They brushed lips and Keppler watched her stroll back in the direction she had come from. Then he waded towards the Stadtmitte station. From there he could take a subway train to Wannsee and be back in his office within an hour. As he walked, he let himself experience the fear he knew he could never show while Helen von Ackersberg was with him. However confident he made himself sound to her, inside he knew that there were any number of risks involved in his plan. Desperation was a terrible thing. Fear gave him a rare moment of insight, even compassion. Compassion for his country, which was about to reap the whirlwind, to be thrown on the mercy of the nations it had cruelly oppressed for six years. For Helen, who had lost her husband, whether she loved him or not, and her security. And lastly for himself, the boy from the poor district of Wedding, only two or three kilometres north of here, who had wanted so much to succeed, who was so determined to catapult himself out of poverty and mediocrity and powerlessness that he had hitched his star to the seductive devil called Adolf Hitler.

Keppler's personal pact with the devil – the devil with the funny moustache, who had talked so well on the radio about discipline and recovery and national salvation and giving talented young men like Keppler their heads – had lasted nearly a dozen years. Now, along with thousands of others who had made the same pact of blood, he was scrabbling for any escape route he could find. He was like a rat in a trap. The only difference was, he had built his own cage.

CHAPTER SIXTEEN

'AGAIN. What is the SS equivalent of a full colonel? Quick!'
'Standartenführer.'
'Lieutenant-Colonel?'
'Obersturmbannführer.'
'Major?'
For the dozenth time that morning, Sutton went through this catechism, one of many that had become daily routine.
'All right. Parrot-perfect,' said Simpson with a malicious grin when they had got down to the lowest rung of the SS ladder. 'You're becoming quite well prepared for survival in what's left of the Third Reich, George.'
'I'm supposed to be a bloody Swede.'
'Certainly you are. And if you know what a Hauptsturm-bloody-führer is, and how to recognise his plumage, you've got a distinct advantage. Knowledge and familiarity *smooth the path*, George. The papers our people have provided you with are excellent – probably better than the real thing – but this information saves time, saves the Nazis becoming too curious and therefore suspicious about you and your friends. Now. When was Gustav Salvesen last in Germany, eh?'
'February '44. Checking Red Cross shipments. There had been pilfering at the docks. Actually, he was in Riga, which is actually in – '
'Tsk. Riga is part of the Greater German Reich so far as the Nazis are concerned, George. Even now. Be careful. They're touchier than ever these days.'
'Look, this is nit-picking.'
'The Gestapo thrives on it! Be prepared!'
'Dib-dib, dob-dob. I never was a scout. My dad couldn't

afford to buy me a uniform . . . And I'm going to have a cigarette.'

Simpson sighed. 'Okay. The old chip on the Sutton shoulder is coming out. Time for a change of tack, I think.'

Sutton lit up and drew the nicotine deep into his lungs. The safe house where they were being briefed and trained was a nondescript suburban villa in a leafy outer district of the city. This room, where he spent most of his time, was large enough, but bare and dark in the afternoons. The place felt like a prison cell, for all its bourgeois comforts. He and McCarr had been here for three days now, going through their paces for fourteen hours a day, sometimes separately, sometimes toge-ther. Helen von Ackersberg had gone back to Berlin for a few days, but was due to cross back into Switzerland the next day. Sutton found himself worrying about her. He told himself that his concern was purely professional, that if there was no countess, there was no trip to Berlin. But if he had been interrogating himself as a suspect on a charge of personal feelings about Helen, he'd have booked himself by now.

There were voices at the door. Simpson re-appeared with McCarr and the German-born, London-based SOE officer who was working as their language coach.

'Oh, Christ,' said Sutton, making a jokey sour face. 'German conversation.'

McCarr shrugged. 'You promise not to talk about your cricket, I'll keep off the Red Sox. A deal?'

'A deal. But what does an Irish-American-Swede actually talk about?'

'The price of potatoes, I guess.'

The language coach, known to everyone as 'Herr Krausner', sat down and motioned sternly to the pair of them to get ready. He was a left-wing émigré, a hawknosed, thin man in his late fifties. He had fled Germany in '33 for Czechoslovakia, then managed to get to London in early '39, when Prague fell, keeping just ahead of the Gestapo all the way. That was all they knew about Herr Krausner. He had fierce, sad eyes that missed nothing, and he refused to speak anything but German in their presence. It was part of his job.

'*Also, meine Herren,*' he began. '*Wir sind im Zug. Es kommt der Schaffner herein. Er steht in Ihrem Abteil . . .*'

They're in a train. The conductor appears and while he checks their tickets he probes a little.

Recreating the experience of travelling as suspect foreigners, Herr Krausner put them through their paces. The conductor leaves the compartment. Now, talk. Talk about anything – all in German with a slight Swedish lilt. Go . . . How does that feel? Familiarise yourselves. Until you are absolutely certain that you are alone and cannot be overheard, you must never speak English, no matter how strong the temptation. You stub your toe . . .

'*Scheisse!*' they both chorused.

'*Gut. Oder vielleicht "gottverdammt!". Kein* shit! *oder* damn!, *nichts von all denen . . .*' Herr Krausner intoned solemnly. Their lives could depend on not letting an English word slip out under stress.

Fresh air in the garden for twenty minutes. Sutton smoked yet another cigarette under an arch of espaliered pear trees, alone. He felt his spine chill when he heard a voice behind him. He had heard no approach.

'Sutton,' the voice said softly. 'George.'

He turned abruptly, found McCarr a bare three feet from him. The man could certainly move quietly, despite his heavy build. Sutton tried to keep the irritation and humiliation from his face, failed.

'Hello, Joe,' he growled.

'Sorry. I wanted to talk to you.'

'Everybody wants to have private chats with good old George these days. I'm assuming you didn't want to cut my throat or you'd have done it by now.'

'Oh, no-o-o. No that.'

The American smiled shyly, then put his hands deep in his pockets, paced around, keeping his eyes on the ground. Suddenly he looked up.

'You know, I like you, George,' he said. 'I guess you think I'm just a gorilla, a gung-ho special ops guy who likes killing people.'

'Well – '

'Now listen, George. Please.' McCarr raised one big hand. The fingers were surprisingly long, and though they were strong enough to crush a windpipe they also indicated a certain sensitivity. 'You know why I ended up in this business? You want to know?'

'Yes. All right.'

'Good. I'll tell you. I volunteered because I don't like the Nazis and what they do to people. You know I was a student at Princeton. I went on a jolly vacation trip to Europe along with some fellows from my frat back in '38. We didn't have a political thought in our sweet heads. I mean, I couldn't really have given a shit about Hitler, Mussolini, the rest of them . . . they were like a bad joke. I hope I'm not boring you with tales of my American innocence.'

Sutton lit a cigarette from the butt of his old one, shook his head.

'No. Though if you were, I'd still listen.'

'That's all I need to know,' said the American. 'Well, we got to Germany, right? My mother's family are from there, all nice, God-fearing people, old-fashioned patriots, fine. So I gawped at the quaint castles, chug-a-lugged my way round a few beer cellars. Thought the uniforms and the swastikas were weird, but so what? I knew this wasn't New England. It wasn't even New Jersey. Then,' he drew his breath in sharply, looked away for a moment, 'I and my fellow Princetonians were in Munich, and we were coming back to our hotel with a skinful. What do you think I saw suddenly on that pristine, clean German sidewalk? I'll tell you – I saw an old guy who looked like Mr Greengrass, who runs the drugstore along the street from my folks' place. Kindliest, sweetest old guy you'd ever meet. But this man was lying there on those scrubbed cobblestones, and there were four young creeps in brown uniforms kicking the living shit out of him. I ran closer and the other guys followed. The brownshirts, they were laughing, yelling stuff like: *'Juda verrecke!'* Rot the Jews, you know? Anyway, I got there and I launched straight into them. They looked at me like I was crazy. I hit one. He went down.'

'The others acted at first as if they couldn't believe what was happening. When they saw the other Americans coming – we were all oarsmen, big fellows – they ran off, leaving their friend on the street alongside the old guy. He was lying in his victim's blood. I put one foot on this asshole, told the guys to fetch a cop – and an ambulance. The cop came. You know what he did? He said he was going to arrest *me*. Then the ambulance arrived. They took one look at the old guy, and then tenderly lifted up the asshole in the brown shirt and loaded him into the ambulance. *They left the old guy there!* They weren't allowed to pick up Jews. Jews had their own hospitals, their own doctors, and what the hell was he doing out on the streets at night anyway . . .'

McCarr's eyes were intense with memory, no longer laughing-Irish or even OSS-tough but slits of outrage and anger.

'I was kept at the police precinct overnight, then turned back onto the streets. They laughed, those jolly Bavarian guardians of public order. Oh, they thought I was very funny. They warned me to stick to tourism; if I didn't stop interfering, I'd find myself on the next train out of the country. Which was okay by me. I headed for France, anyway. It wasn't until I got across that border that I could breathe, and the urge to throw up went away. It was like . . . escaping from hell. It was that strong a feeling, that much relief.'

A bird, perhaps a lark, started to sing in the silence that followed.

'I never saw anything quite like that,' Sutton said quietly. 'I knew it was going on, I had a lot to do with their policemen and I didn't like them or their reputation. But I never actually witnessed anything.'

'I was lucky. It gave me a fire, and that's never left me,' said McCarr. 'Sure, I'm good at my job. I don't let myself get too emotional. But it's always there, in the background. Outrage, I guess. It keeps me going when all else fails, when I start to feel that creeping cynicism, when I don't like the people I have to work with. I can tell myself: remember that little Jewish guy lying in his own blood on that street. You're doing this for him and millions of others. And maybe you don't like present company, Joe, but at least we're all fighting the same evil.'

There was a defiant note to that last part.

'I'm sorry,' Sutton said then. 'I've been doing my best. I'll try harder, Joe.'

'Just relax and enjoy, eh?' Now McCarr's manner was pure locker-room. He reached out and punched Sutton on the shoulder. 'Let business take care of itself.'

They both turned, heard Simpson whistling as he walked across the lawn towards them.

'Everything all right, chaps?' he boomed. 'Not having a bust-up, are we? Can't have you two point-scoring all the way to Berlin.'

Sutton smiled, threw away his third cigarette of the break. He glanced at McCarr, then gave Simpson one of his best, stony, don't-bullshit-me looks, the kind of face-off he had perfected in the old days at the Yard.

'No point-scoring. Joe was reminiscing about his experiences as a tourist before the war.'

'Ye Gods. Who does he think we are? Thomas Cook's? Well, boys, I'm telling you that the countess will be back tomorrow night. If you're good, we'll let you have tea with her. Now, how's that?'

'You know what,' said Sutton. 'I don't know whether it has to do with your public school education, but I'd say you've got some strange and unhealthy attitudes towards women. The countess to me is simply a work colleague, no more or less interesting than Joe here.' He paused. 'But with better legs.' He stopped to think again. 'All right,' he conceded. 'I admit it. With better everything.'

'Both boys tucked into bed,' said Simpson, sliding into the bench seat opposite Dulles. The American had thoughtfully chosen a corner booth, away from the smoky hub of the taproom. Thoughtfulness was Dulles's forte, his particular twist to the craft of spying.

The restaurant was no more than a well-kept pub, done out in plain, traditional style, serving beers and dry, chalky Swiss wines and known for some of the best *schnitzels* in the city. It was discreet, and it was only a few hundred yards from the villa where Simpson was overseeing the training for the Keppler mission.

They had made a deal at the outset to save British face. The British had exclusive charge of the preparations, but in return Dulles got a nightly briefing from Simpson. All the briefings so far had been polite but faintly tetchy; for Simpson, the humilation of Helen von Ackersberg's double role and the forced inclusion of McCarr still rankled. Also, which he couldn't tell Dulles, Lord Frawley's fury and panic over the telephone with London had been awesome. Frawley had agreed to letting the Americans in, but only as a means of damage-control. It was obvious that if he got a chance to outwit the Yanks even now, Frawley would take it. These and many more things worried Simpson, who for all his involvement in the murky parts of Intelligence work would have liked to believe in honesty between friends and allies.

Dulles nodded. 'You look like you need a drink, David. What can I get you?'

'I'd very much like some beer, actually. Thirsty work playing games with our friends, being the life and soul of the party and keeping everything cheerful. Like a day's hunting. We always had beer at home after an afternoon spent following the hounds.'

'I don't believe they serve English bitter ale here. A stein of the local brew do you?'

'Fine,' Simpson agreed with a slightly nervous chuckle. 'I've got used to the stuff. Alcoholic soda-pop.'

Dulles ordered the beer, plus *schnitzel* and *röstli*.

Simpson lit his pipe.

'All's well,' he said after a while. 'Sutton's was a bit more forthcoming today. He and McCarr seem to be getting on fairly well now.'

'Glad to hear it. Joe knows how to handle people. More goes on in that big Irish head than you'd credit just to look at him.'

'If you say so. To tell the truth, I'm more worried about Helen von Ackersberg.'

'Oh. In what way? Something come up while she's been in Berlin?'

'Hard to pin it down, Allen.'

'Come on – '

'Very well.' Simpson hesitated for a moment. A frown crossed his pleasant, unlined features. 'I have some doubts about whether she's entirely reliable. When one really thinks it over, she *is* the mistress of a Gestapo officer. And she's been in Europe for a long time in dubious company. I know she comes from impeccable stock and all the rest, but . . . you know, women . . .' Simpson concluded rather lamely.

Dulles shrugged.

'David, I know there's a lot of grey areas in the life of a woman like that. Hell, even I don't know for sure exactly how she feels about Keppler. All I can really say is that her work for us has been absolutely solid, everything that could be expected from a good operative. This situation is nothing so unusual, you know. Women sleep with men, men with women – and the man may be a powerful figure, with his own attraction – and, well, however strong the connection in bed is, that doesn't mean he or she might not have another loyalty. Maybe I'm not explaining this too well, but these things have been going on for centuries in our kind of world.'

'Of course.' Simpson said stiffly. He was all at once standing on his dignity. Bad enough to be forced into cooperation by a service he still considered junior. Now he was being taught to suck eggs, as good as being accused of naïvety. 'I'm tired, and perhaps that's making me rather over-anxious. We're stuck with our countess, I suppose. She'll be all right. This is one of the few occasions when I wish I were bloody well Prime Minister. If we weren't leaving Berlin to the Reds, we'd be practically there by now. Personally, I'd solve the whole problem by sending in an armoured division with a few of our best special ops chaps along, ready to snatch Keppler and half a dozen cartloads full of bloody documents.'

'It's a question of politics, David. Nobody wants to annoy Uncle Joe Stalin. As a consequence the Russians are going to scoop the pool so far as the Nazis' secret records and personnel are concerned. Keppler isn't the only prize trapped there in Berlin, waiting for the Reds to come,' Dulles said with the bitter resignation of a man who has put his case a hundred times and still failed to convince his superiors. 'We expect Zhukhov and Koniev to launch their offensives any moment. Our people will have to leave very soon, even if it means shortening their training. If the Red Army manages to cut off Berlin from the west before Keppler is spirited out of the city, we – and our people inside Germany – will be in very deep trouble. I'd also like the western allies to be heading hell-for-leather for the Reich capital. You know my opinion on that issue.'

Simpson did indeed. He had deliberately drawn Dulles onto this subject. He knew the OSS man was personally supervising contacts with German commanders on the Italian front, hoping to negotiate a separate surrender there, and that he was running into a lot of problems with his political masters. Dulles was eager to have the Anglo-American forces move into what was left of German-occupied Italy before the communist parti-sans took over. Simpson felt a little better now. He had got back some of his sense of superiority.

'All right,' he said. 'It's really not that important. I'd like to have two or three months rather than a matter of days to knock this particular happy band into shape, but since things are as they are, it probably doesn't make a lot of difference when they leave.'

Dulles nodded. 'And maybe there's an element of truth in what you say about the countess. That's one reason I'm grateful we've got two men going with her,' he said. 'For my part, I can vouch for Joe. He's steady as a rock. Remember, he's the only one of the party we actually got to choose for the job. Helen has to go along, because she's vital to this mission, whatever her faults; same goes for Sutton – he's a bitter man, and that's never a good thing, though I admit he knows how to keep the lid on himself. Most of the time. We're doing the best we can with the human material we've been handed, David.'

Simpson munched a piece of his *schnitzel* and signalled his appreciation of the food with an ungentlemanly stab of the fork.

'The way things are going, British forces should be some-where around the Hanover/Oldenburg area by the time our group makes its bolt for safety,' he said.

'US forces will almost certainly be closer.'

'Naughty, naughty, Allen. You know that was part of the agreement. If possible, they are to make contact with a British unit. It's only fair. We don't want some cowboy colonel with pearl-handled revolvers causing trouble. And another thing,' he added, warming to his theme, 'the plan was to have a senior SS officer piloting some Red Cross officials through an inspection tour of the fatherland prior to popping them on a boat back to Sweden. I want everyone to stick to that plan. I want your assurances McCarr won't try any rough stuff just because they run into a road block or because he doesn't like some Nazi's face, Allen.'

'That won't happen,' Dulles retorted crisply. 'It's not Joe's style. How do you think he's survived those trips into enemy-held territory? By acting like Popeye the Sailor Man?'

'Pardon? I'm afraid – '

'Never mind. Joe's been trained for violent situations, but he's no thug. And, of course, he may *need* to use his training. You can never tell.' Dulles was smiling, but there was authority in his voice. 'Things are pretty chaotic over there. Our reports tell us there's executions, kangaroo courts, gangs of deserters roaming around, not forgetting escaped prisoners and DPs. Order and authority are breaking down. Red Cross papers, even the power of a man like Keppler, don't mean as much as they did just a while ago. Don't forget that.'

'I stand by what I said. And George Sutton is in charge. Especially when it comes to handling any negotiations. You know how important it is for McCarr to understand that,' Simpson said.

'Fine. And there are some really mean, crazy sons-of-bitches out there,' Dulles insisted with untypical fervour and equally untypically coarse use of language. 'The Nazis are starting to eat each other. Everything's up for grabs. We have to be prepared for any eventuality.'

'Don't be dramatic, Allen. It doesn't suit you.'

'I tell you, when the lights go out in Germany, a lot of people are going to want to take advantage of the darkness.'

'Really, you Americans are wonderful people,' Simpson chortled unkindly. 'I suppose you've been closer to all that anarchy than we have. You've had your Wild West and your Chicago gangsters.'

'Quite right,' said Dulles, and he wasn't smiling 'That's why decent Americans care passionately about laws and freedom, Because we know how important they are. We have plenty of people in our country who don't care about either of those things.'

'Yes. That's why you're over here. Fighting for laws and freedom,' Simpson ribbed him gently.

'That's why most of us are here, yes,' said Dulles, suddenly feeling tired and unaccountably depressed. The Englishman thought he was smart, but really he was more naïve than he could know or Dulles had the energy to explain. 'There are hyenas too, already picking over the battlefield.'

'Muscling in on the action.'

'If you prefer to put it that way. Anyway, David, I can tell you those people, those beasts of prey, are all around Europe. I can feel it in my bones.'

CHAPTER SEVENTEEN

JOHNNY COLETTI sat in a comfortable cane chair and sipped fine French wine from his host's cellar. Opposite him, Jean Paoli nursed a glass of Vichy water – for his stomach, he said – and looked thoughtfully out over the curve of the Gulf of Lyons. His villa in the hills just behind Marseilles had a commanding view from the coastal marshlands to the Côte d'Azur. They had travelled here from the docks in Paoli's big Citroën, complete with armed chauffeur and bodyguard, more for show than because there was any physical danger. Coletti was meant to know that his Corsican allies were both powerful and considerate in every way. To emphasise this, even in Paoli's home two muscular, well-armed sentries lounged just inside the double doors leading onto the terrace, in sight but out of earshot.

Silence came easily to Coletti. He could be an entertaining guest, but he was no empty chatterer. Paoli knew this. He chose his conversational gambit carefully.

'Peace is welcome,' he said. 'There is distress here, of course, but not so bad as in Italy. A man can make a living, and the authorities . . .' He shrugged expressively, and his size made the movement like the beginnings of a volcanic eruption. 'Ah . . . After the Germans, it's good to have some honest French politicians to deal with again!'

Coletti laughed politely. 'In Rome it's the same. We are even considered a bastion against communism. I know there are Reds in the government, but that will soon change. Sensible men know who are the real friends of order.'

Yes, this kind of light-hearted general conversation was right, Paoli decided. Comfortable for both of them. He had not asked why his young friend from Rome required his help,

144

nor did he yet feel it right to give Coletti an opportunity to indicate the nature of the favour that must inevitably accompany such help.

Jean Paoli's huge bulk necessitated that he sit on his terrace on a kind of throne, a specially-made, outsized chair constructed of teak reinforced with steel. He knew his men joked about it behind his broad back. He knew they said, 'Be quiet, the king is surveying his kingdom', when he sat out here alone, drinking his water or his herb tea in the afternoons. He did not mind so long as he was certain that they all feared and respected him. At the age of sixty-four, weighing more than three hundred pounds, the head of the most powerful faction within the *Union Corse*, the Corsican Mafia, had a kind of pride that went deeper than mere touchiness. He had wisdom and tolerance. Only if he sensed, or was told by someone he trusted, that a man's jokes implied lack of respect would he take action. Then the man in question would simply die, if necessary painfully, depending on the nature of his offence and whether others needed to be intimidated by example.

'More wine, my friend.'

'Another glass. It is a very delicate vintage, *padrone*.'

'You are very kind. It is the best my humble cellar can provide.'

'I'm sorry your health forces you to drink that water.'

'One grows old, as we all must. The body becomes vulnerable in certain ways. I am glad that I can still enjoy the occasional cigar. They do not affect the liver.'

Coletti nodded. He wore a simple leather jacket with slacks and a turtle-necked sweater. He looked precisely like a sailor on shore-leave, his cover since stepping off the freighter *Candida*, which had arrived here from the Roman port of Ostia three hours previously.

'I have a small gift for you, *padrone*,' he said with a smile.

'Please this is not necessary . . .'

Coletti understood the etiquette. He merely continued to smile and reached easily into the inside pocket of his jacket. He produced a long, flat package.

'Compliments of myself and the professor,' he said, passing the package to Paoli. 'One kilo. Pure, finest morphine, straight from the factory. As you know, there is much more where it came from.'

Paoli's hooded eyes, almost hidden in bulging folds of lard, glinted briefly with unconcealable greed.

'We have been waiting for a long time,' he said softly.

'When my business is completed, I promise you at least twenty more kilos at a very good price. Your analysts will vouch for the quality of this gift. It's special stuff.'

Paoli took the hint. From his pocket he also took an envelope, which he handed to Coletti, wheezing audibly with the effort of leaning forward.

'Our part was not so difficult,' he said modestly. 'Many of us work in the hotels and restaurants of Berne. Those Swiss are short of labour. They welcome obliging people like ours. Corsicans speak French, honour women, and work for low wages.'

Coletti knew that the task had in fact required a great deal of ingenuity and bribery, and therefore money. It was why he had promised so much morphine in exchange for this first favour. Lucky Luciano's terse instructions had been: 'Pay the bastards any price. Give them dope and they'll get whatever you want. Anything at all.'

There were three grainy photographs in the envelope. The first showed a man and woman together in the garden of a café beside the lake. She was quite fair – a note in French scribbled in the margin of the print said she had auburn hair – with an aristocratic look, attractive for her age. The man was beefy and dark-haired, with a moustache. Coletti studied him carefully as a possible adversary. Yes, physical ease and strength, a hidden capacity for violence, he read into that body and face. The second picture was of a blond-haired man around six feet tall, who had just got out of a car. He looked very serious, and there was a restrained power there too. But this was not a naturally violent man. The third picture was uninteresting. It had been taken in the street from the rear and proved only that the auburn-haired woman had a very cute behind.

'The two in the first photograph are American,' Paoli explained. 'The other man, the man getting out of the car, is an Englishman. You know them already?'

'I am grateful for your help,' said Coletti, avoiding Paoli's question. He had heard about the American man, McCarr, just before leaving Italy. Charlie Lucky had issued very specific

orders as a result. It was an interesting situation, and interesting odds. Two men, a woman, and Keppler. 'And I am
impressed,' he added graciously.

It was true that he was grateful to Paoli for doing as he
asked. He was even more grateful that after this he needed
only one more favour from his tricky Corsican allies. They
need know nothing of the real nature of his business, or of his
final destination. Once he reached Paris, he would be among
his own people, good Sicilians who had absorbed *Omertà*, the
ancient law of silence, along with their mother's milk. Aid
for further stages of the journey would cost him nothing but
promises of future favours for his helpers' families. They would
be honoured to speed him on his way with all the means at
their disposal.

'The truck leaves for Paris at ten-thirty on Tuesday
morning,' Paoli continued. This was the second, lesser favour.
'The driver is a trusted friend of mine. Papers have been
prepared which identify you as his co-driver, replacing a sick
man. This is in case there are any spot-checks by the police or
customs men. I trust you find these arrangements satisfactory.'

'Yes, *padrone*. And naturally the truck's load is completely
legitimate. It would be ridiculous if some minor infraction of
the law were to lead to complications with the French police.
I can't afford delays. Even pay-offs take time, as you know.'

Paoli winced gently, as if hurt by his guest's suspicions.
'Completely above board,' he rumbled. 'Fresh spring flowers
from the sunny South, for the Paris markets! Even if the truck
is searched, which is very unlikely, you will have no problems.'

'I apologise. I know you would not let me down, *padrone*.'

Paoli patted the package containing the morphine, smiled
broadly to show that all was well. 'Nor you me.'

The talk continued, polite and guarded, moving on to wider
business. Part of Coletti's job in Italy, after leaving America
in '38, had been to maintain Luciano's contacts with the illegal
drugs trade in Italy. This racket was based on cooperation with
legitimate and in some cases highly respectable pharmaceutical
companies that produced a certain legally-stipulated quota for
medicinal use in hospitals. Of course, it was no trouble for
their chemists to process more morphine than was strictly
necessary for the relief of suffering humanity, and with a few
bribes placed in the right quarters, plus some creative ecord-

147

keeping, that surplus could simply disappear onto the black market. Perhaps one could blame it on the war and the accompanying decline of moral standards, but the demand by addicts for such drugs was increasing very fast. France and Italy were good markets. Soon, when the final peace came, America would be wide open for Italian-produced drugs. Profits were already excellent. Once drugs could be smuggled into America, there would be no limit on the money to be made.

Luciano, even from his prison cell, had thought ahead with his usual genius for planning. When the boom in narcotics really began, Coletti, his organiser and enforcer, would be a prince of crime in his own right, grander even than the gross Corsican potentate who sat on his terrace with him, listening to the whispering Mediterranean breeze and trying to lengthen his life with Vichy water.

'The professor, I see, is a very busy man,' Paoli said when Coletti had told him some selected details of the morphine operation centred in Rome. Now the Corsican knew enough to whet his appetite, but not so much that he would be able – or dare – to cut out Coletti and make his own deal with the suppliers.

'He is becoming a very rich one. And the Italian tax-collectors don't know a thing. One day he will retire to Capri and befriend pretty little girls. Or perhaps little boys,' Coletti added drily, 'like that Roman emperor who had a villa there a long time ago.'

Paoli, to show his appreciation of Coletti's sense of humour and unexpected erudition, threw back his huge head and laughed. His many chins moved from side to side in an orgy of quivering flesh. A few tears ran down his sallow face, so funny did he find the joke. Then he looked at Coletti shrewdly.

'My friend, there is company available for you if you want it. I know these trips are lonely.' Before Coletti could reply, he continued smoothly: 'A dancer from a cabaret in which I have an interest. Very beautiful, absolutely clean. Officers and my guests only!'

A pause. Coletti was always polite, considerate. He stroked his chin, as if thinking over the kind proposition.

'Ah, *padrone*,' he said at last. 'You are very kind. Truly a marvellous host. But I have so much to plan. I must keep my mind clear.'

'She can be slow, she can be quick.'

'I prefer my women to be quick and slow at the same time, if you understand my meaning. *Padrone*, it is not my mood. Please excuse me.'

Paoli nodded gravely. 'Of course.'

Coletti was a rare bird, he thought. Most men would not have dared to refuse the offer of a woman. It was a test of virility. But Coletti was sufficiently secure in his manhood. Probably he could have one without paying whenever he chose. Paoli even felt a twinge of envy for this man's youth, good looks, reputation. His self-containment. Even when young, Paoli had not been especially a lady's man; he had been forced to buy them for the most part, and by the time his slow climb through the hierarchy of the *Union Corse* had reached its pinnacle, where power alone can act as an aphrodisiac, he had already passed the age of fifty and the bulk of two hundred and eighty pounds. When he had sex – even with his long-suffering wife, who hardly counted – it was like a mediaeval knight in full armour trying to stay on his horse.

They stood, shook hands.

'If you should change your mind in the middle of the night. Or before breakfast . . . ?' said Paoli.

Coletti just laughed. There was no disrespect in it, only good humour.

'You are such a dedicated young man,' Paoli murmured. Too dedicated, he thought. Briefly he considered whether to arrange for Coletti's disappearance somewhere on the road between here and Paris. It would be possible to make the murder look like an accident, or a move by a rival Corsican family, and it would open the way for Paoli to move in on the Italian drugs trade. Just as quickly, he decided against it. Lucky Luciano, the Sicilians' *capo di tutti capi* was said to love this young man, and no matter how convincing the explanation, he would probably avenge his death indiscriminately, striking at all those in any way under suspicion. Were Luciano to do that, he would certainly include Paoli among his targets.

The fat chieftain nodded to one of the bodyguards waiting by the terrace doors. The man picked up his rifle and readied himself to guide Coletti to the room at the top of the house, with the finest panoramic view and the sweetest breezes, where he could spend his stay under Paoli's protection.

They had passed through Lyons, France's second city, at dusk, driving as fast as they could. The truck, a pre-war Renault, was in astonishingly good condition. The driver explained to Coletti that it had been requisitioned by the Germans after they occupied the southern zone of France in November '42, and used for running supplies and munitions to isolated Wehrmacht garrisons. The Boches had reasoned that the Resistance would be less likely to attack an unmarked French vehicle. Clever people, the Boches, the driver commented. But evidently not so clever as the British or the Americans. Especially the Americans, he emphasised with a meaningful wink.

Coletti dozed, stared out of the window, even when it rained, and let the driver chatter on. He took his turn at the wheel so that the driver could catnap. His occasional contributions to the conversation were general, non-committal. The Corsican obviously suspected that Coletti was a deserter from the U.S. forces, probably the navy. Coletti did nothing to confirm or deny that impression; his evasions were carefully guaged to leave a healthy element of mystery. The Corsican spoke not very good Italian with lots of dialect words from his own island. Coletti, when he spoke at all, put on his best Roman airs to confuse the issue still further.

The outskirts of Paris slipped on them with the first rays of daylight. In the suburbs, grey-faced men and women walked or cycled through the pot-holed streets. Things were still hard, and war had meant neglect. Many cars on the roads still carried billowing propane bags, a reminder of the petrol shortage. Rickshaw-style pedal cabs were plying their trade. But the girls were as pretty and as miraculously chic as ever, and at least the people were not afraid. France was slowly becoming France once more.

On Coletti's instructions, the Corsican stopped on a nondescript street corner in a shabby working-class district not far from the vegetable markets. Coletti calmly removed his suitcase from the space behind the seats, opened the door and swung himself and his luggage down onto the cobblestones.

'Thank you, my friend,' he said.

The Corsican in the cab smiled the feral smile of his people.

'No trouble. I hope you find some Coca-Cola, eh? Or is it a girl you're looking for?'

Coletti smiled non-commitally. 'Who knows in Paris?' he said. He waved the truck off into the dawn, watched it disappear, looked around to double-check his bearings.

A few minutes later, Coletti put down his suitcase, looked up and down the street to ensure that he was alone, knocked gently on the peeling paintwork of a café door. A face, haggard and suspicious, appeared at the window just to his right. The face showed no sign of emotion or recognition, but within seconds there came the sound of a bar being lifted inside and bolts being drawn back.

The door creaked open a few inches. A chain still kept Coletti out.

'Yes?'

Coletti took out of his pocket a yellow silk handkerchief monogrammed with the letter L, and showed it to the man. It was Charlie Lucky's symbol, by which family people knew him. Such handkerchiefs had made the American agents who landed on Sicily before the Allied invasion honoured guests everywhere, to be given every assistance. 'Luck sent me here,' he said quietly. 'Would you refuse a lucky man?'

'Sir – '

The chain fell away and the door swung open. The man who ushered Prism inside was small, thin, careworn. He looked fifty, though Prism knew him to be fifteen years younger. A child was wailing upstairs. Another was scolding. Yet another seemed to be dancing, thumping out a clumsy tom-tom beat on the first-storey floor. The dawn chorus of a poor man's family.

They exchanged greetings in the Sicilian dialect of the region where they both had been born, strangely formal and yet comfortable.

Dominico Gitti behaved with gap-toothed affability, a little forced, for he was not an affable man by nature. At least, his struggles had not encouraged good humour to take root and flourish. He led Prism between the tables of his small café and into a dingy kitchen that reeked of cheap oil and unclean humanity. There his plump wife, the mother of his brood, nursed a tiny baby as she toiled at the stove.

'Coffee for our honoured guest,' Gitti said with a swagger, still smiling at Prism but his voice a whiplash of male authority. 'This is our good fortune, our privilege. Coffee for a member of our family, for a true man of respect.'

Prism's bed that morning was a cot in a shuttered room at the back of the building, away from the spring sunshine and the street noise. He slept from ten until five. His slumber was fitful, but refreshing enough to carry him through the night's journey to his next destination.

CHAPTER EIGHTEEN

'WE CONSIDERED other methods, especially landing you by parachute,' Simpson said. 'This is hard to do in Germany, because there are no Resistance people to receive you, and anyone wandering around in the drop area by chance is almost certain to be German, therefore hostile and liable to turn you in to the authorities.'

He picked up a swagger-stick from the table in front of him, swung round and pointed to the battle-map of Germany on the wall.

'Also,' he continued, running the tip of the stick down the western front which was running from Holland in the north, through the Ruhr area, bulging into southern Germany, 'there are so many bloody soldiers milling around the countryside between the western front and Berlin that, quite frankly, it would be impossible to pick a spot where you could be sure there wouldn't be an armed patrol in the vicinity. That – in case you're still worried – is why we're relying on the fake papers and sending you in on a common or garden, ordinary, public railway train.'

The main line up from the Swiss border ran through Austrian territory for a few kilometres along shores of Lake Constance, then into Germany proper. The usual route for international travellers, rather than local traffic, lay via Munich, Nuremburg, Nauen. Simpson had marked it in red crayon on the black-and-white map.

'Your papers are *very* good.' Simpson beamed. 'Better than the real thing!'

Sutton had heard that joke from every forger, every passer of counterfeit currency and jewellery, he had ever charged. He raised his eyes to the ceiling and sighed.

'And of course, above all, you'll be travelling in the company of the countess who is, of course, Swiss by birth and German by marriage, and a bona fide German Red Cross official. Hard to beat her for credibility, which will rub off on you. She will be your big advantage.'

'It's the first time I ever went in this way,' McCarr said doubtfully. 'I guess I'm prejudiced against it. I – listen, how old is that map?'

Simpson looked faintly insulted. 'Oh, I suppose three or four days. This would be the military situation at the end of last weekend, Joe. It'll have changed a bit, but not that much.'

'And how long is it going to take us from the border to Berlin?'

'We think between twenty-four and thirty-six hours,' Simpson said.

Helen von Ackersberg's forehead creased in doubt. She was sitting at the back, still wearing her coat, as if she had just popped in to say hello, whereas in fact she had been here for three hours and was staying the night.

'It's still theoretically possible that it will only take twenty-four hours,' she said. 'The railroads are still functioning, but they're not at all what they used to be. It took me forty hours just a few days ago – admittedly via Vienna – but it can only get worse. First, the system is overstretched. Alongside all the military uses it's put to, and the other normal traffic, stock has been diverted to bring at least some refugees west to escape the Russians. Second, there's been a lot of damage to tracks and rolling stock from air attacks.'

'There around Nuremburg,' McCarr said, 'we seem pretty close to the American line of advance. It would be very dumb if we ran into our own troops and got ourselves liberated.'

'I know.' Simpson took a sip of water and swallowed it carefully. 'Things are moving fast, Joe. According to the latest reports, the Germans have made plans to re-route rail traffic through Prague if Allied forces cut the Munich-Berlin line. That will certainly cause quite a bit of further delay if it happens. You'll just have to take things as they come, be prepared to adapt.'

'Heinz knows we can't give a really precise time. As I explained, we have made a number of alternative arrangements in case things become too uncomfortable for him at his apartment.'

'Fine.' Simpson looked at Sutton. 'George? You're very quiet. Don't you have any problems?'

Sutton stroked his chin. 'No. I'm sure we'll be perfectly all right. I never did like flying much, anyway.'

'Very cool, George.'

'If you say so. I call it being resigned to my fate.'

'A matter of, if a bullet's got your name on it, you've had it, eh? Come off it.'

Sutton shrugged. 'What I mean is, I think I'm fated to live. Wandering the earth like the Flying Dutchman.'

When Sutton awoke, it was like a drowning man being hoisted abruptly out of the water just when he had accustomed himself to the sensation of death, resigned himself. There came in quick succession shock, surprise, and a vague and almost disconcerting sense of disappointment. Then he knew he was in a small bedroom, that he was in Switzerland, that soon he was going to Berlin.

A whiff of scent. He put on the light and saw Helen von Ackersberg, dressed in a towelling robe, her hair loose, looking down at him.

'George. Gustav. Whatever,' she said.

'Gothenburg is so beautiful. It has a population of four hundred thousand approximately. I wandered the streets of the old city as a child,' muttered Sutton. 'What do you want from Gustav? Or do you want something from dear old George the policeman?'

'I'm sorry.'

'You said it. George-Gustav, I mean.'

The countess smiled awkwardly. 'Mind if I sit down? I'd like to talk a little. I feel we hardly know each other.'

'Maybe you should only know Gustav, for security reasons. He'll tell you how it was to study foreign languages at the University of Stockholm under Professor Sørensen. Or how he decided against a career in the family shipping business and gave himself over to good works such as the Red Cross.'

She sat down on the bed, tossed her hair.

'For this short time I'd like to talk to George Sutton. About Heinz Keppler. And me.'

Sutton reached for the packet of cigarettes on his table, took one out. 'Oh?' he said in a flat voice.

'I want you to know some things I couldn't say with the others present,' she told him.

'Fire away.'

'Okay. Look, I don't usually smoke these days, but . . .'

Sutton handed her one of his Gold Flake cigarettes, lit it for her. She coughed and her eyes widened.

'Jesus. I used to smoke *cocktail* cigarettes.'

'These vicious little nicotine-sticks go with cheap beer and dirty streets. Scratch my surface, and so do I, countess,' said Sutton.

'Is it your class feelings that make you hostile to me?'

'No.'

'Politics?'

'When I think about it, yes. I find myself relaxing with you, then I remember the company you've kept these past few years.'

'I didn't like what I saw in Germany. That's why, after my husband died, I decided to give information to Allen Dulles and the OSS people here. I had the opportunity to travel. Fate gave that to me. The same fate you believe will keep you alive.'

'Did you worry about how you were using Keppler?'

'I managed to put things into separate compartments. He wasn't a serving soldier at the front or anything. It wasn't as if I was harming him. I was doing something against the Nazi system and for decency. You know Heinz isn't really a Nazi. I know he could work just as well and loyally for America, or for a democratic government in Germany if he was given the chance.'

'Countess, he'd work for anyone who paid him right.'

'God, you're a bitter man!' she snapped, then flushed and looked away. 'You've come a long way. I know that, George. Heinz said –'

'Of course. Yes. Heinz. He was the reason for our little talk, wasn't he?'

'George, please.' Helen took another puff on the cigarette. 'I guess you get used to these. They're an acquired taste. Like you. Anyway – Heinz said you were very smart but limited by your background. Especially so in England, where you have to go to one of those private schools – the ones they call public schools for some reason – to get anywhere. Heinz said in Germany you would have been promoted much faster.'

'To what? Commandant of a nice, cosy concentration camp?' Sutton shot back in a soft hiss. 'Or perhaps I'd have run a jolly team of good blokes whose job was to knock off a few hundred innocent civilians when the Führer was in a bad mood. Thanks, but I'd rather stick to being Sergeant Sutton, ex-D.I. at the Met, whose cockney accent and lack of breeding got in the way of his career.'

'I understand the way you feel. Heinz came from pretty humble beginnings too, you know. He worked his way through college by working on construction sites. He really did join the police force out of a feeling of duty. He talked about that a lot.'

Sutton laughed. 'Well, I became a copper because I thought it would be interesting, because the job wasn't badly paid and offered security. Yes, and I reckoned I would be doing something for society in my humble way. I'd say when I was eighteen years old that probably came somewhere close to the bottom of the list. I'd be very surprised if it was any different for Keppler.'

'Well – '

'Listen. I don't trust Keppler. I know his type. In some ways it's got nothing to do with him being a German. In England he'd have made a career too. No one would've liked him much in the force, but he'd have got his promotions through low cunning and hard graft. And not caring too much how he got a result, as long as he got one. But since he *is* German, he's had a chance to go beyond what's normal, decent. He's been corrupted.'

She nodded gratefully, apparently thinking Sutton was offering an excuse. 'So you do understand how a man like that is affected by the system.'

'You've got me wrong,' Sutton said fiercely. 'You see, no one *has* to be corrupted. You've got to be rotten to start with. Maybe if you're a cop who's got bad tendencies, you start beating up drunks for the pleasure of it, or you take a bribe or two, intimidate people, frame people so you can get the convictions you need. In a decent system, though, there's every chance you'll get caught and punished for it. You don't get the chance to turn really bad. In an organisation like the Gestapo, though, your rottenness gets a chance to grow. In fact, they encourage it. There are no limits.'

She bit her lip. 'He isn't all bad. He's clever, he's hard-working. And he's fun.'

'Do you love him, then? Is that the explanation for everything?'

'Wow. And I thought Englishmen were shy.'

'Not in Stepney, they're not.'

'I . . . it's very hard to explain. Yes, I think I did at the beginning. He was good-looking, strong . . . He knew his way around Berlin and I was a woman and I didn't know much about survival . . . I was infatuated. I'd been living in Germany for more than ten years, married to a pillar of society. I'd become used to certain things, I guess . . . even half thought of myself as German. I was very mixed up.'

'You're good on excuses, countess,' Sutton interrupted her softly. 'I bet Keppler is too.'

'Christ, you can be a bastard. You lured me into a trap with that one.'

Sutton didn't answer straight away. He was busy studying the curve of her neck and jaw, the fine, strong bones of her shoulder. The robe had fallen away slightly and in her agitation she hadn't retrieved it. The Countess von Ackersberg really was an attractive woman, even a beautiful one. Her problem was her self-deception, her bowing-down to power, the lack of any clear moral basis for her choices. She cared enough to risk her life for the Allies – or had there been a reason even for that? – yet there was also something about Keppler and what he stood for that fascinated her.

'Don't look at me like that,' she said, taking a final pull on the Gold Flake before depositing it in the ash tray with a victorious gesture. There, I smoked your strong cigarette, she was trying to say. There, I'm tough too. It was almost touching.

'That'll put hairs on your chest. Why did you really come here to my room?' Sutton asked. 'Did you want me to help you to feel all right about yourself after your latest trip to Berlin, or what?'

'Maybe I did. But most of all, I wanted to get to know you better. It's certainly not easy. What you call conversation is what other people call interrogation. Do you ever take it easy. With a friend? With a woman?'

Suddenly the countess reached out and put her hand in his. Her eyes were a speckled turquoise. It was beautifully timed and calculated. Sutton felt slightly ashamed of himself, and he also felt an unexpected stirring in his groin. You can huff and puff as much as you like, George my boy, he thought, but the body never lies. Why did it have to be happening now, though, for a woman like this one?

'I'm not going to be much comfort to you tonight,' Sutton said. 'We've agreed about what we've got to do. We'll all work together. We'll trust to our Red Cross papers and to fate. What more do you want?'

He gently pulled his hand away. *There, that wasn't too hard, was it?* he told himself.

'It's time to go to sleep, Helen,' he said. A brief smile flickered over her face. It was the first time he had used her first name since she had come into the room. 'The land of nod. I need my kip. That's English-style English for sleep.'

She got to her feet obediently, stood straight, as if despite everything the talk had given her some strength. She stretched. Her robe fell open and he could see her breasts, firm and small, the delicate nipples showing through her silk night dress. She caught herself, smiled in subtly challenging apology.

'It's like being back in the dorm at school,' she said with a giggle, wrapping herself up again. 'All kids together with teacher watching over us. You forget the real world of grownups where, you know . . .'

'Yes. I think I do know. G'night.'

'Good night, George.'

When the countess had gone, he lay back in his pillows with the light still on, wondering whether to smoke another Gold Flake. He could smell her perfume, still see in his mind's eye her nipples, the curve of her breasts.

You forget the real world, she had said.

Like hell you do, thought Sutton. It was just that even though you remembered the real world and tried to bring it to your rescue, as he had tonight when confronted with Helen von Ackersberg, it didn't stop you from continuing to want what you knew to be dangerous, risky, unreal.

CHAPTER NINETEEN

T HE ARTIFICIAL LIGHTING in the interview room brought out Charlie Lucky's prison pallor. He was forty-eight, but today he looked older, tireder. His smile was broad, nevertheless, and his aura of effortless power had not diminished.

'Mr Hoover. Mr Tolson.'

Not such a big number with the 'man of respect' stuff this time. More businesslike, more Lower East Side. Maybe the previous meeting had shown him how futile all that was.

'Luciano. I want to know what's going on. With your man.'

Charlie Lucky gave Hoover a puzzled look. Was this man serious with such a question?

'He's on his way to the heart of Germany. No problems, none at all, on that score.'

'I don't ask for details,' Hoover said carefully. 'I just want to be sure he's on the move. I know the other people cross the border in the next couple of days. More I can't say: that information was hard enough to get. From here on in, everything depends on your people. I can do no more.'

'My man's moving nicely. Coming in from a different direction,' said Luciano. 'He's steady. Like an arrow. A homing-pigeon. 'Cept he ain't no pigeon. A hawk, more like.'

'Sure, Luciano.'

There was a pause. Charlie Lucky sat at his ease, serious and yet relaxed. Like he was the one giving the audience and Hoover was the supplicant. Some kind of a change had occurred since their last meeting. Hoover did not know what it was, and he did not yet have the courage to ask.

'Luciano,' he said finally. His pink-mauve tongue flicked over his lips like a fly-catching reptile's. 'There's no documentation involved in any of this. I'm clear about preventing blackmail. I'm not entered in any books or registers or records here. I agreed that with Warden Morhous. These visits to you can never be proved to have happened. But I want you to know I already spoke to Governor Dewey about the first part of our deal. You'll be paroled. He wants it quick: he'll be starting his run for the presidency in '48. He wants it quick and clean and soon. Time to recover if there's any problems with public opinion about a hoodlum getting out so early, all that.'

'Fine. And the deportation order? I said, I don't want to live the rest of my life in Italy. A good place for a vacation, but . . .' Luciano shrugged expressively.

'A whole lot harder. I can . . . put pressure in those quarters. In my position, you know, nobody likes to cross me. When I have the material. Then I'll do anything and everything we need. I'll put the extra pressure on Dewey and Immigration. Do we have an understanding? It's parole down and freedom from deportation on delivery. That's important. So you know what's riding on our success in this issue.'

Luciano's eyes were opaque as he looked back at Hoover. He knew, of course, that parole had always been on the cards; it had been mentioned by the men from Naval Intelligence he had done business with over the past three years. Staying in the U.S. was something else. Only a federal official of Hoover's power and ruthlessness could fix that, in light of the automatic deportation order that faced him on his release from jail. And the trouble was, Hoover was playing it smart and keeping him dangling, as an extra incentive.

'I know what's riding, Mr Hoover,'he said.

'Okay.'

Hoover got to his feet, indicated that the ever-silent, watchful Tolson should rap on the door to summon the guard who would escort Charlie Lucky back to his cell. It had been a short, sharp interview. He wanted to get away.

The mobster stayed right where he was.

'There are three other people involved, Mr Hoover,' he said softly. 'You didn't tell me the whole truth about that. And one of them is an officer in our Intelligence service. A hero. Hear me? A hero.'

Hoover looked anxiously at Tolson, who had his hand inside his suit jacket, resting on his shoulder holster. Tolson was quiet, but he could read situations. Luciano's softness was dangerous, a sweet rose with thorns.

'I never specified, Luciano. We had a deal, that was all. You get the documents and Heinz Keppler. I didn't tell you how.'

'You think I'm a miracle-worker. Nice omelette. Don't need to crack eggs.'

'Are you reneging on our agreement, Luciano?' Hoover hissed.

Charlie Lucky looked at him steadily. 'I'm saying my man can get you what you want, Mr Hoover,' he said. 'If he can't, no sonofabitch can. Not the secret service. Not the Seventh Army. Not the Lord God Almighty.'

'As long as we understand that. I never knew you people were so fastidious,' Hoover said. 'I don't recall such forethought when federal officers got in your way in the past.'

Luciano threw up his hands, as if to say, if you don't know the difference, I can't tell you.

'My man will do what he needs to do, according to my instructions,' he said.

The subtle Sicilian evasion in the mobster's answer passed over Hoover's head. 'It sounds like I should hire him myself,' the FBI director said. At a nod from him, Tolson moved cautiously to the door and rapped the signal for the guard to come. They waited.

A short while later the guard walked in, looked around nervously as if uncertain who to ask for instructions. He beckoned to Luciano, who gestured at him to wait, as high-handedly as if he were a flunky and not a turnkey.

'Well, Mr Hoover,' Charlie Lucky said 'You're a very fortunate man, because for the moment you got him hired. The future is negotiable, naturally, like everything else in this world.'

It was his parting shot. He was still laughing when he left the Director of the F.B.I. standing alone by the doorway of the interview room. Lucky had found the meeting both repugnant and amusing. Repugnant because of the outrages Hoover was prepared to commit to get what he wanted. Amusing because Charlie Lucky had already issued some extra instructions to Johnny Coletti before Coletti had finally moved out of contact.

Say what you like about the *capo di tutti capi*, but he had his own sense of what was fit and right. And some of his best friends were Jews. It would give him great pleasure to give a lesson in morality to John Edgar Hoover, guardian of rectitude, cannibal of men's secrets.

CHAPTER TWENTY

THE SURPRISING THING was how easy it felt at first, moving into the territory of a ruthless dictatorship that was fighting for its life. The train was almost empty after Saint Galen. There were a few German passengers, very few Swiss. Some of the Germans were Swiss residents darting into the Reich on errands; others looked like diplomats or men on official business. The tunnel into neutrality had narrowed. Freight traffic had been banned since before the new year after pressure from the Allies.

From the moment they arrived at the main station in Berne, there had been a rule that they speak only German to each other. The countess had done almost all the talking, in her sing-song *Schwyzer-Dütsch*, the dialect that was as distincitve as Scottish English or Appalachian American. That was natural enough for a Swiss accompanying two Swedes. McCarr and Sutton carried off the task of appearing strong, silent and Scandinavian, McCarr in a sober business suit and overcoat, Sutton equally conservatively dressed and with his gold-rimmed spectacles. They had an entire compartment reserved for themselves. They talked quietly and sparingly as the little engine chugged its way through valleys radiantly alive with alpine flowers all along the slow line to Lake Constance and Germany.

The border appeared suddenly, though they had been warned by the thin blue edge of the lake on their left. A rusty sign indicated the beginning of the territory of the Greater German Reich. They were on the lake shore of what had been Austria and was now under German control.

German customs officials had boarded at the last station inside Switzerland and were already moving along the train,

164

quiet, pink-faced men in late middle age wearing the inevitable uniforms and high-peaked caps. The train jolted to a brief halt at a tiny village station inside Germany and other men got on. They wore trench coats and hats; these were younger and had a ruthless, military look to them. Gestapo.

The customs man came first, while the Gestapo men restlessly roamed the corridors, slamming doors and glancing suspiciously into compartments, whether they were occupied or not. From the sounds in nearby compartments that he had thought were empty, Sutton wondered if they were looking under the seats for spies.

The customs official, a wiry veteran of around sixty with a limp – this war or the last one? – and an Austrian accent, was correct, thorough, and incurious. The real checking work was obviously left to the Gestapo.

Two of the men in trenchcoats entered the compartment almost immediately the customs official had taken his leave with a polite 'servus' in the graceful style he had probably been trained to under the old empire. These men were very different: one tall, pale, flat-faced, in his early thirties, the other broad and stocky, with the ruddy features of a South German peasant.

'Please. Your papers, *Herrschaften*,' the tall one said unsmiling even for Helen von Ackersberg. He wore too much cologne; it was like an invisible field of scent around him, an aggressive fog.

He examined their passports, Red Cross documents.

'So. You are travelling to Berlin, Countess von Ackersberg?' There was a slight sneer when he pronounced the *von*, enough to make his point, which was that he didn't think much of aristocrats, not enough to get him into trouble if the countess had powerful friends.

'Yes,' she answered in that comforting Swiss singsong, smiling easily. 'As liaison between our people and the International Committee of the Red Cross. There is, sadly, much work to do for myself, Herr Salvesen and Herr Forlander.'

'I see you have been to Berlin many times,' the Gestapo man said.

'I have. I live there much of the time, as you can see.'

He squinted at Sutton and McCarr. 'The gentlemen not so often.'

'No. Not nearly so often.'

The Gestapo man turned to Sutton.

'I see from the visas in your passport that you have visited Riga, Herr Salvesen,' he said.

Sutton nodded. The man smiled thinly.

'I was born there,' he told Sutton, in no way implying that the experience had given him much pleasure. 'I have not been back there for ten years. Tell me, how is the place?'

'Still a fine city when I last saw it,' said Sutton, glinting myopically at the Gestapo man from behind his lenses. 'Of course, many Swedish architects and masterbuilders worked there in the old days. So unfortunate, the destruction . . .'

'The Latvians let a good German town go to blazes. And now, what do the Russians care?'

'Ah. Yes, of course.'

Flat-face and the silent peasant exchanged glances. The train was drawing into Bregenz, the small tourist resort that sat prettily on the lake on ancient Austrian land.

'If you will excuse me, *Herrschaften*, I must take your papers with me and leave the train for a moment. A few formalities. My colleague will wait outside in the corridor.' Flat-face pursed his lips. 'To ensure that you are not disturbed in any way.'

He gathered up their passports and Red Cross documents, stepped outside with his companion. A whispered conversation and flat-face opened a door and jumped down onto the platform like an athlete. The other man waited outside the door of the compartment, impassively glancing up and down the corridor from time to time, a thick-necked bird on guard. The many passengers joining the train knew him for what he was and did not jostle or push or show irritation at having to pass his bulk. They kept their heads down, squeezed past very carefully. An old woman tried to enter the compartment, despite the reserved sign; peasant warned her off in terse monosyllables and she went off down the train as quickly as her frail legs would carry her.

The countess seemed the calmest of them at this first test. She leaned forward to where Sutton and McCarr were sitting opposite her, murmured: 'Look natural, boys. This has happened before, several times. They just like to show they are being conscientious.'

166

Sutton nodded, self-consciously relaxed back in his seat and lit a cigarette, a Swiss brand now.

'If you say so.'

'I say so.'

Joe McCarr was looking out of the window to his right. A group of home guards were standing on a grassy bank maybe twenty yards away, clutching their rifles, trying to look as if they knew how to use them.

'I think,' McCarr said very softly, 'that we're about to find out whether friend Keppler is still one of the Führer's favoured ones or whether we've walked into a trap. This is our first hurdle. I hope it's not our last.'

They waited for five minutes, hardly exchanging another word. Flat-face re-appeared, and the peasant stuck his head out of the window for a brief exchange. Both men seemed quite casual. The identity papers were handed over from flat-face to peasant, who returned to the compartment.

'*Alles in Ordnung,*' he said, handing them back to each passenger in turn with a flourish.

'Excuse me,' said Sutton with a shy smile. 'You seem to have given me Herr Forlander's papers in error. If you will permit, I shall give them back to him.'

The Gestapo man grinned. '*Natürlich.*'

Sutton handed McCarr Herr Forlander's papers, received his own. Perhaps some kind of routine border trick with foreigners, perhaps not, he thought. A man who would accept another's identity in a situation such as this would be betraying something about himself. Well, if the Gestapo had been trying him on, he hadn't fallen for it.

'*Tack,*' McCarr said his thanks stiffly in his basic Swedish.

Sutton acknowledged him with a nod of the head.

'So,' said the Gestapo man briskly, 'please keep to your itinerary and report to the appropriate authorities on your arrival in the Reich capital. *Gute Reise!*'

He gave a lazy Hitler salute, left the compartment, sliding the door firmly shut behind him.

'Jesus, Maria and Joseph,' muttered McCarr. 'First hurdle over.'

'Seems so,' Sutton said.

The countess smiled. 'This was the key test. The border people are specially trained and have a direct line to Gestapo headquarters at the Prinz-Albrecht-Strasse in Berlin. The documents obviously passed muster. It looks like you were wrong about Heinz, and about Müller,' she added, making a wry face at Sutton.

Sutton shrugged. A couple of minutes later, he noticed a nondescript man in a coat and worker's cap look into the compartment, as if searching for a free seat in the crowded train. The man disappeared for a moment, then came back, unclapped one of the little seats stored in the wall of the train, with an expression of irritated resignation on his face. He was looking right into their compartment, and something about him indicated that he was settling down there for a long journey.

Sutton kept his eye on him, and noticed McCarr was doing the same. The big American said nothing, but Sutton sensed they were reading the same thing into this development.

The man in the corridor opened a newspaper, yawned.

'Poor fellow out there. Still, he was lucky to get a seat,' said McCarr carefully.

Sutton shook his head. 'I don't know. He seemed to know what he was doing.'

Helen carried on looking out of the window, apparently oblivious to the message passing between them.

The lake, bereft of its peacetime pleasure-steamers and sailing-boats, stayed placidly just where it was, while the *Eilzug* to Friedrichshafen battled forward along the shore and into war.

CHAPTER TWENTY-ONE

'NEED TO GO somewhere, lieutenant?' asked the fat master-sergeant from Cleveland.

'Reckon I do, sergeant.'

Master-Sergeant Randy Spalding grinned. The trim, dark officer in his neat uniform looked a little out of place in the middle of the battle-zone. No one looked like that unless they'd just arrived from the States or from some cosy desk job behind the lines, way behind the lines. But then again, this man looked tough, alert, self-contained. A fighter. If he'd been an obvious jerk, there was no way Spalding would have stopped his jeep for him here on the edge of town, officer or no fucking officer.

'Okay, sir, Where you headed?'

'Well, I can't rightly say. I arrived to join my unit, and it wasn't here. I'm told we're about ten miles east, close to the frontline.'

'I'll do my best to get you to them, sir. We're headed in that direction. You give Grabowski here your bags and jump in the back.'

'Thanks, sergeant. I wouldn't want to miss getting back to war. You understand that.'

The officer's smile had just enough self-mockery to win Spalding's heart.

He clambered in the back seat and they conducted a roared conversation, competing with the scream of the jeep's engine as it wove its way between the pot holes in the road, past occasional wrecked vehicles, clusters of bewildered German civilians.

'Name's Spalding. Randy Spalding.'

'Eddie Avery. Glad to meet you,' Coletti answered casually.

169

'This your first time in combat, lieutenant?'

'No. I was on Sicily.'

The answer was a safe one. He had handled liaison between local families and U.S. forces before and during the invasion. He had personally dealt with American intelligence and combat officers; he knew the terrain they had covered and the course of the swift, bitter battle for his ancestral island intimately. Even if the master-sergeant had fought there, he was unlikely to catch Coletti out on details.

'Hey, I missed that,' bellowed Spalding. 'Still over in England. Didn't see a German till I hit Omaha Beach. Seen too fuckin' much of 'em since, sir.'

Coletti laughed. 'The Krauts look darned sorry for themselves right now.'

'There's some pretty women . . .'

'Sergeant, you know the regulations against fraternisation with the enemy.'

Spalding turned round to check the lieutenant was smiling when he said that, saw he was, and laughed uproariously.

'Hell, we're just red-blooded guys. I reckon: Best way we can make the Krauts surrender, we fuck their women stupid. Those Krauts know what's happening, they can't summon the balls to fight no more! They just desert, run home to catch their old ladies at it.'

'An interesting point of view. You written to General Eisenhower on the subject?'

'Hah! You got a sense of the ridiculous, lieutenant. Say, you from New York?'

'I spent a lot of time there. I'm from the Mid-West originally. Minnesota.'

'And I'm from Cleveland, Ohio. Grabowski here, my driver, he's from Allentown. He can sure make this jeep go, but he's got a Pennsylvania steel girder 'stead of a brain. Ain't that right, Grabowski?'

The PFC in the driver's seat nodded solemnly. He had muscles everywhere from his ankles to his earlobes, and a head the shape of a tank-trap.

'Yup. Don't hardly need a helmet, sir,' he said with pride in his voice. 'A shell hit me, I just butt it right back at the enemy.'

It was his only remark for the next ten miles or so, while

they careened through drab Westphalian villages separated by clusters of poor-looking pine trees. Some areas were quite well-preserved; others bore witness to the desperate flurries of fighting and to scorched-earth actions by the retreating Germans.

'It's real messy around here, sir,' Spalding explained.

'You know, the armour's moving forward, their wheels ain't touching the ground, just bypassing the Kraut garrisons. Plenty of Krauts give theirselves up the moment they catch sight of us, but you never know when you'll hit a bunch of fanatics. Them SS boys.'

Coletti noted the mixture of loathing and awe in the master-sergeant's voice.

'Many of them, sergeant?'

'Yeah. Quite a few here and there. Goes on like this, though, we could be through to Berlin in no time, pickin' flowers all the way. Krauts'd open up like the Red Sea did to the people of Israel. 'Cept for the SS, they got no stomach for this fight any more'

'The Russians are even closer to Berlin.'

'Sure, sure. That's what the Krauts are so shit-scared of, lieutenant. Those Russkies are feeling *real* mean, they're in no mood to fuck around.' Spalding laughed, dug Grabowski in the ribs, to which the man with the steel girder for a brain showed no reaction either. 'We said to the Krauts, you just let us through to Berlin 'cos we're in a hurry, they'd fuckin' well *push* the tanks there. They'd *carry* us the whole way.' He let out another booming peal of laughter. 'Say, we getting close to where you need to go, lieutenant?'

Coletti nodded. Just two, three more kilometres. So close that he was already pre-occupied with his next move. He was going to have to move fast once he got to the lines, keeping in front of the American advance all the time. He knew from his trip in uniform since Liège, and from talk during his overnight stop with family people near Marl, that the Fifth Army had really burst through to the South-East, was driving for the Elbe and meeting little resistance.

'Right, sergeant. Things sure have changed since Sicily. The Krauts fought really hard there, gave us a whole lot of trouble.'

The road-block was on a thickly-wooded stretch of road just beyond the next bend, about a kilometre short of a village whose church-spire they had already glimpsed across the open fields a way back. It was manned by four MPs under the command of a sergeant who looked to be about six-eight, with the huge feet and ridiculously elongated body of a pro basketball player.

They pulled up. Spalding, obviously angry, sat with his arms folded. On his orders, Grabowski kept the jeep's motor running while the giant and his assistants walked over. They had automatic weapons; by their jeep a light machine-gun on a tripod was trained on the newcomers.

The MP sergeant looked down at the lieutenant and saluted.

'You . . . ah, in command here, sir?' he asked in a slow, deep Mid-Western drawl. He had a slight speech impediment, as if he had to catch his breath once in a while. Maybe the air was thin at that altitude.

'No, sergeant. I'm trying to join my unit, and the sergeant here, offered me a ride.'

'Okay . . . ah, sir. Well, I'm going to have to ask to see all your . . . ah, ID and travel warrants, anything like that. We got orders. You know . . . ah, since the Battle of the Bulge, where there was all those Krauts running around in American uniforms. We . . . ah, gotta be careful.'

'Fine. I guess it's good you guys are so vigilant.'

Spalding still had his arms folded, and the engine was still growling. At a glance from him, Grabowski revved the motor. It snarled shrilly like a mean dog on a leash. Sheer frustration: no one had rank to pull here. MPs were MPs. Even a four-star general would be technically obliged to do just as he was asked.

The MP sergeant checked Spalding's papers first, then Grabowski's. He took his time. He was either a real asshole or extremely conscientious, maybe both.

'Ah, sir . . . ?' he said after he had grudgingly handed back their documents. 'If you don't mind.'

'No trouble, sergeant.'

Coletti smiled, reached into the pocket inside his tunic. There were the documents of Eddie Avery, and also his knife faced with cotton wool to soften the touch of searching hands and lightly but securely taped to his shirt.

He handed over the ID. The sergeant looked it over, examined the orders. Then he looked at the other MP, swallowed his adam's apple.

'Ah, sir . . . I see here that your unit is . . . well, I know you're way out of your area.'

His voice trailed off uncomfortably, but his eyes were progressively hardening.

'Sir, you . . . ah, ah, shouldn't be around here, sir.'

Coletti shrugged. 'Then I'm lost, sergeant. It's a long way from Italy.'

He was keeping his eye on the light machine-gun, inwardly cursing that he had been stopped at this late stage on ID that would have stood up perfectly if he had been checked anywhere before, say, Düsseldorf. He had known that the last stretch, the dash to the lines, would contain unavoidable risks. Well, all he could do now was to manoeuvre himself into a situation where there was no machine-gun, where six other soldiers weren't staring at him.

'Sure, sir,' the giant said. 'Look . . . ah, we got our command post just up ahead. The captain could maybe look over your papers and put you on the right . . . ah, track. You understand. I got orders to be real strict.'

'Of course.' Coletti laughed, cast his eyes mockingly to heaven. 'My first time in Germany. Snafu. And I realise you're only doing your job, sergeant.'

'I'm . . . ah, real glad you understand, sir.'

The giant had visibly relaxed. But the machine-gun and the others were still there. If it had been two, even three against one, maybe this would have been the time. But the village, from what Spalding had told and from his own reading of the map, was very close to where he needed to be. Better from there. He knew the route from there, had it pictured in his mind very clearly.

'Okay,'

Coletti got slowly out of the back of the jeep.

'Get the lieutenant's bag, Grabowski,' snapped Spalding.

'Shit, sarge,'

'Move. The MPs wanna take him for a little ride to daddy's house.'

'Thank you, sergeant,' Coletti said with dignity.

'You're welcome, sir.' Spalding stared balefully at the giant

MP sergeant. 'I'm based with ordinance at Wesel. Spalding's the name, remember. You need help, we'll be there.'

'That's very kind of you. I'm sure I can handle this and be on my way in no time.'

Coletti strolled nonchalantly over to the MPs' jeep. The barrier across the road was raised and with a howl Spalding's jeep rushed through, Grabowski low over the wheel like a racing-driver. The master-sergeant called out something inaudible but clearly obscene, and Coletti was left there alone with the stuttering giant and his three merry men.

'Now, sir, if you'll . . . ah, please sit in the front of the jeep.'

Coletti could see there would be armed men behind him.

'You're serious, aren't you, sergeant?'

'Have to be.'

'Well, I think I'd better talk to your commander, son.'

'Yes, sir. I think you'd better.'

The village was half in ruins, whether from bombing or artillery action it was hard to tell. The jeep drove almost right through the place, then turned into a courtyard. There was another jeep parked by the front door of the simple stone building. Chickens were scratching in the yard. A pair of bored MPs with rifles sat on the steps. One was eating a sandwich. They stared silently at the giant, then at Coletti, without particular interest. Coletti had thought again of doing what he needed to do while they were still in the jeep, but had concluded that the odds were too long with two heavily-armed men at his back. They had confiscated his service pistol, of course.

How many MPs were there here?

They walked past the two at the door, into the low-ceilinged house. The late-afternoon sun was pleasant. Two or three soldiers were sitting gloomily in a room to one side of the hallway, guarded by another MP. They looked as if they had been caught AWOL. Or did it count as cowardice in the face of the enemy around here?

'Okay. Just a minute, sir. Fletcher, Spatz, you wait here with the . . . ah, lieutenant.'

Fletcher and Spatz stood between Coletti and the outside door, looking amused. The sergeant ducked to avoid the ceiling, went and knocked on the door straight ahead. He opened it and stuck his head in, for which he needed to bend almost double.

'Captain Feder, . . . ah, sir,' Coletti heard him say, 'we have an officer we picked up on the road. He's way off from his unit, and I believe his personal details . . . ah, don't fit too well. I thought I should . . . ah, ah, let you talk to him, sir.'

Coletti didn't catch what the officer said in reply, but a moment later the giant turned and beckoned.

'Lieutenant. Ah, the captain would like to see you, sir.'

Coletti walked past him through the doorway.

As the door closed behind him, he was aware of a number of things at once. The giant had also entered the room and was standing at ease but watchful behind him. The captain, seated at his desk chewing on a spent cheroot, was plump and officious. And at the captain's back the window was open to let in the soft, spring air. He could see an uncut lawn and a run-down kitchen garden about forty yards long which ended in a low fence, beyond which was thick forest. All this he registered while being careful to stand respectfully and slightly sheepishly in front of the captain.

'Lieutenant Avery? Or so you claim,' the captain rasped in a light, Ivy League tenor. His eyes were beady, his face unsmiling. 'Now, you're supposedly from Minneapolis and yet you speak like a New Yorker; you look like a Greek or an Italian; you're wandering around nowhere near your unit, acting as if you were on vacation.' He shook his head. 'I'm entitled to a little extra explanation, I think.'

'Well, sir, I guess you are,' said Coletti slowly, making it look as if he was in a position of genuine embarrassment. He felt no fear now; his escape route was planned, and if the giant could not be made to leave, he would just have to make do. But a plan was crystallising rapidly in his mind, one he was sure would succeed.

'Well, may I have the privilege of hearing your reasons, lieutenant?' the MP captain said with a smirk, relighting his half-smoked cheroot.

'Of course, sir.' An awkward pause. 'Sir,' Coletti then said in a firmer voice, 'I have to ask first if you are acquainted with an outfit by the name of G-2.'

The captain's eyes narrowed. He nodded.

'Okay. Then maybe I can explain what I'm doing here,' Coletti continued crisply. Those nights spent plying American agents on Sicily with heady, oily *grappa* that loosened their tongues, made them boast, were paying off. He knew enough of the jargon, enough of the basic command structures and departments, to bluff his way through, at least with an Ivy League ignoramus. 'But first,' he added, 'I'm afraid I'll have to ask you to withdraw the sergeant here outside into the hallway. This is extremely sensitive material we have to discuss. Sir.'

The captain's eyes flicked towards the giant. Coletti heard the man behind him swallow hard and at a great height. The captain put his cheroot back in the ash-tray, took out his service pistol and laid it on the table with what he obviously hoped looked like a tough-guy flourish.

'I'm prepared if the lieutenant tries anything, sergeant. He's been disarmed? Right, now you just move outside and wait. If I need you, I'll holler!'

'Right . . . ah, sir.'

The door clicked closed. The captain watched Coletti very carefully.

'Shoot, lieutenant.'

'As you know, sir, we have been engaged in secret operations in and around the battle zone for some time,' Coletti began.

The captain clearly did not know anything of the kind, or had only heard the vaguest gossip, but still he nodded sagely.

'Okay. Well, sir, I am travelling under a false identity, belonging to an officer killed in action quite recently.'

'Uhuh. But can you give me any proof? Is there anyone I can call to check this out?'

Coletti looked doubtful. 'Maybe . . . sir, I have concealed in my uniform a separate ID document. Perhaps that will satisfy you without recourse to my superiors.' He grinned in feigned embarrassment. 'You know, I shouldn't have told you this much. I'd be in real hot water . . .'

'All right. We'll see. Please take the document out and throw it on the table. Slowly does it, eh?'

'Sure,'

Coletti put his right hand into his inside breast pocket, as if

176

searching for a further, secret place, felt the knife and deftly untaped it.

'Hell, sir . . . we deliberately make these things hard to find.' Coletti told him with a laugh.

The captain leaned forward expectantly, a foolish smile on his face to match Coletti's. He was just momentarily off guard, the pistol on the table forgotten and his attention totally with the other man's fiddling.

'Take your time, lieutenant – '

The knife left Coletti's palm at a speed of something close to a hundred miles an hour and passed right through the captain's throat until the point stuck out the back of his neck. The man's eyes grew huge and glassy, the eyeballs rolled. His arms flapped like a big baby bird's and a curious metallic wracking sound emerged from his open mouth, as if he had just swallowed a handful of paper clips from the pile on his desk.

Coletti took the two steps necessary to get close enough, launched himself swiftly but soundlessly across the desk, grabbed the back of the captain's head with one hand, put the other over his mouth. The precaution may have been unnecessary: the eyes were already those of a dead man, but Coletti waited to the count of three before releasing the head and pulling out his beloved knife, pushing the captain back in his chair as he did so. Blood began to spurt over the mahogany desktop. Coletti, sliding way to the side and landing on his feet, reached out and let the captain down to the floor.

Then he jumped through the window and began to run down the garden, putting his knife back in its pocket as he ran, very fast, his muscular legs working with exhilarating power, towards the forest.

The MPs were incredibly slack and stupid for this kind of war. They wouldn't have lasted a minute on the streets of Palermo or even New York, Coletti thought as he ran. He calculated it was fifteen seconds before the first shot was fired, from the giant standing in the open window, probably straddling the captain's corpse. By then Coletti was beyond the first stand of trees and heading down a hillside, grateful for the gathering twilight and knowing that on the far side of the thick wood ahead lay another village, and a place where he would meet another friend, the guide who would escort him through the lines and into Nazi Germany.

He felt triumphant, invincible, unstoppable. Johnny Coletti had become Prism.

CHAPTER TWENTY-TWO

T HEY HAD SAT for four hours in a siding at Nuremburg that morning, and according to the word that went through the train they had been lucky to get moving again so soon. Twenty-nine hours after leaving Swiss soil, their train was puffing through Northern Franconia, approaching the ancient border between Bavaria and Thuringia, the division-line between the protestant north and the catholic south of Germany. The towns were bomb-damaged, the countryside by contrast mostly safe and even prosperous looking. The only sign of crisis was the heavy, curiously aimless traffic on the roads.

The original tail, if that was what he was, had been taken off and replaced at Munich. The one now in the corridor outside their compartment was quite young, in the uniform of a sergeant in the Luftwaffe Auxiliary, and he was good. If his predecessor had not been a little too obvious they might never have suspected they were being watched at all, but now they did, it was easy to sense the extra edge of vigilance that distinguished him from the other passengers. They would have to test him, though, when they got closer to Berlin. To be sure, and to take the necessary steps. Sutton had already begun to feel reluctantly grateful for McCarr's presence.

The countess had gone to the W.C.

'All right,' McCarr murmured in German, 'this man's the one. We don't change trains again before Berlin. D'you think he may have an offsider?'

'Impossible to tell. It depends why he's watching us, doesn't it? If it's just routine surveillance, maybe he is alone.'

'Or maybe they're short-handed. We'll try him out when the train stops at Hof. Just do what I say.'

They were sitting in brooding silence when Helen von Ackersberg returned. Her face was flushed.

'That Luftwaffe boy *stared* at me,' she said. 'He looks really *hungry*.'

Sutton forced a smile. 'It's been a long, lonely war.'

If the man was Gestapo, the presence of a pretty woman in the party gave him a marvellous excuse to be shameless in his observations. And maybe he really *was* hungry too, which would help.

McCarr had been looking out of the window.

'We need to go through a little routine at Hof. I was just explaining to our friend Gustav. I'd like everyone to follow my moves, please.'

'Cloak-and-dagger?' She laughed nervously.

'Good professional practice, that's all.'

She pouted. 'You're not as much fun as you look.'

'I'm working, Helen. My personality changes when I'm working.'

The train slowed down to make its entry into Hof station. The town seemed undamaged; it was flattered by the sharp spring light. A man was talking loudly outside their compartment, having buttonholed the Luftwaffe sergeant. The sergeant listened impassively while he was told that the Americans were coming, the Russians were coming. Who would get here first? The man had heard the 'Amis' were heading for the border of the Protectorate, the place that had once been Czechoslovakia. What did the sergeant know about the situation? If – God help Germany, and of course our boys in uniform, under the leadership of our Führer, would surely stop the advance – if the Amis did come, it would at least be better than the Russians. In East Prussia, the Russians had murdered and mutilated harmless German officials, raped their wives and daughters in front of their eyes. *Jessasmariaundjosef*, such barbarians . . .

The train settled to a halt at the station. The by now familiar crush of bewildered peasant, sallow war cripples, anxious, confused refugees, mostly women with children and old people with nothing but a few possessions saved from their abandoned homes. Sutton had got used to these sights. At first he had been curious, had even experienced a kind of satisfaction at the fate of the Germany he had come to hate. Now there was nothing but weariness, leavened with a dull, useless compassion. The Blitz had been bad, but at least Londoners had not been driven from their homeland. Families and communities had stayed for the most part stubbornly intact.

'Boys and girls,' McCarr said, 'we're getting off the train.'

'That's crazy.'

'I said, follow my moves. This compartment is reserved. Someone once said: the socialist revolution here failed because the workers couldn't get a permit for it from the appropriate authorities. Our seats'll be safe. Come on.'

The countess responded without protest or comment. She got to her feet, patted her hair in front of the little mirror set above the men's seats, led the way out of the compartment.

Once they were on the platform, McCarr gave them a glance which was slightly but noticeably furtive.

'We've got to find a phone,' he said.

'A phone?'

'A phone.'

They followed him past the stationmaster's office and the *Imbiss* snack bar. There were two phone booths around the side, set in a narrow brick cul-de-sac. Both were in use.

'We'll just wait here,' said McCarr. 'Look like you're pros, but you're on tenterhooks, just a mite nervous. Understood?'

They had to wait several minutes for a booth to become free. Fifty yards away, the engine hissed and growled impatiently. McCarr told them not to worry. It would be in the station for at least fifteen minutes. Maybe four hours again. Trust, just trust.

He ducked into the booth, dialled a number, said a few urgent words, put the receiver down again.

'Follow,' he said after he had re-emerged, and began walking briskly down the platform towards the gate marked *Ausgang*. They followed.

At the gate he turned, seemed to fumble in the pockets of his raincoat. Then he looked vaguely along the platform in the direction they had come from before smiling innocently at a po-faced ticket collector.

'Excuse me,' he said. 'We have urgent business in Berlin. Have you any idea when the train is anticipated to arrive there?'

'You a foreigner?' asked the man.

'Swedish.'

The Bavarian chuckled grimly.

'In Sweden the trains run on time.'

'I suppose they do.'

'Sir, you are in Germany. We have a few obstacles to normal operations. So maybe tonight you will arrive in the Reich capital. Maybe tomorrow morning for breakfast. Maybe Wednesday week. Friend, the *Deutsche Reichsbahn* still pays me to stand here and take tickets and look as if I know what's happening. In fact, the timetables of the *Reichsbahn* are no longer in the hands of its operatives, but in the hands of God.' He crossed himself solemnly.

'Thank you,' said McCarr.

'*Bitteschön*. You Swedes, you are clever. You kept your noses clean and now you reap your reward.'

McCarr nodded, smiled politely but non-committally, as anyone would expect from a man of the Red Cross, with his diplomatic status to maintain.

When they were on their way back down the train towards their compartment, he said: 'The Luftwaffe sergeant stuck to us all the time just now. As unobtrusively as he could, but nevertheless, like glue. We're in trouble.'

'I know that,' said the countess. 'Did you really think I didn't? What are we going to do about him? Can we give him the slip?'

McCarr looked down at the concrete platform floor, sighed thoughtfully.

'Oh no, countess,' he said softly. 'He's the one who has to disappear, poor asshole. *Verschwinden muss er, armer Schwein*.'

The planes came out of the late-afternoon sun, very suddenly and very fast. Someone nearby had the knowledge and just, only just, the time to identify them as Typhoons, the doughty American fighter-bombers that could outpace anything except the Me 262 jets. The engine was hauling up a gentle, wooded incline north of Hirschberg. There was nothing to be done.

The first rockets arced into the woods to their right, exploding in searing orange balls among the tops of the pine trees. Almost immediately a kind of clinging, peculiarly acrid smoke began to seep through the half-open windows.

Another voice yelled: '*Phosphor!*'

The train lurched, seemed to buckle back down to its climb for a few moments with extra vigour, then began to slow down. There was the shriek of high-powered aircraft engines above them, followed by a rush of air and a deafening explosion very close by. The carriage rocked wildly, tipped. Women were screaming – or perhaps there were men also. How could you tell?

The train halted as if a huge, invisible fist had been planted into its head.

Suddenly the train corridor was full, doors were being flung open. It was two or three seconds later that the big hit came, only yards up towards the front of the train. A horrible booming, whooshing sound and the smashing of glass, explosions, and the corridor was filled with that terrible smoke. The screams really began, not screams of fear but of hideous, animal pain. A high-pitched wailing: '*O Gott O Gott O Gott . . .*'

The carriage kept swaying, as if they were slowly toppling over, but in fact when Sutton got unsteadily to his feet and looked around, he realised that it was only listing to about ten degrees or so. There was a strong smell of noxious, poisonous burning. An image flashed into his mind of nights spent fire-watching during the big German bombing raids on the London docks in '41; when chemical warehouses had been hit, the smell had been like that, except that it had been far away.

'Let's get out,' he said to McCarr, who was regaining his feet, rolling like a drunk.

'I got thrown against the window,' McCarr explained. 'Luckily my head didn't go right through. I'll be okay in a minute . . . Helen . . .'

They both peered through the smoke. The countess was sitting just where she had been before the rocket's impact, bolt upright in her seat. Amazingly, she had stayed there, having seized hold of an armrest as a ship-wrecked sailor clings to a spar. The trouble was, she still hadn't let go of it, and her face was set in a frozen smile.

'Helen!' Sutton shouted.

She looked at him. 'Yes.'

He didn't hit her across the face. He pinched her cheek

hard, said slowly, 'We've got to leave this train. The fire's spreading. The engine's making a hell of a noise . . .'

'Yes.'

'Oh, Christ. Give me a hand, Joe . . .'

They grabbed hold of her and pushed her out through the compartment door and into the corridor. Once out there, she stood upright, still not saying anything too sensible, but at least not falling down.

'You take her outside,' said McCarr. 'She's in shock. I'll get the luggage . . .'

'I'll help you.'

'Help her. She needs it. I'll be better off alone. Room to move, you know. Go . . .'

Sutton nodded, realising that McCarr was right. Someone had to get Helen out, someone had to try to save the cases, and there was no point in wasting more time arguing. He began to cough. The fog of smoke was getting thicker. He took the countess's arm, pushed her along. Closer to the main door the crowd thickened, but most were already outside by the side of the track. Glancing through the window, Sutton saw one of the victims of the direct hit being carried away from the stricken carriage. The victim – impossible to tell its sex – was still partially on fire, smouldering in patches. The gap in the face that had once been a mouth was open in a full-throated, piercing and inarticulate bellow. One of the helpers was yelling, 'For God's sake, don't throw water on him! That's the worst thing you can do! No water!' Sutton turned away and forced Helen out through the door, prepared to follow himself.

In the corridor by the compartment, McCarr put a handkerchief over his mouth, reached inside and grabbed the first suitcase – Helen's, as it happened – swung it down. He realised he was crying from the fumes. First case out beside him. Someone pushed past, and he flattened himself against the partition. Strange, the screams and the wounded out there in the pale sunlight, in here people behaving more or less normally. He made to reach in again, saw that a passenger had either managed to open a window or smash one, to let the smoke out and air in. The smoke had begun to billow out, the air inside was clearing a little. Quick, move quick. This was deceptive. As if to hurry him on, an official railway voice outside, one of the conductors, was bellowing: 'Please leave the train! There is danger from the boiler! Please leave the train!'

Then McCarr saw the Luftwaffe auxiliary sergeant, the tail. He had forgotten him in the immediate crisis. The sergeant was lying on the floor of the corridor seven or eight feet to his left, his head at an awkward angle, his body limp as a doll's. McCarr realised how lucky he had been himself. The tail had not just fallen awkwardly – the way he had been thrown had broken him . . .

By the man's side was a Roman Catholic priest in a neat black clerical suit and a black wide-brimmed hat. He was kneeling, listening intently. Before he could control himself, McCarr was saying, '*Kann ich etwas tun?*' The priest, bespectacled and square-faced, with an aquiline nose and a deep cleft in his chin, shrugged in apparent despair, looked carefully at McCarr and then nodded. 'He has lost consciousness. We could make him more comfortable, my son. It's too dangerous to move him.'

The professional in McCarr cursed himself for getting involved. This was the power of the priesthood over an Irish boy they'd had until he was seven, just like the Jesuit brothers' textbook said. Despite the urgency of his tasks, McCarr found himself regretting his cynicism. The priest was here, not panicking where all around him were saving themselves. Thirty seconds maybe, one decent act for human being, even if the man had been his enemy.

Moving forward fast, McCarr knelt, supporting the Luftwaffe sergeant's young head. The priest felt his heart, seemed to fumble with the man's clothing, then suddenly stood up, surprising McCarr with the athleticism of his movement, its almost brutal decisiveness.

The realisations came in quick succession. First McCarr became aware that the sergeant's neck was broken and that the man was dead. And when he looked up in accusing enquiry at the priest, he saw that the priest had a gun in his fist.

'Slowly,' the man said. 'Slowly back up the corridor. We're leaving the train all right. Don't bother with the luggage. Come on, move!'

McCarr nodded, looking straight at him, his gaze calm. If inwardly he was seething, he was disguising it well.

'All right,' he said. 'But just a moment. There's one small thing I need to do.'

He straightened up, looked down at the body of the Luftwaffe sergeant, then at the priest, smiled, and kicked the corpse hard in the side of the ribs, so that it shivered and the arm flopped.

There was a fraction of an instant when the priest's attention was caught in the surprise, his disbelief at such an unexpected act of sacrilege so strong that he lost the advantage. It was hardly more than the blinking of an eye, but for McCarr it had to be enough. His right foot came around again, high and hard, aiming for the priest's vulnerable groin and just missing. The kick glanced against the man's hip, spinning the priest away a bit and hurting him, for his mouth tightened in a grimace of pain. At the same time, McCarr's right hand reached out towards the gun.

'Please leave the train!' the conductor outside bellowed. 'Everyone must please leave the train. The boiler is overheating!'

'I'm all right now,' Helen said. 'Where's Joe?'

Sutton had led her over to the edge of the pine forest some fifty feet from the track. The movement had seemed to bring her to her senses. At least, she was clear-minded enough to share the concern that had started to nag at him in the last minute or so. He stared at the carriage, expecting to see a suitcase appear through the door or one of the shattered windows, but nothing had shown itself. Everyone else seemed to have moved away, except for a few inside helping those still injured or trapped. The conductor, hatless and his face covered in soot, was walking up and down the length of the train, calling out the message for everyone to leave, get away. The bubbling and hissing from the engine, just a carriage's length away from where Joe should be, was getting more ominous by the moment.

Another minute passed. Sutton looked at the countess. 'Will you wait here? Don't move.'

'Of course,' she said. her voice was shaking but normal enough. 'What are you going to do?'

'I'm going over there to see what's going on.'

'Be careful.'

He nodded, set off at a diagonal that took him back towards the train and also forward towards the crippled, angry engine. Great clouds of steam were rising from it, mingling with the smoke from the rockets and from scores of tiny fires throughout the front of the train. He quickened his pace, oblivious to the fact that everyone else had fled, ignoring the urgent shouted warnings of the conductor, and began to run the train's length, staying a few feet from the windows so that he could see inside. He passed the foremost-but-one carriage where he had expected to see Joe and was wondering whether to risk searching inside the endangered train, when he heard a shot and stopped dead in his tracks. He could see Joe McCarr through the swirling smoke, his face twisted in a rictus of effort, his big hands busy and straining. With a shock Sutton realised that one of the American's hands was pressing on a man's neck and that the man's head was outside the open window, being forced back farther and farther. The other hand was clasping a wrist. In the man's right hand he recognised the shape of a gun.

Sutton began to run towards the open carriage door nearest to the place where Joe was fighting for his life. He was just about to swing himself up and into the corridor when the great sound came, and hot, sharply-metalled wind blew him into the air, spinning and spinning, away from the door and down a different corridor, with sudden darkness at the end.

The explosion had died down to a dull, continuous roar in his head. George Sutton began to see shapes. In his half-consciousness he believed he was seeing milky ways of fire in the tops of the trees. He opened his eyes some more. There *were* flames in the treetops. Parts of the forest had caught fire. And there, all of a sudden, blocking out most of the view, was a round, unfamiliar middle-aged face, concerned but smiling, topped by a female version of a Tyrolean hat. It was a kind face, the face of a woman who had cared for others, professionally or as a mother, all her life.

He heard the woman say in a thick dialect that he could barely understand, 'He's come round. You're a very lucky woman.'

'He's not my husband,' said Helen von Ackersberg irrelevantly.

'All the better!' The older woman laughed.

He could see the countess now, looking far less vague. She touched him on the cheek.

'All right?'

He nodded. And he was very lucky that the woman had spoken German; otherwise, in his dazed state he might have talked to her in English. He was waking up fast. Now he was worrying whether he had rambled in English while he was unconscious. How long had it been? And where was Joe?

'Where is he?' he asked.

The countess looked down at him sadly. 'We don't know. The engine blew up.' She paused, bit her lip. 'I don't think the outlook is very bright.'

The middle-aged woman took her hand rather than Sutton's in an spontaneous gesture of female solidarity.

'*Ach, Scheisse*,' said Sutton, raising himself on one elbow. Herr Krausner would have been proud of him.

The countess turned to the woman. 'I think Herr Salvesen is fine now,' she said. 'He is starting to curse and swear and that is a good sign. Thank you so much. I can look after him now. There are other injured people, I think.'

'Of course. You are still a fortunate person, wife or no wife,' the woman said with a wink. 'And he is a fortunate man.'

Then she waddled away, stately and reassuring in her coat and hat. How had she managed to keep them?

'What's going on? How long was I unconscious?' Sutton asked. Already he could see the wreck of the front of the train, the fires still burning fiercely; the twisted shape of the half-destroyed engine.

'About ten minutes. As you can see, it's a bloody mess. That's what's going on.'

'There will be a lot of official people here soon, won't there?'

'I suppose so. There's a road about a quarter of a mile over there,' the countess said, pointing to her left. 'One of the railway people went up there to see if he could find help. God knows, they'll have seen the attack and the clouds of smoke if they've any sense at all.'

Sutton sat fully up, winced. 'Helen, we have to get away.'

'It's okay. We're far enough from the engine that even if it goes up again, we won't be harmed.'

'No. You don't understand. We have to just get right away from here and all these people. We mustn't be here when the police arrive.'

'Don't panic, George.'

'Panic has nothing to do with it. I saw Joe just before the explosion. He was fighting someone. I was going to help him when the engine went up.'

The countess paled. 'Who?'

'I don't know for sure. Logically, the tail. Something must have happened.' Sutton looked around. The cover of the woods was only a few yards away. It was a big conifer forest, dark and dense as a jungle.

'What does it mean?'

He was on his feet, unsteady but on his feet. 'We can't hang around. Those Red Cross papers won't do us much good. Let's go. Joe is dead,' he added harshly.

She opened her mouth to say something else and Sutton seized her arm fiercely, so savagely that he realised how much anger he still had left. 'Come with me. If we're here when this place starts swarming with cops and medical teams, and they start drawing up lists and contacting headquarters, we could end up in serious trouble.'

'George – '

'Trust me. We've taken enough chances. I don't know for certain what it is, but I can *smell* something wrong.'

'What shall we do? Where shall we go?'

'First into that forest. Then we'll see. Go!'

He went and she followed him. No one seemed to care. Among the trees it was a secret world. As they moved up the gentle slope, their footfalls muffled by the thick carpet of pine needles, they could hear the shouted orders, the moans of the injured, the hissing and roaring from the burning wreck. It felt good to leave all that behind. Somehow it didn't seem to matter that their situation was now far more dangerous than it had been – exactly how much more, even Sutton couldn't guess at. There was for the moment a sense of freedom, and a half-conscious awareness of how the loss of Joe McCarr had drawn them together into a more challenging and intimate relationship.

As Sutton and the countess climbed, the sun began to sink in the west. Over there somewhere the Allies were pushing forward inexorably into the heart of Germany. Over there lay safety, the protection of the Anglo-American advance. But there could be no going back now. The sunset's crimson light, latticed by the tall pines' branches, picked out the path ahead of them, almost urging them on their way, as they moved purposefully eastwards.

CHAPTER TWENTY-THREE

THEY HAD GONE a couple of miles by the time night began to fall. The moon was no more than a thin crescent; there would be little light tonight once the last of the sun had gone. Sutton and the countess stood in a clearing on the ridge they had been following for the past fifteen minutes, and stared out over the darkening valleys. A spare pall of smoke showed the direction of the train crash site. There were still dim echoes of sound audible.

Sutton had a half-full packet of cigarettes in his coat pocket. He lit one, took a puff, handed it to the countess.

'Not a cocktail cigarette either,' he said. 'But then, this isn't a cocktail party.'

She accepted it, drew eagerly until she was suddenly sated, handed it back.

'George, what was going on back there?'

He breathed in deeply. The air was wonderful here. He felt he just wanted to fill his lungs with it, hold it, let it out, fill again forever.

'I don't know, to tell the truth. I've been giving it some thought during our little walk, and I still haven't got it clear. Tell me something,' he said, jabbing with the cigarette at the evening air. 'How do the German police handle foreigners? Would there be some kind of routine police surveillance of, for instance, foreign Red Cross personnel?'

'I don't know. Quite possibly,' the countess said bleakly. 'I'm not a policeman.'

'Keppler is.'

'He's not here. I don't recall him saying anything about such a thing.'

'Not his department.'

191

'Not directly.'

There was a tense silence, and then Sutton said, 'And Joe's not here either. I rushed us off. There wasn't time to do the proper thing, to mourn him. We were too busy surviving.'

The countess nodded. 'To survive is the only thing we can think of. It is what Joe would have done in our shoes. You mourn when you're in a safe place with plenty of time.'

Sutton looked at her with respect. She talked sense. His respect was not diminished when he realised that there were tears running down Helen Ackersberg's cheeks even as she spoke her sensible words. He reached out, she fell into his arms and they stood there for a long time, just holding each other.

'We can't wait around,' Sutton murmured finally. 'We have to use the light while it lasts, try to find a road, a village, get some bearings, before it gets too dark.'

'Yes. Of course. I'm sorry.'

'It's a big responsibility,' he said, shading his eyes with his hands so that he could look west and north-west along the ridge.

'Responsibility? What do you mean?'

'The job of crying for both of us,' Sutton said, 'because that's what you just did.'

He moved round, taking his eyes away from the sun, carried on inspecting the distance as far as he could see, then pointed. 'That's a tower. A wooden tower. I can see the top on the far side of the ridge, where it starts to slope down to the east. What is it? A prison camp, a military base or something?'

Helen followed the direction of his finger, looked carefully, shook her head.

'No. Such guard-towers are sturdier, more open. That is a foresters' tower, a lookout. In case people get lost, or they need to look out for forest fires, that kind of thing.'

'Let's head for it,' said Sutton. 'It'll give us a view to the east.'

It took about five minutes at fast walking pace, almost a run, for them to reach the tower. It looked far from sturdy – the countess had been right – and clearly hadn't been repaired or even minimally shored up in years. Nevertheless, Sutton clambered gingerly up the rickety, primitive wooden ladder to the platform.

'There's a lake about five, six miles away. A road beyond that. Others may be hidden in the forest.' Sutton paused. 'Also, some farm buildings. A mile away, something like that. A few outbuildings. We should head in that direction. As quickly as we can.'

The farm was run-down to look at, scruffily mediaeval. They could hear hens settling down for the night as they reached the edge of the clearing. They waited while a dog began to bark somewhere among the farm buildings. Then it stopped. Probably not a trained guard dog.

'It's hard to tell which is the house, which the cowshed and the stables,' said Sutton.

'It's there,' the countess said, pointing to a long, low half-timbered building that was indistinguishable, to Sutton's eye, from the others.

'How do you bloody well know that's the farmhouse? Second sight? I'm a city boy born and bred.'

She laughed softly. 'I'm not particularly expert myself. I used to spend as little of my time as possible on my husband's estate. It's just that if you look closely you'll see there's a telephone wire running into the building.'

'An unlikely thing in a place like this, a phone.'

'Could be the farmer's richer than he looks. German peasants have a way of concealing their wealth. It comes from the days not so long ago when the local robber baron would roast you over a slow fire to squeeze out your last *gröschen* in taxes. If he saw any signs of prosperity, that is. Anyway, sometimes in these lonely spots the state or the army subsidises phone installations, so that the locals can report on suspicious goings-on or forest fires, or whatever. Or so the foresters can use it in emergencies.'

'Thanks for the lecture. I'd guess it also means that the road can't be far away.'

'True. And there will be soldiers on the road, George. Heading up towards the front line. They move them at night to avoid the Allied bombers. I know that.'

Sutton nodded. 'It would be good to shelter here for the night. Early to bed, up before the sparrows and keep on walking.'

'To where?'

There was a long pause. 'We can choose to go forward. Or we can try to go south or south-west. Until we either intercept the Americans or we reach the Swiss border. We don't have our luggage, but we do have papers and money. Either way, whether we give up or we continue to Berlin, we could get picked up, arrested, shot out of hand, anything. Especially me. It's a choice.' Sutton said slowly. 'And it takes a unanimous decision.'

The countess settled down slightly with her back against a tree. 'In a way, it's up to me.'

'I can't make you do anything you don't want to. You've got a life to look forward to.'

She laughed, and this time the sound was harsh, hopeless.

'Sure. A hell of a life. No husband. The Russians have his land now, and they'll never give it back. There's no money outside the Ackersberg estates, you know, and the estates are gone.'

'At least you've got your family. Are they in Switzerland or in America?'

There was a pause, then the countess said, 'George, I think I had better come clean with you. My mother's dead. She died when I was twenty. She killed herself by jumping out of a tenth-storey window. That's why I came back to Europe. As for my father – ' she spat the word out like it was a piece of rotten fruit – 'he died two years ago, in the Louisiana State Penitentiary, near Baton Rouge. He was no Swiss patrician. He was from Basel all right, but his only background in high finance came from working as a messenger in a bank. But he was smart. He took off for the States and was able to make a lot of people believe he was a respectable Swiss financier. You see, he *looked* the part, and that was good enough for most Americans. I suppose that's where I learned that appearances are nine-tenths of reality. Anyway, Daddy dear rode the stock market boom as if the devil was after him. He borrowed a lot of money he had no intention of paying back. In other words, he was a con-man and a thief. So now you know. I'm a straw woman, George. All I've got in the world is Heinz Keppler. He's my only asset, my future . . . oh, and this coat. I've got two thousand Swiss francs sewn into the lining. That's all.'

'You've told a lot of lies,' Sutton said gently.

'It's a family trait,' she said. 'And if you really want to

know, when I came back to Europe, after Mummy died and they put Daddy in clink, I was a dance-hall hostess in Berlin. One of those places in the Friedrichstrasse where the men aren't interested in dancing, and where the title 'hostess' doesn't mean you're hot on seating arrangements or a good conversationalist.'

'You said you'd been to a good college.'

'Oh, that at least was true. I did two semesters at Vassar. Daddy was having a good year then. He had good years and bad years. All through my teens I'd spend a year or two at a nice expensive prep school, with vacations at the mansion in Connecticut or Long Island, wherever he'd managed to rent one furnished. Then Daddy would go broke again and I'd be pulled out . . . and then he would bring off some spectacular "business" coup and it would be back to another fancy prep school, never the same one because my family had blotted their copybook. I did 'em all – Brearly, Spence, Chapin. Needless to say, at the end of the second semester at Vassar the usual thing happened. He couldn't pay my room or tuition, and it was just after that he was arrested.' Helen von Ackersberg took a deep, painful breath. 'He got twenty years for a big swindle down in New Orleans. Something to do with offloading shipments of pork he knew were bad. He was pretty far gone by then, old Erich Zweig, stooping really low. People died – poor people – because of that bad meat.'

'No family, no husband,' said Sutton. 'Only Heinz Keppler. And the contents of your coat.' He smiled at the irony of it all. 'We seem to have an awful lot in common, countess.'

'Please, I said to call me Helen.'

He touched her on the shoulder. 'Just my sense of humour. I like the way it trips off the tongue, the word "countess". What was the count like?'

'Ackersberg was a good man in his way. When we met, I told him I was about to start a degree in English at Humboldt University and that all my family were dead. We met at a charity ball, by the way, not at a dance-hall! I don't think he believed me, but he was kind enough to pretend that he did. I never did start the degree, he never asked why, and anyway we were married soon after.'

Sutton nodded. 'All right, shall we take a closer look at the

195

farm, see if we find some shelter? That barn over there is a bit apart from the others and well away from the house.'

'Okay. It's good to get these things out in the open. You know, even Heinz – '

'Tell me some other time,' Sutton said, and his voice was suddenly sharp. 'I don't think I can listen to your problems with Keppler as well as all the rest, love. If we ever get to Berlin, we're going to have to depend on him, aren't we? So let me keep some of my illusions.'

'Of course. I'm sorry, George. It was nothing serious.'

They left the cover of the trees and set off slowly across the paddock. There was a big cart horse grazing in the far corner. Sutton cocked an ear for the dog. It had sounded old, lazy, the kind that barked half-heartedly at the slightest noise or scent, so often indiscriminately that his master paid no mind any more, but you could never be absolutely certain.

The barn was tumbledown, still partly filled with hay left over from the winter. The cows themselves were two buildings away, in a more modern-looking shed, milked and barred in for the night. A tiny chink in the blackout curtain betrayed the fact that the farmer had retreated into his house.

The bales were sloppily stored, mostly grouped in one corner, making a natural hideout. They picked their way in the darkness, guiding themselves by touch into the space. There was just enough room to lie down.

'All right?' Sutton asked.

'Fine. I guess we can use our coats for blankets.'

The hay was stale and grey with age. When they did lie down, careful not to touch in that way that contains far more than casual, natural physical contact, the silence was a tangible energy. Outside, the Thuringian countryside was gently stirred by winds, but inside the barn there was a quiet as intense as the loudest noise.

'George,' the countess said very softly. 'I want to say something. I need to.'

'All right. Just keep your voice down, love.'

'I know you said you didn't want to hear about Heinz, but – well, I need to explain something.'

A wait. Then: 'Go ahead, countess.'

'Thanks.' For a moment she searched for the right words, the right tone. 'I . . . don't love Heinz any more. In the early

196

days, of course, he seemed an attractive man, everything was very good – in bed and out. It's all right if I'm frank? Anyway, I realised after a while some things about him and the nature of his job, and I didn't like them. Neither did he, and I can't say exactly why but things went wrong. Are you listening, George?'

'Yes.' His voice was throaty, impossible for her to interpret.

'Well . . . we . . . Heinz and I . . . we don't make love any more. Heinz can't. He says he feels so bad about everything, so guilty and so worried. It is psychological, to do with his guilt because, you know when there was the conspiracy to kill Hitler, his friend Arthur Nebe, the boss of the Criminal Police, was involved. He wanted Heinz to be part of the plot, but Heinz couldn't bring himself to betray everything he had once believed in. Or so he said. It was around that time I started to doubt my own feelings for Heinz.'

'Why tell me this?' Sutton interrupted. He had to stop the breathless torrent of words pouring out of her. His question was just a device, because he knew perfectly well what she was leading up to.

The countess sighed. 'It's obvious, isn't it? You're not so dumb you don't realise, George. I'm a normal woman. I respect strength and I need comfort. I want you, George. I want a man, but in particular I want *you*.'

Sutton felt the countess reaching out for him in the darkness. He searched for her hand and held it. Suddenly, without warning, she rolled over onto him. She lay pressed against him tightly, breathing heavily and almost sobbing with the relief of the touching, the pressing of her body against Sutton's. Her skirt had ridden up around her thighs. When she let go of his hand it was only to christen it with her lips and then press his palms and fingers against the warm flesh. Her free hand slid inside his jacket.

'I – want – *you* . . .'

The softness, fragrance, the violence of the need that overwhelmed them both felt natural, right. Sutton responded, moving headlong into territory where the heart, the head, the body were all one.

As his finger reached the silk hollow where the countess's thighs met her belly, and he began to do what she wanted him so much to do, he thought of his night at Mornington Crescent

197

with Rose Wesolowski, and knew that it had been no more than preparation for this. That had been ninety percent opportunity, ten percent mechanical lust. This was the real thing. Then thought seemed to disappear, and his mind became a receiver, with no past and no future, just an organiser of impressions. Soft, hot skin, wild scents, sounds and sensations. Immersed in a primal dream, guarded by the darkness of the Thuringian hayloft that black-satin spring night, Sutton and Helen von Ackersberg made love with the blind, compelling instinct of animals.

He took her, she took him, every way, meeting no resistance to their invention in the yielding hay, until the countess wrapped her long legs around Sutton, feeling his jet and her final leap into total abandon beginning. And they bucked their way together into an exploding rush of fulfilment, of pleasure that seemed to have no beginning and no end.

CHAPTER TWENTY-FOUR

SUTTON COULD FEEL the warmth of Helen von Ackersberg's breast against his bare chest. He sighed, half-woke, registered a rooster crowing somewhere close, began to be aware of the special, damp chill of the hour before a spring dawn. He wasn't expecting the touch of a cold wet tongue on his neck, and it brought him to his senses with the force of an electric shock.

Something poured foetid, sour breath into his face, there was a panting and a blur of clumsy movement among the hay. Sutton's eyes snapped wide open, and he found himself staring into the mottled, bloodshot eyes of an extremely elderly Dobermann pinscher. Elderly, but that didn't mean harmless. They eyed each other warily. The dog may have retained some distant personal or race memory of his breed's fearsome reputation for savagery, but if so it had obviously decided to let its instincts lapse on retirement, because it broke the silent standoff by licking him again, this time on the end of his nose, and whimpering appealingly.

Sutton's first instinct was to snort with laughter and relief. It didn't last long. How had the dog got here? Then he heard a door slam across the farmyard, and he knew he had to move quickly, and rouse the countess too. He shook her, hard.

'Wake up, Helen. Quick. Don't be frightened of the dog. Just wake up, wake up, get ready. I'll be back in a moment.'

Then he was on his feet, pushing the unresisting – just slightly offended – dog out of the way, tucking his shirt into the waistband of his trousers as soon as he could button himself up. Within twenty seconds he was on his way to the door of the barn in the miserly light, knocking over an iron bucket as he went – that hadn't been there last night or one of them would have tripped on it then – and picking up speed towards the house, the soles of his shoes slapping against the dewy grass.

The door to the farmhouse was slightly ajar. A hurricane lamp in the corner gave out enough light to show him a short, wiry man in his seventies with fierce eyes and a silver moustache, thick and curled at the corners like the old Kaiser's. He was talking wildly into the old-fashioned wind-up telephone on the kitchen table, saying, '*Ja*. In the barn. I already told you six times. You come quick – '

The old farmer saw Sutton, reached out with a knotty left arm for the shotgun that lay on the table next to the phone, yelled one last time: 'This criminal is now in the house! You come fast!' Then he laid the phone down, so that whoever was on the other end could still listen in, and levelled the gun at Sutton.

For a moment they eyed each other in silence. It was not unlike Sutton's eyeball-to-eyeball confrontation with the dog, except that this veteran had a gun, looked as though he had used it a few times in his life, and had no intention of throwing it away and giving Sutton a lick.

'*Hören Sie!*' – listen! – croaked the farmer, bizarrely addressing himself as much to the telephone as to Sutton. Perhaps even the illusion of contact with authority gave him strength. 'I will shoot! I have called the police and they are on their way! Put your hands up and surrender!'

Framed as he was in the doorway, Sutton knew he presented a wonderful target, a target the old man's trembling trigger finger could start firing at as much by chance as design if he stayed much longer. The game was up. There was no stopping anything. The only important thing was to get the hell out of here.

'I'll shoot!' the old man repeated his threat once too often.

Sutton was now almost certain that he wouldn't, unless he made a move towards him. So he took his life in his hands, turned, and began to sprint back towards the barn, shouting for Helen. She appeared at the door of the barn, looking surprisingly composed, fully dressed and carrying his coat.

Still without a word, he scooped her by the arm and they began to run through the farmyard. There seemed to be a track leading through some trees, and it seemed the only route that could lead to a road. Ducking behind a cattle byre to avoid passing the house and the armed farmer, even though it meant a considerable detour, they headed on towards the pink beginnings of dawn in the east. There must lie the road. There their luck would show itself; there their fate would be decided one way or the other.

They ran for two, three hundred yards, forgetting the old man. Sutton slipped on his coat without breaking his stride, and still neither said a single word. They didn't need to. There was as much naturalness, as much unspoken understanding, in all this as in the previous night's love-making. He found himself thinking, I don't care about Keppler, or this woman's past, or anything, all that much, but may God grant me some life beyond this to enjoy her, because I've never known anything like it before.

It was another couple of minutes before they sighted the road, a fairly well-surfaced highway, more major than Sutton had expected. Perhaps this farm was not so remote after all. They would head for the trees that he could see on the far side, perhaps then follow the road under cover of the woods towards a village, see if they could find their bearings that way. It would be harder going than just walking the highway, but then it would be foolish risking running into a police wagon.

At the junction, Sutton thought he heard a faint shot from the farmhouse. The old bastard must be venting his frustrations, he thought. He turned to the countess to tell her too.

Then the headlights pinned them like helpless night creatures, caught in the open with nowhere to hide from the day.

Sutton pushed Helen ahead towards the trees, but already as he looked to his left and saw the figure standing up in the Kübelwagen jeep, he knew it was useless. How did the cops get here so damned quickly? he thought dully. Then he realised that there were several vehicles behind the Kübelwagen and that they were painted in army field grey. Sutton cursed under his breath as he stood with his arm firmly linked in the countess's, watching the machine-gun that was trained on them from the jeep and examining the booted figure who was climbing out of the front seat and beginning to walk over towards them.

When he came within a few feet, they could see clearly that

he was an officer, that he seemed young, and that he had a patch over his left eye. He was also languidly unbuttoning his holster as he walked.

'What's going on? What are you doing springing around the road like March hares, eh? You're a month too late, and far too grownup to play games.'

His accent was strong, South German or possibly Austrian. Close up, his sallow face was twenty-five going on sixty.

Beside him, Helen von Ackersberg drew herself up. Sutton could feel her pulling all her strength together, inflating herself like a beautiful, lifelike rubber doll, bringing in the air from the ground up. She was her father's daughter, he realised more poignantly than every before. Child of the Swiss con-man, the oh-so-convincing phantasm of middle-class solidity to whom even the most devious of Wall Street predators and Florida real estate sharks had entrusted their cash without a qualm.

'Good morning, Herr Hauptmann,' she said. 'I am the Countess Helen von Ackersberg.' She slowly pulled out the precious Red Cross papers and Swiss passport that were in her coat pocket, held them out to him. 'This,' she said, indicating Sutton, 'is Herr Gustav Salvesen, a Swedish national and representative of the International Committee of the Red Cross. We are on official business.'

The army captain took off his cap, scratched his cropped head.

'Interesting,' he said then, taking the papers and sorting through them like a hand of cards. 'I like your style. I ask you what you are doing hopping about the highway at five-thirty in the morning and you simply tell me you are a countess, and he is a Swedish Red Cross official, and that is that. Obviously you consider that sufficient explanation.'

'Perhaps it is, Hautpmann. However, I might also add that we need to be in Berlin within the next twenty-four hours, on a humanitarian mission, and that we should be grateful for any assistance you could grant us.'

He grinned, looked at Sutton. 'Salvesen, eh? I was in Norway earlier on in the war, you know. A year's garrison duty. And very pleasant it was too.'

Sutton made an effort to nod politely.

'*Du has tur som är ved livet. Jag slar vad am att du hellre vore hemma med en öl, eller hur*?' the Hauptmann said haltingly, and chuckled.

Sutton smiled. 'Of course, Norwegian is as different from Swedish as Dutch is from German,' he said.

'Well, one learned a few phrases,' the Hauptmann said mildly. He clapped his hands together, as if he had made a decision, turned to the driver and the man with the gun, who were both watching the scene from the leading vehicle. 'I intend to take this gentleman and lady into Nauen and see what I can do for them. They are important people who have lost their way and we can't have them running around the countryside. Something might happen to them.'

'Of course not, Hauptmann,' the driver said crisply.

'Shift yourself. I have decided that I shall drive them myself. Corporal, you and Private Spatz will ride behind in the truck. The Swiss lady will sit in front with me, the gentleman behind.' He made a cavalier bow.

'Is it wise for Herr Hauptmann – '

'Do as I tell you, corporal. These people are perfectly harmless and one of them is a countess. Shoo! – '

'Yes, Hauptmann.'

'Herr Hauptmann,' Helen began, 'perhaps if I might just have a chance to discuss this with my colleague . . .'

'Oh, I'm afraid not. This *is* in the nature of duty for me. Protective custody would be too strong a word, but I'm afraid I have to say my invitation is also a kind of an order.' He gestured smoothly towards the Kübelwagen. The man with the machine-pistol was standing by the running board, with the gun pointing down towards the road but obviously ready to fire, just in case.

'Of course, Hauptmann. I'm sure you're a busy man. Perhaps you will be able to put us on a train at Nauen?'

'Perhaps.'

Sutton was installed in the back of the jeep, the countess settled into the passenger seat next to the officer, who introduced himself as Hauptmann Otmar Panowsky, from Vienna, and assured them that he was 'at their service' in that careful, smiling Austrian way that was impossible to penetrate.

'Get in the truck behind, Spatz,' he told the soldier with the machine-pistol. 'Just watch carefully, all right?'

'Yes, Hauptmann.'

The man saluted smartly, bringing his right hand up to his temple in the old army way – no Hitler salutes here, despite the fact that it had been technically compulsory since the July plot against the Führer. The captain returned the salute, offered cigarettes around, lit each passenger's carefully, and within a few moments the column moved off down the road. The Hauptmann drove at its head with obvious enjoyment, explaining that he loved to take the wheel but needed an excuse such as this. One could not leave a countess to the mercies of a corporal-driver, after all.

They had gone two kilometres or so when they were forced to pull over almost to the verge to allow a police car to race past.

'Aha. The gentlemen of the Criminal Police. Or is it the Gestapo?' said the Hauptmann conversationally. He laughed. His laugh had an unnerving, knowing quality. 'We just got away in time. Or rather, *you* did.'

Helen glanced at him, trying hard to seem puzzled and hurt. 'Hauptmann, we have nothing to fear. Our papers are perfectly in order. I have had frequent dealings with your police.'

'Maybe.' He turned as he drove, grinned at Sutton. 'Your papers may be in order, my dear man, but your knowledge of your native language is all over the place.'

Sutton stiffened, clenched his fists in frustration, aware of the man in the truck behind with the machine-pistol.

'I misunderstand you,' he said. What else could he answer?

'Absolutely. You know what I said to you back there?' Panowsky explained gaily. He did not wait, because he was not expecting an answer. 'I told you were lucky to be alive. And I bet you'd rather be at home with a cold beer. In Swedish, not Norwegian. You see, I have also served in Finland, where Swedish is the second language, spoken by many, many people. I picked up a good smattering. Easier than learning Finnish, which is heathen nonsense, with no relationship to any known civilised language.'

Helen kept her eyes on the road ahead and said: 'It's very hard to explain.'

'Now, you are a real Swiss,' the Hauptmann said. 'A cool customer – at least under these circumstances,' he qualified his statement gallantly. 'As for explanations, I don't want any.

I don't really care who you are, you or your friend. Jews on the run. Allied airmen who took a dive. Spies. Ambassadors from Mars, for all I know.' He frowned. 'It's too late in the day. If you're trying to get *into* Berlin, you're crazy anyway. Everyone else with any sense is desperate to get out of there before the Russians arrive. As a pair, you have a certain insane style about you.'

'Thank you,' said Helen, glancing back at Sutton. He was staring ahead in stupefied silence.

'Of course,' Panowsky added after a few moments had passed, 'I'm not doing this just because I like your style.' He lit a cigarette skilfully, one-handed. 'You see, I had a brother once. He was a student in Vienna – a medic, so they were letting him do a year or so before they stuck him in uniform and shipped him off to the slaughter.' He took a deep breath of nicotine, and now his pale-blue eyes were hard. 'Well, my brother – Franz-Xavier, his name was – nineteen years old and a real idealist, he and some of his friends at the university decided they were going to agitate for a free Austria, and so they produced some leaflets to that effect, put them into a few solid citizens' mailboxes. They were arrested quick as a wink, of course. And beheaded. Just like that. Hardly old enough to shave, any of them.'

'I'm sorry.'

'My kid-brother's misfortune is your good luck. I'm not handing anyone over to those bastards. Joe Stalin, Winston Churchill, could walk around the corner and I'd give 'em shelter and send them on their way. And I may as well tell you now that you are in luck, because we have been ordered to a place just south of Berlin. We have instructions to report there, sit on the *Autobahn* and wait for the Communist hordes I just hope for all your sakes that they're not already there. If you can stand my company, you're welcome to come along. All that protective custody nonsense was for my men. And because it speeded things up'

Sutton grunted. He would have to trust Hauptmann Panowsky. There was no choice. 'I can tell you one thing. The Russians are the last people we want to meet. You can cross them off your list.'

'My dear pseudo-Swede friend, I told you I don't want to know anything. I may be kind-hearted, but I'm not quite suicidal. In the unlikely event that we're stopped and there's any trouble with your papers or your Scandinavian credentials, you're on your own.'

'That's pretty reasonable.'

In the grey little Thuringian town, Hauptmann Panowsky stopped to make his phone calls at district headquarters and they waited in the vehicle, surrounded by the men of the captain's unit.

'So we could say our mind was made up for us,' the countess said. 'Last night, we were wondering whether to press on to Berlin or turn back, and here we are.' She ran her fingers through her hair, tossed it free, making an expression of faint distaste at how greasy it was, yet also aware of the lustful glances that the Hauptmann's soldiery were casting in her direction. 'Unless, of course, our captain's stringing us along and he's on the phone to Gestapo headquarters at this very moment.'

'That's a chance we have to take,' Sutton said. 'I think that if he'd been intending to shop us to the Gestapo, he'd have put us under proper guard. I know the type. He may seem very casual, but he's a military man to his fingertips.'

She nodded. 'If that's so, then we're about to travel to Berlin in the safest way possible.'

Hauptmann Panowsky finally emerged from the squat, modern barracks that housed the district headquarters. He had a brief discussion with the corporal-driver, slapped him on the back, walked over to the *Kübelwagen*.

'We're in luck,' he said. 'The Russians have not yet arrived in Berlin. I assume they are waiting for us to take up our positions. Sporting fellows, the Ivans.' He paused. 'Listen, I could take you to the station. They tell me there is a train to Berlin due to leave around mid-day, but one can never tell, of course, these days. And there are risks. A train was bombed by the Americans only yesterday.'

'You've convinced us, Hauptmann. We'll come with you if your offer's still open,' Sutton said.

'Of course it is. The trip will be tedious and uncomfortable, especially for you in the back seat. But don't worry, Herr Salvesen.' Hauptmann Panowsky swung himself into the driver's seat with his habitual unsettling laugh. 'I can give you Swedish lessons on the way if you like.'

CHAPTER TWENTY-FIVE

THE WINDOW was creaking in the wind. That was Coletti's first thought when he half-awoke. Then he remembered that there was no window. It had been thirty-six hours since he had arrived in Berlin and knocked on Mario Liggio's house in the working-class district of Moabit, close to the huge, mock-Gothic prison building. During the few hours that he was not personally staking out Heinz Keppler's apartment, he slept here in this windowless basement. It was cold, but dry and well-insulated. No noise or damp or smell leaked in or out. Here in this room, someone had told him, Don Mario sometimes kept men who had cheated, insulted or otherwise displeased him. Here they would stay until he decided what to do with them. It was a good, secure room, a place to hide and be hidden. Coletti knew that other men had suffered and perhaps died in this dark, comfortless place, but the thought did not distract him or lessen his vigilant lust for life. So what was this sound? In the pitch-blackness, his fingers encircled the knife beneath his pillow, and he watched and listened.

A faint scratching and shuffling persisted like a mouse on flagstones. The handle of the basement door was turning slowly. He did not move, except to bring the hand holding his knife to his side with the very tiniest of rustles against the fresh cotton sheets. Whoever was coming in must be light and timid, unknowing or crazy.

For his part, Coletti was at peace with the situation. He had been awake for some time already, considering his plans for the day to come. This immediate, local contingency puzzled him. Was anyone stupid enough to believe that his knife ever strayed beyond the reach of his arm?

The door opened a few inches. Coletti tensed, or rather he

put his body on alert, a well-tempered machine ready to fire into life. If necessary, he decided, he could roll onto the floor and throw his knife as he rolled. He had done that before; it would be no trouble.

The hand that then came into view was slim and dark, and it carried a candle-holder with a flickering night light. In that moment Coletti felt grateful that he was not the kind of man who needed to panic or over-react. No, this was a problem of a different kind, not one that could be solved with a knife.

He had experienced intimations of this particular problem the previous evening, when there had been long, lingering looks while he ate his meal of cabbage soup and coarse pasta. This was a case not for violence but for the utmost diplomacy, the most subtle manipulative skills.

'Good morning, kid,' he said very softly, with a degree of amusement but carefully avoiding any suggestion of seduction. 'Stay where you are. Don't come in any further. That's an order.'

She opened the door quietly but very quickly and stood on the threshold.

'I couldn't stay away from you,' she whispered.

'Little Maria, this is bad and dangerous. I'm a Sicilian man and you, though you were born in Germany, are a Sicilian girl.'

'Don't call me a girl,' she hissed petulantly. 'I'm a woman. And you have been to America. You're different, you know everything. My father – '

'Your father would kill us both if he knew you were here in this room. Do you realise that?'

Maria Liggio took a step into the room, tossed her head in a way that was intended to be provocative but ended up plain gauche. But the way she put the candle down on the packing-case by the door was disturbingly definite. She was slender, still girlish, it was true, but soon she would be seventeen and she was ripening quickly. Her hair was dark but her skin pale, and Coletti thought fleetingly, with a sharp stab of longing, of the northern girl from Rome, and all the other fair-complexioned ones before her. This was a pity, but business came first, and in such an old-fashioned Sicilian household as this, even the most superficial matters of the heart involved life and death.

'Maria. Don't move. You must go.'

She laughed throatily in a way that betrayed knowledge beyond her years. Coletti felt glad that he was not her father. This girl was trouble. Quite how much trouble, she proceeded to reveal.

'I could cry out. My father would find us.'

It was ridiculous, this child's game, but Coletti felt a momentary anxiety. He was still holding his knife under the cover of the pillow. It was so tempting just to throw it, stop her, solve the problem, explain everything later, maybe even Don Mario dealt with if he caused trouble. A man should bring up his daughter better than this, or pay the consequences.

'You would regret that very much. I don't think you realise how much,' he said.

'My father loves me. And you are an important man. He is frightened of you, and so he would not harm us.'

'His honour would matter to him more than either of those things,' Coletti insisted as gently as he could.

'I know exactly the kind of man Don Mario is. A very fine man, and a good one, but as proud as the biggest boss in Palermo.'

His words seemed to sink in. The girl frowned, bit her lip.

'Then let me talk to you for a while,' she said, changing her tone of voice. Now she was really a girl, a little girl. 'I want to talk to an important man, who has lived in America. And who is handsome and strong. Not like those stupid German boys.'

'Maria, I think you have spent too long with German boys,' Coletti said, and gave her a fatherly smile to put things on the right footing. 'If they're anything like American boys, they don't know how to behave with a good Sicilian girl. Let me assure you, on the other hand, that I certainly do. That is why I am telling you to go back to your bed.'

'Please talk to me about – '

'Go back up to bed. One day I'll be back. Then I'll spend time with you and tell you about America.'

It was a lie, but a permissible one. On second thoughts it might not be untrue at all. When the war was over and peacetime business was established, he might well come back. Not skulking, furtive, but openly and like a prince. Just get to bed, girl, he thought, and save everyone a lot of trouble.

'You'll talk to me. Just to me. Will you?'

'Of course.'

A half-truth this time. Such a girl as this, though she might come from the best of families, was too wild for his taste. Too wild to marry, that was. And to use her for a romantic, sexual interlude would be unthinkable.

'I . . . I would very much like to go to America. I want to find a strong, handsome man like you who will take me there.'

Coletti smiled to himself in the semi-darkness. 'I think soon America will come to you, little one. Mind you behave yourself.'

Impulsively the girl stepped forward, reached over and kissed him on the forehead, at the same time resting her hand on his bare shoulder. She smelled slightly smokey – the family still had open fires at night – and the womanly part of her scent was as fresh and pure as spring flowers. Coletti groaned inwardly. If circumstances had been different, and if she were not who she was, what a blossom to pluck and enjoy.

He pushed her gently away, and as he did so the sheet moved and rode up slightly to reveal the blade of his knife lying next to him between the pillow and the undersheet.

The girl murmured a childish oath to a saint, recoiled. The look in her eyes told him that she was both frightened and excited.

'I tell you. Go to bed, girl,' he said, and could not resist adding: 'When you're married you'll learn something about the world of men. It's not the same as the world of women.'

She crossed herself, but still hovered between the door and the bed, staring at him and at the spot where the knife had been, even though he had quickly covered it with a sheet. When he put a finger to his lips to advise silence, and winked, she smiled with small white teeth as if a favourite uncle had just made a joke that was theirs and theirs alone to share.

'I'm not so terrible,' said Coletti. 'At least only to my enemies. Now, be off with you to bed and dream of the husband you're supposed to be keeping yourself pure for.'

Maria left without another word.

To his relief, Coletti's diplomacy had ultimately proved successful. He lay for some moments on his narrow bed, staring into the darkness, the smile fading on his lips now that it no longer served any purpose. This family would come to no good. He would not use them in future. Liggio spoiled his daughter: it was his weakness, the one thing that undermined his pride and cunning. A man who was not in control in his own home could not be relied on to perform his allotted tasks without faltering. This one factor undermined everything that made Liggio of use to the men of respect, the ones they called the Mafia, the 'Friends'. *Cosa Nostra* or 'Our Thing'. Worse, it could make Liggio a potential danger.

It was now almost four a.m. In half an hour he was due to relieve Liggio's nephew, who was keeping up the vigil outside Keppler's apartment in the Kantstrasse while Coletti grabbed this sleep. Mario Liggio had supplied papers and suggested special details that enabled Coletti to move around the city of Berlin in safety – more safely than most of its legitimate citizens, he reflected.

Coletti leaned over, located and lit the kerosene lamp by the side of the bed. Before its fumes permeated the room, he fancied that he could smell the girl's elusive, sweet perfume. He shook his head and slid quietly out of bed, deciding that more sleep was neither necessary nor possible tonight. She was a little fool, that Maria, he thought as he dressed. Sooner or later, the Americans would arrive here in Berlin. When they did, some crazy, fast-talking G.I. would sweep her off her feet, and Don Mario would probably end up in front of an army court, on trial for killing a member of the Allied occupying forces. Everyone concerned would have his profoundest sympathy, he decided, wherever he might be.

And in the light of Liggio's faults, such an outcome might save much trouble for future *capo* Johnny Coletti, not forgetting Prism's busy, clever blade.

CHAPTER TWENTY-SIX

THE AGEING tram rattled along the wide cobbled boulevard. Panowsky's unit had dropped them close to the autobahn, a kilometre or so east of Michendorf. Helen knew that the most suitable route lay through Potsdam, following the main flow of commuter traffic into Berlin itself.

Potsdam, the old royal seat of Prussia – the kings' and Kaisers' Versailles – was a town of wide streets, elegant buildings, official prosperity. In the crowded tramcar, Helen von Ackersberg and Sutton stood holding grimly on to straps with the rest of the commuters, rubbing elbows with civil servants and men in uniform, and at this time of the morning women with string bags and shopping baskets, many of them obviously once well-off, even pampered, now reduced to scouring the stores for rationed foods and presenting themselves in threadbare finery. It was amazing how, even in a city preparing for one of history's greatest sieges, life went on with something approximating to normality. Who had done the shopping in Troy, in Jersualem, in beleaguered Atlanta with Sherman's battle-crazed Yankees at the gates? Maybe the same sort of women who still stubbornly maintained the rituals needed to feed their families, keep life going for another day or two before Armageddon finally struck. Thousands of Berliners would die with their underwear clean and with food in their bellies.

Through the window Sutton glimpsed the grey-blue elbow of the Havel, the river that snakes across the western rim of Berlin and broadens out until it became a lake which the Berliners call the *Jungfernsee*, the virgin's lake.

'How much longer?' he asked the countess.

'Thirty minutes or so. We have to cross the Glienicke bridge

212

into Berlin itself. From here, providing the tramway isn't blocked, through the southwesterm suburbs to the centre. Heinz's flat, you know – '

'Yes, I know his flat. If it's the same one in the . . . ah . . . Kantstrasse.'

'The same.' She squeezed his arm, ran her tongue along her lips as if they were dry.

'Of course, I only went there once. For drinks with some other men from the conference,' Sutton added almost apologetically.

She nodded, a faint smile of guilty complicity spreading slowly over her face. Then she stiffened, turned to look at Sutton directly. 'I'm afraid.'

Somehow he knew what the countess meant. She was talking not about the risks of the mission as such, but about how it would feel to see Keppler again. She and Sutton had had virtually no chance to touch, let alone talk, since waking up together in the farmer's hayloft the previous morning. And yet so much had changed, the balance of their world, their desires and expectations, had tipped dramatically. Where to, Sutton had no idea. But if the countess was frightened, it showed she knew it too.

'Wise woman,' he said. 'There's plenty to fear.'

'I suppose I'd been keeping up a facade, relying just on maintaining the equilibrium, the appearance of normality.'

'Normality can become an obsession,' Sutton said. 'The worse things get, the more you cling to it.'

She gave a short, snorting laugh, more like a gasp of relief coming up for air. Her eyes told him she was not sure she wouldn't go under again, into whatever form of drowning happened for her some or even most of the time.

'I suppose we have to speak in code,' she said with a gesture of helplessness.

A man in uniform with an attaché case under his arm looked at Helen sharply. He wore an army major's shoulder-flashes, had wire-grey hair and intensely inquisitive eyes.

The countess squeezed Sutton's arm again, to his surprise nuzzled into his neck and kissed him. The shock of contact went through his whole body. It was all he could do to stop himself from crushing her to him on the spot.

'I needed that anyway, darling. Also, that officer heard

me. I'd rather he thought we were adulterers than spies,' she whispered. 'Excuse me, won't you?'

'Pardon granted.'

She withdrew her lips, as if regretting her impulsive expression of feeling and said, just loud enough for the attentive major could hear: 'Soon I'll tell Heinz. I'll ask for my freedom. Then we won't have to speak in code any more, darling.'

The major's look of suspicion was replaced by one of amused disapproval. Then he looked away.

The tramcar slowed down to walking pace, allowing its passengers to see that the approaches to the bridge across the river had been stacked with sandbags. Two machine-gun emplacements were already in place just in front of the first spans of the steel structure. Close up, the uniformed figures working on the bridge's defences were revealed as boys no older than thirteen or fourteen.

Sutton's watch told him that it was eleven-fifteen when they finally reached the corner of Weimarer Strasse and Kantstrasse. There was a bombed-out lot, a delicatessen that still seemed open for business of a kind, and a grilled doorway leading to a dive called the *Groschenkeller*. His and the countess's clothes were becoming creased and worn-looking. They fitted in easily among the war-weary Germans, many of whom had spent yet another night in cellars and air-raid shelters. Every night the British sent a squadron or two of Mosquitos over Berlin to keep the city's defences on their toes. Both of them were also authentically footsore; they had been forced to get off the tram because the lines had been destroyed by bombing in Schöneberg. They had managed to catch an S-bahn train that went right through to the Zoo station in the city's West End, near the Kurfürstendamm. From there it was ten minutes on foot to the street where Heinz Keppler had lived for nearly eight years.

Several buildings in the neighbourhood had been completely destroyed. Others were half-exposed to the elements. Life carried on in the cellars, in apartments where with the coming of the warmer spring weather Berliners had plugged the gaps in the walls with boxes, sacking, anything to give a degree of shelter. On the entrances to shattered apartment blocks here, as in the rest of Berlin, were scrawled messages of new addresses. 'Family Stolz at Augsburger Strasse 13 II . . . Family Vogel/Breidenstein Schöneberg Kufsteiner Strasse 43', and of simple defiant survival: 'The Vietheers are still alive'.

'Now, just keep walking naturally, with your head down, as if we know exactly where we're going. The apartments on the third storey, about a hundred yards along on the right.'

Sutton nodded, took her arm. They began to move briskly along the street, silent but absorbed, like one of those married couples with a joint routine but separate lives.

'I look up very casually,' the countess murmured. 'Just as if I'm looking at the sky to check the weather . . . you keep looking straight ahead, George . . . and . . .' She caught her breath. 'Keep walking,' she said quietly but very, very insistently. 'Keep on and keep natural. We're going somewhere else, somewhere very different . . .'

They reached the next corner, turned off up the cross street, ready to double back eastwards towards the Zoo station.

'We have to get away from here, very fast,' she said, almost tumbling over her own words. When Sutton looked sideways at her he saw that her eyes were bright with fear and a kind of excitement. 'There was a signal Heinz and I agreed on. Flowers in the loungeroom window of the apartment. It meant the Gestapo bloodhounds were sniffing too close and he had to make for the cottage. Müller's probably got men up there waiting for us.'

As they walked, the countess explained that they would have to find their way down to the south-west of the city again. The new rendezvous was at Nikolaussee, a thirty-minute journey on the S-bahn from here – if it was still running.

Now the situation had changed incalculably. The police tails on the train journey could have been normal procedure with a foreign group such as theirs. But the presence of Gestapo at Keppler's flat put a dangerously different complexion on all that. Not necessarily, but possibly. They had reason to be grateful for Keppler's careful planning and the countess's obedience. They also had reason to be very, very careful.

They returned to the Zoo station, entering by the subway next to Aschinger's eating house. There were some patrols in the ticket hall, police and army, checking papers. Fortunately they seemed mainly concerned with picking on stray soldiers and long-haul passengers, especially a large group of refugees that had just arived from the battle zone east of the city. A little girl stared gravely up at a tall N.C.O. who was questioning her mother. She wore a fur-trimmed coat with a pixie hood, and the rucksack on her back apparently contained nothing much besides a large, well-loved china doll, whose one remaining eye seemed to stare at Sutton unblinkingly with the same kind of high-gloss terror that he had seen in the countess's eyes when she had realised that Keppler was not at the apartment.

The hall smelled of humanity close to the end of its tether but trying desperately to believe in order and safety. The weary passengers displayed their papers almost gratefully, as if they provided some guarantee of the right to survival, and the near-hysterical bellowing of the loudspeakers announced ever-changing details of arrivals, departures, cancellations. Just behind them in the line for tickets there stood a swarthy man of indeterminate age, dressed in an oversized cap and poor worker's clothes. One leg dragged behind him, there was a patch over one eye, and the left arm of his jacket was pinned up where flesh and sinew should have been. The man's eyes were dull but somehow satisfied. It struck Sutton that perhaps the safest thing to be in embattled Berlin was an amputee. Nevertheless, he felt a kind of guilty relief that he had his ticket in his pocket and was on his way to the platform where a train was promised, and that – so far – he had a whole body.

The lake, with its thick cloak of trees, sparkled coolly in the afternoon sunshine. The city of Berlin, its millions bracing themselves for the savage military whirlwind from the east, was only a few kilometres away, but here was another world; an idyll of woods and water caught before it dissolved in violence.

'Even last autumn you would have seen the sailing boats out there,' the countess murmured as they picked their way through the birch trees that fringed the water, following a shady path still slippery from days-old spring rains.

Sutton made no comment. There was something deceptive about this piece of heaven. It wasn't entitled to be this way. Maybe he believed that nothing was. Perhaps he just couldn't take life, and happiness, at face value.

There was a hut scarcely bigger than a garden shed further

on. It had a wooden window box filled with blooming primroses.

'Not that. Another two or three hundred yards. You can't quite see it yet,' she said. 'God, we're like strange guests turning up for the weekend from far away.' She giggled. 'And we've taken *so* much trouble to get here . . .'

Suddenly, as they drew level with the little building, the shutters on the hut's only visible window were flung open. Like a cuckoo poking out to signal the hour, an old man's wizened, weatherbeaten face appeared.

'Fräulein,' the man said wheezily. 'So you are back to hide from the Russians with your friends, eh? I think they will find you anyway, God help us all.'

'Herr Nautschke,' the countess responded with a tight but genuine smile. 'It has been quite a long time, hasn't it?'

'And much has happened. I am old. I don't care what happens to me. It is you young people I feel sorry for. I know this is for our sins. Good-bye and good luck to you. And the gentleman.'

He looked at them both with a kind of demented pity, then slammed the shutters as abruptly as he had opened them.

Sutton waited until they had gone twenty yards or so down the track.

'Who was that? You know him?' he demanded.

'Of course,' she said. 'Relax. That's Herr Nautschke. He's lived here for nearly thirty years, ever since he was invalided out of the First War. Mustard gas got his lungs. He's okay. A little crazy, very sweet.'

'Do you trust him, Helen?'

'Herr Nautschke loathes the Nazis. He's never made any bones about it, even to Heinz. Heinz never cared. In a way that made things safer here. He always brought the old boy coffee, schnapps, maybe a can of black-market ham. Kept him sweet.'

They continued on their way. Round a bend in the path and down a grassy dip, and the house came into view. It was right on the lake shore, a structure hardly bigger than Herr Nautschke's except that it had a sizeable boatshed built on to it. The surroundings were neglected. Where there had once been a garden, brambles and weeds had choked off the shrubs and were threatening to block the path. The countess

217

explained that Keppler had not been near the place since the previous September. It was rented in a false name; understandable for an occasional love-nest and very useful for other reasons besides.

They had no need to knock. As they approached the door, it opened. A tall, well-built figure in shirtsleeves and dark civilian trousers stood four-square on the threshold to greet them, like any German householder at his leisure. The eyes were red-rimmed, the face paler and puffier than Sutton remembered, the blonde hair noticeably sparser, but the superior, careerist's smile was unforgettable. This was Standartenführer Heinz Keppler.

'Welcome, Helen. Mister Sutton, a pleasure to see you again, though under rather strange circumstances.' Keppler said calmly but with a slight hoarseness in his voice. He spoke fluently in English. The accent was almost perfect American, but a little archaic, such that it would probably be considered charming at first but after a while would drive his listener crazy. 'Well, they say beggars can't be choosers.'

With that he took two steps forward, put his hands on the countess's shoulders and kissed her. Sutton saw her flinch. He knew Keppler was marking her out as his woman in front of a possible rival. It was a primitive, animal exhibition. If Sutton hadn't known what he did about Keppler and the countess, and if there hadn't been the time in the hayloft, he might have been impressed.

She pulled back, smiling too broadly, patting her hair.

'George . . . Mister Sutton . . . is exhausted. Heinz. We've had a tough time getting here,' she said.

'You tell me your troubles, and I'll tell you mine,' said Keppler with a dry laugh. 'At least I seem to have persuaded your people that I am not without value as a commodity in the great end-of-the-war bargain sale. Come in, come in.'

Inside, when they filed through the low doorway, the reek of nicotine and alcohol and male physicality was almost unbearably intense. Keppler had obviously not been out for some time. Two camp beds, one unmade, were set up in the corner of the room, with an opened brandy bottle on a small table between them.

'Come in, come in,' Keppler repeated with a nervous

bonhomie that seemed completely inappropriate, until Sutton
realised that the man was actually a little the worse for alcohol.

'How long have you been here,' he asked Keppler.

'Two days. Ah, nearly three days. Things were getting a
little hot at the office . . .'

'So where are the documents?'

Keppler shrugged evasively. 'First a brandy. Why don't you
take off your coats, take it easy for a little while?'

Sutton shook his head. 'No drink, thanks. And I'll keep my
coat on. Look, how safe are we in this house?'

'Ah . . . where in the world is safe, Mister Sutton?'

Keppler poured himself a generous schnapps. 'There's
Gestapo-Müller on my tail, and then there are the Russians
just a few kilometres away and heading for Berlin, cutting
through our defences like the proverbial knife through butter.
You tell me where is safe.'

'You said the Russians are on their way. What do you
mean?'

'You haven't heard? I mean that according to radio reports,
the Russian offensive against Berlin began this morning. The
news is still vague. They are trying to play down the scale of
the fighting, but it's clear that the Red Army has made its big
push, the one we've been waiting for these past weeks. They've
crossed the Oder river and are heading straight for Berlin.'
Keppler smiled crookedly. 'You arrived in the nick of time,
my friend.' He looked at his watch. 'In fact, we should be
checking the latest bulletin.'

He crossed the room to the cheap sideboard. Sutton noticed
one of the crude but functional 'People's Wireless' radios of
the kind sold at a government-subsidised price to millions of
Germans, all the better for them to stay in contact with Josef
Goebbels' own very special version of the truth. Keppler
switched it on. After some martial music came the professionally enthusiastic voice of Nazi radio commentator Hanns Fritz-
sche, tinnily proclaiming 'heavy fighting on the Oder front'
and German 'tactical successes' in eastern Slovakia.

'How much can we trust the radio reports?' Sutton asked.

'Ironically, they have become more rather than less accurate
as the situation has worsened. There has been a policy decision
in the Ministry of Propaganda to tell the people the worst,

219

appeal to their patriotism and their fear of the enemy, especially the Russians. I have friends in the ministry who – '

'Listen, both of you,' Helen von Ackersberg hissed. The newsreader was announcing that the Americans were at the Elbe, sixty miles to the west, that fighting was going on in Magdeburg. He was less clear about the British. They seemed to be pushing forward north and east of Hanover. Despite the clichés about 'courageous resistance', it was obvious that the German front to the west of Berlin was in a state of disintegration, and that all the real resistance was to the east, where the army was fighting with grim determination against an overwhelmingly superior Russian enemy.

'Why didn't the British and the Americans make straight for Berlin?' Keppler asked accusingly.

'I don't know. But the Russians are our allies, you know.'

Keppler chuckled sourly. 'They were ours once, as well. You will have a hard time shifting them once they are established in Berlin. Possession is nine parts of the law, isn't that true?'

'Probably. But there's not a lot we can do about it at the moment. Our job is to save our hides and get to safety in the west.' Sutton looked at his watch. It was ten past two. They had another five hours until it got dark; five hours of sitting here, a static target. It was not a comfortable feeling. 'I want you to show me the documents,' he said.

Keppler had finished his brandy and was about to pour himself another. He looked at each of them in turn with mingled guilt and defiance.

'And you'd better stop drinking. Even the way you are now, you're a liability, Keppler,' Sutton said with sudden brutality.

Keppler bridled. 'I asked your superiors to send you because I wanted an insurance policy, Mister Sutton,' he growled. 'Not a nursemaid.'

Without speaking, Sutton reached over, seized the bottle by the neck, hurled it into the big concrete sink in the corner. There was a tinkling crash, the sound of liquor ebbing away down the waste. Keppler raised his fist automatically, his face suddenly scarlet with rage, but Sutton moved around quickly and grabbed him by his shirtfront.

'Don't,' he said. 'Just don't. So far as I'm concerned you can stay here and drink yourself stupid, wait for the Russians or the Gestapo or whoever. The point is, if you carry on getting smashed, you endanger us, not just yourself. You want to make something of it, you're only too welcome.'

They were matched for weight. Keppler was probably a little stronger under normal circumstances, but the alcohol had taken its toll. The man's heart was beating hard against the knuckles of Sutton's right hand, but somehow the crisis passed. The tableau stayed frozen for a long moment. Keppler seemed to know that Sutton wasn't about to lash out yet. He let his fist drop and said, 'This is no time to fight.'

'No. And it's no time to get paralytic with alcohol.'

'Spoken like a man who knows.' Keppler's half-smile was knowing and subtly superior.

Sutton said nothing. He let go of Keppler's shirt, wishing the man had chosen to fight, yet at the same time knowing that his wish was foolish, adolescent. There was still a lot to be sorted out between the three of them; the countess's presence was causing unspoken tension. Would it be better to have that out now, or leave it until they reached safety?

'Okay. No more booze?' Sutton said. 'Agreed.'

Keppler shrugged again. It was too much to expect explicit surrender.

'And now let's have a look at those documents. Are they around the house?'

'They are outside. All right, I'll get them for you. I'll finally give up my hostages,' Keppler said. He was smiling. but it wasn't hard to see the apprehension in his eyes. He hesitated. 'Müller, you – even Helen – no one has known where I hid those precious documents. That's been my strength.'

"Well, sometime between now and nightfall, you're going to have to reveal all. I want it to be now, Keppler,' Sutton said softly. 'I want to know I haven't wasted my time, and that other people haven't wasted their lives.'

'There have been no deaths.'

'Oh, but there have, Keppler. There was an American – a good man – and someone else, probably a Gestapo agent, on the train. I make that at least two deaths already for the sake of Heinz Keppler's life.'

Thoroughly but concisely, Sutton explained about Joe McCarr, about the rocket attack on the train, about their escape and the trip to Michendorf with Hauptmann Panowsky. He left out two things in view of the delicacy of the situation:

he didn't mention the countess's old role as an American agent, or her new status as the lover of George Sutton.

Keppler was obviously shocked by McCarr's death, but more so by the fact that the party had been under observation from the time they had crossed the German border. 'Müller is uncanny,' he repeated several times. 'Quite uncanny. He suspected me, I knew that. I told myself he had his hands full, or he was holding back because he wanted to see how I'd done it, what I had arranged. But that he should have had so much of it worked out already, prepared in advance . . .'

'We lost the tail, Keppler. But we can't afford to make any more mistakes. That's why you have to stay sober and all of us have to move fast once we get out of here.'

Keppler's expression was momentarily vacant. His eyes showed terror. 'Of course. I wish I shared your confidence about the tail. Müller is uncanny.'

'The files,' Sutton reminded him gently but firmly.'I want to see those documents. This is business, after all, and I need to check your credentials before we go any further.'

'I understand that,' Keppler said. 'Come with me, Mister Sutton. Outside.'

CHAPTER TWENTY-SEVEN

OUTSIDE the cottage, Sutton and Keppler and the Countess von Ackersberg stood still for some time, staring out over the lake. First, because the air was sweet with the scent of spring rain and pine. Second, because each of them had heard the same low, insistent rumble coming from the east.

'It's the guns,' Keppler pronounced finally. 'Those goddamned big Russian guns. The Katyushas. The Stalin-organs. They can't be more than forty kilometres or so away. Fifty at the most. I give them three, four days to surround Berlin.'

'A while ago, everyone seemed to be convinced that the eastern front would hold for longer than the west. Because all your troops are terrified of surrendering to the Russians,' Sutton said.

'They are terrified, it's true. But there are too few of our soldiers left, Mister Sutton. The best of them have been killed; the rest are either unfit and untrained, or so weary they can hardly lift their weapons. The Third Reich and its people are at the end of their tethers.'

'Except for the likes of Gestapo-Müller.'

'Except for him,' Keppler agreed. 'But then he's spent his war either behind a big desk or taking first-class trips around Europe to inspect his torture-chambers.'

Sutton didn't say, and what about you, though he was tempted. Instead he just murmured: 'The documents. Okay?'

Sutton followed as Keppler walked slowly round to the boathouse facing the lake. There was a small, decaying wooden jetty that didn't look as if it had been used for years, even decades. The countess had decided for the moment to keep her distance. She sat down on the grass in front of the house, where she could see them and the lake, and drank in the sun while she watched, baring her legs to the spring warmth.

'You met Herr Nautschke?' Keppler asked.

Sutton nodded, left a silence for Keppler to fill.

'At first, when Helen and I used to come here for weekends – she will probably have told you that we did that very covertly – I felt uneasy to have the old man so close. Then, as time went on, his eccentricity and his outspoken opposition to the régime became a comfort, a kind of security. We had discussions, I hinted that perhaps I agreed with him about many things. We trusted each other. I am saying that, rightly or wrongly, I have felt safe here, Mister Sutton. I love this place, it would not be an exaggeration to say that.'

All the time he was speaking, Keppler was rolling up his sleeves to reveal muscular arms running only very faintly to plumpness, covered in fair down. Also, on the right forearm a number had been tattooed. Keppler caught Sutton staring at it, smiled self-consciously.

'We were all co-opted into the SS, you know, four or five years ago. We had no choice in the matter. We had to have this blood group tattooed on our arms. Awful. Embarrassing. But it was SS regulations. No tattoo, then goodbye to our jobs, eh?'

'A small price to pay,' Sutton said.

Keppler frowned, decided to ignore the sarcasm. He moved onto the rickety jetty, tentatively edged forward for two or three feet, then carefully went onto all fours, finally graduating to lying on his belly with his right arm dangling into the water. Keppler's face screwed up with effort and irritation before the frustration gave way to triumph.

'There! I've got it!' he said. 'Still there, thank God.'

Sutton had lit a cigarette and observed keenly while Keppler hauled on a rope with both hands, for what seemed an infinity, until a shape began to emerge from beneath the surface of the water, just close to one of the jetty's piles. Eventually Keppler moved up onto his knees and hauled his prize clean out of the lake. What he had brought out of the water was oblong, about two foot six by two, wrapped in thick waterproofed oilskin. He pulled it back towards the shore, until he had his feet safely on land, braced himself, then took out a pocket-knife and began to saw through the rope so that he could free the entire package.

'I was very careful, you know. I prepared all this very thoroughly,' Keppler told Sutton as he worked, glancing over his shoulder at the Englishman from time to time. 'We moved many, many big boxes of files from January onwards – high-security material that needed to be preserved at all costs. Experts handled the packing, the transportation, and took most of the responsibility for picking out the storage sites – places like caves, mineshafts, you know? – and ensuring that the documents were protected from long-term damage and decay. Through chatting informally to these people I found out how it would be possible to store this selection of papers under water. Of course,' he added with a laugh, 'I didn't let them know that was what I intended to do. I merely coaxed all the specialist knowledge I could out of them, hiding my real questions amidst a whole host of flattery and pretence of scientific curiosity. Anyway, this specially treated oilskin, for instance, will not start to deteriorate for at least a year, probably more, and I have several layers, plus special casing.'

'How long's the stuff been here?'

Keppler didn't reply immediately. He finished sawing through the rope, with a grunt of satisfaction, began to unwrap the oilskin. 'Five weeks, I managed to bring it out here before things got dangerous. It would, after all, have been stupid to keep it at the apartment where the Gestapo could search at any time.'

'So these are just copies?' Sutton demanded sharply.

'My dear fellow, no,' Keppler said. He had removed the last of the oilskin covers to reveal a sealed tin box with a simple catch lock. He sprung it open. 'There are two sets – the originals and a set of copies.' he explained carefully, taking out an almost disappointingly ordinary-looking attaché case. 'Come and see, feast your eyes and know that your journey has not been wasted as you feared.'

'But surely the files can be checked and found to be missing if you took the originals?' Sutton squatted down by his side. Keppler had opened the case and there, sure enough, were two cardboard folders, one marked as the original, the other as a copy. All so banal, so deceptively, bureaucratically harmless.

Keppler smiled, shook his head. 'No Mister Sutton. This

would be true of most of the Interpol documents. They have
been carted off down to Munich and stored just outside the
city. But 'sensitive' material – material that might have looked
bad if discovered by the Allies – was burned. I selected the
exact material to be burned. I signed it all out and witnessed
that it had been destroyed, personally. Do you see the beauty
of it all?'

Sutton nodded. He did, yes. So Gestapo-Müller had only
suspicions to go on, but no proof. Whether ultimately that
made a great deal of difference to Müller, he doubted very
much.

'Neat,' he said. 'For a man who was so careful you seem
very nervous.'

'I know my superiors, I know my colleagues. Müller has
suspected for some time that I was disaffected, perhaps looking
for a way out. He has been keeping an eye on me – and maybe
on Helen as well. Very different to police life in London or
New York, eh, Mister Sutton?' There was wry defiance in his
look. 'You probably disapprove of all this and of me. This is
not the way you English do things,' he said then.

Sutton shrugged, took a last pull on his cigarette and tossed
it away. 'True, it's not the way most of us do things, no. But
then, these are exceptional times, Keppler. There are some
things I can't take for granted either, even from my own
people.' He shaded his eyes with one hand, looked out across
the lake. A couple of kilometres away, perhaps, he could
make out a boat, moving quite quickly, which meant it was
probably a launch or even a speedboat of some kind. 'In fact,'
he said, 'there's nothing at all any of us can take for granted.
What do you think of that boat, for instance?'

'Who knows?' Keppler tried to seem confident, to imply
that he had seen the boat and dismissed it as a danger, but
the veneer was wearing thin already. 'It does seem to be
moving fast. Even now, one sees them around. Not on a
pleasure trip, of course. Only official vessels can get the
gasoline.'

'No. It doesn't look like a pleasure boat.'

'For God's sake, Sutton!'

'I don't like the look of it. All right,' Sutton said with a
firmness that surprised himself, because really he had nothing

to go on but instinct. 'Here's what we do for now. You give that case to me, and then you go inside and get ready to leave.'

Keppler opened his mouth to protest, then thought better of it. The speedboat was still coming, very fast.

'Do as I say, Keppler. I promised I'd get those documents – and you – out of here. *Move.*'

Sutton reached out and put the documents back in the case, snapped it shut in a commanding gesture that brooked no denial, picked up the precious container and got to his feet.

Helen had also seen the launch. She was standing watching with her hands on her hips. She called out once to the men, and Sutton acknowledged that they had realised the danger and were coming. Keppler began to run towards the cottage door. Sutton followed him, glancing back as he went. The boat had eaten up almost half the distance and was still approaching as if being drawn to that spot by magnetic attraction, not deviating and not slowing down.

The countess frowned. 'What is it?'

Keppler said: 'I don't know. Mister Sutton thinks . . .' He shrugged awkwardly, then looked back at the lake and saw the same steady progress that Sutton had seen. He pushed past Helen von Ackersberg, his bravado rapidly disintegrating, muttering, 'We may need to hurry. I'll get my coat and my travel bag.'

The countess quickly came to Sutton's side, gripped his hand. 'George, I'm frightened all over again. This is happening so fast. I haven't even had time to talk to Heinz about us.'

'That's the least of our problems,' Sutton snapped. Then his tone softened. 'Look, there'll be plenty of time for explanations later. If we manage to get out of here in one piece. Where's Keppler's car?'

'He keeps it in a rented garage up by the street.'

Still the launch kept coming. Keppler came out of the door carrying a leather overnight bag and wearing an overcoat and Homburg. The effect was of a tipsy bank clerk wandering home after a few drinks too many with the boys from the bank on a Friday night, except that Keppler was also fiddling with a pistol, which he shoved into his coat pocket as he walked up to Sutton and the countess.

He faced the lake. There was a faint sheen of sweat on his forehead and the bridge of his nose. Haste and fear.

'Well?' he said.

Sutton hardly needed to answer. The launch was travelling very fast, straight as an arrow, heading for them and was now maybe five hundred yards distant.

'We go,' he said. 'What the hell do you think?'

They began to move off up the path they had entered by less than half an hour before. There was a flash from the deck of the launch, the sunlight catching a telescope or some binoculars. The launch changed direction very slightly, as if anticipating their escape. Sutton cursed between clenched teeth. He only had a moment to reflect that his brain was also working like a beautiful machine, that it had been years since he had felt like this, physically and mentally challenged – and with something to lose, to put that extra fine edge on the danger.

The countess saw Herr Nautschke's body first; it was half-hidden by an unruly privet bush, but there was still a rivulet of fresh blood in the grass beside the path.

Sutton knelt down, felt for the pulse, turned the body over and saw the hole in the chest, the rictus of surprise on Herr Nautschke's face that in death had softened into a strangely peaceful smile. The old man was as light as a child, so easy to move that they could have taken him with them to the car, Sutton thought.

Then, as he looked at the body, several things happened almost simultaneously: he realised from the raggedness of the hole in the shirt around the chest-wound entry that Herr Nautschke had been killed with a knife; someone with a megaphone began to address them from the launch, which was only fifty yards away out on the lake; and Heinz Keppler turned around, aimed out onto the water and fired two shots.

The amplified voice telling them to stay where they were and surrender became a little more muffled as the speaker ducked down behind the rail of the launch's bows. Sutton got back on his feet, swung around and yelled to Keppler to hurry and not waste time taking pot-shots at the boat. It occurred to him, though he didn't mention it, that there must be reinforcements coming from somewhere else, and that for the moment they were probably eager to take the three of them alive. 'Run, for Christ's sake!' he bellowed at Keppler, pushing the countess on up the path and seizing Keppler's shoulder, ready to spin around and set him on his way too.

Keppler glanced to his right at Sutton, his eyes bright with anger and fear, a cramped smile on his face, and let off another shot at the bobbing, wildly revving launch. *'Die Schweine!'* he exulted. *'Ich habe die Schweine!'*

Suddenly he seemed to slip, staggering around on the balls of his feet to face Sutton with a look of surprise taking over from the hysterical gunplay. He was staring over Sutton's shoulder, still mouthing the word *Schwein* over and over.

The man with the gun was a tall, well-built heavy wearing the usual trenchcoat but instead of a Homburg a fly-fishing hat. Perhaps it had been his gesture to camouflage. The gun was smoking, but he seemed quite calm and curiously unthreatening as he covered Helen von Ackersberg and gestured for Sutton and Keppler to fall in line, and for Keppler to drop his gun.

Keppler did not fire – he seemed transfixed – but neither did he do as he was told. The man gestured once more with the gun that was trained on Keppler, smartly and irritably, then with a tiny shrug and a blink squeezed the trigger. As he made to fire, though, something strange happened with his stomach; it flipped out like a belly dancer's pelvic thrust and his square face stiffened and then collapsed. The next moment he began to topple forward, with a blur of dead weight on his back and his pistol firing once, uselessly, into the earth.

The blur on the Gestapo man's back composed itself into a figure that was teasingly familiar to Sutton, in its shabby coat and trousers, with one arm still pinned up. It was the man from the queue at the Zoo station. In the animation of the violence his face was no longer exhausted and dead-looking but very much alive, actually handsome and set in a feral grin. The attacker rolled once with the Gestapo man's body, and the next moment Sutton saw the automatic hurtling towards him and an authentically American-accented voice yelling, 'Catch!'

Keppler fired once more at the launch, then clutched himself just under the armpit to the right of his ribs, wincing with pain. Sutton fired too, and pushed Keppler on. The countess, he noticed, didn't need any help. Whoever this interloper was, he was just fine with her. Within moments the killer had pulled a knife with a flashing hilt from the corpse and was on his feet like a wrestler, seizing hold of Keppler's arm. 'There's a car on the road! Just head for the car!' he yelled.

And they all obeyed. Within twenty seconds they were in sight of the road. The countess, suddenly realising there might be an unwelcome reception party there, stopped and turned hesitantly to where Sutton and the interloper were frog-marching the injured Keppler at a fast walking pace. The man told Helen to head on. There would be no one at the road. He said that with great confidence.

What was waiting for them at the road was a dark, sleek Mercedes sedan, parked in the shelter of some trees at the spot where the lane to the cottage became too narrow for it to have progressed any further. Both the driver's and passenger's doors were open, and as they came closer they could hear a crackling, disembodied voice coming from the front. The presence of a large aerial on the roof told them it was a two-way radio, police issue. The panic in the voice indicated that someone at headquarters was trying to contact someone else – perhaps the former inmates of this car – as a matter of urgency.

When they came close, the countess let out her first gasp, that almost turned into a scream. She had seen another man in a trench coat lying eight, ten feet from the driver's door, just lying on his back with his throat obviously cut, arms and legs splayed wide as if he had been pinned out to dry in the sun. So that was why the stranger had been so sure there would be no one at the car.

Sutton and the stranger pushed Heinz Keppler into the back seat, Helen followed. Then, without a word exchanged between them, Sutton took his place behind the wheel, tossed the priceless briefcase into the back with the countess, and started the engine. The stranger waited almost until Sutton accelerated the car forward, half-hanging outside the pass-enger door, his intense eyes staring all around them, checking the road. Then, when the car finally moved off at speed, he swung himself inside next to Sutton and slammed the door firmly shut.

The powerful Mercedes turned left on a shouted instruction from Helen, who was already searching for something to staunch the bleeding from Keppler's chest. It raced up the cobbled street, heading north-west towards the sun.

Suddenly, apart from the roar of the engine and Keppler's increasingly laboured breathing, there was silence and time. They had gone about two hundred yards when Sutton turned to the stranger.

'I think I'm pleased to meet you,' he said by way of greeting. 'But who in God's name are you?'

CHAPTER TWENTY-EIGHT

'Turn right here into the Havelchaussee. Head for Staken,' the countess told Sutton after they had gone about a mile. 'Yes, I know that means we have to stay close to the lake, but it's not for long. We don't have any other choice. We take the fastest route out of the city before they seal it off. Once that happens, even if we manage to keep out of the Gestapo's hands, we're stuck here, waiting for the Russians. Do you want that?'

'You've convinced me.'

Sutton waited for a slow-moving army truck to finish crossing the junction and followed her directions. They had kept the radio on so that they could monitor police traffic. The Gestapo had only just found out that two of their number were lying around the lakeside with lethal knife wounds – plus the old man, which would confuse them. So far, the Mercedes with its Gestapo numberplates and prominent radio aerial had cleared their path miraculously through the crowded highways, giving them precedence over all pedestrians and cars except the heaviest, proudest military vehicles. All that would be thrown into jeopardy when headquarters told its patrols to watch out for one of their own cars, and the Mercedes became an object of suspicion rather than a laissez-passer.

'So, Eddie Avery,' Sutton said. 'Who put you on our tail?'

'I can't tell you,' Johnny Coletti said simply. 'Eddie Avery isn't even my real name. It doesn't matter. All you need to know is that it's my job to get that case – and if possible Herr Keppler – safely out of Germany.'

'How did you get here?'

'I picked you up in Berlin, I told you.'

'That's not good enough.'

232

'Listen.' Coletti's eyes flashed in sudden anger. 'There's only one thing I want to know from you, and that is, what happened to Joe McCarr? I was told to expect him here in Berlin.'

Sutton faltered for a moment, disarmed by the man's apparent conviction. What was the point of fighting him? This man was obviously American – certainly not German – and he knew all about McCarr. It was understandable that he felt surprised by the man's sudden appearance, but why did he feel so uneasy? Maybe it was the way the man spoke only a dozen words of German, showed no signs of recognition when dramatic messages flashed on the police radio. How the hell had he got here through all that Nazi-held territory?

'Joe McCarr was killed when our train was attacked by American planes north of Hof. The Gestapo were after us even then,' he said with an edge of bitterness.

Coletti nodded solemnly. 'I'm sorry.' He stared ahead for a short while, then turned to look into the back. In that moment he saw the countess's grim, duty-bound concentration as she wiped bubbles of blood from the corner of Heinz Keppler's mouth with a bandage they had found in the car's first aid kit. He also saw the briefcase stored between the seats to her right. Also, Keppler's overnight bag. Good to keep a check on where everything was, because the moment he was planning for could come any time. He smiled tightly at Helen von Ackersberg, playing his chosen role as the coarse but caring man of action. She returned his gaze without affection or gratitude.

'Did you kill Herr Nautschke?' she said quietly.

'Herr who?'

'The old man.'

Coletti ran a finger through his dark hair, nodded with the best impression of self-doubt that he could manage. He considered lying, blaming the death on the Gestapo officers, then realised that both she and Sutton had noticed the nature of the knife-wound on the old man. In any case, it was not so hard to feign regret at the murder of the harmless pensioner. In many ways, he had summoned up memories of Coletti's own father's last days of shuffling, babbling senility. The poor old guy had just been in the wrong place at the wrong time. He had been working in his vegetable plot and had seen Coletti working his way around towards the cottage. At least the old man had died quickly, and Coletti could tell himself that in a

few days, weeks, the Russians, the bombs, old age would have
done for him anyway, maybe far more painfully.

'Listen, he surprised me. He was going to cry out . . . I was
stalking the Gestapo guys . . .' He shrugged helplessly. 'Hell,
he was a German, after all, and he could've screwed up
everything.'

The countess showed no sign of having heard his excuses.
She continued to wipe away the blood.

'How's Herr Keppler?' Coletti asked, though he knew the
man was dying. Very swift treatment would perhaps have
saved him; under these circumstances, with a bullet obviously
smashed into his lung or heart, he would probably go slowly,
choking on his own blood. This was going to cause some
inconvenience. But mingled with that concern was Coletti's
relief that he wouldn't have to bring the physical body of
Keppler westward for Charlie Lucky. God knows, the *capo di
tutti capi* had hemmed his servant they called Prism around
with enough conditions; it was good to lose one. But he would
try to fulfil the rest, or Charlie would not react well on his
return.

The countess was whispering softly to the German, who was
trying to reply but finding it hard to make sense as blood and
bile accumulated in his chest and throat, turning his speech
into incoherent plops, like boiling mud in a hot spring. His
face was pasty, his eyes wide open, staring up at her with
desperate intensity. Keppler had no hope either; even he was
aware that death would come very soon.

Sutton was negotiating the obstacle-course of the outer
Berlin suburbs very skilfully. Coletti respected that, and the
coolness that went with it. He would also have to be careful.
This man was no fool, and would not knowingly provide him
with the opportunity he sought.

'This has been a mess. I think our people at home are gonna
give us a hard time,' Coletti said conversationally. He had
decided to turn the enigma of his appearance in these people's
lives into an advantage. This way he didn't have to explain
anything, but could give the impression of knowing everything.
Explanation, exchanges of information, were all on his terms,
and there was no chance that he would trip himself up by
making a serious mistake of fact.

'Our people at home can take a running jump,' Sutton said.

'They'll be bloody lucky to get anything. I even think they might have suspected the Gestapo were on to Keppler. Think about what that *means*.'

Coletti laughed humourlessly. 'Listen, they always want perfection. And do they tell you all the problems you're gonna have to face?' He shrugged, looked out of the window. A sign pointed to Falkensee just a kilometre or so away, with a branch indicated for Nauen. From what he remembered from the map, that would start to take them due west towards the Allied lines. Fine. It was a pity he couldn't understand the radio, but he trusted Sutton's and the woman's knowledge of the language and sense of self-preservation. Until they were in open country and close to the lines, he was better off with them than without. He hated dependency, reliance on others, but he also knew how to accept it when there was no other choice.

Helen von Ackersberg's voice came from the back seat. It was clear and dignified, as if she were putting her own feelings aside and acting as a spokeswoman. She was paying the last of a debt, in fact, Sutton realised.

'I think I'm understanding what Heinz is trying to say,' she told them. 'He says he should have known Müller was on to him. He shouldn't have brought us here. He – ' she took a deep breath and spilled it out, 'he's very, very sorry, George. He wants you to know that.'

Perhaps it was simply the inevitable deterioration of his wound, and then maybe the increasingly pot-holed bad roads were the cause, but just after they had turned off the main highway at Perleberg, Keppler began to vomit blood into the wads of cloth that Helen von Ackersberg held out for him. He made a sound that was chillingly rhythmic and uncontrolled, like a dog trying to void its stomach in the grass. She looked anxiously around, the caring part of her ashamed at her impotence, her practical part concerned not to get his blood all over her coat and be marked out by it later, when suspicious eyes might be cast over them.

'Where are we?' asked Coletti.

'Getting close to the Elbe,' the countess said. 'We have to get over the river or we'll never manage to make contact with the Allied advance.'

'It's quiet. Strange.'

'Maybe because this is not the quickest route away from the Russians,' the countess said wryly. 'But it's good enough to get us where we need to go. We were too conspicuous to risk staying on the main highway any longer than we needed to.'

'The lady's a strategist.'

'The lady knows this road from years ago – and she wants to survive,' she dismissed Coletti. 'Oh God . . . I think Heinz is unconscious . . .'

'He's finished, isn't he?' Sutton said.

There was no answer for a moment, then he glanced over his shoulder and the countess nodded and said. 'Yes. There's no hope. If he doesn't haemorrhage and go out quickly, he'll just bleed right over everything and go slowly.'

Sutton reached his decision with a swiftness and ruthlessness that might have shocked him even a few weeks ago but seemed natural now. There were two things he had to do, he knew, and now was the right time to do them.

Up ahead was a sign warning of forestry vehicles turning onto the highway. As he expected, it meant the opening to a foresters' track used to transport equipment and felled trees to and from the road. He slowed down a little, hoping it was enough, without warning swung the car over onto the soft verge just before the track, and was still doing between thirty and forty when the Mercedes hit the rough, compacted dirt of the new surface. It bounced, and he could hear the countess gasp. 'Sorry,' Sutton said, 'I had to take my chance quickly.'

He brought the car's speed right down, kept going along the track until they had rounded a bend and were out of sight of the road. He stopped, engaged the hand-brake, finally cut the engine.

They sat in silence for a few moments. Then the countess said, 'What happens now?'

Sutton caught the stranger's eye, saw the man recognised at least one of the things he was planning.

'Helen,' he said with a sigh, 'we're going to leave Keppler here. We have to.'

Coletti was nodding silent agreement.

'We'll make him as comfortable as we can. There's really nothing else to be done, love.'

There was a brief flicker of horrified defiance, a last flash of peacetime, humanity, and perhaps an old loyalty. Then she nodded slowly, glanced down at Keppler. His eyes were still closed, and he showed no sign of having heard the conversation or grasped its meaning.

'Please . . . finish it,' the countess said then, biting back tears. 'I'd hate for them to find him, even for a few minutes . . .'

Sutton nodded slowly, waiting his chance.

'We should do this fast,' Coletti said with ill-concealed impatience. 'I think we don't have so much time for all the usual niceties.'

The radio was still crackling away in the background, fainter but still audible. The messages being sent in and out at the moment were to do with some other emergency, but every now and again Sutton heard the description and number of the car given out on the waveband. Even halfway to the Allied lines, they weren't safe. Müller wouldn't ease off until he had them and the stolen documents cold. *Who was this stranger who called himself Eddie Avery and admitted even that was a lie?* Sutton was aware that he might never know; he was also certain that the only real triumph would be not to know this man but to survive him.

'All right,' he said, and motioned for Coletti to get out and wait. 'Just a moment. I think the lady needs me.'

Coletti shrugged, got out.

Sutton leaned over between the seats, put his arm around her neck and pulled her close. Then he began to whisper his instructions to her, quickly, urgently and choosing his words with extreme care. The last thing he whispered, before he pulled away from her, was, 'Now have your cry. Cry your eyes out. The more the better.'

He was already outside and opening the back passenger door when Helen von Ackersberg let out an authentic, choking wail of despair.

'Here,' Sutton said, summoning Coletti over. 'Give me a hand easing him out of the seat, will you? Helen, this isn't easy for any of us. Let go of him.' And don't overdo the tragedy bit, he thought.

Finally they got Keppler out, a little clumsily but without too much delay. The dying man coughed, his eyes rolled, a dribble of blood ran down his shirt front. Sutton took him under his left arm, Coletti his right, and they dragged him away towards the trees. Coletti made to set him down when they got just inside the forest, but Sutton insisted they take him a little further, out of sight of the countess. They laid him down among the pine needles facing west towards the setting sun.

Sutton took out the automatic pistol that the stranger had thrown to him during the battle at the lakeside, checked that it had shots left in the clip. Then he braced himself, looked at Keppler. He told himself that he was killing the man for the sake of all their safety – and to save him pain – but as he began to steady the gun and take aim, there was a sudden and powerful twinge of ancient, primitive conscience. *He was killing a man and taking that man's woman.* Every religious scripture, every ethical code known to the human race forbade that. Never mind the fact that he was killing to save life, that she had certainly stopped loving Keppler, that it was all over between the two of them. To kill him suddenly seemed impossible. Involuntarily he let the gun waver. His hand was beginning to tremble.

Then Sutton felt a hand on his sleeve. The stranger had silently drawn a knife from his clothing, was also staring down at Keppler.

'I know the problem,' said Coletti quietly. 'I can do this job with no pain and no noise. It's easier for me, okay?'

Sutton found himself nodding. Coletti immediately squatted down, gently pushed aside Keppler's coat, slit the white shirt open. Sutton had to watch. First, because he owed it to Keppler; second, because he had to study this Eddie Avery, to see how he operated before the show-down came.

Coletti felt under Keppler's ribs, nodded to himself, then turned and looked up at Sutton with a strange blankness, as if surprised that the Englishman was still there and looking on so impassively, but made no comment. Then, like the professional he obviously was, he unceremoniously slipped the blade into Keppler's body, at the apex of the rib cage where his hand had been probing a moment before. He frowned with the precision and the effort of it. Keppler twitched, his eyes opened white and wide, then a final crimson trickle came out of the side of his mouth. Coletti waited, pulled out the knife and wiped it on the grass. Then he reached over one hand and closed the eyes.

'We ought to take his personal stuff, to ensure the body can't be identified,' Sutton suggested. 'We don't want someone finding him and the cops realising we've been in the area.'

'Right,' Coletti said coolly, without even bothering to look at Sutton.

Sutton said softly, 'You're used to abandoning dead soldiers, I think.'

Still Coletti didn't face him or show any sign of emotion. 'It happens,' he said after a couple of long beats.

Busily his hands checked the pockets of Heinz Keppler's suit, overcoat, extracted a wallet, a passport, some keys, and a photograph of Helen von Ackersberg, smiling, against a background that looked like a funfair or maybe a stadium. She looked happy. At last Coletti turned and got to his feet, handed it all over to Sutton solemnly, possibly with a hint of insolence.

They walked back to the car in silence. Sutton half-smoked a cigarette on the way, offered it to the countess, who was still sitting hunched in the back seat, more composed now. She accepted the cigarette, took a couple of puffs and handed it back.

'All right?' Sutton said.

She looked at him coolly. 'I'll survive.'

Sutton showed her the items taken from Keppler's pockets. 'I'm sorry. It seemed like a good idea to remove any identification. And I thought you might want these anyway.'

The countess nodded, and a shadow of bemused sadness came over her face as she accepted the last of Heinz Keppler. 'I – I'll put them in the overnight bag with the other things, all right? I would like to keep them.'

'A good idea. You're very brave,' Sutton said. She had done what he had told her to do; their exchange of signals confirmed it. He felt a warm flood of relief surge through his body.

Coletti was already waiting in the front passenger seat, tapping his fingers on the dashboard in tune with some imaginary beat. It was beginning to get dark. Sutton gratefully touched Helen von Ackersberg's hand, went around and got behind the wheel.

When he switched on the engine the radio also came to life;

fast-talking, precise German voices dipped in and out of a pool of static.

The Mercedes, luckily for them, had enough petrol left to get them some distance west of the river Elbe. It was more than enough for their needs, if what Sutton suspected was true.

CHAPTER TWENTY-NINE

WITH THE COUNTESS still acting as guide, they soon turned onto an even smaller country road. The Mercedes' smooth suspension saved them too much discomfort, but it was noticeable that the highway was not just littered with pot-holes but had subsided badly. Maybe mining. Or maybe heavy vehicles passing this way, tanks to the front line or trucks hauling big artillery. On the positive side, the road was almost empty, which was relaxing and also enabled Sutton to drive fast even though, at the countess's insistence, he had to drive on sidelights to conform with blackout regulations. The thought of being challenged by some officious local cop or home guard patrol for a blackout violation had a certain grim humour to it, except that it could also cost them their lives.

When they eventually passed over the barrier of the Elbe, by a rickety country bridge, they saw military vehicles parked by the side of the road, some faces in the dim beam of the Mercedes' lights. Someone briefly stepped out a few feet and waved, but made no serious attempt to force them to stop. Before he put his foot down and roared on into the darkness, Sutton saw shadowy figures on the bank and on the bridge itself; almost certainly sappers wiring the structure, ready to blow it up when the enemy came. Why should they stop to check a fast Mercedes with police number plates, even if they had been warned to look out for one? There was a war on. Why ask for extra trouble?

They drove towards Uelzen, about forty kilometres on. It was one of the names they had heard on the radio, one of the places threatened by the Anglo-American advance. Helen von Ackersberg had fallen asleep in the back, and Sutton was beginning to feel the exhaustion getting to him too. The dark landscape had a look of waiting, of passivity about it as if resigned to its fate.

The Mercedes was climbing over a low range of hills when Sutton's fatigue suddenly vanished. On the Gestapo waveband a voice was repeating that the stolen Mercedes containing the murderers of two officers near Berlin had been spotted crossing the Elbe on the Uelzen road. The local Gestapo were requested to take all, repeat all, necessary measures to seal the roads and apprehend the felons, believed to be enemy agents, dead or alive.

So the men at the bridge had reported them after all, Sutton thought. This was a new danger, but it was also a gift, the extra gift that he had been praying for. It was the signal to put his plans into operation. He turned up the radio, grateful that the countess was asleep and had not betrayed them by her reaction to the tightening Gestapo net.

Sutton drove on for a short while more, gradually letting his head droop onto his chest, half-closed his eyes, and deliberately let the car veer to the right towards some trees as they moved into a long, rising bend.

Coletti seized his arm, shook it. 'Hey, you wanna kill us?' he barked, half-anxious, half-humorous.

Sutton snapped to with a grunt, eyes stupid with apparent surprise, corrected the car's course just in time to prevent them from ploughing off over the hill.

'Christ, I'm sorry,' he mumbled. 'Getting tired. Maybe I should take a rest. Just five minutes to walk around, clear my head . . .'

'Will you turn that radio down?' Coletti said. 'What's with that stuff anyway? Are they still after us?'

'No,' Sutton said. 'I was keeping it on just in case. First place I can, I intend to pull over and take a quick break. All right with you?'

The man beside him had been so impatient just a short time before, when they had dumped Keppler. Now, suddenly, he was easy.

'Sure,' he said. 'We're close to the battle zone, right?'

'It's just the other side of Uelzen, yes.'

'Listen, anything you say, anything you say.'

Johnny Coletti didn't betray his relief, merely made a little conversation to sweeten his assent. Sutton's decision to pull over and rest solved all his problems. He had thought of settling things when they had disposed of Keppler, but had decided it would be safer to keep Sutton and the woman around for a while longer. Now things had changed; they were close to the front line. For the past mile or two he had been considering whether to say he needed to take a leak, or that he would spell Sutton. Now strategems were no longer necessary. Sutton had delivered himself into the hands of Prism.

The man Sutton was capable and cunning) Coletti could tell. But he had his Achilles' heel, in the form of the Swiss countess, the fancy lady from the photograph with the cute behind and the now-deceased Nazi boyfriend.

If the woman was threatened, Sutton would offer no resistance. All Coletti had to do was to engineer a situation in which the Englishman had to choose between her and the documents in that briefcase, between his desire and his orders. This was where Coletti's – Prism's – common ground with ordinary people such as these ended. To choose a *woman*, particularly one who was still fresh from another man's bed, over duty and ambition was so alien to Prism that it made him angry, it almost made him want to kill out of sheer contempt.

But he wouldn't kill Sutton and the woman unless it was forced upon him. Charlie Lucky's last message had been very clear. To 'my honoured friend Prism' it had said, get what my man here in the States wants, and be sure of that, but also know that I'm a patriotic American and it offends me to kill Allied personnel without reason. Kill when necessary, and by all means kill Germans, but leave the OSS man and those with him alive if possible. If you cannot, I will try to understand – so soft, so diplomatic, Charlie Lucky's threats – but from the young man who is as close to me as a son I would then demand a painstaking, exact explanation. Prism, he had continued, is such a perfect killer that *he can afford not to kill*. Charlie Lucky had underlined that, like a schoolteacher labouring the point to a promising but headstrong pupil. Lucky was testing, teaching; for his part, Prism would show the boss of bosses that he was capable not just of devastating violence but also of tact, restraint and the management of men. For his future as Lucky's successor, these skills too would be vital. He knew that and was prepared to be humble.

The Mercedes pulled over into a farm track shielded from the road by spreading chestnuts. Sutton sighed, doused the lights and stopped the engine, collapsed softly onto the wheel and rested his head there for a few moments.

'Helen?' he said then. 'I'm taking a break, a little walk around.'

There was a sleepy reply from the back. The countess's head appeared between the seats. 'But we're almost in Uelzen.'

'I was dozing off, threatening to crash the car,' Sutton explained. 'How much real sleep have we had these past nights?'

Shit, thought Coletti, amused despite his readiness, they're already like an old married couple, talking about how terrible it is when you get kept up at nights, such a wild social life here in war-torn Germany.

Sutton switched the radio off, stretched and yawned. 'Thank God we don't need that noise any more.'

Coletti smiled, nodded. He turned to look at the countess, making like he was concerned. 'You okay?'

She said she was, wouldn't go any further than that. So she still didn't like him. The important thing was, he had seen that the briefcase was handy and that she was still clutching the late Heinz Keppler's little leather overnight bag to herself like a security blanket. If she and Sutton ever got it together, Sutton should throw away that bag, maybe burn it, show her not to be attached to her old lovers.

'I'm going to stretch my legs,' Sutton said.

A cloud of alarm passed over Helen von Ackersberg's face. She held the bag even tighter with one hand, reached out ready to open her door with the other. Anything but be left alone in the car with big, bad Johnny Coletti.

By contrast, Sutton was relaxed and in no hurry. Except that before he got out he reached over into the back seat and picked up the briefcase, grinned in his tired way at both the others and made a joke of it, said, 'I like to keep the family jewels on me at all times. For safe keeping. You know how it is.'

'Sure I know.' Coletti had anticipated this, had prepared for it in his mind. Let Sutton do what he wanted for now. Coletti would still get his way.

It was a very dark night, and what light there was had been

further reduced by the overshadowing trees. It was perfect. Coletti nestled down in his seat, gave a little wave of the hand as if to say, you do what you like, I'll just wait here in the car, see if I care.

Sutton swung the briefcase out in front of him, eased himself out of the door and onto the grass outside, stood up so that the top half of his body was out of Coletti's vision. A tiny flare showed he was lighting one of his cigarettes, was occupied fully with that. The countess was out of the car too. Coletti turned, checked her, saw she was standing a little hesitantly on her side of the car, maybe wondering if she was being dumb, not wanting to look like a scared little girl to Sutton.

Go. It's now. This opportunity may never come again. This is Prism's moment, he knew with a certainty that thrilled him.

Coletti was out the door, quickly and almost soundlessly. The countess was still standing there, not even reacting to any sound, when he reached one arm out and his sturdy hand went over her mouth, the other arm coming round with the blade to point it at her throat. It was a complete, easy movement. She stiffened, dropped the leather bag, made a gagging noise, bit a little into his palm, and then Coletti said, 'Okay, Sutton. Please turn around and pay attention.'

He could hardly see Sutton's face from where he was standing, but enough to tell the expression of shocked surprise, the flash of real horror before the Englishman's features hardened to face the danger.

'Right. Let's make this quick and easy, eh? You know I can use this knife, you know how I am. I'm telling you to do things one at a time,' Coletti said calmly. 'First, take that gun from your pocket and hold it up – pointing down, okay – so I can see it. Then throw it onto the ground near me. *Now.*'

Sutton did as he was told, slowly and without the slightest sign that he was going to try any surprises.

Coletti nodded approvingly. 'Very good. Now the briefcase. Throw that over here too.'

There was a silence. Then Sutton said, 'No.'

'Sutton, don't be stupid. I'll kill her. I'm asking you again. Just once more.'

For a moment, he worried that he had misjudged Sutton, that he would have to carry out his threat, or that Sutton would suddenly make a dive for the trees in the darkness and to hell with the woman and her cute behind.

'I don't trust you. I want her safety guaranteed.' Sutton grimaced. 'Then . . . I'll . . . hand . . . it . . . over.' The words ground out like he was chewing on broken glass. 'This is crazy. Who are you?'

'Never mind that. Don't worry, you did what you came to do, this is no dishonour,' Coletti said. He thought about the deal. He could still kill her, then go for Sutton. In the dark it would be so easy to outwit him and finish him. But it was not necessary. He would make a deal, and honour his word to both Charlie Lucky and to Sutton.

A short wait, to allow everyone some dignity.

'We have to do this carefully,' he said. The woman kicked back at him suddenly, bruising his shin. He simply squeezed her harder, moved the point a millimetre closer to her throat so that she would feel the prick, even have her skin break. She went limp in his arms. 'Hey,' he said quietly with a short laugh. Then to Sutton: 'I see the gun. I'm moving over to it. Stay where you are.'

He moved to where the gun lay, taking the unresisting countess with him, using his strength to manhandle her like a store mannequin. He put his foot on it, touched it. When Sutton had checked the magazine clip before Keppler died, there had been three shots left. Fine. It could stay here, waiting for the next step, with his foot in contact, keeping it safe,

'Next, put the briefcase down and step back five paces. Good . . . Now take five paces to the right.'

He flung Helen von Ackersberg with all his strength away from him, straight towards where Sutton was waiting, and in that confusion he ducked. Swapped his knife into his left hand, swooped and picked up the gun with his right. Within an instant he was advancing on the briefcase, pointing both weapons towards Sutton, who had grabbed the countess and swept her towards the cover of a tree-trunk.

He had the briefcase. He slipped his knife into his jacket pocket, felt his fingers encircle the leather handle, picked it up and played with the weight of it.

'Stay there. I won't hurt you. I'm going to leave you here is all. I regret that, but I have to travel quickly.'

Neither of them said anything. The woman was sobbing, Sutton was holding her, his face a mask of failure, of hatred for the winner. Maybe he was wondering how he was going to explain this back in London. Listen, Pal, don't worry too much, Coletti wanted to say; you'll have an easier time telling your guys the bad news than I'd have had with Charlie Lucky, and that's for sure. I had to pick a guy who doesn't need to screw up at this point in his life, I'd pick me.

'You . . . you said you'd help us,' the countess said. 'You bastard.'

Coletti let out a whistle from between his teeth, began to move back towards the car, still covering them with the automatic .

'You said you'd help us!' she repeated, her voice rising to a yell.

Coletti tossed the briefcase onto the passenger seat and got behind the wheel.

'I lied, countess.'

For a full minute after the car had accelerated up the road, Sutton and Helen von Ackersberg stayed pinned against the tree-trunk. Then Sutton let out his breath in a sigh of relief.

'Thank God,' he said. 'Thank God he was the kind of man he was. It wouldn't have worked otherwise. You were magnificent.'

'I was scared to death, George. You're already talking like I was acting. That fear was for real, all right.'

He kissed her quickly on the lips. 'We'd better get ourselves away from here,' he said, pulling back and listening to make sure the sound of the Mercedes' engines had faded.

The countess followed Sutton over to the area where the car had stood. He took his matches from his coat pocket, sheltered one with a cupped hand and lit it, searching the ground. It went out. Three matches later he found what he was looking for: Keppler's overnight bag.

'Here we are!' Sutton picked it up, looked inside, grinned at the Countess. 'The documents are safe. There was only one thing I was really frightened of. I didn't think he'd look in here, but I was worried he'd look in the briefcase to check. We put the folders back, but he might have been just that

247

little bit more thorough and taken a peep. Not his style, but he might have.'

The countess shook her head. 'He didn't suspect anything could have happened while you were away laying Heinz to rest. He must have thought I was just too grief-stricken to do anything so *distasteful* as work a switch.' She laughed. 'But he didn't know Erich Zweig's little girl. And he didn't understand that people can love, and grieve, and still keep their survival instincts in good working order.

'No, he didn't know that – and the poor bastard never will, not even if he survives what's waiting for him just along the Uelzen road,' Sutton said. 'Still, at least we let him choose his own fate. I'd say that's more choice than he's ever given any of his fellow men.'

They ducked through a gap in the hedge and headed for the nearby woods, feeling their way in the darkness. It was going to be a long, hard night's journey for a man, a woman and Heinz Keppler's suddenly very precious overnight bag.

Coletti took the bends tightly, relishing the car's speed and handling, oblivious of the ruts in the road. Another couple of miles and he would think about ditching the Mercedes, with regret, and heading westward on foot, one anonymous, pathetic refugee among tens, hundreds of thousands. First priority would be to make it to Bremen, then to Hamburg. There he would be given shelter, food and papers by his friends, the local friends of 'Our Thing', and arrange for the delivery of the briefcase and its contents.

He hoped that Sutton would survive, in a dispassionate kind of way. The man had been brave enough, resourceful, but ultimately a sucker, for a woman and for a well-told lie.

Thinking of Helen von Ackersberg, Coletti also found his mind supplying an image of Lisa, the woman from Milan. He felt himself harden and a small fire come to life in his belly. Then he forced the vision of her pale, soft body from his mind. There were still challenges to be faced before he granted himself that particular pleasure. Rewards came after achievement, not before. Nevertheless, Coletti was still feeling the afterglow of his lustful thoughts about Lisa when he rounded the final bend at sixty miles an hour and saw a barrier across the road.

It was just a striped bar between makeshift supports; he saw a man holding a lamp and waving frantically; he saw others with rifles, a machine-gun mounted on a jeep by the side of the road.

Coletti instantaneously processed what he saw and realised that there was no question of stopping or turning the car around. His right foot hammered the accelerator to the floor, and the Mercedes roared as if in triumph, punching the barrier into the air like matchwood. There was a thud against the front fender, and a wobble in the car's course which he brought under control again immediately. A body? He asked himself. Maybe a foolish German who had not got out of the way quickly enough, or had been stupid enough to believe that his body would stop him. Coletti's heart soared in that instant, until he saw what lay ahead.

Less than a hundred yards away, the mobile Gestapo unit had placed a requisitioned truck right across the narrow highway. A man can think many thoughts in the time it takes to travel such a distance. He can realise the foolishness of human pride, he can understand how the man who uses deception can also become its victim, he can feel himself plummet from the highest peak of exultation to the depths of despair, humiliation and futile rage. He can even think the usual things, such as whether to drive for the wheels, for a clean impact, or keep going and risk having his head sliced off. It would make no difference, of course. He was going to die either way.

Sutton had fooled him. Sutton had let him take – what? – certainly not the documents . . .

Johnny Coletti, known in professional criminal circles as Prism, hit the five-ton truck at eighty-three miles an hour. Deepening his final agony was the knowledge that Charlie Lucky, his second father, perhaps his only real one, would be so very disappointed in him.

They heard the distant sound of impact, stopped for a moment and turned to stare over the rolling landscape. They were making good progress up a steep path towards a wooded ridge, had come some distance from the highway in just a few minutes. The countess took a tight grip on Sutton's hand, looked at him enquiringly.

Sutton nodded, 'I think it must be him,' he said, panting

slightly from the climb. 'God knows what happened when he hit the road block or whatever it was. Sounds like the petrol tank went up.'

An area of forest and sky to the north-west was suddenly suffused with an errie orange glow. Billowing smoke leaked quickly into the vast, velvet blackness of the night.

'If we're lucky, it'll take them all night to realise he was alone in the car. If we're really lucky, they may never realise it at all.'

'Maybe we deserve some good luck, George.'

Sutton smiled and shook his head.

'You make your own luck, love,' he said. 'Come on, let's go. We need to keep moving cross-country, away from people. We're not safe yet, and I honestly don't know when we will be.'

CHAPTER THIRTY

SUTTON CAME out of the main post office building in the Rue Notre Dame and crossed the street to the café where Helen von Ackersberg was waiting for him. He walked with his head slightly bowed and his shoulders hunched against the brisk westerly wind that had blown up that morning off the English Channel.

They had been in Calais for five days now, staying in a small *pension* near the central station. For five days they had waited, making love and talking, drinking cheap wine and eating simple meals of bread and cheese and soup like all the other shabby refugees and war-scarred natives crammed into the battered but lively French port. Even living modestly, they had used up a surprising amount of the countess's precious Swiss francs. Note by hoarded note, the francs had emerged from the lining of her coat as they had bribed, charmed, cajoled and footslogged their way west across Europe. Three days previously, men and women had embraced each other in the streets here at the news that Adolf Hitler was dead and Berlin in Russian hands. Now there was a kind of breathless hiatus as everyone waited for the final, official end to the Führer's war.

The countess made to rise when he came in, but Sutton motioned for her to stay where she was and ordered a coffee from the proprietor, a short, bulky man who was a walking advertisement for the fattening qualities of his wife's home-made *pain au chocolat*.

Sutton kissed the countess on the cheek. 'Sorry I took so long,' he said. 'The first call was easy, but I had to wait bloody ages until I got through on the second one.'

She stroked his hand. 'Well? Don't keep me in suspense, George. I think we've both had enough of that.'

'Everything's arrived safe and sound. That's the first thing. As for the call to Rudwick, when I finally spoke to him he nearly had a fit.'

'Wasn't he relieved to hear from you and know you were all right?'

'It was quite a bit more complicated than that, as you can imagine, love.'

The countess stared thoughtfully at her coffee cup. 'Yes. It's easy to imagine.'

'You don't look happy.'

'Oh, it's all right . . . Perhaps part of me had been thinking that the package hadn't arrived, and then you wouldn't be going through with this.'

'Well, it did, and I have to go,' Sutton said.

'You're totally convinced you're right, aren't you?' she said with a sad smile. 'We could have given ourselves up to the first British troops we saw, near Uelzen more than two weeks ago. We'd probably have been in London the next day, if you had followed your bosses' instructions. But no, you'd decided you weren't going to. George Sutton, I thought you were pretty stubborn, from the moment I set eyes on you, but – '

'You didn't realise I was completely pig-headed,' Sutton joked. Then his voice became harder, fiercer. 'I'm sorry, Helen. I can't, I won't, become a refugee from my own country. After all, I've done nothing wrong.'

'No, George. Of course not. I would never want you to be an exile. I know all about that,' Helen von Ackersberg said. But here in this foreign place, she thought, life for two lovers is not so bad. The people are kind, and it feels peaceful and safe. Say the word, George, and we could just disappear, forget Rudwick and England and Heinz Keppler's documents, all the rest. Aloud she said to Sutton with a determination that equalled his own, 'I won't leave you, no matter what you do. I didn't leave you before, and I won't now.'

'Don't be stupidly loyal. There's a risk.'

'But I can't live without you,' the countess answered quickly and her eyes flashed. 'You're brave and honest, you're clever, and you're the best lover I ever had,' she ended a little too loudly.

A Frenchman sitting at the next table obviously understood the last part and grinned broadly, managing to express both surprise and delight at such a compliment being paid to an Englishman, of all people.

Sutton and the countess laughed, held hands, and the tension was broken. She had waited an hour for him to make his phone calls from the Post Office. It had not been easy on nerves already stretched taut by danger and exhaustion.

'It's true, George,' she said then. 'I suppose I always thought that only dishonest men, men who dominated others by deceit and manipulation and force, were strong – a legacy from my father. Now I've found one who's got strength *and* integrity, and I'm not going to let him out of my sight. We stand or fall together. In any case, my presence may reassure your bosses.'

Sutton shook his head, 'If the worst came to the worst, you could be vulnerable, Helen. They could use you.'

'If the worse comes to the worst, then we can forget everything – you and me, a future together, anything close to a life worth living. I'd rather be with you whatever – captive or free, dead or alive, kill or cure.'

'It won't come to that. I won't let it,' Sutton said flatly. He looked at his watch. 'It's four-thirty. I suggest we go back to the boarding-house, have an afternoon nap, treat ourselves to a little fish dinner on the other side of the harbour. We'd better be in bed by ten or so. The boat leaves bright and early in the morning.' He shot her a wry smile. 'Rudwick's boys will be waiting on the other side of the water, and that's when the fun will really begin.'

'So it's you and me? Together?'

Sutton nodded, squeezed her hand. You and me. Together. You're my woman and I don't want anyone else.'

She searched his face for meanings. He seemed a little distracted, unsettled.

'George, I know I make brave noises, but do you trust me?' she asked.

Sutton knew how hard it was for her to ask that question, how hard it had been all her life. 'I know you make brave noises, but you also do very brave things, Helen,' he said. 'Don't ever let yourself forget that.'

'But do you trust me?'

253

'With my life,' he said, with such certainty and feeling that all her doubts were swept away.

Helen von Ackersberg registered light filtering through the small high window of the boarding-house room, stirred under the thick peasant quilt, reached out sleepily for the warm, hard body she had become accustomed to find next to her. Her hand encountered only crumpled sheets, a pillow, then the rough distemper of the far wall. Her eyes flicked full open like a startled deer's, and she rolled over to face where George Sutton should have been. He had gone. For a moment she listened without real hope for the sound of a W.C. flushing, or running water in the ancient, noisesome bathroom just along the corridor. But there was only the everyday clamour of a working port – cars and buses honking at each other, a policeman's whistle, the greedy, keening protests of seagulls wheeling overhead.

'George . . .' There was suddenly a sickening clarity to all this. She was already searching her memory for the hints, the clues she should have been vigilant enough to have picked up before it was too late. 'Oh, George . . .'

The next shock came when she realised that it was quite late; they had been due to wake at five-thirty. From the noise and the light, it was obvious that the day was well advanced, past the waking time, past the sailing time of the Dover ferry – for her, at least.

Sitting upright, the countess stared carefully around the room. Keppler's overnight bag was gone, of course. She hardly needed to look to know that. Her gaze searched Sutton's side of the bed for other clues; then the table, the chipped dresser with its jug and bowl; finally came to rest on the inside of the door. A note had been pinned to one panel, next to the doorknob.

She swore under her breath in Swiss dialect, in her anger and fear remembering a few of her father's pet phrases, the ones he had used in those fearsome arguments with her mother, or when chewing out the bailiffs who came after his routine bankruptcies to repossess the furniture, the cars, every candlestick and salt cellar and expensive little girl's toy and silk dress and Saville Row suit . . . all illusory, all worthless mirages gone with the dawn like this one. So George Sutton had conned her, and now he had left. How about that? The countess cradled her head in her hands for some time, sinking deep into a very familiar kind of pain. Eventually she found the strength to ease herself out of bed and pad naked across the threadbare carpet to the door.

The note was even marked with the time: 5 a.m. This was such a very precise exercise, wasn't it?

Darling Helen, it said, *I've done the dirty on you and gone to England alone. In the end I decided I couldn't take you with me into the lion's den. I wanted to, but it wouldn't have been right. Please don't try to follow me, because I didn't even tell the truth about the boat – I'm catching the first train along the coast to one of the other ports and crossing from there.*

God knows, it hurts to do this and to know I may never see you again, but it would hurt a lot more if I knew I'd caused you to come to any harm. Please believe that I meant every word I said yesterday – I trust you, and now I need you to trust me. If you decide that this is too much and you have to leave, I'll understand. If not, stay where you are – we calculated we had enough money for a month, didn't we? – and with any luck you'll see a weary Englishman at your door some day soon. Weary but free. Whatever happens, just remember
I love you
GEORGE

Mechanically Helen went over to the wide windowsill where she had left her watch the night before, picked it up and saw that the time now was five minutes past eight. Three hours. He had been gone for three hours, and she hadn't stirred or sensed anything. By now he could be on board any number of different ships – the ports of Boulogne, Dunkirk, Ostende were all within easy reach.

With the realisation that her lover must now be far away, the countess could no longer hold herself back. She cried tears of loss. Then she cried tears of relief that he had promised to come back to her if he survived this challenge. Finally, she sat quietly on the big, soft bed and said a long, awesomely intense and detailed prayer for the safety of George Sutton when he set foot once more in his native country.

CHAPTER THIRTY-ONE

THE BELGIANS at Ostende hadn't given a damn about his credentials; any potential consumer of scarce rations who wanted to leave their hard-pressed country was welcome to do so without let or hindrance. As Sutton had anticipated, however, the passport control officer at Dover was thoroughly disconcerted. He took a long time to check through Sutton's Red Cross papers, the forged Swedish passport covered in German entry stamps and permits. Then he took in Sutton's frayed suit and travel-stained shirt, the fact that his only luggage was a small overnight bag bearing the initials 'HLK', and said, 'Could you explain your purpose in the United Kingdom, Mr Salvesen?'

The huge, hangar-like hallway was teeming with returning troops, a few of the civilians who had now started to travel between Britain and the continent again.

'I think there may be someone here to meet me, actually,' Sutton said, his voice pure London without a trace of Swedish accent.

'Ah, yes . . . just a minute, sir.'

The official, unwilling to leave Sutton on his own in case he sneaked through the barrier, waved frantically to a man in a dark double-breasted suit who was standing by the main exit from the immigration hall, watching everyone who left the building. Eventually the man saw he was wanted, frowned, then walked quickly over. He was in his early thirties, with a blue chin and thick, dark hair cut very short at the neck and round the ears. He moved with loose power, like a boxer in training.

'Yes?' he said. The accent was hard to work out. A suburban middle-class, rugby-playing sort of voice.

'This gentleman's name is Salvesen, sir,' the passport official explained. 'He did say someone was going to meet him, and I understand you were on the look-out for someone of his description.'

'It's all right. I'll take over,' the man said with crisp authority. 'Come with me, Mr Salvesen, and we'll sort you out. Thank you,' he acknowledged the passport official and took Sutton by the arm.

The man did not introduce himself. He was hardly talkative, though friendly enough, as he guided Sutton through the main exit and then off to the left, through a door marked 'Private' and up a bare corridor.

'We've been waiting for you, of course,' he said after a while. 'You'd never have got into the country otherwise.' He let out a snort, half-humorous, half contemptuous. 'You'll be interested to know that this is the VIP way through onto British soil.'

Sutton, holding on to Keppler's overnight bag as if his life depended on it, did not return the stares and slightly bemused 'good mornings' of the warehousemen and customs officers who passed them in the corridor. They must have wondered why this strange, tramp-like creature was being hurried through formalities that took all but the most privileged a matter of hours. No one questioned the authority of the dark-haired man with the fighter's body.

They emerged through a double door into a loading-bay of some sort. Several lorries and vans were parked opposite the entrance, obviously waiting to pick up loads of imported goods once they were released from the clutches of H.M. Customs and Excise.

Sutton stood and looked out over the yard. The sun was shining, as it had been all the way over during the four-hour ferry trip. So deceptive. Everything was deceptive. You had to work hard to stay ahead.

'Waiting for a bus, are we?' he said to his companion, who was suddenly a little nervous.

'Very good,' the man chuckled, looking up and down expectantly. 'Bloody good.'

'Where are we going?' Sutton asked then.

'Oh, you'll see. Debriefing, that kind of thing. You know.'

Then a maroon-coloured, unmarked Morris van drove

quickly through the gates and up to the loading bay, rapidly turning in a tight arc and backing up.

'Here we are,' said the fighter. 'All right, old boy?'

'Not very elegant,' said Sutton, seeing the back doors being opened from the inside just a couple of feet below the bay platform, a face staring up at him.

'Good enough for you, you bastard,' the fighter said, and gave him a big push, so that he toppled off the edge and into strong, violent arms.

It was all very quick and efficient. Sutton hadn't known exactly how they would do it, how long they would keep up the charade of welcoming home the courier from Berlin, the disappeared one, the survivor. On balance, he'd expected longer than this, but it was too late to complain now. The doors were slammed and locked behind him, and he was on a cold steel floor, sliding around like a helpless baby while the van careened out of the yard with a scream of tyres. He was mad to have come here, he almost decided at that point. The countess had been right. Why hadn't they just lost themselves in Europe?

After a couple of minutes they moved out onto a main, straight road, and Sutton stopped being thrown around the back of the van. For a moment he lay there, clutching the overnight bag to his chest and wondering if he should get up. Then a very big man climbed up from a seat behind the driver's cab, scrambled over and squatted down beside him. The man's face was an atrocity in itself, a plastic surgeon's nightmare, all cauliflower ears and pudding nose and fat lip. Compared with him, Bignal of blessed memory was Cary Grant.

The big man put one hand on Sutton's chest and leaned. Sutton groaned.

'Give me that bag,' the man said. 'I'll take charge of it.'

Sutton didn't respond immediately, so the man cuffed him around the face. It wasn't a punch, but neither was it a little slap. It held the promise of worse to come. Sutton winced and handed the bag over. He hoped the man wasn't authorised to open it immediately, and was comforted when he simply placed it beneath his seat for safekeeping.

'You just fucking behave,' the man said. 'You just fucking lie there and behave. Don't you fucking move or I'll make your face look like Coventry Cathedral. All right?'

'Fine,' said Sutton. 'I think we understand each other perfectly.'

'Welcome to Britain,' the man said, sitting back down on his seat.

Sutton might have lost consciousness at some stage during the journey – sleep would have been too flattering a description – but he was well aware of his surroundings when he felt the van jolt onto a cobbled surface and drive for a long distance down what sounded like an echoing, sloping tunnel. He was back in London.

The van stopped suddenly. A short while later, the back doors were flung open. The big man got off his seat, leaned over and scooped up Sutton, pushed him out to where the fighter and another man were standing. The third man, presumably the one who had driven the van, held a Smith & Wesson revolver, service issue, in his right fist and it was pointing at Sutton.

'Come on,' said the fighter. 'Walkies.'

They were standing in a kind of a catacomb, a high-ceilinged stone vault that looked very old. There were Edwardian electric lamps set into the wall for lighting.

'I said walkies!' Fighter nodded to big man, who pushed Sutton forward. Big man had the overnight bag in one meaty hand.

They walked about a hundred yards along the cobbled catacomb, round a bend, and then fighter opened a green-painted door in the wall with a key from a bunch on his trouser belt. 'In we go.'

A winding stone staircase led down and down into the bowels of the city. Just when Sutton was beginning to wonder how deep they could humanly go, they were confronted by another steel door, which this time wasn't locked. Fighter led the way through into a long, narrow, dungeon-like room with no windows and strip lighting down the middle. There were strange metal harnesses, chains, implements in alcoves in the wall. Christ, thought Sutton, a bloody torture chamber. In England!

Fighter must have seen the look on his face. He guffawed. 'Oh, you're in trouble, Sutton or Salvesen or whoever you are, but don't think this is the Spanish bloody Inquisition. It's

259

used most of the time as a railway maintenance workshop. We've had it for a while now and we use it for occasions such as this one. It intimidates the punters. Good eh?'

'Impressive,' said Sutton. 'And who is "we"?'

'Never you mind. Sit down.' Sutton stayed standing where he was, because he needed to stretch his legs. '*Sit down!*' fighter repeated. Big man pushed Sutton down onto a stool near the wall, and they waited.

He hadn't been sure who to expect to walk in through the inner door five minutes later, but on reflection Simon Marjoribanks, the priestly but brusque figure who had been introduced at the Downing Street meeting as 'a senior adviser to the Home Office, can't say more than that', would have been a logical prediction. Rudwick's coy description had been a way of saying that Marjoribanks was high up in one of the Intelligence organisations, probably M.I.5, and that he had supplied resources and muscle from his own empire. How else could they have funded and organised a private adventure like this one? Sutton hadn't thought these heavies were police officers. They were too professional, too cold, and altogether too damned sure of their right to do whatever they pleased. No, this had been Marjoribanks', the cloak-and-dagger merchant's contribution. This was not at all the style of Frawley, the politician, or Rudwick, the senior policeman. They kept this kind of thing at arm's length.

Marjoribanks stood and stared at Sutton as if he were a piece of meat on a slab, didn't speak. He was wearing a pin-striped suit and leather gloves with a red carnation in his buttonhole.

'Well, this is a bit of a change from Number 10, Downing Street,' said Sutton. 'What's the matter? Couldn't you hire the room this time? Hasn't Mr Churchill conveniently absented himself so that you can play out another little charade with George Sutton?'

Marjoribanks grimaced in a cold approximation of a smile. 'You've got a lot of cheek in you for a man in your position, Sutton,' he said. He gestured to big man to hand over Keppler's bag. 'You said you'd be bringing this with you. Excellent. It's all we're really interested in,' he added, and weighed it up, almost fondled it, in his gloved hands. 'Little weight, much moment,' he joked donnishly.

There was a rumbling somewhere below. Sutton guessed this workshop had also acted as store and locker-room for one of London Transport's nightshift service teams that worked on repairing the underground railway during the small hours. An excellent choice for an interrogation centre. And if necessary, of course, the victims could be disposed of down a tunnel. Another suicide on the underground line? All too common these days, what with the war and the high divorce rate.

Marjoribanks carefully unzipped the overnight bag, delved inside, began to rummage. Then he looked at Sutton, his thin face suddenly white with anger.

'What the hell is going on here?' he snapped. He took a pace forward. 'Where are those bloody files? We want them. What do you think you're doing, Sutton?'

Sutton waited, just long enough to keep the man off balance, not enough to drive him to violence.

'Oh, I've got them,' he said. 'You don't think I'd have been stupid enough to bring them straight here, though, do you? I mean, luckily I put two and two together a while ago. And made five. Which, as it happens, was the right answer – and the exact number of times Ambassador Kennedy sent his secret courier to Berlin on behalf of you and the other would-be collaborators. Now that's all I'm saying. Before I go on, I want Sir James Rudwick here, standing in this room.'

Marjoribanks looked at the big man, then back at Sutton. 'This is very hard to believe. Do you realise I could have this man do you real damage?' he said with soft menace. 'Have you any idea of what that means?'

Sutton shrugged. 'You know what I think?' he said. 'I think that if I talk, I'll probably end up down a big hole somewhere. That's a powerful incentive not to tell you what you want to know, threats or no threats. Quite honestly, if we're talking about life or death, the prospect of a thorough spanking from the jolly giant here isn't going to tip the balance in your favour, believe me. No Rudwick, no files.' He folded his arms and fixed Marjoribanks with a steady stare. 'Get him here, and I'll explain everything. It'll save all of us a lot of time and trouble.'

Marjoribanks wrung his hands as if cleansing the leather of the contact with the rubbish that had replaced the documents in Keppler's bag. He returned Sutton's gaze for some time, then turned to fighter.

'You and the chaps stay here with our cocksure friend,' he said. 'I'll be back in a few minutes.'

He strode out through the door, slamming it behind him. Sutton settled down to wait yet again. He hoped that he looked more confident than he felt. Getting Rudwick here would be a big step forward, he was sure of it, but it was only the first stage.

Less than an hour later, the door opened and in walked Marjoribanks, followed by the familiar figure of Sir James. Rudwick trod slowly, as if to the scaffold, and couldn't look Sutton in the eye. He made no attempt to shake hands or even come close. He stood at Marjoribanks' side, keeping fighter between himself and Sutton.

'Goodness, George,' he mumbled. 'What a bloody nuisance. Can't you just let us have the files, so we can all rest easy?'

Suddenly the man Sutton had looked up to, been in awe of, for almost twenty years was revealed as a pathetic, silly old buffer who had got in too deep with people far more ambitious and far nastier than himself. Now he couldn't get out. Well, too bad, Sutton thought with a surge of anger and contempt. Too bloody bad that you made that mistake five years ago. Too bad that you were coward enough to let the likes of Marjoribanks take the unpleasant, decisions regarding the fate of George Sutton and friends. You never even intended to see me again until I forced them to bring you here, Sir James. You didn't want to know what happened to me. You just didn't want to be involved. Well, now you're involved all right.

'R.I.P. in my case, Sir James,' Sutton said after a long pause. He let his gaze travel around the room then come back to rest on Rudwick. The police chief had gone an unhealthy shade of pink – heart-attack pink. 'Because,' he continued, 'I know far too much about everything. We all do – or rather, did, in the case of Joe McCarr. He's dead now. You remember him? The brave man from OSS who volunteered to go with us to Berlin?'

'Look, George, I don't know the details. I just did these fellows a favour by arranging for you to take on the Keppler job, that's all. If I'd known – '

'Bullshit!' Sutton snapped. 'You were in it up to your neck

right from the start in July 1940, after Dunkirk, when the plot was hatched.'

'Wait a minute. I suggest we operate on what the Americans would call a need-to-know basis,' Marjoribanks said. He looked edgily at fighter. 'You boys go outside and have a smoke,' he said. 'Just give me that gun in case Mr Sutton tries anything on.'

The three men left the room. Now Sutton was alone with Rudwick and Marjoribanks. It was Marjoribanks who broke the silence.

'All right,' he said. 'How much do you know, Sutton? Let's see why you're so bloody cocky, shall we?'

'Give me a cigarette first.'

Marjoribanks, who didn't smoke, snorted with irritation. Nevertheless, he stuck his head round the door and got a box of matches and a pack with three Navy Cut in it from one of the heavies outside. He tossed them in quick succession over to Sutton, who caught both skilfully.

'Not bad,' said Marjoribanks.

'I used to play club cricket. I intend to again.'

Marjoribanks pursed his lips but made no comment, just waited for Sutton to answer his original question.

After he had lit the cigarette, Sutton got to his feet. Marjoribanks released the safety-catch on the Smith & Wesson, but the prisoner kept his distance from the two of them with a fastidiousness that was not lost on Sir James. Rudwick fixed his eyes on the ground, and kept them fixed there as Sutton began to speak.

'The first time I really started to think something was more than a bit strange was when I was in Berne and Simpson got a bit chatty,' he began. 'All his talk about favours to Lord Frawley, et cetera, et cetera. Why Frawley all the time? Why wasn't it all just being organised through the usual channels? Then I was really pissed off that you let us walk into a Gestapo trap – it was no thanks to you that Helen von Ackersberg and I got out of it. Joe didn't, of course . . .'

'George, please understand – '

'Shut up, Rudwick,' Marjoribanks growled. 'Let's hear out Mr Sutton's story, for what it's worth.'

Sutton drew gratefully on his cigarette. 'Then there was something else. A man, an American, who turned up in Berlin when we were in real trouble with the Gestapo. He all but saved us, at a price. He was an obvious criminal type, a psychopath, and he wanted Keppler's files too. God knows who he was working for. We had to sort him out. No point in going into the gory details.' He shrugged. Marjoribanks had a supercilious smile on his face but his look was hard, searching, probing both for detail and for information about Sutton's strengths and weaknesses. It was good to let Marjoribanks know that he had already faced one formidable opponent and bested him. Force and cunning were the only things the likes of Marjoribanks respected. Sutton could not extricate himself from this situation by force; his only chance lay in cunning, as it had back in Germany with the violent stranger. 'Anyway, by that time I'd started to ask myself what the hell was really going on,' he continued. 'It all seemed so chaotic, open season on the Keppler files for anyone who got a whiff and could get a man into Germany. There was no sense of anyone working for anyone except himself. But it had all appeared pretty straightforward and legitimate when Sir James first put it to me, you see. Official business. A bit strange, certainly secret, but official business all the same.'

Sutton had left out one really vital building-block, and that was the existence of Harry Stone, scrap metal dealer and receiver of stolen goods. He had to keep quiet about his little chat with Harry, when he had gained that all-important information on Albert Lapentière, the criminal with the high political connections who had acted as Kennedy's courier and whose knowledge had cost him his life – just as Sutton suspected he might pay with his if he didn't protect himself. So long as he didn't tell them about his very beneficial relationship with Harry Stone, he stayed ahead of these bastards in every way that mattered. Harry didn't know it, even now, but he was George Sutton's ace in the hole.

'You're a master of deduction, Sutton,' Marjoribanks said sarcastically. 'More importantly, though, presumably you read the files.'

Sutton nodded. 'Eventually. In a bombed-out basement near Bremen, actually. And, of course, they were extremely interesting. They proved that there was nothing official about my mission at all. I'd been duped into thinking there was, but in fact it was a private affair, made to look official, organised by a very frightened, grubby bunch of ageing pro-Nazis to save their own skins. Including you, Rudwick, and you, Marjoribanks, and Frawley – all of you traitors.'

'It was never as simple as that, George,' Rudwick said, so quietly that he was almost inaudible. All the fierce bulldog power had gone out of him; he had collapsed like a stale balloon. 'We thought at the time that Churchill was leading the country into disaster, continuing to resist Hitler in a war it seemed we couldn't win. It's all very well to look at things now with the advantage of hindsight. You have to understand the way it looked in 1940. It seemed as if the country was going to bleed itself dry. In the long term the only people who would have benefited were the Communists. Hitler had promised to guarantee the British Empire, George! Imagine. We could have turned the Germans into *allies* against the Reds, instead of enemies – '

'You planned to overthrow the Prime Minister, the greatest Englishman of this century, if necessary by force, and hand over England to the Nazis!' Sutton snapped. 'That's about as plain and bloody simple as it could be!'

'Now, now, children,' Marjoribanks cut in. 'Let's not get personal. I don't deny anything I did in 1940. But that's not the point. Could you get a move on, Sutton? I don't want to spend all day listening to this self-righteous drivel. I'm a busy man.'

'I think you'll spend as long as you need to,' Sutton said slowly. 'I certainly intend to, and when I speak, you'd better listen.'

Marjoribanks gestured with the Smith & Wesson, as if to say, I could put a stop to this conversation just by pressing the trigger, but Sutton knew it was bravado. The man from M.I.5 was hooked; he just hated to admit the fact.

'I can see why the thought of those documents becoming public made all of you fill your trousers, anyway,' Sutton went on. 'I saw the list of the people involved, and I saw how Joseph Kennedy had been used as an intermediary, and that's when I realised two very important things.' He paused, making sure he had them hanging on his words, before he went on. 'First, the files were more than just an embarrassment. The revelations would have ruined a dozen very important careers in this country and in America. All Ambassador Kennedy's

265

hopes and ambitions would have been destroyed, he and his family disgraced. Second and more important for me personally, gentlemen,' Sutton said softly, 'it was obvious to me that anyone who had anything to do with these files could not be allowed to live to talk about them. That went for Keppler, Joe McCarr, Helen von Ackersberg, and George Sutton.'

'But we let the Americans in on the whole thing!' Rudwick protested. 'That proves something, George!'

'All it proves is that they outwitted you and gave you no choice. I'm sure you had no intention of allowing the files to go to them. And if Joe McCarr never re-appeared, why should they? You would have said, how sad, a joint Anglo-American team went into Berlin and never came back.'

Sutton turned to Marjoribanks. This man was the key. The rest of the conspirators were probably like Rudwick, overcome with guilt and fear, feeling power slipping away and old age creeping on. Marjoribanks was different. Although he too was no longer young, it was clear that his ambition and hunger for power were limitless, and he would remain utterly ruthless and self-seeking until they nailed the lid on his coffin. No regrets for Marjoribanks, no heartstrings to be tugged. 'Well? What do you say?' Sutton demanded. 'You wouldn't have let us live, would you?'

Marjoribanks stood like a statue, his eyes unblinkingly staring at Sutton, as if trying to suck the life out of him on the spot. Then he shook his head slowly. 'I can't comment. You can't expect me to give you more ammunition, Sutton. Let's just say it was difficult to know what to do with you if you came back safely – and it still is. Now, for Christ's sake get on with what you have to say.'

'All right. I don't want to spend any more time with you people than I have to,' Sutton said, crushing his cigarette butt under one heel on the concrete floor. 'You realise I've got the files hidden somewhere safe.' Marjoribanks shot him a wry half-smile with just a dash of professional appreciation in it. 'Well, here's my offer. You release me and guarantee the safety of myself and Helen von Ackersberg; Rudwick ensures I get out of the army immediately, plus receive the gratuity I was promised. In return I'll supply you with the originals of the files. The one set of copies existing stays right where it is, as my life insurance. If *anything* happens to me . . .'

'We can't allow that,' Marjoribanks snapped. Then he realised he had over-reached himself. 'I'm not saying we agree to your terms in the first place, but if we did, we'd have to insist on your handing over all the existing copies as well as the originals.'

Sutton shook his head. 'Those are my terms.'

'No guarantee?'

'Not the kind you're thinking of.'

'But George, you can't do that. How would we know you wouldn't let us down?' Rudwick said. 'I mean, old boy, I trust you absolutely, because I know you but – '

'What makes you think you know me?' Sutton said wearily. 'You thought I was the perfect pawn. Old George, who was down on his luck and would fall for any story you told him. Really buggered up his career with his boozing. He'd do anything to get back his old job at Scotland Yard. And you could offer the moon and sixpence, because with luck Marjoribanks and his boys would make sure you never had to deliver, wouldn't they, Sir James?'

Rudwick turned away, shamed into silence.

'And what happens if we don't agree, Sutton?' said Marjoribanks, glancing at Rudwick with a look of unconcealed contempt.

'Easy. In that case, every paper in Fleet Street gets a copy of the files. The left-wing press especially would be only too delighted to crucify a gang of treacherous right-wing members of the British establishment. It would be the political sensation of the century. At the very least, it would cost you your careers. If you were unlucky, you could end up on trial for high treason.'

Marjoribanks nodded. 'Rudwick's right, though. There would be nothing to stop you from blowing the whistle on us anyway, once we let you out of here.'

Sutton was relieved the M.I.5 man had given up all pretence of innocence. It meant he might be getting somewhere.

'Strictly speaking, I suppose you're right,' Sutton said. 'But there are plenty of reasons why I won't. For a start, I'm pretty sure that if I did expose you, you and your friends really would move heaven and earth to have me killed. Also,' he reserved an especially cruel smile for Marjoribanks, 'even if I was prepared to risk that, I don't see the point. If you were a threat to the country's future, I'd give it serious thought. But really you're has-beens. You belong to the past. Very soon normal life will start again. There'll be younger men coming back from the war, full of energy and wanting your jobs. There'll be elections for a new government, and you'll be swept out of your cosy billets in parliament and the civil service. In a few years no one will even remember your names. You'll all be rotting away in retirement, wondering what hit you. Why should I release information that will only tear the country apart, divide it between right and left just at a time when we need unity and hard work if we're going to make a success of the peace?' He paused, spelled it out deliberately. 'You're yesterday's men. You're just not important any more. It's not even worth anyone's while to destroy you.'

Rudwick looked like he'd been slapped. Marjoribanks' supercilious smile was wearing thinner all the time, but being the man he was he had a long way to go before he lost his nerve.

'I'm only sorry I can't see you punished, Marjoribanks,' Sutton said to him. 'You're part of our Intelligence Service, with the kind of powers that policemen and politicians and ordinary government servants can only dream of. That's why you have to be carefully watched and immediately sacked and if necessary prosecuted when you overstep the mark. You overstepped it by a mile five years ago, and you've continued to since as a matter of routine. What about the little operation that brought me here? Maybe a future government will have the guts to make sure you're put under some kind of proper control. Maybe you and those like you will stop believing that your special knowledge puts you above the law. I wouldn't bet on either of those things, but for the sake of future generations I can hope.'

'I could shoot you now and no one would ever know,' Marjoribanks said with icy venom. 'We could find the Ackersberg woman within a few days if we really wanted to. I'd guess she's got the files. I could have a dozen men over the other side of the Channel within twenty-four hours, Sutton. And I mean professionals, who know what they're doing and don't care how they get their results as long as they get them.'

Sutton slowly took another cigarette out of the packet, rolled it in his fingers, put it between his lips and lit it. He counted to ten, timing the apparently casual gesture to the second.

'She hasn't got them, Marjoribanks,' he said then. 'Now leaving them with her would have been stupid of me, wouldn't it? Believe me, the files are where you'll never find them. They're very small needles in a very very big haystack.'

Marjoribanks' face was heavy with anger and loathing. He was furious as only a man addicted to others' obedience can be. 'I'm getting tired of this. I might just keep you here for a couple of days. In the dark. Without any food, or drink, or your precious cigarettes. I think you might learn a bit of sense then. You're an arrogant bastard, Sutton.'

'That may be,' Sutton said. 'That's not the trouble, though, is it? The trouble's not that I'm arrogant – you could forgive that in one of your own kind, in fact you'd expect it – but that I come from the wrong class. I was born in Stepney and I don't talk proper. But let me tell you something. Tomorrow morning bright and early I'm going to get up and go for a ride on a bus. I'm going to ride all over London, and at various places I'm going to get off the bus and walk around. While I'm walking, someone will see me. I won't acknowledge him, he won't say or do anything that shows he knows me.' Sutton put his hands in his pockets and smiled at Marjoribanks like a poker-player before he shows his winning hand. 'If he doesn't see me, though, or if he has reason to think I'm there under duress, or if I'm being watched by your blokes, that man will immediately release those files to the press, just as I promised.'

There was a silence that seemed to last so long it began to choke the room. Sutton felt his heart thumping against his ribs; the strain of keeping up the relentless facade of self-assurance was beginning to tell. He prayed Marjoribanks couldn't sense his fear, or read his mind.

The M.I.5 man was blinking furiously, tapping his foot, a child on the verge of a tantrum. Finally he said to Rudwick, like a man talking to a pet dog, 'Come outside.' He took Sir James by the arm, led him to the door. 'We'll be a while, Sutton,' he said over his shoulder as he opened the door to leave.

Before Marjoribanks closed the door behind him, and bolted it, he switched off the light, plunging the room into suffocating, claustrophobic darkness. It was an act of sheer spite, because he knew he was going to have to accept Sutton's demands. At least that was what Sutton told himself as he settled down to wait out the final decision. The alternative didn't bear thinking about.

The door opened and the light came on with a loud snap of the switch. Sutton had no idea how long it had been since Marjoribanks and Rudwick had left him alone. His eyes had accustomed themselves to the light and he saw the fighter standing just inside the door, poised on the balls of his feet, armed with the Smith & Wesson. A glance at his watch told Sutton he had been alone in the darkened room for four and a half hours. He couldn't remember much. Maybe he had gone mad after all, maybe he had just fallen asleep.

'Come on, Sutton,' said fighter. His smile held a trace of irony, but there was still enough straight savagery and violence in his face and body for Sutton not to take anything for granted.

'Walkies.' He gestured playfully with the gun. 'Final walkies.'

Sutton went through the door ahead of him, ascended the steps one by one with the gun at his back. The other two heavies, plus perhaps Marjoribanks and Rudwick, would be waiting for them at the top. Big odds. Too big. If they had decided to liquidate him anyway and to hell with the consequences, he was finished. A gallant gesture, and a failure. The climb seemed to go on forever. He didn't see his whole life flashing before his eyes, but he did manage to review a few of the better moments, just in case.

At the top of the stairs, when they emerged into the cobblestoned cavern, there was in fact only the big man and the driver, and the maroon van. The big man grinned. 'There you are,' he said, and managed to make it sound like a death threat.

Then Sutton felt a hand over his mouth and a cloth and a sickly smell. As he spun back down a crazy Alice-in-Wonderland shaft into unconsciousness, his final coherent thought was, *that bastard Rudwick didn't even have the nerve to face me just once more.*

Sutton awoke in darkness, with a chill in his limbs and a

270

serious headache. For a moment he thought he was back in that claustrophobic underground room, but then he realised he was lying on damp grass. There was the sound of traffic quite close. He opened his eyes very slowly, saw a dark sky and clouds. He moved his head to the left, saw only bushes, to his right and saw a wooden fence. He painfully lifted himself onto one elbow, peered through the slats in the fence, found himself staring at a city street, a fairly major thoroughfare by the look of it.

Within a couple of minutes he was on his feet, unsteady but able to stay upright. He knew it would be a while before the effects of the chloroform wore off. They must have knocked him out so that he would never be able to work out the location of the underground interrogation room. Well, they had bloody well succeeded, because he had no idea where he was even now.

He guessed he must be in one of the big London parks, but it still didn't help him to find his bearings. Sutton wandered for a while along the fence, looking for a gate, arrived at one and found it locked. He climbed it with difficulty – twenty years ago, he reflected, he could have done it without a second thought – and dropped down onto the pavement. A couple of minutes later, he came across a group of soldiers walking with the kind of intense, directed speed that meant they were either on the way to the pub before it shut, or meeting some girls. Sutton stopped them, asked where he was.

'Doncha know your own city?' said the one who acted as spokesman. He had an American kind of accent, though they were wearing British-style uniforms. They must be Canadians. 'Behind you, you got Hyde Park. This here,' he explained as if to an idiot or to the drunk he obviously thought Sutton was, 'is the Bayswater Road. Okay? That way,' he said, pointing to his right, 'is Lancaster Gate. And that way,' he pointed left, 'is the way to the badlands of Shepherd's Bush. Got that?'

Sutton thanked him. So Marjoribanks' boys had dumped him about half a mile from the boarding-house in Holland Park where he had slept for those few nights in London after he had agreed to go to Berlin. How thoughtful of them.

At Notting Hill Gate there was a corner shop still open. Sutton checked his money, found he still had the fifteen pounds he had changed into sterling at Ostende, plus some

271

change. He limped into the place, feeling fragile and exhausted but determined, bought a picture postcard of the Houses of Parliament and asked the shopkeeper if he could sell him a stamp for it. This wasn't a post office, therefore couldn't stock stamps, was the polite answer, but when the man behind the counter saw the look of bitter disappointment on Sutton's face, he asked if it was a matter of urgency.

'My girl's waiting to hear from me,' Sutton explained. 'I need to let her know that I'm all right and I'll be seeing her very soon.'

'Well . . . I keep some in the office for my own business use. You know. I suppose I could let you have one, since you want to post your card so badly.'

'I need enough stamps to cover postage to France,' Sutton said.

'Ooh-la-la,' the shopkeeper said with enthusiasm, suddenly animated. '*Parlez-vous*, eh? I was in the last lot, you know. Three years in Flanders, most of the time in the trenches, up to me you-know-whats in mud. I know all about French girls, I can tell you.'

The man was kind-hearted and straightforward, a bit ridiculous with his attitude towards foreigners and his patched cardigan and his carpet slippers. Nevertheless, he was typical of the best sort of Englishman, the sort it was good to meet when you had just been through an encounter with the Rudwick and Marjoribanks and Frawley variety.

'I'm very grateful,' Sutton said.

'No trouble.' The shopkeeper eyed him with a kind of shy concern. 'I hope you can get a decent night's sleep once you've got your card in the post.'

'Oh, I'm all right, thanks,' Sutton reassured him. Suddenly he wondered what he must look like. His clothes were like a scarecrow's, his hair was wild and matted, and for all he knew his face was bruised and scarred. The British really were an amazingly accepting race, he thought thankfully.

'Sure?'

'Sure.'

The shopkeeper shook his head in mild disbelief and went out the back to fetch the stamps. When he had gone, Sutton wondered fleetingly whether he should have bought a card to send to Harry Stone too, then decided against it.

All in good time, he told himself. Suddenly there was not so much hurry. Tomorrow is another day, as the saying goes. And George Sutton, ex-copper, ex-drunk and ex-husband of Jeannie, was looking cautiously forward to a lot of tomorrows, days he didn't intend to spend alone.

EPILOGUE

Sydney, Australia, February 1962

THE TALL, bronzed man who came walking down the concrete pathway that led to the water was pushing sixty, but he was fit and seemed happy enough. He was whistling 'Night and Day' when he reached the mailbox at the end of the path and fished out the contents.

George Sutton stood for a while with the mail – three letters and a slim airmail package – tucked under one arm, and looked out over the clear, turquoise water. Later, he thought, he might go out in the boat. He would wait until Helen got back from in the city. She was picking up young George from High School on the way back; the three of them could catch a breeze, or use the outboard to make their way to one of the thousands of little inlets on the Pittwater. It would be too late to sail out to Palm Beach and the ocean proper. That would have to wait until the weekend.

The old house was a white, single-storey clapboard place surrounded by a beautiful verandah and set high up in the bush overlooking the creek. It boasted one of the most stunning views in Sydney – which meant one of the most stunning views in the world. Sutton had bought it ten years ago after opening his second sporting goods shop. He owned seventeen stores at present. Not bad for an old cricketer with an eye for the main chance. Now semi-retired, he could have afforded a much bigger, more modern home, but he was happy here. It was handsome, comfortable, and a bit run down. Just like him, Helen joked.

He climbed the forty or so steps back to the house slowly, not because he couldn't have taken them faster, but to savour

274

the garden – always kept well watered and now flourishing in the brilliance of an Australian summer – and to enjoy the panorama below him. A kookaburra eyed him solemnly from the branches of a gum tree at the foot of the lawn. The birds only 'laugh' to mark out their territory at the beginning and close of each day, and are otherwise very dignified. Sutton saluted it with a wave. He and the kookaburra shared this little kingdom, five acres of demi-paradise, a long way from the world's troubles.

The phone was ringing when he reached the kitchen. He picked it up on the seventh ring. It was Helen, calling to ask if they could afford it if she bought a new cocktail dress from her favourite designer. Fine, he said. He had been going over the latest turnover figures just after breakfast, and 'the countess' – as he still called her sometimes, to the vast amusement of their Australian friends – could have bought up the whole bloody store if she'd wanted. The economy was booming under Prime Minister Menzies, and the country was sports-crazy; it had been a record summer for sales so far.

'I thought we might go for a sail when you get home with Georgie,' Sutton said. 'There's a nice breeze. We could anchor up at the Basin, go for a swim . . . Oh, bugger his exams. I didn't get where I am by passing exams. We'll see when you get home, eh?'

'George, you spoil that boy.' Helen Sutton's accent was still a little reminiscent of America, a little of Switzerland, but it also had a strong trace of the Australian twang. 'It's always me who has to keep his nose to the grindstone.'

Sutton sighed. 'You're right.'

George Jr – 'Georgie' – was just fifteen, born not long before they had decided to emigrate. Sutton was honest enough with himself to acknowledge that the boy was the apple of his eye. He had come late in his father's life, when it had seemed all bets of a family were off, and he was correspondingly adored. Helen's disciplinarian pose was also little more than that: a pose. She worshipped Georgie too.

So much happiness, Sutton thought. His mind went back to a hillside in Germany a long, long time ago when Helen had asked him if they had deserved happiness yet. He had answered then that you made your own luck. Well, that was true. They had worked hard in business and in their marriage, but there was also a mysterious factor that couldn't be explained. Maybe that was the bit Helen had wondered about, had wanted to summon up. Germany, England, the war, death and duplicity, it all seemed like a dream now. But it wasn't. There were times when he still woke up in the middle of the night for no reason, seeing a long, narrow room under ground, with metal chains on the walls, and a hard-eyed figure in a pin-striped suit and a carnation and leather gloves staring at him. Or when he couldn't get that dark, violent American out of his mind, with his knife and his 'I lied, countess'. Nothing ever felt complete, even thought those who had survived the killing were nearly all of them dead now.

Sutton went to the fridge and poured himself a glass of cold milk. Then he strolled onto the sun deck and settled into a wicker chair, taking care to sit half in the shade. Even now, when summer was past its peak, the sun's rays could roast the careless sunbather.

A couple of bills. A letter from his bank. And the cuttings from England. His monthly ritual.

First he lit his pipe, the occasional pleasure that had now taken over from cigarettes. Then he took his sip of milk. Then he opened the package. For fifteen years now he had been employing a Fleet Street cuttings agency to airmail him all the month's obituary notices from the London *Times*, which he kept cross-referenced and alphabetically arranged in a small scrap-book. He knew the names he was looking for. Slowly he had ticked them off on the list he kept in a locked drawer in his desk. Slowly they had all been marked down as 'deceased'. All except one.

As usual, Sutton browsed a little. He was a man hopelessly addicted to information, evidence, stories – perhaps that was why he had once been a policeman – and there was material aplenty in these death notices, especially if you read between the lines. Suddenly, as he worked his way through the alphabet, one caught his eye.

It turned out that the notorious Sicilian-American gangster, Lucky Luciano, had died in Naples at the age of sixty-four. The man had been the biggest gang boss in America – only recently had the press started to speak of the 'Mafia', but if it had existed, then Luciano had been one of its most powerful men. Sutton read on. He had been let out of jail in America on parole in early 1946 for unexplained reasons, and then deported, despite heartfelt protests on his part. There was a photograph, smiling, playboy's face but with the eyes of a snake. He reminded Sutton strongly of that young man with the knife in Germany. Their faces were not all that alike, but if they had been judged by their eyes, the mirrors of their souls, Luciano and he might have been father and son. Sutton would never forget that man's eyes. When he had last seen them, they had been staring at him from the driver's door of a Mercedes, filled with a triumph that was fearsomely intense but also terrifyingly empty. On to another obituary, Sutton said to himself. This is too morbid for a sunny summer morning in innocent, life-loving Sydney.

Sutton's heart skipped several beats when he saw the notice a couple of pages on. He checked, he double-checked, and knew that it was true. Rudwick had gone in '49, Frawley in '56, others at intervals up to two years ago. Now, at last, Marjoribanks was dead. Sutton had waited almost seventeen years for this moment.

Slowly he read the brief, discreet notice. Marjoribanks had been in retirement in Hampshire, died after a long illness, etc. etc. on January 21st at the age of seventy-five. He had been knighted on retirement in 1951, for services to the Home Office. Some veiled comments by the obituarist about Marjoribanks' 'colourful' assignments with various departments. Very droll.

Still shaking his head in disbelief, Sutton got up from his chair, carefully put down the scrapbook. Then he walked through into his study, fished out a key from his ring and opened the drawer in the right-hand part of the bureau that he always kept locked. In it lay a typewritten list of a dozen or so names – all the English conspirators named in Heinz Keppler's files. All were crossed through in red, except Marjoribanks. Sutton leaned over, took a red pencil from the mug on the top of the desk, and scored through the one remaining name. The list was now complete. *They were all dead, every one of them.* As dead as Hitler, as Mussolini, as Heinz Keppler, as . . . History. And he, Helen and Georgie were free at last from the tiny but still-lingering fear of the sudden visitor in the night, sent by an ageing government-licensed thug who had never forgiven or forgotten.

Sutton then slowly and systematically tore up the piece of paper, tearing and tearing until the scraps were small as confetti. He took the pile in his cupped hand, tossed it right over the edge of the verandah so that it scattered on the thick tangle of bushes and lantana below. He smiled at the water, the boats, the sun and the sky, and he said aloud to no one in particular: 'Thank you.' Tonight he and Helen would go out and celebrate.

Finally he looked at the time. Ten-thirty. A rough calculation told Sutton it would be ten hours later in London, which made it eight-thirty in the evening there. One more human being needed to be freed of the burden of the past, and he knew exactly where that human being would be at this time of night. He had kept the number of the place in anticipation of this moment. He had it in his little black book.

As he dialled to get the international operator, Sutton thought of the ironies of history. The old Ambassador Kennedy, for all his Irish, millionaire's reasons, had helped the conspirators. Perhaps he had thought that if Britain made peace with Nazi Germany, America would be saved the horrors of war, could stay neutral and slumber on in her comfortable isolationism. Perhaps. Now there was his bright and handsome son, forty-five years old and President of the United States, the American King Arthur with his Camelot of wit, talent and brains, symbol of the U.S.A. come into its own as a sophisticated and awesomely effective world power. Sutton wished John Fitzgerald Kennedy, and his country, well. That was another reason why he was glad to be able to phone London this day – to deal with the final disposal of the evidence that would have damned the Kennedy family in the eyes of many, and now no longer had to be preserved for George Sutton's own reasons.

It took half an hour for the hook-up to London to be arranged. It seemed to take almost as long again before a slightly tipsy Cockney voice came on the line.

'Hello,' said Sutton. 'It's good to hear your voice. How's the old country? It's me, George Sutton, and I'm a happy man today . . .'

Everyone in the Coach and Horses had gathered round, of course, when the call from Australia had been announced.

Couldn't help being curious, could they? Even the teenage boys in their sharp Italian suits and winkle-pickers had sneaked closer, almost forgetting the iron laws of cool in the process.

Finally Harry Stone put the phone down and belched.

'Bloody hell,' he said.

Ernie, the landlord, made a disgusted face. 'Harry, you're an animal.'

'Well,' said Stone, 'at least I can earn me keep. I've made your fortune for you these twenty-five years with the money what I've passed over this counter, so kindly shut your face.' He grinned fuzzily. 'And I'll shout you a little drink in a minute. But first I got a job to do. A job for my old mate, George, who's gone off to Australia. Christ, do you know it's eighty-seven degrees out there at this very moment?' he added. 'You wouldn't fuckin' believe it, would you?'

Stone donned his Crombie coat with difficulty, put on his mismatching trilby, dragged his bloated body to the door and out into the street. The cold February air hit him like a blast of a reality he didn't want to know about. He stood swaying and wheezing, looking up and down the street from the one or two remaining bomb sites to the big new blocks of council flats and a little further west to the looming office buildings. Soon this whole area would be gone, turned under the bull-dozers like an ancient city turned under the plough. Then the world Harry Stone and George Sutton had grown up in would be gone for ever. That was why Harry got drunk most nights, and he had a suspicion it was part of the reason why George had gone to Australia. That and a bit of bother, the bother that had led to that parcel arriving from Calais in the last days of the war, and George giving his loyal old childhood mate Harry some very strict and clear instructions – which he was now about to fulfil to the final letter.

He had to squeeze between parked cars to reach the gate to his scrapyard. In the old days there had been no cars; now everybody had them, even the ones who lived off the dole. It was a national bleeding disgrace. Harry unlocked the gate, locked it again behind him – even when he was a bit Brahms and Liszt, he was still careful – and went to his office, his beloved little old shack with the elderly safe in the corner. It was to the safe he went, and the safe that he opened after adjusting its combination lock to release the door.

The parcel was in there, a bit dusty, but still as firmly sealed as it had been in May 1945. He had posted the other parcel to an address George had given him, but kept this one in the safe. George had been very specific about where it had to be stored. He and George had seen each other a few times – '57 the latest, Harry thought, for a quick jar in the pub – but he'd never told Harry what was in there, and Harry had been too discreet to press him, let alone take a peek off his own bat. Maybe now was the time? Stone fingered the brown paper, itching to rip it off and examine the contents. Instead, he just clawed around and tore the paper a bit. Underneath was a grey cardboard folder marked with an eagle and swastika. Peculiar. Maybe some war memento George had picked up somewhere. Hang on, though: as far as he knew, George had spent his entire period of war service in Scotland except for that trip to Calais well after the place had been liberated.

Harry was starting to get confused, and he needed another drink. Bugger the bloody contents. He'd promised George he'd be trustworthy and follow his instructions to the letter, and he was going to do just that. Stone closed the safe, locked up the office and the yard. Then he set off away from the pub.

He didn't need to go far. The nightwatchman from the big building site up the road was sitting warming himself by a forty-gallon drum filled with wood shavings and rubbish from the construction, and as usual he greeted Harry warmly. He didn't get many people to talk to, unless you included the tramps, and they had a vested interest in enjoying his company, because of his big fire.

'I need to get rid of something, mate,' Harry said. 'There's a drink in it for you.'

The nightwatchman, a big Pakistani with a full beard, nodded. 'For you, Harry, it's all right,' he said in his distinctive singsong.

'Good.' Harry stood there in front of the blazing drum, took a deep breath, and tossed the whole package right into the centre of the flames. He cheered, and so did the night-watchman, who liked a celebration and didn't give a damn what it was about. Harry stood there for ten minutes, befuddled but loyal and grittily resolved to make sure the entire parcel was reduced to ash.

Eventually he was satisfied.

'Ta very much, mate. You're a white man . . . if you know what I mean,' Stone said, and slipped the man half a crown. 'Ta-ta for now.'

Then he set off back down the street where he had played football as a kid, where he and George Sutton had been friends and rivals. Just about all that was left of those days now was Harry's scrapyard and the old pub. He quickened his step as best he could without losing his foothold on the icy road. In another hour, the Coach and Horses would be closing, but Harry Stone intended to sup well from the cup of forgetfulness before Ernie's deep voice sang out the dreaded 'Time, gentlemen, please'.

At least he had proved that friendship counts, and that even criminals can be trusted when it's a matter of life or death.

A wind blew up as he approached the pub. He turned and saw that it had blown the fine ash from the watchman's fire over the icy road.

'Wa's the matter?' he shouted. 'Don' you wan' to burn? You burn, or my friend George'll be very cross, he will.'

Then Harry Stone laughed, slapped his fat thigh, and lurched the last few yards up to the Coach and Horses. He'd buy a round for the whole bar, to commemorate old George Sutton and his phone call from Downunder and his peculiar bloody parcel from seventeen years ago, for Christ's sake. There'd been so much bloody fuss about it at the time. Now it was just a lot of ashes blowing about in a dirty London street.